W9-BWO-309

# The Art of Betrayal

**Also available by Connie Berry**

A Kate Hamilton Mystery

*A Legacy of Murder*

*A Dream of Death*

# The Art of Betrayal

*A Kate Hamilton Mystery*

CONNIE BERRY

NEW YORK

This is a work of fiction. All of the names, characters, organizations, places and events portrayed in this novel are either products of the author's imagination or are used fictitiously. Any resemblance to real or actual events, locales, or persons, living or dead, is entirely coincidental.



Published in the United States by Crooked Lane Books, an imprint of The Quick Brown Fox & Company LLC.

Crooked Lane Books and its logo are trademarks of The Quick Brown Fox & Company LLC.

Library of Congress Catalog-in-Publication data available upon request.

ISBN (hardcover): 978-1-64385-594-3
ISBN (ebook): 978-1-64385-595-0

Cover design by Alan Ayers

Printed in the United States.

www.crookedlanebooks.com

Crooked Lane Books
34 West 27th St., 10th Floor
New York, NY 10001

First Edition: June 2021

10 9 8 7 6 5 4 3 2 1

*For David and John*

Myths do not happen all at once. They do not spring forth whole into the world. They form slowly, rolled between the hands of time until their edges smooth, until the saying of the story gives enough weight to the words—to the memories—to keep them rolling on their own.

—V. E. Schwab, *A Conjuring of Light*

# Chapter One

Long Barston, Suffolk, England

The fourth of May was one of those glorious spring days in England that almost convince you nothing evil could ever happen again. Mild, green-scented air wafted through the open door of Ivor Tweedy's antiquities shop. A curious bumblebee meandered inside, had a quick look around, and buzzed out again in search of the window boxes along Long Barston's main street.

I was perched on a stool behind the counter, polishing silver, when I heard a soft cough.

She stood framed in the doorway, clutching a large striped tote bag as if it held her firstborn—a ridiculous image because the woman had to be in her late sixties. Her thick, iron-gray hair was pulled into a coil at her neck, and she wore a pair of those light-sensing eyeglasses that never quite achieve transparency. She was obviously ill at ease, which in itself wasn't unusual. Antiques shops often attract timid souls hoping to raise a little cash by selling grandma's pearls or grandpa's collection of vintage cameras. They come expecting to be cheated.

"Hello." I pulled off my latex gloves and came around the counter, feeling like a kindergarten teacher on the first day of school. "Welcome to The Cabinet of Curiosities."

The woman stepped into the shop. I couldn't see her eyes behind the darkened lenses, but she seemed more wary than timid, which set off alarm bells. Twice in my life I'd been offered stolen property—in both cases, the items brought in by dodgy-looking men in their twenties. This woman looked respectable, even old-fashioned. She wore a well-cut linen skirt, a crisp white blouse, and flat orthopedic sandals. An expensive but well-worn Gucci handbag hung from one bone-thin arm. "I was expecting the owner, Ivor Tweedy."

"I'm afraid Mr. Tweedy is recovering from surgery. I'm filling in while he recuperates."

"You're American." Her lips thinned in disapproval.

"I am." *Obviously.*

Once, this woman had been quite beautiful. I could see it in her bone structure, the line of her mouth, the way she held her head and shoulders.

She studied me for a moment. Her eyes shifted to the small-paned front window. "Is there somewhere more private we could speak?"

"Of course." I grabbed the binder Ivor used to record sales and commissions. "Just let me lock up." I closed the shop door, shot the bolt, and flipped the "Open" sign in the window to "Closed."

"My name is Kate Hamilton. And yours?" When she didn't answer, I tried another tack. "Have you brought something for appraisal?"

"Not for appraisal, no." Now that she'd been out of the sun for a few minutes, her glasses had partially lightened, allowing me a glimpse of pale, hooded eyes. "I have something I wish to sell."

I led her through a maze of display cases to an alcove furnished with an early Regency pedestal table and two folding campaign chairs that, according to Ivor, had traveled with Wellington into the Battle of Waterloo.

Once we were seated, the woman settled the carryall on her lap and peeled down the fabric, exposing a large, roundish object swathed in Bubble Wrap.

"Be careful. It's heavy." She handed the bundle to me.

"Well, let's take a look." I placed the object on the table and used the edge of my thumbnail to peel back a strip of clear tape. That's when I felt it—the tingling in my fingertips, the flush of heat in my cheeks, the pounding of my heart against my ribcage. I've experienced these symptoms from childhood in the presence of an object of great age and beauty.

Some would call it a gift. I've always thought of it as an affliction. My father, who taught me about antiques, had half-jokingly called me a *divvy*—an antique whisperer—born with the ability to spot the single treasure hidden among the trash that frequently passes for antiques. He wasn't right, of course. My eyes can be fooled by a masterful fake as easily as the next person's.

It's the internal sensations that never fail.

The client watched me, her bony fingers clasping and unclasping in her lap.

I peeled back a layer of plastic and took a sudden breath.

Even before the wrapping was fully removed, I knew what was inside. The technical term is *húnpíng*, a distinctive type of stoneware jar found in the Han dynasty tombs of early imperial China.

The final layer of wrapping slid away. Each húnpíng is unique—some fairly simple, others wonderfully complex. This example was nothing short of dazzling.

The bulbous jar had the earthy gray-green glaze known as celadon, typical of the period. The lower two-thirds of the vessel featured a procession of mold-pressed figures—leaping chimera; riders astride coiling, dragon-like creatures; peak-helmeted warriors wielding long pikes, ready to strike. The fullest part of the jar culminated in a wide mouth supporting a fantastical, multistoried architectural complex with triple-tiered, tiled roofs and curved corner eaves surrounded by gates and pillars, each entryway watched over by a pair of oversized guards. I tilted the jar to peer at the bottom. Unglazed, unmarked—typical of the Han period.

"Do you know what this is?" I asked.

"Some kind of urn?"

"It's an ancient Chinese funerary jar from the Han dynasty. In English we call it a *soul jar* or *spirit jar*."

"Han?"

"They ruled much of China for four centuries, roughly 200 BCE to 200 CE.

"Is it valuable?"

"If authentic, very."

"Oh, it's authentic. How much is it worth?"

"My guess would be thirty or forty thousand pounds, but to be sure I'd have to consult someone who specializes in early Chinese ceramics. I'm not an expert."

She blinked and shoved her glasses higher on her nose. "How long would that take? To consult, I mean."

"Two or three days, perhaps a week." I clicked open my pen. "First, I'll need your name and the history of the piece, as far as you know it."

Her shoulders stiffened, as if I'd asked to see her bank balance. "My name is Evelyn Villiers. My husband bought the urn forty years ago in Hong Kong. He traveled a great deal for business and often purchased pieces for his art collection. If necessary, I can tell you the name of the shop and exactly what he paid for it. He kept meticulous records."

"That would help," I said, tossing my earlier caution to the wind. This woman actually had documentation. "It's a wonderful piece. May I ask why you're selling?"

"Not for the money, if that's what you're thinking." Mrs. Villiers snapped open the clasp on her handbag and pulled out a white handkerchief. "My husband died eighteen years ago. We had one child, a daughter. When I'm gone, she'll inherit a large trust fund from her father. I can't stop that, but I refuse to let her inherit his art collection as well. I've decided to sell now, while I'm able." She met my eyes, as if daring me to criticize.

Criticism was the last thing on my mind—pots calling kettles black and all that. My own daughter, Christine, and my son, Eric, had recently (and unexpectedly) inherited twenty thousand pounds each from their Scottish aunt, a sum I'd persuaded them to invest in a money-market account in Ohio. Eric's share would help pay for his doctoral degree in nuclear physics. Christine had intended to spend hers, meaning it would have been gone in months, with no more to show for it than a handful of receipts—and very possibly a lady's

Rolex. Christine's latest boyfriend, the son of an Italian manufacturing executive, had a Rolex. *Doesn't everyone?*

Mrs. Villiers cleared her throat, and I put my parenting issues aside. Whatever had caused a rift between this woman and her only child had been a tragedy, and I wasn't about to take advantage.

"We'd love to help you sell the jar, Mrs. Villiers, but you might want to consider Sotheby's or one of the other large auction houses in London. Buyers from all over the world receive their catalogs. Wealthy Chinese collectors are paying top prices for objects like this. I'm sure you'd realize more from them than you could from us."

"No public auctions. No catalogs." Mrs. Villiers pinched her lips together. "I insist on doing this privately, without publicity. That's why I came to you . . . well, to Mr. Tweedy. Just write a check. Whatever you think is fair."

I felt my cheeks turn pink. Ivor's checking account currently held just about enough to cover expenses for the month of May. "I'm afraid we're not in a position to purchase the piece outright. If you're sure you want us to handle the jar, I suggest consignment. We find a buyer. You get the proceeds minus a reasonable commission. Why don't I show you our standard contract? If you're satisfied, we'd be happy to handle the sale." I turned to the back of the binder, snapped open the rings, and pulled out a printed legal document. As I organized the papers, I tried to make conversation. "Will you be going to the May Fair on the green this evening?"

She mumbled something that sounded like *wagon bell.*

I looked up. "Sorry? I didn't catch that."

"I said if you can guarantee my privacy, I have more to sell. A lot more."

That was *not* what she'd said, but I let it go, swept away by the glorious possibilities. What Mrs. Villiers was proposing was nothing short of a miracle—a source of high-quality antiques without any financial investment on Ivor's part. This woman wasn't offering an odd piece now and again, but an entire collection, and if the húnpíng was any indication of the quality, a collection that would place The Cabinet of Curiosities among the highest tier of England's private dealers. I couldn't wait to tell Ivor. "What sorts of things did your husband collect?"

"Like the urn—pottery, porcelain, paintings. Special figurines as well—nearly fifty pieces. I can't remember the name, but they're marked on the bottom with crossed swords."

"You mean *Meissen*." My heart kicked up a notch.

She brightened. "That's right. Meissen."

The famous Meissen factory near Dresden was the first European manufacturer to crack the closely held Chinese secret formula for true hard-paste porcelain. Europeans called it "white gold" in the eighteenth century, beloved for its translucency, resilience, and pure white hue. The Chinese had been producing porcelain since the seventh or eighth century, exporting it all over the world. Then came Meissen with its crossed-swords mark, creating stunning pieces that surpassed even the Chinese ones in beauty. I couldn't wait to set my eyes on them.

"And jewelry," Mrs. Villiers said. "Wallace loved fine jewelry."

She obviously hadn't shared that interest. Except for a small heart-shaped locket around her neck, she wore no jewelry of any kind.

"We have a tiered commission structure," I said. "The higher the sale price, the lower the percentage." In the description column I wrote *Chinese Húnpíng Jar, Han dynasty, approx. 16" high and 11" wide. Value to be determined.* "Now, if it's all right, I'll take a few photographs. That way you can take the jar home until I've arranged for an expert to examine it."

"No. I want you to keep it."

"All right—if you're sure." I turned the consignment form toward her and handed her my pen. "Read through the contract carefully. The payment terms are in the final paragraph. Print your name, address, and telephone number there, and sign at the bottom."

While Mrs. Villiers examined the contract, I used my cell phone to snap several images. I couldn't believe our good fortune. I felt like pinching myself. Finally, laying the jar carefully on its side, I took a shot of the unglazed bottom.

Mrs. Villiers turned over the final page. Placing her index finger at the top, she drew it down slowly, stopping briefly at the final paragraph. At the bottom, she printed out her information and added her signature.

*Mrs. Evelyn Villiers*

*Hapthorn Lodge, Hollow Lane*

*Little Gosling, Suffolk*

She'd included a phone number. Her signature was a squiggly line.

Standing, Mrs. Villiers smoothed her skirt and gathered her handbag and the now-empty carryall. "Thank you for your assistance."

"My pleasure." I held out my hand, and she took it. "I'll put a copy of the contract in the mail. And I'll telephone you when I've arranged for the appraisal."

"I'd prefer to take the contract now." Was there a slight challenge in her voice?

"Of course." I'd rather have had Ivor sign the contract, but I knew he trusted my judgment. I signed, adding "Subject to Appraisal," and handed her the top copy. "I'll be in touch soon."

"I never answer the telephone. Text me at this number, and I'll contact you." Picking up the pen I'd provided, she scribbled a different number at the bottom of the contract.

Something floated in the air—a vague uneasiness. Why didn't Mrs. Villiers answer her phone? To avoid telemarketers?

I stood at the front window and watched her cross the High Street and turn left toward the river. She scurried past the shops—shoulders hunched, head bent—until she disappeared down a side street. Had she driven herself, or was someone waiting for her?

That was the least of my questions about Mrs. Evelyn Villiers.

I checked my watch. If I left immediately, I could be at The Willows by eleven thirty.

Time to break the good news to Ivor.

# Chapter Two

The Willows, a private convalescent facility about forty minutes east of Long Barston, sat at the end of a tree-shaded drive. I found one of the designated visitor spots and parked my leased Mini Cooper—midnight black with built-in sat nav and automatic transmission. The rambling, red-brick Victorian house looked every bit as impressive as the photograph on the glossy brochure I'd seen the previous December when I had accompanied Ivor to his presurgery consultation in Ipswich.

"Perfect alternative for someone in your circumstances," Ivor's surgeon had said. He'd unfolded the brochure and pointed a well-manicured finger at photos of spacious private suites, smiling nurses, and a glass-walled dining room. "Assuming you can afford it, of course."

Ivor could afford it—just. The twelve-thousand-pound fee would wipe out his savings, but with no wife or children to care for him at home, and with a residence ill-suited for someone recovering from bilateral hip-replacement surgery, he had no alternatives. He would recover in the hospital for five days, then transfer to The Willows. The surgeon had suggested a two- to three-week stay, after which Ivor could return to his flat above the shop, navigating its uneven floors; narrow, twisting staircase; and high porcelain tub with the help of occasional NHS-provided home care. In the meantime, I would manage his antiquities business. After the previous December, when Ivor had sacrificed an ancient glass head of the Egyptian pharaoh

Akhenaten to help me track down a ruthless killer, the least I could do was keep his antiquities business afloat during his recuperation.

This was my third visit to The Willows. The first was the day before his scheduled surgery, when Ivor and I had presented ourselves for a tour led by a brisk young woman who'd identified herself as secretary to the deputy hospital administrator. The house had been a cottage hospital until 1996, she told us, when its remaining patients were transferred to the newly renovated NHS facility in Ipswich and the property sold to a private medical practice. Besides residential post-op rehabilitation, The Willows offered outpatient physiotherapy and, in a separate wing, temporary respite care for dementia patients.

The sun reflected off the tall windows. Shielding my eyes, I squinted at the ivy-clad exterior. A peaked central porch was flanked by wide bays framed in glossy, white-painted trim. On the left, a coach house had been converted into administrative offices. On the right, a low brick wall led to a stand of beech trees, leafy shrubs, and a small rose garden. A nurse in a crisp white uniform and navy wool cape maneuvered a wheelchair-bound patient toward the garden. The effect was purposely retro, conjuring images of "the way things were" before soaring costs, an aging population, and a shortage of qualified doctors made timely, personalized medical care no more than a memory.

Inside, the reception room had the look of a small deluxe hotel rather than a medical facility. Deeply cushioned furniture faced a marble fireplace. Soothing landscapes in oils hung on ochre-painted walls.

Ivor's room was on the ground floor, facing the back garden. While a pretty, young aide changed the linens on his hospital bed, Ivor sat in a huge leather chair by a sunny French window, tucking into his elevenses—that quintessentially British custom of a mid-morning snack. His cheeks were pink, his sparse white hair frizzed out like a halo, and his eyes that electric blue that reminded me of Kashmiri sapphires. My heart soared. He was looking so much better than he had in the hospital.

"Kate, my dear girl!" Ivor raised his flower-sprigged teacup and waggled his eyebrows. "Join me?"

"No, thanks. How are you?"

"Ha! I'd be better if *Attila* here didn't find it necessary to torture me several times a day."

"Oh, go on wi' you." The aid, whose name badge said "Jay'den," winked at me. "He's walking the length of the hall now. We're right proud of Mr. Tweedy. At this rate he'll be leaving us early 'n' all." She fluffed the pillows on his bed and shook a playful finger at her patient. "The physio will be back at two, mind, for your range-of-motion exercises."

Ivor grimaced and rolled his eyes.

"How are things at the shop?" he asked when she'd gone.

"I closed early. Hope you don't mind."

"Your call, Kate. I warned you we don't get many walk-ins." Ivor dipped a biscuit in his tea. "Sure you won't join me?"

I declined and spent the next few minutes catching him up.

"The good news is I sold that small bronze statue—Perseus holding the head of Medusa—to a collector in Canada. He wanted it so badly he didn't even bother to haggle."

"A true collector. You can always tell."

I had to laugh. "My father used to get a glazed look in his eyes. And he'd start whistling."

"So what's the bad news?"

"The auction."

"Ah." Just before I'd arrived in England, Ivor had placed a group of objects from Roman Britain—a wax writing tablet, a silver-and-gold pepper pot in the shape of a woman's head and shoulders, and a bronze drinking vessel with gladiator scenes—with the new auction house outside Long Barston, on the road to Sudbury. The owner and his son had been all enthusiasm, he'd told me, talking about their upscale clientele and exceeding estimates. They'd set a value of ten thousand pounds.

"How bad was it?"

"We got half."

"Ah, well." He attempted a philosophical smile. "You can never tell with an auction."

Ivor was right. Some auctions generate a buzz that boosts prices through the ceiling. Others, with the same type and quality of merchandise, feel more like a wake. So many factors are at play—the economy, the news cycle, even the weather.

"Well, here's something to cheer you up." Dragging the visitor's chair closer, I dug in my handbag for my cell phone and pulled up the images I'd taken of the húnpíng jar.

*"Blimey."* Ivor shoved his glasses higher on his nose. "I haven't seen one of those in decades."

"My parents had one in their antiques shop once, but it was plain—just a jar, really. Still worth a bundle, if only for its age."

"Where did you find it?"

I told him, beginning with my early suspicions and ending with Mrs. Villiers's tantalizing suggestion that we handle the sale of her late husband's entire art collection.

Ivor sat for a moment, not speaking. "I know Evelyn Villiers—well, know *of* her."

"That's what I was hoping."

"Terrible tragedy, the death of her husband. It was in all the papers. Must have happened—oh, fifteen or more years ago."

"Eighteen, according to her."

"Yes, well. They had a fine house near Little Gosling. Wallace Villiers was managing director of an investment firm. One daughter, Lucy. Doted on her, sent her to the best schools. She was seventeen, young for her age. According to news reports, Lucy had a clandestine relationship with her father's chauffeur, a dicey lad in his late twenties. Her parents found out, raised a fuss. Then Mr. Villiers discovered that one of his paintings, a rare seventeenth-century landscape, had gone missing. He accused the chauffeur of stealing it—on what basis, I never knew. Lucy defended him. There was a terrible row, ending tragically in Wallace Villiers's death from a cerebral hemorrhage. Evelyn took it hard. Blamed her daughter."

That would explain her bitterness. Still, it had been eighteen years ago. Lucy would be in her mid-thirties now. Had there been no reconciliation? "Was the painting ever recovered?"

"I never heard."

"Was the young man found guilty?"

"Released for lack of evidence."

"And Lucy?"

"Left the area, I believe. Memory's a bit fuzzy there." He frowned. "What is it, Kate? You look troubled."

"Not troubled exactly."

"You'd better tell me."

"It's just I got the impression Mrs. Villiers was"—I shrugged—"oh, I don't know. Ill at ease, maybe, or fearful."

"You suspect the húnpíng is a fake? I doubt that. In my opinion, from the photograph, it's exactly what it appears to be—a very fine and very old example of ancient Chinese pottery."

"She says she has documentation—sales receipts. I haven't seen them."

"So you're suspicious."

"Not about the jar."

"About the woman? She's reputed to be a bit odd. A recluse. Never leaves her house."

"Well, she left her house today. I told her I'd have an expert examine the jar. Do you know of anyone?"

"As a matter of fact, I do." Ivor gave me one of his deceptively angelic smiles. "Bring the húnpíng here. I'll take a look. In the meantime, do some research yourself. There's a reference book on ancient Chinese pottery in the book room at the shop—on the left, third shelf from the top."

Ivor took a deep breath and closed his eyes. He was tiring.

As if on cue, the pretty young aide returned. "Time for a lie-down, Mr. Tweedy. You'll need your strength for the physio. And our afternoon stroll."

"I can't wait." He pulled a face. "How are you and Vivian getting along?"

"Like Thelma and Louise—Vivian's words. I'm afraid to ask what she means."

Vivian Bunn, owner of Rose Cottage, the picture-perfect, thatched-roof cottage where I'd taken a room for the next six weeks, was an endearing elderly woman of the type commonly referred to in England as Boadicea in tweed.

"May Fair's tonight," Ivor said, looking wistful. "First one I'll have missed in more than thirty years."

"If I win a teddy bear, it's yours."

"Much obliged." Ivor's blue eyes twinkled. "Your detective inspector will be there?"

"Of course." I gathered my handbag and slipped my cell phone in the outside pocket. "Take care, Ivor." I stopped halfway to the door. "Is there anyone who might know more about the Villiers family?"

"Come now, Kate." Ivor cocked his head. "Who knows everything about everyone in these parts, hmm?"

I couldn't help smiling.

Ivor winked. "Give Vivian my regards."

# Chapter Three

I parked the Mini beside Rose Cottage, one of several on the Finchley Hall estate. A climbing rose grew up and around the planked-wood door. Flowers in the front garden bloomed in profusion—columbine, foxglove, bellflowers. Mounds of pink and white peony bushes drooped under the weight of their blooms. Snatches of *A Midsummer Night's Dream* came to mind—"oxlips and nodding violets;" Queen Titania, asleep on a bank of wild thyme.

I stifled a yawn. It couldn't be jet lag. I'd been in England more than a week now. Still, a bank of wild thyme sounded tempting.

I let myself in with my key. "Vivian? Fergus?"

Silence. Fergus's leash, usually hanging on a hook by the door, was gone.

A note lay on the kitchen table: *We're at the Hall with Lady Barbara. Everything's fine. Don't worry. We'll see you at the fair.*

Now I *was* worried, of course—Vivian's aim, no doubt. A self-proclaimed non-gossiper, Vivian loved nothing better than implying she had tantalizing secret information she couldn't divulge—just before letting you drag it out of her. Ivor was right, though. Vivian Bunn knew everything about everybody within thirty miles of Long Barston.

Tossing my car keys in my handbag, I climbed the stairs to my room under the thatch. After my stay in Long Barston last December, when I knew I'd be spending most of May and June in the village, I'd searched online for a short-term lease. I'd just about settled on a self-catering cottage in a nearby village when Vivian put her sturdy leather brogue firmly down.

"*Pay* for accommodation? Nonsense. I have a spare room. I won't hover. You'll have your own key, so you can come and go as you please. Kitchen privileges so you won't feel obliged to keep us company."

Fergus, Vivian's elderly, obese pug, had snorted his agreement. *No brainer.*

Rose Cottage *was* the perfect solution, within walking distance of Ivor's shop, near the friends I'd come to care about in Long Barston, and (most importantly) a mere stone's throw from Tom Mallory, the handsome detective inspector I'd first met in Scotland and had fallen hopelessly in love with.

There—I'd admitted it, if only to myself.

The double bed, with its rose satin comforter and chintz pillows, looked tempting. Instead I settled myself at the desk under the small-paned dormer window and opened my laptop. I typed *Wallace Villiers* into the search bar and waited. A series of news articles from 2002 appeared. I opened the one on top.

*The Telegraph, 12 March 2002*

*Colin Wardle, the 27-year-old Suffolk man accused of murdering prominent investment banker Wallace Villiers, has been released after the coroner pronounced the cause of Villiers's death as natural.*

*According to eyewitnesses, Villiers confronted his daughter, Lucy, 17, and Wardle, his chauffeur, at 1 a.m. outside his Edwardian house near the village of Little Gosling. An altercation ensued, leading to what the coroner described as "a neurological event." Police and emergency responders were called but found Villiers unresponsive.*

*Wardle insisted he'd acted in self-defense. "Mr. Villiers was a good employer," he said at the inquest, "until he found out about me and Lucy. Wasn't good enough for her, was I?" Wardle testified he had arrived at the house that night in order to rescue Lucy from what he described as "a toxic environment." Miss*

*Villiers told police they were traveling to Scotland, where they planned to marry.*

*Two weeks earlier, Wallace Villiers had reported the theft of a valuable 17th-century painting, naming Wardle as the perpetrator. Wardle denied the charges, and when Miss Villiers testified that the two had been together the night of the theft, the charges were dropped.*

*"It wasn't Colin's fault," said a defiant Lucy Villiers at the inquest.*

A grainy photograph showed a dark-haired girl with a thin face, sloping chin, and small round eyes.

*Speaking outside the coroner's court in Ipswich, a tearful Evelyn Villiers, wife of the deceased, said, "That young man insinuated himself into our family, preyed upon our daughter, and turned her against us. He took the painting, and now he's taken Wallace's life. One day he'll pay for what he's done."*

*When questioned about Mrs. Villiers's statement, Wardle said, "She's suffered enough."*

Had Lucy married Colin Wardle? If she had, I could understand Mrs. Villiers wanting to make sure he would never get his hands on her husband's art collection.

There were depths here I couldn't plumb.

An elopement, a betrayal, a death.

The uneasiness I'd felt earlier in the day came back in spades, but now it centered on the húnpíng. Was it safe? I'd left the funerary jar on a shelf in Ivor's stockroom. The shop had security—roll-down metal grilles on the windows plus a coded and monitored alarm system—but the jar was on consignment. The least I could do was conceal it.

After checking my e-mail to see if either of my children had written (they hadn't), I changed into the cotton sundress and warm cardigan I'd planned to wear that night with Tom. Even mild summer evenings in England can be chilly.

A delicious sense of anticipation washed over me. Tonight was the May Fair, the traditional spring fête, held in Long Barston since the fifteenth century. Tom was meeting me on the green. Afterward, we'd share a late dinner at his house in Saxby St. Clare. And the best part? His mother, Liz (definitely *not* a fan of mine), was out of town, visiting her brother in Devon. I felt a warm glow thinking about that. Perhaps she would decide to move permanently to Devon.

*Dream on,* said the voice of reason. Liz would be home in ten days or so. We hadn't spoken since that December afternoon at the Suffolk Rose Tea Room when she'd announced that Tom had adored his first wife and had no intention of ever marrying me. I was so shocked, I lost my temper and stalked out, but not before telling her to stay out of my life.

*Well done,* quipped my conscience, piling on the guilt.

I was transferring a few essentials from my handbag to a small leather belt purse when my phone pinged. A text from Tom: *Will be there by 7:30. Love you.*

The warm glow returned. Grabbing my jacket, just in case, I flew down the stairs.

I *would* have to apologize to his mother.

But not tonight.

* * *

I parked my car in the alley behind Ivor's shop and used my keys to open the reinforced security door leading into the stockroom. After flipping on the lights, I punched in the alarm code. Ivor's stockroom, an open, brick-walled space, served as a combination receiving facility, mail room, and warehouse. There was the húnpíng, right where I'd left it.

My *affliction* began as it always did with tingling fingers, a sudden flush of heat, and a dry mouth. I used to worry about the violent pounding of my heart but gave up on the grounds that the episodes never lasted long and there was nothing I could do about them anyway. The more alarming symptoms usually settled into what I'd come to think of as a pleasurable buzz. Spending time with Ivor's treasures every day, I quite enjoyed the sensation—that and the familiar scent of old wood and old dust with notes of linseed oil and a finish of mildew.

Ivor's shop smelled like my childhood.

The late-afternoon light slanted through the window grille, illuminating the dust motes in the air and casting a crisscross pattern on the wood floor. The húnpíng sat . . . *in repose* was the phrase that came to mind. Apt as it turned out, because while none of the jars known to exist had ever held physical remains, scholars believed they were intended to attract the life energy of the deceased, acting as a sort of portal through which the departed soul could enter paradise. I ran my fingers over the network of fine crazing in the gray-green glaze. This jar had lain in an earthen tomb for almost two thousand years. What had become of the person for whom it was created? How did he or she die? Who mourned?

My heart thumped alarmingly. Blood swooshed in my ears.

Ivor was right. This jar was the real thing.

I found the lighted magnifier I always carry with me and bent to examine the complex lid composition. Tiny molded figures had been tucked among the pagoda-like structures: a bearded sage holding a tablet; an acrobat; a musician; a grinning juggler. And creatures—a flock of birds, wings spread in flight; a dog dozing on a lower roof; a parrot; a tiger with a bird caught in its teeth. Exuberance. Joy. This was a scene fit more for a wedding than a funeral.

Then, among the other figures, I saw him, a robed man standing alone in the shade of a parasol tree. His eyes were shut, his mouth open wide in agony. The single note of grief amid celebration was stunning. Did the figure represent the deceased or the mourner?

A thought pinged in the back of my brain: *a wedding, a betrayal, a death.*

My head swam.

*Oh man.* What was it about the UK that brought on these flights of fancy? Fortunately, these experiences don't happen often, but when they do, a word, a phrase—even simply an emotion—coalesces in my brain, as if the atmosphere in which an object existed has become permanently embedded in the cracks and crevices. For the record, I reject all notions of paranormal powers or second sight. Just because something can't be explained doesn't mean it's supernatural.

Shaking off the thought, I positioned the húnpíng behind a rosewood letter box and covered it with a felt polishing cloth. Then I located Ivor's book on Chinese ceramics—right where he'd said it would be.

After resetting the alarm system, I stowed the book in my car and headed for the village green.

# Chapter Four

St. Æthelric's Church stood on the north side of Long Barston. The large, roughly triangular green south of the churchyard marked the divergence of two roads. The main thoroughfare, the High Street, turned northeast, widening beyond Long Barston to join the A134 toward Saxby St. Clare and Bury St. Edmunds. The narrower road curved in a west-northwesterly direction toward Little Gosling, first in a string of tiny medieval villages leading eventually to Cambridge.

The walk to the green from Ivor's shop took less than ten minutes. By the time I arrived, the May Fair was in full swing. Tent awnings billowed in the breeze. Children darted excitedly from stall to stall as parents chatted in small circles, keeping one eye on their offspring. All the usual attractions were there—hoopla, coconut shy, white elephant stall, plus a variety of opportunities to eat and drink.

Small food stalls served fish and chips, kabobs, pizza by the slice. The local Chinese takeaway offered jasmine smoked pork ribs and their famous shrimp rolls. The Finchley Arms, the oldest pub in the village, had set up a beer tent with the proprietor, aging hippie Stephen Peacock, pulling pints into disposable plastic glasses. At the other end of the green, The Three Magpies, Long Barston's increasingly popular gastropub, offered wine and a selection of gourmet flatbreads. Near a guess-your-weight kiosk—*people pay money for this?*—a mob of children surrounded a tent advertising candy floss, ice lollies, and something mysteriously called "Nobbly Bobblys." The largest tent belonged to the Suffolk Rose Tea Room, providing tables and chairs where weary fairgoers could sit for a spell, enjoying tea and cakes. Since Tom wouldn't arrive for another hour, that's where I headed, figuring I'd find Vivian.

I spotted her right away. She and Fergus, her ever-present pug, shared a table with the local peeress, Lady Barbara Finchley-fforde. Vivian, a well-upholstered single woman in her late seventies, wore her year-round uniform, a baggy tweed skirt and twinset. Lady Barbara—slim, elegant, and a decade younger—had chosen a shirt-waist dress in a lavender floral design, with a matching bouclé jacket.

Vivian was speaking, her hands slicing the air in aid of some point. Fergus lay in a puddle at her feet, panting softly. Lady Barbara's silver-blonde hair was pulled back in a ponytail, emphasizing the hollows beneath her fine cheekbones. She appeared to be weeping.

As I approached the table, Fergus lifted his head and gave a friendly woof.

Wanting to give Lady Barbara time to compose herself, I reached down and patted Fergus on the head. "And how are you this fine evening, Fergus?" He wagged his corkscrew tail. I spotted a cake crumb caught in the fur near his mouth. "Enjoying the party, I see."

Lady Barbara reached out her hand. "Kate, dear. I'd hoped to see you tonight."

"Is something wrong?" I pulled up a chair. Lady Barbara, one of the bravest women I knew, wasn't one to feel sorry for herself. Or exaggerate her troubles.

Vivian answered for her. "It's the National Trust." She finger-combed her gray pixie cut. "They're pulling out. Leaving Barb in the lurch."

"Now, Vivian, we don't know that yet."

"What do you mean 'pulling out'?" I asked.

Vivian opened her mouth, but Lady Barbara laid a quelling hand on her arm. "They're enthusiastic about Finchley Hall, Kate. They understand the historic significance of the house and have already talked about preserving what they call 'the faded postwar ambiance.' The problem is money. Funds are tight—a temporary state of affairs, they hope."

Finchley Hall, the family seat of the Finchleys for nearly five centuries, was in remarkable shape for its age. In other words, it was slowly crumbling and would continue to crumble unless someone invested a fortune in repairs and renovation.

Lady Barbara's smile was disconcertingly hopeful. "I understand about the money. Of course I do. The National Trust cares for so many wonderful properties. There is a limit to what they can take on, but what will I do if they delay too long—or worse, turn Finchley Hall down altogether? My father would turn over in his grave if I sold the estate to some developer who would bulldoze everything to build a housing estate. I couldn't do that."

"Of course not." I could see her dilemma. The upkeep on Lady Barbara's increasingly derelict Elizabethan manor house (not to speak of the outbuildings) had to be mind-boggling. After the Second World War, when many of England's stately homes were demolished, victims of the struggling postwar economy, crippling taxes, and a changing social structure, Finchley Hall had been granted a reprieve when Lady Barbara married the scion of a wealthy Welsh mining family. When his fortune reached its dregs, he had attempted to offset mounting expenses by hosting university interns—at a fee.

I knew the sad history because my daughter had been part of the final group of interns. But after the shocking murders last December, the internship program had been abandoned, and Lady Barbara, the last of the Finchley-ffordes, had been forced to face her dire financial condition. Her only remaining source of income was the Finchley Hoard, a treasure trove unearthed on the estate in 1818. But she'd promised her father she would never sell the Hoard, and she'd kept that promise by gifting it to a local history museum. At the same time, she'd made the agonizing decision to transfer ownership of her ancestral home to the National Trust—with two provisions. The first would allow her to occupy a private wing of the house as long as she was able to live independently. The second would grant her previous employee and best friend, Vivian Bunn, life tenancy in Rose Cottage, the thatched-roof jewel box that was now my temporary home.

"When will the National Trust make their decision?" I asked.

"They've promised to contact my lawyer by the end of the month."

"And that will be final?"

"Who knows?" Vivian huffed. "They implied funds *may* be available at some *unspecified* later date. Load of good that will do." She snorted and popped the remains of a clotted cream–slathered scone into her mouth.

"Viv's right." Lady Barbara pushed an iced fairy cake around her plate with a fork. "But where does that leave me?"

"Could you sell something? To tide you over, I mean."

Two sets of elderly eyes stared at me as if I'd uttered an oracle.

"Like what?" asked Lady Barbara.

"I don't know. Something you don't need. Something that won't be missed when Finchley Hall is open to the public. How about the attic? You must have some valuable things up there."

"You mean you'd sell them for me at the shop?"

"We could, but you might not realize a profit for months—even years. I suggest putting a few items up for auction. That way you'd get the money right away."

"Let me consider it, dear. I'll let you know."

A stout woman in a frilly apron plopped a teacup in front of me, took my prepaid ticket, and poured out from an enormous metal pot. "Milk and sugar on the table," she said. "Biscuits and cakes at the counter."

I thanked her and turned back to my companions. "Do either of you know a woman named Evelyn Villiers? She lives in Little Gosling."

"Why do you ask?" Vivian tilted her head. So did Fergus, at her feet. The resemblance between mistress and dog was remarkable.

"She came into the shop this morning."

"She *came* to the shop?" Vivian shot Lady Barbara a look.

"You saw her?" Lady Barbara's brow furrowed.

"Yes. Why?"

"Because Evelyn Villiers hasn't been seen in public for years."

"*Years* and years," Vivian added. "She's a recluse. Never leaves her house. Not since her husband died."

"Well, she left her house yesterday. She brought in an ancient Chinese funereal jar she wants Ivor to sell."

"Oh my." Lady Barbara raised a hand to her cheek. "Something must have happened."

"How do you know she never leaves her house?" I asked. "Maybe she just never shops in Long Barston."

Lady Barbara shook her head "You don't understand."

"Do you know Yasmin, the mail carrier?" Vivian asked.

"Of course." Yasmin Green, the mother of two handsome, rough-and-tumble sons, was a lovely young woman of Afro-Caribbean descent who lived in Long Barston with her husband, Ralston, an ex-footballer for Ipswich Town, a huge hulk of a man known locally as the "gentle giant."

"Yasmin's mother-in-law, Ertha, used to *do* for the Villiers." Vivian leaned forward, lowering her voice. "After the inquest, Evelyn locked herself in her room and refused to come out, even to eat. Ertha left trays outside her bedroom door. Then Ertha was dismissed—no notice, no explanation. Something snapped in the poor woman's mind. Refused to have a funeral."

"No funeral?"

*"Cremation."* Vivian mouthed the word as if it were slightly off-color. "No ceremony of any sort."

"What about her daughter?"

"Lucy." Vivian shook her head. "Sad story there. Her mother blamed her for causing her father's death. They say the girl had planned to run off with the family chauffeur. Broke her father's heart. Literally. Keeled over on the spot."

"Did they marry—Lucy and the young man?"

"We never heard," Lady Barbara said. "Lucy was sent to live with an aunt somewhere in Essex. Best thing, all in all."

Vivian stood, wrapping Fergus's leash around her hand. "Come on, Barb. Time to try on our costumes."

"Dress rehearsal?" I asked. All week Vivian had been hinting about her part in some sort of theatrical performance on the green.

"It's a pageant," Lady Barbara said. "'The Green Maiden,' a local folktale, acted out every May all over this part of Suffolk." She threw me a cheerful look. "We're peasants."

"Begins at nine," Vivian said. "You'll attend, of course."

"Wouldn't miss it."

Fergus grunted as he scrambled to his feet.

Vivian regarded her pet fondly. "I've entered the dear boy in two competitions this year—Most Handsome Dog and Waggiest Tail. He's bound to win at least one blue ribbon."

Lady Barbara tucked her handkerchief in the sleeve of her jacket. She blinked as the tent flap blew open, letting in the near-horizontal rays of the sun. Thanks to corneal dystrophy, a genetic eye condition common in the Finchley family, her vision was slowly dimming. She'd never go completely blind, I'd learned, but she would eventually lose her independence.

"Consider my suggestion," I told her.

"I will, my dear. Thank you."

Vivian took Lady Barbara's arm. "Well, I think it's a grand idea, selling a few bits and bobs. You could use that new auction house on the road to Sudbury. Keep things local."

"Of course." Lady Barbara's face lit up. "We attended the grand opening about a month ago, Kate. It's a perfect idea. That way the village would benefit."

I remembered the disappointing return on Ivor's items. *Auctions are always a risk.* I'd ask Tom to check out the owners of the auction house, make sure they were reputable.

As I watched them make their way toward the church, I thought about the oak-paneled walls of Finchley Hall, hung with portraits of long-dead Finchleys, gazing out in their velvet-and-ermine condescension. *Fidelis, Fastu, Fortitudo*—the Finchley motto.

Loyalty, Pride, Courage.

With Lady Barbara there was no false pride. The Finchleys hadn't always been saints, but like her father and grandfather before her, Lady Barbara's first consideration was always for the village families who had depended on the Hall for generations.

My phone vibrated. A text from Tom: *On my way.*

A tiny, joyful explosion went off in my heart.

# Chapter Five

Watching Tom stride across the green, I marveled at life's unexpected joys. Some women never meet the man of their dreams. I'd met two. First my husband, Bill, older by eleven years and the father of my children—easygoing, kind, safe. And now, almost four years after Bill's tragic death, a completely different man—Tom Mallory, a widower my own age. He *was* kind, but I couldn't honestly say he was easygoing and safe. There was an intensity about him, a fierce energy that intrigued and excited me. With his high cheekbones and aquiline nose, he looked like a monk; and yet when he gave me that charming half smile, when his hazel eyes crinkled at the corners, he took my breath away.

Our problem wasn't attraction, but proximity.

I lived in Jackson Falls, Ohio. He lived in Suffolk, England.

"I've been looking forward to this all day." Tom pulled me into his arms. "You look amazing."

He looked amazing himself in a pair of jeans, a crisp white shirt, and a tobacco-colored sport jacket. He smelled amazing too—that faintly woodsy aftershave I would always associate with our first meeting in the Scottish Hebrides.

He pulled back to look at me. "Lovely dress, Kate. Matches your eyes."

My coloring I'd inherited from my mother—dark chestnut hair, blue eyes—*"blue as the waters of the fjords,"* my father used to say.

Tom looked concerned. "Will you be warm enough?"

My calf-length sundress had a drop-shoulder Bardot neckline. One of my friend Charlotte's picks (I'm hopelessly unfashionable). Fortunately, she'd insisted on pairing it with a cashmere cardigan, which I'd tied (unfashionably) around my waist.

"The sweater will do just fine. And I do have something warmer in the car, just in case."

"Where did you park?"

"In back of the shop, but I'm fine now." I threaded my hand through his arm. "I like the jacket. Looks like you stopped home after work."

"To shower and change. After the day I've had, I needed it."

"Tell me about it—if you can." Tom worked in the Criminal Investigations Division of the Suffolk Constabulary. His team covered everything from fraud and burglary to rape and homicide. He was currently on a special assignment.

"It's drugs, Kate." We passed the White Elephant stall. "I wish I could say we're making headway, but it wouldn't be true. We arrest one dealer—they're just kids, really—only to find ten more taking his place. The answer is to find and disrupt the county lines."

"County lines?"

"A term for the drug trafficking routes from the cities into the countryside. The urban dealers recruit vulnerable teens, those excluded from school or in care, some as young as ten or eleven. They give them free drugs, get them addicted, and then force them to sell to their peers through a practice called *debt bondage*. Almost impossible to track because they communicate with disposable mobiles and apps."

I watched the fresh-faced children lining up for candy floss. "And this is happening here?"

"All over Britain. No village too small. The dealers call it 'going country,' but there's nothing bucolic about it. Last year the National Crime Agency estimated the annual profits from county lines in the range of five hundred million pounds." He took a long breath and let it out. "Look, are you hungry? I'm starving. Let's have a bite to eat and talk about something more pleasant."

"Fine with me. What'll it be? Shrimp rolls at the Chinese takeaway or flatbread at The Three Magpies?"

We decided on The Three Magpies. The tent was crowded with patrons waiting to order. Since we were having a late supper after the fair, we ordered a small Thai chicken flatbread to share with two glasses of Riesling. With all the high-top tables inside the tent taken, we carried our food outdoors and sat on one of the slated benches lining the green.

The sun lay low on the horizon, a shimmering coral ball floating in a lapis and amethyst sea. A mild breeze ruffled the plane trees near the church and brought the scent of lilacs.

"How's Ivor?" Tom asked.

"Much better. Driving the staff mad."

He laughed. "And the shop?"

"Quiet." I took a sip of my wine and balanced the glass on the wide wooden arm of the bench. "Ivor said the walk-in trade won't pick up until the end of May, when tourist season kicks in. But even then, tourists are mainly browsers. My main work is to follow the online sales. When something sells, I pack it up for shipment and make sure the paperwork's right. A percentage of what Ivor sells is shipped abroad. That means bills of lading, cargo manifests, export declarations—stuff like that."

"Sounds complicated." Tom took a bite of the flatbread.

"It's not life or death, which is what you're dealing with."

Taking my first bite, I almost moaned with pleasure. The chicken was warm and tender, perfectly complimented by a hint of peanut sauce, cilantro, and a bit of heat. *Fabulous.*

"Sometimes we get lucky," Tom said. "Last week we intercepted a shipment of synthetic carfentanil from China—enough to kill tens of thousands, Kate."

"I'm glad you're on the job."

"And *I'm* glad you're here." He pulled me close. "What do you hear from Christine?"

My daughter, Christine, was studying history at Magdalen College, Oxford. She and Tom had met the previous Christmas at Finchley Hall.

"She has a new boyfriend—Italian."

"Decent chap?"

"Christine thinks he's wonderful. But then she always does."

"Maybe this time she's right." He said it lightly, but we both understood the subtext. Christine's taste in men tended toward the flashy and unreliable. Her last boyfriend, a real charmer, had involved her in covering up a serious crime. "And your mother?" He was changing the subject. I was grateful.

"Mother has a boyfriend too—if you can call it that at her age. Dr. James Lund, a retired physician. He lives at Oak Hills Senior Community, just a few units down from Mom. They've been spending a lot of time together recently."

"Serious?"

I turned to look at him. "You mean will they get married?"

"People do."

"I know they do." I made a face. "I just find it hard to imagine being the matron of honor at my own mother's wedding."

"Where you're concerned, Kate"—he gave me that heart-melting half smile that always turns me into a teenager—"I can imagine all sorts of things."

My stomach swooped. Since my brain didn't seem to be working, I just smiled and took another sip of wine.

"Want the last piece of flatbread?" he asked.

"You take it."

He polished it off in a single bite and wiped his fingers on the paper napkin. "What about Eric—still in Italy?"

"For now. He'll complete his research at the nuclear waste facility by the end of the month. I'd hoped he might stop through England on his way to Ohio, but he doesn't have time."

"I want to meet all your family—especially your mother. I know how important she is in your life."

"She's the wisest person I know."

We watched a couple pushing a pram across the green. Their toddler, a little boy, clutched a dripping ice cream bar with both chubby fists. They smiled knowingly at each other. Their main purpose at the moment was keeping him safe, happy, and relatively clean. In time they would realize their hardest job would be preparing him to leave home and begin his own life.

My mother had done that for me. Now I had a chance to repay that gift by letting her follow her heart. Easier said than done. I was used to having her all to myself.

Tom had never said much about his relationship with his mother. I flushed, remembering again the day I'd lost my temper and stalked out of the tearoom, leaving Liz Mallory in possession of the field. A Pyrrhic victory if there ever was one.

"What is it, Kate?" Tom was getting way too good at reading my thoughts.

"I was thinking about mothers—well, your mother, specifically. I'm not proud of our last meeting."

"Let it go. It was her fault."

"I'll have to face her."

"And you will, but not tonight. Come on. Let's have some fun."

"May I ask you something first? What do you know about the death of Wallace Villiers?"

"Villiers?" Tom frowned. "The name's familiar."

"He died eighteen years ago in Little Gosling."

"That's right—Villiers. I remember now. I'd just entered the force. Sarah was pregnant with Olivia at the time—about to deliver, if I remember."

Tom's wife, Sarah, had died of cancer four years earlier. Their only child, a daughter, was currently finishing up her gap year in East Africa, at an orphanage for babies with AIDS.

"I knew about the Villiers case, but I wasn't personally involved. Why do you ask?" He stood, gathering our paper plate and napkins.

"Evelyn Villiers, the widow, came in the shop today." I grabbed both wineglasses and joined him. "She brought a piece of ancient Chinese pottery she wants to sell—it's called a húnpíng jar. In fact, she implied she'd like us to handle her late husband's entire art collection."

"That's a good thing, right?"

"Yes—but there's more to the story. She said the reason she's selling is so her daughter can't inherit. Apparently, she blamed Lucy for causing her father's death—sent her away to live with an aunt in Essex. I'd like to do some research. The last thing Ivor needs is to get involved in a family dispute."

"I believe Villiers died of natural causes. I could request the file—if we still have it."

"Could I see it? Is that possible?"

"Let's find out if we have it first." Tom tossed our trash in one of the large garbage bins.

I smiled as I placed our wineglasses with others on a tray stand. I'd known Tom less than a year, been in his company less than a month and a half, all told. But in that short time, my life had changed. As a widow, I'd been stuck in the past, throwing myself into my antiques business to fill the time. Now I had a future—even if I couldn't yet see it.

The dying sun warmed the air. Nearby, children lined up outside a petting zoo enclosure, waiting for their turn to touch the shy, patient lambs and mischievous little goats. A cool breeze brought the mingled scent of farm animals and cotton candy, familiar from all the summers I'd taken Eric and Christine to the Ohio State Fair.

"Bet I can beat you at the coconut shy." Tom grinned.

"You're on."

He did beat me when his third ball knocked down two coconuts, but I got my own back at the Hoopla when my wooden ring circled a bottle of Merlot on the third attempt. Pure luck, although the label looked suspiciously like England's version of Two-Buck Chuck.

At eight thirty, we watched the dog show. The blue ribbon for Waggiest Tail was taken by a gregarious Airedale Terrier—well deserved. Fergus did win a blue ribbon, though—Most Handsome Dog, Golden Oldie Division. From the expression on Vivian's face—and his—I think they were offended.

The sun had dipped below the horizon, leaving a chill in the air and a rosy afterglow in the fresh-ink sky. I slipped on my cardigan and threaded my hand through Tom's arm. A bubble of pleasure caught in my throat. I never imagined I could be this happy again.

A man trotted past us, dressed in medieval clothing and carrying a lute.

"The pageant will be starting soon," I said.

Tom glanced at his watch. "Twenty minutes. Let's find a place to watch."

* * *

Some families had brought lawn chairs. Others spread blankets on the green, where sweaty, exhausted children could sleep off their sugar highs. Tom and I reclaimed our park bench and settled in. As the twilight deepened, a handbell choir from St. Æthelric's entertained us with tunes from *Camelot*.

The Green Maiden pageant began at nine sharp. Several portable light stands illuminated the stage.

Tom put his arm around my shoulder. I leaned back against his chest.

"Look," I said as the first actors took the stage. "There's Vivian and Lady Barbara."

They were dressed in rough, earth-colored woolen tunics. With her round face and stout figure, Vivian looked every inch the part. In contrast, Lady Barbara, even with a tattered shawl tied around her thin shoulders, couldn't have looked less like a peasant if she'd been wearing a tiara. Vivian gave me a surreptitious wave as they milled with the other peasants in front of a painted canvas backdrop depicting a line of timbered houses and a stone bridge. A banner read "Year of Our Lord 1044." Three musicians in medieval clothing were playing "Greensleeves."

In the first act, a young man wearing knee britches and a leather jerkin dashed onto the stage, waving his arms and looking generally gobsmacked. As the peasants gathered around to see what all the fuss was about, a second man in similar clothes appeared, leading a girl wearing a faux-leather shift by the arm. Her skin was the color of moss. Seeing the green maiden, the peasants fell to their knees and crossed themselves.

I leaned over. "Where's the dialogue?"

"It's pantomime," Tom whispered.

A bit of flirting between the green maiden and a peasant youth ended in a wedding when the singularly miscast clergyman—Stephen Peacock from The Finchley Arms—made the sign of the cross over them.

In the next scene, a thatched canopy was carried onstage—a cottage, I supposed. The green maiden, dressed now in a long tunic and wimple, sat with her husband at a rough wooden table. His hand grasped an oversized tankard, but he appeared to have passed out. The green maiden produced a vial from within her tunic, cackled at the audience, and poured a measure of red liquid into the tankard. Waking up, her husband swilled his ale and belched. The crowd roared with laughter. The husband stood, clutched his stomach, and staggered off stage. Immediately, a mob of angry villagers carrying clubs and ropes surrounded the cottage. Inside, the green maiden cowered. *Oh, dear.* Four men unfurled a length of blue cloth and waved it gradually above their heads. Rising water? When the sheet dropped, the green maiden lay dead. Four men carried her offstage.

Everyone clapped.

"Is that it?" I asked. "Is it over?"

"Not quite," Tom said. "First we get a nice speech by the lord of the manor, then the curtain call."

The medieval lord—Mr. Cox, the local butcher—swaggered on stage in green velvet doublet and breeches, far from historically accurate, but oh, well. He gave a nice speech about accepting those who are different from ourselves. Finally, the entire cast filed out.

The crowd applauded wildly. The cast members were taking their final bows when a disturbance arose, stage left. Someone appeared out of the shadows.

The audience screamed and sprang to their feet, partially blocking our view.

A woman staggered toward the players, clutching her belly. Parents grabbed their children and their blankets and ran for their cars.

"What it is, Tom? I can't see."

He took my arm, and we pushed our way toward the stage. People were shouting.

"She's been hurt! Somebody call for help."

"Look at the blood."

Several cast members tried to help the injured woman, but she pushed them away. She appeared to be focused on the actress playing the green maiden. Reaching out with both hands, she took hold of the actress's tunic, nearly pulling the young woman to the ground.

The crowd parted. The front of the woman's white blouse was soaked with blood.

I gasped. "Tom—that's Evelyn Villiers."

She crumpled to the ground.

Tom rushed forward and felt for a pulse. "Kate, call nine-nine-nine."

"Already on their way," someone called out.

A siren screamed. Lights flashed as an ambulance rounded the corner from the main road. The sound faded as the emergency vehicle bumped over the grassy area and came to a halt. Several men jumped out. One grabbed what looked like a portable TV but was probably some kind of medical device.

"Stand back," one of them called. I recognized Ralston Green, Yasmin's footballer husband. At six foot five, he was hard to miss.

The EMTs worked for what seemed like an eternity. At last Ralston stood and peeled off his latex gloves. "Deceased," he told Tom quietly. "Stab wound to the abdomen. Probably bled out."

*Dead? Evelyn Villiers is dead?* I wanted to ask if they were sure.

"Crime scene manager's on his way," Tom told them. "Notify the coroner's office. As soon as we get photographs, he can remove the body."

"Yes, sir." One of the medics pulled a radio from his belt and moved toward the vehicle.

Tom approached the cast members.

The actress playing the green maiden, a young woman of perhaps eighteen or nineteen, was crying. "She looked me straight in the eyes. She was trying to say something."

"It sounded like *mice*," Vivian said.

"Or *mice end*." The maiden gulped down a sob and wiped her eyes on her wimple.

"You must mean *Meissen*," I said.

Lady Barbara stepped forward. "Yes, that's it. I heard her quite clearly."

"Meissen?" Tom asked.

"The German porcelain manufacturer."

"Why would she be thinking about porcelain when she'd been stabbed?"

"I can't imagine," I said, but I was thinking about our meeting at the shop. "She said her husband collected old Meissen."

Tom addressed the green maiden. "Why do you think she singled you out?"

"I don't know, do I?" the girl wailed. Her green makeup had smeared. "I've never seen her before in my life."

A police van pulled up behind the ambulance. White-suited men hopped out, pulling on gloves and shoe covers. The crime scene team.

"Move back." One of the team members pushed the crowd away from the body as another began rolling out the blue and white crime scene tape.

"Start taking down names and details," Tom told a young, uniformed policeman. "First the cast members, then anyone who saw the incident. Backup is on the way."

Turning to me, Tom whispered, "Are you sure that's the woman who came into your shop?"

"Positive—that's Evelyn Villiers." I felt out of breath—probably shock.

Tom's mobile pinged. "Mallory." He listened, his hazel eyes darkening. Cupping his hand over the receiver, he looked at me. "Someone's broken into Ivor's shop. There's blood on the floor and in the alley."

*"What?"* An icy hand clutched my heart.

"On our way," Tom said into the phone. Turning to the constable, he said, "Keep the crowd back. Crime scene team's in charge now."

"Will do, guv." The young police constable looked slightly green around the gills.

"Come on, Kate." Tom seized my hand. "Let's go."

# Chapter Six

As we rounded St. Æthelric's Church, I had to jog to keep up with Tom's long strides.

My breath came in short bursts. *"Someone's broken into Ivor's shop. There's blood on the floor and in the alley."* How was that possible? I'd been there a few hours ago. Everything had been fine.

We crossed the High.

"This way, Kate. Around back." Tom led me through a narrow passageway leading from the High Street to the alley and parking area at the rear of the shops. "Stay to the side. Don't step in the blood if you can help it."

A trail of dark fluid told me this was the path Evelyn Villiers had taken. She'd been bleeding profusely, fatally wounded. My throat tightened.

More sirens.

The rear door to Ivor's shop stood open, guarded by a young female constable in a neon yellow vest and a cap with a black-and-white-checkered band. Near her, a man huddled on a plastic crate, his shoulders slumped, his head bent toward the ground. His shoes—what I could see of them—were bloody. A three-wheeled cargo bicycle sat abandoned near my parked car.

Tom flashed his warrant card. "What happened?"

"Looks like a break-in, sir. And some kind of attack." A slight twist of the young constable's upper lip told me she was fighting to retain control. "Crime scene team is on the way. There's a lot of blood inside. No body. I tried not to disturb anything."

"Well done. Your name, Constable?"

"Weldon, sir. Police Constable Anne Weldon. I work out of Sudbury. Can you tell me what's going on at the green? I heard the radio call about an injured person."

"A woman, deceased."

"This is Mr. Henry Liu," PC Weldon indicated the seated man. "He owns the Chinese takeaway. He noticed the open door and called it in." A slight shifting of her eyes said there was more to the story.

The man stood. His hands were trembling.

"Detective Inspector Mallory. Can you tell me what happened?"

"My restaurant is three buildings down, toward the river." Mr. Liu's voice was clear and cultured. He was average height, slightly built. His black hair was neatly trimmed and smattered with silver. He might have been anywhere between forty and sixty-five.

"We have a stall at the May Fair. We'd run out of shrimp rolls, so I rode back on my bicycle to get more. My wife and I had just packed them up." Mr. Liu pointed to an insulated metal box on the back of his bicycle.

"Was your wife with you?"

"No. We live above the restaurant." He held up a cell phone. "I let her know what happened—so she wouldn't worry."

"She wasn't helping at the tent?"

"My wife speaks almost no English, Inspector. She assembles the rolls in the restaurant kitchen, then we finish them off in the tent."

"All right," Tom said. "You packed up the shrimp rolls. What happened then?" His voice had the reasonable, unhurried tone he used whenever he wanted to put people at their ease.

"I was on my way back to the tent when I noticed the door to Mr. Tweedy's shop was open. Naturally, I dismounted to investigate. That's when I saw the blood."

Bloody footprints, more than one set, led from inside the shop.

"You went inside?"

"I was afraid someone might need help."

"Where were you earlier in the evening?"

"I'd been at the fair since four thirty. "

"What time did you leave to pick up the shrimp rolls?"

He hesitated, suddenly looking lost. "I'm not certain. Around nine, I think. The pageant had just begun."

"And you came through the passageway from the High?"

"Shortest route."

"Did you see anyone—or anything—suspicious?"

I pictured the trail of congealing blood.

"Nothing suspicious." He shook his head. "Everyone was at the fair."

"Was the door to Mr. Tweedy's shop open then?"

"No. If it had been, I'm sure I would have noticed."

"How long were you in the restaurant?"

He looked at Tom blankly "I couldn't say for sure. Maybe forty minutes—no more than that. I was in a hurry to get back before the pageant ended. We expected more customers."

"Stay where you are until we're able to seal off the area. We'll need your fingerprints and shoe prints. It shouldn't take long. Call your wife again if you think she'll worry. In the meantime, Constable Weldon will take down your details."

"Fingerprints? Am I a suspect?"

"We need them for elimination purposes."

"What about my shrimp rolls?"

"I'm sorry. Nothing leaves the scene until it's been processed."

A knot of bystanders gaped at us from the passageway.

"Stay where you are," the constable called out. "This is a crime scene."

"Let me through." A younger version of Mr. Liu elbowed his way past the bystanders. "Dad? What happened?"

Mr. Liu shrugged and gathered his canvas jacket more closely around his body.

Tom stopped the younger man from approaching. "No further, please. I'm Detective Inspector Mallory. Are you Mr. Liu's son?"

"Yes, of course." The son was the spitting image of his father except he was several inches taller and wore a pair of round wire spectacles. "What happened? Is he all right?"

"Your father is fine." Tom moved toward him. "Your name, sir?"

"Liu Zhong. In English, James Liu." He flicked his head toward his father. "Is he in trouble?"

"He reported a crime. As soon as we're finished, we'll escort him back to the restaurant. The best thing for you to do now is—"

James Liu cut across him. "What sort of crime, Inspector?"

"A break-in. Possibly an assault."

"Exactly how is my father involved?"

Tom ignored the question. "Why did you come looking for him?"

"I heard the ambulance. People were running. Someone said there'd been a murder."

"Where do you live?"

"My wife and I are staying with my parents for the present, in the flat over the restaurant."

"Where is your wife?"

"At the tent, where I should be. Look, I want to make sure my father's all right."

"I'm afraid you'll have to wait here. When Constable Weldon has finished with your father, she'll take your statement. Then you can leave."

The temperature had dropped. I buttoned up my sweater.

Tom took my arm. "I need to know if anything's been stolen."

Constable Weldon handed us paper booties.

"Follow my footsteps," Tom said. "And don't touch anything."

We moved slowly, skirting the blood.

"What would Evelyn Villiers have been doing here tonight?" Tom asked.

"I can't imagine. Unless—" I shook my head, unable to finish the sentence.

"Unless what?"

"Well, unless she changed her mind and wanted the húnpíng back, but that doesn't make sense. She didn't have to break in. Maybe she came to talk to me and interrupted a burglary in progress, but why wouldn't she have telephoned me first? And what was she doing in the stockroom?"

"This is where she was stabbed," Tom said. A pool of congealed blood lay soaking into the floorboards. "Is anything missing?"

My eyes swung to the shelves.

The rosewood box had been pushed aside. The felt polishing cloth lay on the floor.

I felt sick and lightheaded. "It's gone, Tom—the húnpíng jar is gone."

"What's this?" Something small, white, and cuplike lay at Tom's feet.

He pulled latex gloves from inside his jacket and snapped them on before reaching down to pick it up.

He held out his hand.

In his palm lay a single white petal.

* * *

I leaned against the picket fence surrounding Vivian Bunn's garden. Tom and I had remained at Ivor's shop until the crime scene team arrived. Since my car was within the cordoned-off zone, he'd driven me home.

"Nothing about this makes sense," I said. "Why was Evelyn Villiers so focused on the girl playing the green maiden—and why would she tell her about a German porcelain factory?"

"That's up your alley, not mine." He wrapped his arms around me. "You're shivering."

I slipped my arms inside his jacket, feeling his solid warmth.

"In the next few days, we'll need you to take a thorough inventory," Tom said. "Make sure nothing else is missing."

"Of course."

"What did you make of Mr. Liu senior?"

"He was horrified. In shock."

"And the son?"

"Slightly belligerent."

"I thought so too. Notice something else about the son?"

The scent of evening primrose met me, light and lemony.

"Like what?" I pulled back to look at him.

"He never asked about the victim on the green."

"Maybe he didn't know."

"When we asked him why he checked on his father, he told us someone said there'd been a murder."

"You're right. What really puzzles me is that flower petal."

"Did someone drop off a bouquet for Ivor today?"

I shook my head. "The only person in the shop the entire day, besides me, was Evelyn Villiers, and she didn't bring flowers. She wasn't even in the stockroom. We talked in that little alcove off the display area."

"The petal was fresh. It must have fallen—or been placed there—recently."

"You mean by Mrs. Villiers?"

"Or the person with her. She obviously didn't stab herself."

"And she didn't steal the húnpíng jar, either."

"The CSIs will analyze the footprints. That should tell us something." He reached out and tucked a strand of hair behind my ear. "You asked earlier why she didn't call you. Would she have known how to reach you after hours?"

"I wrote my cell number on her copy of the consignment form." My throat contracted. "Tom, she was running for her life, trying to find help."

"I'm amazed she made it all the way to the village green."

"And why, after making it all that way, would she say 'Meissen'—not 'Help, I've been stabbed' or 'Call an ambulance'?"

"It has to mean something," Tom said.

"I hate it when things don't make sense. And another thing—how did Mrs. Villiers and her killer get into the shop without setting off the burglar alarm?"

"Had a key?"

"And Ivor's security code as well? Come on, Tom."

"Could you have forgotten to arm the system?"

"No. I specifically remember punching in the code as I left."

I must have sounded defensive because he raised a hand in surrender. "A question, Kate, not a criticism."

"Sorry." I pulled my sweater tighter around my body. "My second week on the job, and Ivor's shop is burglarized." I felt sick, imagining the look on Ivor's face when I told him. "Trust is everything in the antiques business. With the kind of objects Ivor deals in, clients need to know the dealer will take appropriate care. Ivor did that. He was extremely careful."

"Think, Kate. Is there any way Mrs. Villiers might have gotten the security code?"

"You mean did I tell her?" I mimicked the imaginary conversation. "'In case you should want to have a good wander around the shop after hours, just push one-two-three on the keypad.'"

"Ivor's code is one-two-three?"

"Of course not. It's an example." I closed my eyes and made an effort to calm down. "Look, Ivor never mentioned giving a key to anyone but me. And I can't believe he would give out his security code."

"We'll ask him."

A thought struck me. "Tom, how do we know she actually *was* Mrs. Villiers? She gave me her name, but she didn't provide identification—not that I asked. Could she have been someone else pretending to be Mrs. Villiers?"

"You mean she stole the jar and then tried to consign it under Evelyn Villiers's name? Possibly, but why take the risk you'd contact the real Mrs. Villiers?"

"Yeah." I had to agree. "No thief worth his salt would offload a stolen object locally. Besides, the real Mrs. Villiers would still be alive." I took in a breath. "Have you checked?"

"My sergeant is at the Villiers' house now. No one's home. He found the name of a housekeeper. He's asked her to identify the body tomorrow."

"How about the daughter—Lucy?"

"First we have to find her." He bent to kiss me. "Sorry. I must go. Long night ahead. Can you drive into Bury tomorrow to give your formal statement? I have a meeting in the morning, but I should be free after one o'clock. Until then, keep this to yourself, all right?"

"Of course. When will I be able to get back in the shop?"

"I'll let you know. In the meantime, we'll contact Ivor."

"Oh, not tonight, Tom. He'll be sleeping. Let me talk to him in the morning."

"All right. Tell him we'll need to speak with him. Give him my best."

The porch light blinked on, illuminating the flagged path.

"Go on." Tom ran his hands down my arms. "I want to see you safely inside."

A face appeared at the window—Vivian, waiting to pepper me with questions.

I braced myself for the interrogation.

# Chapter Seven

"You poor child." Vivian wore a gray wool robe piped in navy and a pair of well-worn scuffs. She poured me a cup of tea, adding a splash of milk and three unasked-for lumps of sugar. "Another murder—can you believe it? After what happened last Christmas, anyone would think Long Barston was the crime capital of East Anglia." She tsked. "We're Suffolk, not Midsomer County."

We sat in the kitchen with its massive limestone hearth, oak timber framing, and whitewashed plaster. An old Aga cooker radiated warmth. Beyond that, a set of wooden steps curved toward the upper floor.

"And you were just asking about Evelyn Villiers as well." Vivian pushed a slice of apple cake toward me. "Eat something. You look pale."

I took a bite of the cake. It was warm and tasted of cinnamon and allspice. "Thanks, Vivian. All I've had to eat since breakfast is a bite of a flatbread and a glass of Riesling."

She gaped at me as if I'd confessed to anorexia. "You need a proper meal. Give me a minute or two." She stood and began rifling through the pans hanging over the Aga. I pictured her whipping up a "full English"—eggs, bacon, sausage, beans, grilled tomato, and (*eek!*) black pudding.

Vivian loved to cook—or rather, she loved to feed people.

"Please don't bother," I said. "The cake is all I can manage tonight—truly."

Vivian made a moue of regret and settled back in her chair. "They *say* Evelyn Villiers was stabbed in the course of a *robbery* at Ivor's antiquities shop." Vivian had a habit of speaking in italics. "I'll bet it was that Chinese *thingy* she wanted Ivor to sell."

"The police aren't releasing any information."

"I *thought* so." She gave me a smug look.

"All right—just keep it to yourself for now. You may be able to help me."

Her eyes lit up. "What do you want to know?"

"You told me Evelyn Villiers was a recluse, but she must have had a friend, a solicitor, a doctor who would know where I can find her daughter, Lucy."

"Why? Surely the police will locate her."

"I'm sure they will, but I'd like a chance to talk with her about the húnpíng jar. If Ivor's insurance doesn't cover the full value, he'll owe the estate for the remainder. She may agree to give us time to pay up."

"I wish I could help," Vivian said, frowning, "but I never knew the Villiers woman personally. All I know is what I read in the newspapers—and heard from the ex-housekeeper, Ertha Green."

"Would Ertha know where Lucy lives now?"

"She might."

"Would she talk to me?"

"I can ask." Vivian glanced at her watch. "I'll phone her in the morning. Her mind's clearest in the morning."

"I can't see her tomorrow. I have to break the news to Ivor." I polished off the last bite of apple cake. "After that I'm giving my formal statement in Bury."

"How grisly."

My cell phone pinged a text. I pulled out the phone and swiped the screen. "It's my mother. She wants me to call her. Do you mind?"

"Certainly not, my dear." I started to clear my cup and plate, but Vivian stopped me. "Leave this to me. You phone your mother. Then get some sleep."

"I will. Thanks for the tea and cake." Kissing Vivian on the cheek, I slipped my phone in the pocket of my sundress and headed for the staircase.

"Vivian," I said, then stopped and turned back. "Are you sure Evelyn Villiers didn't say anything else before she collapsed."

"She might have been trying to tell us who stabbed her," Vivian said darkly. "Her mouth was sort of opening and shutting, but all that came out was that *mice* thing."

* * *

After undressing and slipping into the cloudlike double bed in Vivian's guest room, I called my mother.

"Linnea Larson here." My mother, ignoring the caller ID function on her phone, always answered with her full name.

"Hi, Mom. It's me. How are you?"

"Tip-top. I was just about to head down for dinner with James. Then Wii bowling. We're practicing for the annual tournament against Wesley Woods. It's a grudge match."

I laughed. "Should I call back?"

"Certainly not. James will wait. Now," she said in a tone that would brook no argument, "fill me in on all the doings in Long Barston."

I did.

When I finished, the line went so silent I thought we might have lost the connection.

"*Another* body?" she said, echoing Vivian. "What does that make it now—three? four?"

"I'm not collecting them."

"Of course you aren't. What does Tom say?"

"Not much yet. Evelyn Villiers was stabbed, but why and by whom no one knows." An image of blood on the front of that crisp white blouse made me queasy. I swallowed hard. "The thing is, I can't figure out how she got into Ivor's shop without setting off the alarm—and why she would try to steal something that belonged to her already."

"But she didn't steal it, did she? Someone else did. Maybe that person forced her to return to the shop. They killed her and took the húnpíng."

"It just seems so unnecessary. Why wouldn't the killer make her phone me and ask for the jar back?"

"That is a point." I pictured my mother frowning, the corners of her mouth turned down. "I don't know the law in the UK, but you do realize Ivor may be financially responsible for the loss. I hope he has insurance."

"Me too." Ivor's insurance coverage was one of the topics I'd planned to address in the morning. "From the little Mrs. Villiers told me, it sounds like her daughter, Lucy, inherits everything. The police are trying to locate her."

"Kate, darling—" From the tone of my mother's voice, I thought she was going to warn me against involving myself in the investigation. Instead she said, "Lady Barbara's comment was intriguing, don't you think? *'Something must have happened.'* For eighteen years Mrs. Villiers lived with her late husband's art collection, knowing it would go to her daughter when she died. Today, after all those years of inaction, she suddenly decided to sell the húnpíng jar and possibly the entire collection. Then she was murdered."

"What are you suggesting?"

"I'm suggesting that when the police discover what changed in Mrs. Villiers's life, they'll know why she was killed."

"I just hope they find Lucy before she reads about her mother's death in the papers."

"You said you took photographs of the húnpíng. Can you text them to me?"

"As soon as we hang up."

"Every jar is unique, Kate—no two alike have ever been found."

"So if this jar turns up for sale somewhere—even in the future—my photographs will prove it's the húnpíng stolen from Ivor's shop."

"Exactly. Your photos may be the only ones in existence. You should send them to the police as well."

"I'll do that." I changed the subject. "How's James?"

"His arthritis is playing up. Otherwise, he's fine. James is partly the reason I called you. He's invited me to join him at his daughter's lake cottage in northern Wisconsin. We leave a week from tomorrow."

"Lake cottage?" I tried to say, "How nice"—I really did—but the words refused to form.

"You don't mind, do you?"

"Of course not, Mom. I want you to be happy." It was the truth. So why was I feeling like I'd been punched in the gut?

She went on briskly. "I'll be sharing a room with his granddaughter. Bunk beds if you can believe it. Carly's twelve, an inquisitive little thing from all accounts. Reminds me of you at that age."

"Poking my nose in?"

"*Curious*—and very bright. I'll say goodnight now, darling girl. Keep me posted."

I clicked off and fell back against the huge square pillow. My mother, off for a week with her boyfriend. What was I feeling? Loss? *Jealousy?* A stab of shame pierced my heart. Who was I to resent my mother's happiness? She'd borne so many losses—my brother, Matt, to heart disease when he was just eleven; my father, killed in a car crash on Christmas Eve, when I was seventeen. After his death, she and I became exceptionally close. We were the only family we had left.

In the early days of my marriage to Bill, my mother had spent time with us—weeks at Christmas and in the summer—helping me raise Eric and Christine, filling in at the shop when I had an auction to attend or a doctor's appointment for one of the kids. She'd helped me price the stock at the antiques shop. She'd helped me restore our lovely Victorian house in the Jackson Falls historic district. When Bill died, I'd needed her more than ever. Tom had said it once: Linnea Larson was the fixed point in my life. My anchor.

Now I was being asked to share her with another family—a big, noisy family with children and grandchildren and cottages on lakes. They would sweep her into their orbit, leaving me on the outside.

A sob caught in my throat. *Stupid. Selfish.* Tears welled in my eyes.

What I felt—resentment, jealousy—was ugly, mean-spirited, and unfair. Not once had my mother even hinted that my feelings for Tom might take me away from her one day.

I blew out a furious breath and wiped my eyes.

*I will not do this. I will not feel this. I will be glad for her.*

Picking up my cell phone, I tapped out a text: *Have a fabulous time at the lake! I love you.* Then I attached the images I'd taken of the húnpíng jar and pushed "Send."

I turned off the bedside lamp and lay in the dark.

Something niggled at the back of my mind. A question.

I heard Vivian rustling about in the kitchen below me. "Come on, then," I heard her tell Fergus. "Walkies."

Jumping out of bed, I called down to her. "Vivian, I'm curious. Who told you the body on the green was Evelyn Villiers?"

She appeared at the foot of the stairs, looking blank. "I don't know. Everyone knew it."

But how? No one had actually mentioned her name—I knew I hadn't. Had someone recognized her after eighteen years?

# Chapter Eight

Sunday, May 5

I arrived at The Willows at nine. Another glorious day was in the offing—temps in the upper sixties and warming with the sun. Definitely not a match for my mood.

The front door stood open.

"Welcome back, Mrs. Hamilton." The cheerful woman behind the reception desk had remembered my name. "Mr. Tweedy will be delighted."

I doubted that, given the news I had to tell him.

The words I'd practiced all morning sounded lame. *Something's happened, Ivor. Try not to get upset, but—*

When I entered, he was sitting in the big leather chair by the French window, dressed in a spiffy paisley dressing gown. "Kate, just in time." His blue eyes sparkled.

"Ivor," I said, summoning my courage, "I have something to—"

"Not now, Kate. Look at this." He shoved a catalog at me. The corner of one page had been turned down. An item was circled in black ink.

I pulled up the visitor's chair and read: *Previously unknown translation of the Little Domesday Book, ca. 1786, covering Essex, Norfolk, and Suffolk.*

"Familiar with the Domesday Book, hmm?" The only thing Ivor loved better than testing my knowledge was catching me in some lapse.

"Of course." I handed him the catalog. "It was the great survey—a sort of census record of England, ordered by William the Conqueror in 1085. Villages, family names, livestock, land."

"And why was it called Domesday?" His blue eyes widened, all innocence.

"I think it means 'doomsday,' the Final Judgment, and if I remember correctly, the name came later."

"Late twelfth century. But why Domesday?"

"Because of the comparison to the book mentioned in the Bible, the one recording the deeds of all mankind—a reminder that the Domesday records were final and could never be disputed. The ultimate authority."

"And the Little Domesday Book?"

"All right, I don't know. Never heard of it."

"Ah, well." He cocked his head, relishing the role of tutor. "The Domesday Book is actually *two* separate and independent documents, both written in Latin. Not many people know that. The Great Domesday Book is a summary of thirty-one English counties south of what was then the Scottish border, *except* for Essex, Norfolk, and Suffolk." He ticked them off on his fingers. "The records for those three counties—the full, unabbreviated records, mind you, not summaries—are preserved in the Little Domesday Book, which is actually the bulkier of the two parchment folios. Smaller in dimensions, but fuller in details because the text is undigested—a virtual treasure trove of historical details, little-known facts, descriptions of local customs, even the musings of the commissioners assigned the task of gathering information." He tapped the catalog. "This is a translation in English, made sometime in the mid-eighteenth century. I just put in a bid."

"You *bid* on it?" This was not good news. "How much?"

"I do have the proceeds from the bronze statue and the auction," he said with dignity, skirting the question. "I may have a shot."

Just over five feet tall, Ivor looked even smaller since his surgery. And vulnerable. I felt a pang of affection for this dear elderly man who'd risked so much to help me the previous December. "But you need that money, Ivor. Some of it anyway."

"I know, I know." He waved his hand impatiently. "But the manuscript is as good as sold, Kate. I know a professor in Essex who will pay—"

His thought was preempted by the entrance of the young aide, Jay'den, looking fresh and cheerful in her crisp blue pinstriped tunic.

"Thought you might like today's newspaper, Mr. Tweedy. Twenty minutes, mind. Then we'll get you ready for physio." She smiled at me. "He's making tremendous progress. His legs are stronger than most people's his age."

"All those years at sea," Ivor chirped. "The deck pitching and rolling."

Jay'den breezed out, and Ivor unfolded the newspaper.

I gaped at the headline: *"Long Barston Antiquities Shop Scene of Brutal Murder."*

His face crumpled.

"I'm sorry, Ivor. I should have phoned last night, but it was late, and I didn't want to wake you. There was nothing you could do anyway."

He made a high-pitched gurgling sound. "Read it to me."

Ivor handed me the paper. I cleared my throat.

> *"The woman who died last night at the May Fair in Long Barston has been identified as Mrs. Evelyn Villiers of Hapthorn Lodge, Little Gosling. Police believe Mrs. Villiers was stabbed inside a well-known antiquities shop on the High Street. Fatally injured, she staggered several blocks to the village green, where she collapsed. Her death is believed to be connected to the theft of a valuable Chinese urn."*

"They mean the húnpíng jar," I said pointlessly.

> *"The owner of a nearby restaurant found the back entrance to the antiquities shop open, saw the blood, and called police. A representative of the Suffolk Constabulary told reporters, 'More*

*details will be made public as we receive them.' Anyone with knowledge of this crime is asked to contact the police station at Bury St. Edmunds."*

"Which nearby restaurant?" The tremor in Ivor's voice got my attention. This was not going to help his recovery.

"The Chinese takeaway." I told Ivor what Henry Liu had said about running out of shrimp rolls and riding his bicycle to the restaurant for more.

"How did these people get into the shop?"

"There was no sign of a break-in. Have you given a key to anyone besides me?"

"Never." Ivor's forehead creased. "Was the alarm set?"

"Yes, of course. I remember wondering what would happen if I messed up and the alarm went off."

"It wouldn't, Kate. It's a silent alarm. Monitored remotely. If the cancel code wasn't entered within a minute, the alarm center would have contacted the police first, then me." He gave me a sheepish look. "Are you absolutely certain you armed the system?"

I couldn't blame him for asking. I laid my hand on his. "I'm as certain as I can possibly be, Ivor. Truly. And even if I had forgotten the alarm, the rear security door locks automatically. They couldn't have gotten in without a key. The police are checking for CCTV camera footage. Maybe that will shed some light."

"Ha! I doubt the village has more than two or three cameras. And those are probably on the blink. You say Henry Liu raised the alarm?"

"Do you know him?"

"Nice family—wife, son, daughter-in-law. Henry's a quiet chap. Keeps himself to himself."

"He was pretty shaken up."

"You were *there*? How did that happen?"

I told him about the May Fair and the play. "The EMTs had just confirmed Mrs. Villiers's death when Tom got the call about the break-in."

"What will happen now?"

"The shop will have to remain closed while the police process the scene." I felt a lump in my throat. "Then I'll be able to have a good look around, to make sure, um . . . nothing else was stolen."

"I should be there, Kate. This isn't fair on you." He was taking this better than I'd expected.

"I'll be fine. My mother asked if you have insurance."

"For cleanup crews and alarm repairs? Yes." His eyes glistened, and I realized with horror he was trying not to cry.

"Theft?" I almost hated to ask.

"Twenty thousand pounds," he said miserably. "With a five-thousand-pound deductible. If I insured everything for its retail value, the cost would be prohibitive. That's why I invested in security." He sat for a moment without speaking. "Reimbursing the estate for the húnpíng will mean selling things, no question. It can be done, Kate, but it will take time. If the insurance company gets involved, there'll be a lawsuit, publicity. My reputation will be ruined."

"What can I do?" I reached out for his hand. "Anything. Just ask."

"Find Lucy Villiers. Talk to her. If the police don't recover the húnpíng, I'm going to owe her a lot of money. See if she's willing to give me time to raise the cash."

"I'll do my best—I promise. Try not to worry. Whatever happens, we're in this together."

# Chapter Nine

I drove straight from The Willows to Bury St. Edmunds.

Tom met me in the lobby of the Suffolk Constabulary on Raingate Street. He looked cool and professional in a pair of tailored trousers and a white shirt, with his police ID on a lanyard around his neck. This time his smile did little to cheer me up. I was still thinking about Ivor raising thousands of pounds in cash to reimburse Evelyn Villiers's estate for the value of the hunping jar. He might never recover financially. He wasn't a young man, and for better or worse, his nest egg consisted almost entirely of fine objects, not pounds and pence in a bank account.

The lobby of the station was lined with posters informing visitors of various neighborhood safety programs and warning constituents about the dangers of drugs. A portrait of the Queen hung over a large clock. Tom introduced me to two constables behind an open glass partition. Then we passed through a door into the inner sanctum, three floors of offices and meeting rooms where the officers of the Suffolk Constabulary, Western Division, fought crime and maintained peace within the limits of an ever-shrinking budget.

Tom had an office on the second floor, with a single window overlooking the covered motor pool. His desk was stacked with papers. A framed photograph of his wife, Sarah, hung on the wall. Beaming into the camera, she held a chubby toddler of about two—their daughter, Olivia, now almost nineteen.

Love and loss. Tom and I had known them both.

I took the chair nearest his desk and handed him an envelope containing the consignment agreement Mrs. Villiers had signed and the copies he'd requested. The original would go to forensics.

Tom spread the photocopies on his desk and scanned the pages, stopping to examine the personal information and the signature on the final page. "I'll be recording our conversation, Kate—routine. The consignment agreement and the notes I've already taken will be incorporated into the case file."

"I'll text you the photographs of the húnpíng jar."

I was about to tell him the victim's name had been common knowledge in Long Barston before the newspaper reported it, when someone rapped on the door. A man entered, and I had a sudden picture of the old boar on my Norwegian grandmother's farm—pink face, leathery snout, chip on his shoulder.

Tom stood. "Kate Hamilton, this is Detective Chief Inspector Dennis Eacles. He'd like to sit in on the interview." Eacles's trousers were held up by a low-slung belt. The fabric of his navy sports jacket strained across his arms and shoulders.

"A great pleasure, ma'am," Eacles said without a trace of a smile. He had a slight northern accent, with the broad vowels typical of Manchester or Leeds.

DCI Eacles, Tom had told me, had been recently brought in from Eastern Division to fill the vacancy when Tom's failure to follow orders in the Finchley Hoard case had cost him his promotion. My fault—a fact he'd never once brought up.

Eacles took the third chair and pulled it slightly behind mine in the narrow room—just enough to make me feel uncomfortable. It brought back my grandmother's warning about that old boar: *"Look him in the eye, girlie. Never turn your back on him."*

Tom turned on a recording device. "Tuesday, May fifth." He looked at his wrist. "Twenty-five minutes past one PM. DI Mallory and DCI Eacles interviewing Mrs. Kate Hamilton concerning the death of Mrs. Evelyn Villiers."

He opened his black notebook. "Let's begin with yesterday morning, Mrs. Hamilton. Can you tell us how you first met Mrs. Evelyn Villiers?"

I told my story again, trying to picture the meeting in my mind so I wouldn't omit any potentially relevant details. When I finished, I said, "She told me to contact her by text. Then she left the shop, crossed the street, and turned toward the river. She appeared to be in a hurry, and I wondered if she'd driven herself from Little Gosling or if someone had given her a ride."

"Do you remember which street she turned into?" Tom asked.

"The one just before the Suffolk Tea Room, leading to Dash End Lane."

"Weavers Street," Tom said.

"Send Cliffe to see if anyone saw the damn car," Eacles growled. "If we're going to solve this case, we need facts."

"Already done, sir." I saw a muscle tighten in Tom's cheek. He flipped a page in his notebook.

I heard Eacles move behind me. "You said you felt uncomfortable about Mrs. Villiers. Why was that?"

"Intuition, I suppose—and her demeanor." Being questioned by someone I couldn't see felt weird, so I addressed my answer to Tom. "When she entered the shop, she made sure no one was observing us from the street. Then she asked if I had somewhere private to talk. She seemed wary, suspicious, but maybe it was just because the jar was worth a lot of money—although she didn't seem to know that. Or because Ivor wasn't there as she'd expected. Or maybe"—I hesitated, trying to put my thoughts into words—"because she wasn't used to dealing with people face-to-face. Vivian Bunn said Mrs. Villiers had been a recluse since the death of her husband eighteen years ago." I looked over my shoulder at DCI Eacles. "Miss Bunn is the woman I'm living with on the Finchley estate."

Eacles grunted.

"Mrs. Villiers specifically said not to telephone her about the appraisal. I was to text her, and she'd call me."

"Does that have some significance?" Eacles asked.

"I don't know. You asked me to tell you why I felt uncomfortable."

Eacles exhaled slowly, like a leaky balloon. "That word she said—*Meissen*. What do you make of it?"

"Meissen is an old and very fine porcelain manufacturer in what used to be Eastern Germany. Mrs. Villiers told me Meissen was one of her late husband's favorites. That's what she must have meant, although I can't imagine why she said it."

"Is there anything else you can tell us?" Tom asked. "Maybe something that didn't seem important at the time."

I thought for a moment, going over my conversation with Mrs. Villiers. "There is one thing. As I was preparing the contract for her to sign, she mumbled something—sort of under her breath. It sounded like 'wagon bell,' but when I asked her to repeat it, she said something completely different. I decided she'd been talking to herself and didn't realize she'd spoken aloud."

*"Wagon bell?"* I felt rather than saw Eacles roll his eyes.

Tom made a note. "What can you tell us about the Villiers's art collection?"

Eacles's chair scraped the floor as he moved into my peripheral vision.

"Only what Mrs. Villiers told me. I got the impression she hadn't shared her husband's passion for art and antiques and was taking an interest now only to prevent her daughter from inheriting." I wanted to add my mother's comment about something having changed recently in Mrs. Villiers's life, but I'd save it for later, when Tom and I were alone.

Tom glanced at Eacles, and some message passed between them. He opened the top drawer of his desk and pulled out a polythene bag. "Mrs. Villiers was wearing this necklace when she died. What can you tell us about it?"

I peered at the heart-shaped gold locket inside. "I noticed her wearing it when she came in the shop."

Tom handed me a pair of latex gloves. After putting them on, I unzipped the bag, took out the pendant, and pressed the release.

Inside, under a rock-crystal window, was a coil of black hair and an inscription: "M. Grenfel, born Mar 5, 1805, died Feb 4, 1853."

"It's a mourning locket—mid-nineteenth century—a floral design embedded with paste stones—not diamonds. The surface and edges are worn, so it hasn't spent much time in a jewelry box." I turned it over to examine the markings. "It's engraved on the back with the initial *E*. For Evelyn, I suppose. This is the kind of thing a young girl might receive on her birthday. It's twelve carat gold filled—pretty, but not especially valuable. Might sell for a couple of hundred pounds on a good day."

"How about this Grenfel person?"

"He—or she—was in their late forties when they died. A great-great-grandparent, perhaps. Or maybe someone found the locket in a thrift store and bought it because they thought it was pretty."

"We'll check the name Grenfel," Tom said. "Maybe Evelyn Villiers had relatives who would know where Lucy is living now."

"What about the aunt in Essex?" I asked. "The one Lucy was sent to live with after her father's death."

"Someone's on that now."

DCI Eacles cleared his throat. "I don't fancy our chances of recovering the stolen item—the *hoon*ping." He stretched out the vowel. "In the meantime, we need to know what's what with that art collection—if there'd been any funny business going on. We need professional advice. There'd be a small stipend."

I stared at him. "Are you asking for my help?"

"If Ivor can spare you," Tom said. "Mrs. Villiers was an elderly woman, living alone with a fortune in art and antiques. An easy target for thieves."

"The *point* is," Eacles said unpleasantly, "*oo*ther items may be missing as well. You said the woman had records. We need an inventory by someone who knows what they're about."

"Have you spoken with Mrs. Villiers's solicitor?" I asked Tom. "There may have been a valuation done at the time of Wallace Villiers's death."

"If there was, I'll let you know."

"We'd be grateful for your help," Eacles said, flattening out the *a* sound in grateful. He smiled, revealing large yellow teeth. *Never turn your back on him, girlie.*

Well, this was something I hadn't anticipated. I'd be helping the Suffolk Constabulary make sense of whatever secrets Wallace Villiers's art collection might reveal. Still, my first priority was Ivor—and locating the húnpíng jar, if possible.

"I'll do what I can."

Tom shut his black notebook. "We'd like you to begin as soon as possible. The forensics team will be finished at Hapthorn Lodge in two or three days. Are you available?"

"I can be."

Someone tapped on the door. "Sorry to interrupt, guv." DS Ryan Cliffe's large placid face peered at us. "It's Lucy Villiers. Looks like we've got a *misper* on our hands." Cliffe handed Tom a folder.

I looked at Tom. "A misper?"

"Missing person." He opened the folder. "Fourth of January 2003. Miss W. Villiers of 34 Lark Court, Dunmow Parva, Essex, reported her niece, Lucy Villiers, missing. As the girl was eighteen and there was no indication of foul play, the search was called off."

Eacles leaned back in his chair, causing the plastic to crack. "That's great. All we need."

* * *

After the interview, Tom and I walked to The Dog & Partridge, a traditional chain pub five minutes from police headquarters.

I grabbed a table in the bar while Tom ordered two coffees.

"Three things," I said when he joined me. "I didn't want to mention them around DCI Eacles."

"No one ever does. That's his problem."

"Well, the first is unrelated to the case. Do you have time to check out that new auction house on the road to Sudbury? I looked them up. One of the owners is an ex-estate agent named Nigel Oakley. The business is actually run by his son and a business partner. Lady Barbara is thinking about placing several items there. I want to make sure they're on the up-and-up."

"I'll see what I can find. What's the second?"

"Vivian *knew* the victim was Evelyn Villiers last night—before the newspaper article this morning. She said everyone at the fair knew."

Tom shrugged. "Things get out. Don't ask me how." He emptied a packet of milk into his coffee and swirled it with his spoon. "And the third?"

"There's a woman in Long Barston—Ertha Green, Ralston's mother. Vivian said she kept house for the Villiers family years ago. I'd like to ask her if she knows anything about the daughter, Lucy. Ivor asked me to find her. Do you mind? If the húnpíng jar isn't recovered, he'll have to arrange for restitution."

Tom reached out and touched my cheek. "I trust you, Kate—you know that. Your instincts are sound, and your judgment is impeccable. You notice things others don't—connections, odd coincidences most people pass over as unimportant. It's a gift. You've proven it. But focus on the art collection. Your knowledge of antiques is what we need. That's why I pushed for you with Eacles. I have to tell you he wasn't keen."

"I got that impression."

"Did I put you on the spot? I know you have your hands full with the shop."

"If you want to know the truth, Inspector Mallory, I'm delighted. I've been dying to see the Villiers Collection." I shot him a smile. "Now I don't have to break in."

He rolled his eyes. "Don't make a joke, Kate. What I'm trying to say is, I trust you, but I'm not willing to take risks."

I started to protest, but he raised a hand. "If you get mixed up in the investigation and Eacles hears of it, there'll be hell to pay. Eacles doesn't like me. He's biding his time, waiting for a reason to push me out. Besides—"

"Besides what?"

"I don't want you taking any chances. Remember last Christmas—the roof at Finchley Hall?"

He looked so earnest, I couldn't help myself.

"I'm pretty sure I'll be safe. Ertha Green's almost ninety."

# Chapter Ten

Monday, May 6

At seven fifteen the next morning, Lady Barbara telephoned, summoning Vivian and me to Finchley Hall at ten o'clock. She and Francie Jewell—her cook, lady's maid, and cleaner, rolled into one—had assembled several potential sale items for me to evaluate. I had plenty of time. Ivor's antiquities shop was still off-limits while the crime scene team gathered evidence. Finding something that would lead them to the killer's identity was unlikely, Tom had admitted. The perpetrator was probably a professional thief. That worried me. If he got in once, he could get in again.

At breakfast, Vivian handed me the local newspaper. "You'll be interested to know the local shop owner who discovered the break-in at Ivor's shop was Henry Liu—and his son."

I refrained from saying *I know.* Why spoil her fun?

Opening the paper, I scanned the short article. The Suffolk police had issued an official statement, giving a quick overview of the case but keeping the details and their lines of inquiry to themselves.

Vivian stacked her breakfast dishes in the sink. "I spoke with Yasmin Green this morning. Your interview with Ertha will have to wait. The old lady is staying with one of her nieces in Torquay—an annual two-week respite for Yasmin and Ralston. She'll be home on Friday."

*Rats.* I'd hoped that Ertha, the Villiers's old housekeeper, could tell me about Lucy and what really happened the night her father died. I admit to curiosity. And Ertha might know Lucy's current whereabouts. If she did, I'd have to wait until the end of the week to find out.

Vivian and Fergus left for Finchley Hall while I was still finishing my breakfast. Dressed in her baggy tweed skirt, moss-green twinset, and sturdy leather lace-ups, she stumped off with her walking stick as though she were about to inspect the troops. She'd probably done exactly that when Lady Barbara's husband was alive. As his private secretary, I was sure she'd kept everything at Finchley Hall ship-shape and Bristol fashion.

Twenty minutes later, as I was leaving for the Hall, I received a text from Tom. The forensics team had a theory as to how Mrs. Villiers and her killer had entered the shop without setting off the alarm. He'd fill me in on our way to Hapthorn Lodge on Wednesday.

Every couple needs at least one common interest. Why did one of ours have to be murder?

The path from the cottage to the Hall led through Finchley Park and the brick-walled Elizabethan garden. With the old rose bricks soaking up and reflecting the warmth of the morning sun, the garden felt milder than the crisp morning air outside. I breathed in the resinous scent of English boxwood. Dwarf cultivars had been planted the previous autumn by the last of the interns, Peter, a handsome doctoral student from the University of East Anglia. The boxwood had already begun weaving itself into dense green mini-hedges defining the half-acre of geometric beds. Those closest to the kitchen were filled with herbs, lettuces, and low-growing berries. Farther from the house, flowers bloomed—dianthus, coral bells, foxgloves, and historic varieties of roses. Semi-dwarf apple and pear trees formed graceful, horizontal tiers against the brick walls. *I could live here*—assuming I had several million pounds burning a hole in my bank account.

Old Arthur Gedge, who'd tended the Finchley Hall grounds since he was a lad, still pottered about most days, but a team of professional landscape gardeners was needed—and soon. Grounds maintenance wasn't the only problem Lady Barbara faced. Updating the ancient electrical system was the most pressing issue, followed by much-needed repairs to the lead roof over the east wing. And that was just for starters. The survival of Finchley Hall depended on the National Trust taking over—and on Lady Barbara's ability to raise significant amounts of cash to tide her over until they did. I didn't want to think about what she would do if the Trust declined her offer.

I found Lady Barbara and Vivian in the private sitting room with its white marble fireplace and faded wallpaper in a vintage design of urns and flowers. Morning sunlight streamed through the deep-set windows, picking out the frayed cushion on the armchair and the missing fringe on the carpet.

For once, they weren't having tea. Lady Barbara looked all business in a simple cotton dress and fluffy silver-gray cardigan, the sleeves pushed up to her elbows.

A cool breeze blew in through the open French door, bringing the scent of fresh flowers. "They're lovely," I said, noticing the generous bouquet arranged in a crystal vase. "From your garden?"

Lady Barbara blushed. "Oh no. They're a gift from that collector in Bury St. Edmunds—the one who helped you track down the missing artifacts from the Finchley Hoard last December."

Ivor was the one who'd put us onto the reclusive collector who suffered from a rare form of albinism. The man had been intensely private—a response, I'd imagined, to the bullying he must have received in his youth. Initially I'd suspected him of dealing in stolen artifacts, an impression encouraged by his refusal to reveal his name and his habit of paying for valuable antiquities with stacks of twenty-pound notes.

"Flowers arrive weekly," Vivian said.

"He really shouldn't," Lady Barbara said, but I could see she was secretly pleased. "I don't blame him for anything. Charles knows that."

"Charles? You're on a first-name basis?"

Lady Barbara blushed again. "That's all I'm allowed to say. You know how he values his privacy."

"He has a title," said Vivian, who loved knowing things other people didn't. "A title even *you* would recognize."

"Imagine that," I said. Vivian's blunt remarks were one of her endearing qualities.

"Enough of that." Lady Barbara flapped her hands at us. "Now, Kate. What's happening with the investigation? Viv said the police asked you to give a statement."

"I did that yesterday. They've asked me to compile an inventory of the Villiers's art collection and check it against the records Mr. Villiers kept." I had no qualms telling them about my new job. If the local grapevine hadn't heard it already, they would soon.

*"Ah-ha,"* Vivian crowed triumphantly. "The police believe Evelyn's murder was connected with the art collection. Exactly my own theory."

I refrained from saying that was fairly obvious. Instead I asked, "Do either of you remember who first mentioned last night that Mrs. Villiers was the victim?"

"I told you," Vivian said. "Everyone at the fair was talking about it."

"She's right." Lady Barbara wrinkled her forehead. "But wasn't it the woman from The Finchley Arms who said it first?"

Vivian held up a forefinger. "Briony Peacock. Of course. She'd actually *seen* him, you know."

"The murderer?"

"No—Henry Liu, on his delivery bicycle. Pedaling for all he was worth."

"When was that?"

"Eight fifteen. She was helping her husband into his twill cassock and linen stockings for the play. Caught the back of Henry as he raced passed them."

"Are you sure of the time?"

"You'd have to ask Briony," Lady Barbara said, "but everyone was in costume by eight thirty. We did a walk-through before the pageant."

*Strange.* Henry said he'd been in a hurry to get more shrimp rolls for the crowd after the pageant, but eight fifteen was a good forty-five minutes earlier than he'd claimed to have left the fair. Could the time difference be significant? Something else Tom needed to hear.

"Go ahead and show her, Barb." Vivian cut into my thoughts. "You can't afford to waste time, and I have rhubarb preserves to put up this afternoon."

"This way, dear." Lady Barbara held my arm as we made our way into the small drawing room with its coral-pink walls, plasterwork frieze, and Portland stone fireplace. It was a small gem, and I was glad to see the portrait of Lady Susannah Finchley, Lady Barbara's seventeenth-century ancestor, hanging over the mantel.

"These'll raise a bob or two." Vivian plopped into one of a large set of early nineteenth-century dining chairs with ebony-strung backs. Fergus, her constant shadow, curled up on the Persian carpet, his chin resting on his paws.

"What do you think?" Lady Barbara clasped her hands together like a child showing off a cherished art project.

I counted the chairs—fourteen plus one armchair. "They're stunning," I said. "You wouldn't happen to have a second armchair around somewhere, would you?"

"Irreparably damaged years ago."

"Christmas 1976," Vivian added. "*Someone* thought it would be rather *amusing* to add an explosive charge to one of the Christmas crackers. Lady Melbury toppled right over—smashed the chair to bits. Nearly blew her hand off as well. Of course, she did weigh all of twenty stone."

Lady Barbara tsked. "Don't exaggerate, Vivian. It was only second-degree burns." She looked at me. "Does having only one armchair affect the value of the set?"

"The chairs are Regency—beautifully constructed, in fine condition." I was trying to be diplomatic, but Lady Barbara deserved the truth. "A complete set of sixteen with both armchairs might be worth thirty or forty thousand pounds. For individual chairs—or in pairs, which is how they'd probably be sold—you might get a thousand for each of the sides, more for the armchair."

"Oh, dear. Not nearly enough. What about this?" She reached behind her and handed me what appeared to be a tray in a brown flannel silver-cloth bag. "My father called it *cinnabar*."

I unzipped the bag and removed a large, red plate, deeply carved in a botanical pattern. It took me a moment to speak. "I've never actually seen a piece this fine. People call it cinnabar, but it's actually lacquerware, an ancient Chinese art form dating back to Neolithic times."

"*This* is Neolithic?" Vivian asked.

"No, no—it's probably sixteenth or seventeenth century. Just *look* at the detail."

Lady Barbara and Vivian examined the plate. The entire surface, even under the lip, was carved through the thick resinous lacquer with flowering trees and plants—peonies, chrysanthemum, cherry blossoms, others I couldn't identify—marked out in meticulously incised detail on a deep amber ground. I turned the plate over. The base was lacquered in dark brown. A series of Chinese characters had been incised along the foot rim.

My fingers began to tingle. My heart picked up speed alarmingly. "This could be an inscription. Or possibly a reign mark, meaning the piece was commissioned by the emperor himself." I let out a breath. Controlling your breathing isn't easy when your heart thinks you're jumping hurdles.

"One of my ancestors served with Lord Elgin during the Second Opium War," said Lady Barbara. "He brought the plate back to England after the sack of the Old Summer Palace in Beijing."

Vivian peered at the plate. "Lord Elgin? Wasn't he the chap who removed all those marble statues and friezes from the Parthenon in Athens?"

"That was his father, the seventh earl," Lady Barbara said. "Larceny seems to have run in the family." She opened a drawer and took out a folded piece of paper. "Major Thomas Finchley, in his own handwriting." She unfolded the paper and handed it to me. The old hand-cut sheet was so fragile the creases had begun to separate.

*Saved from the flames at the Imperial Gardens, Yuan Ming Yuan, 20 October 1860, by Sir Thomas Finchley, Major in Her Majesty's Royal Marines.*

A thought struck me. What were the chances of finding two very old, very rare, and extremely valuable Chinese antiquities in the vicinity of one small Suffolk village? I handed it back. "It sounds like he thought he was preserving it for the future."

Lady Barbara shot me a disapproving look. "We looted everywhere we went, the British—China, India, Egypt, Ethiopia. That's why I've never had the plate on display. Why celebrate the worst in our national history?"

"I'd like to have Ivor take a look. He'll be able to give us some idea of the value." I was so hot, I was starting to sweat.

"I'm not sure I feel right, profiting from it." She fingered the strand of pearls around her neck. "If I didn't absolutely need the money—"

"Are you well?" Vivian was looking at me with alarm.

"A bit warm at the moment."

"Ah, the *change*," Vivian said knowingly.

I let it go. I'd rather have her think I was menopausal than mad. "Is this what you have to sell?"

"Show her," Vivian said.

I hadn't noticed the large shape in the corner of the room. Lady Barbara removed a drop cloth, revealing what turned out to be a multistoried dollhouse on legs.

*"Oh,"* I said, charmed by the rose-red brick exterior and tiny mullioned windows. "Was it yours?"

"My mother's first. Made in 1933, after Queen Mary's dollhouse was exhibited at Wembley. Not nearly so grand, of course."

I bent down to examine the rooms. The lower floor consisted of a Victorian-style kitchen, butler's pantry, and laundry. The first floor had a tall-ceilinged drawing room, a gracious dining room, and an oak-paneled library, complete with miniature, leather-bound volumes and a tiny stuffed fox in a glass showcase. The upper floor had two bed chambers and a bath with a water closet and footed copper tub.

"This is Finchley Hall," I said, amazed. "Look—it's even got the green velvet serpentine sofas. You *can't* sell this, Lady Barbara. It's part of your childhood, your family history."

"To whom shall I pass it on?" She cocked an eyebrow. "I'll never have grandchildren, you know—or even nieces and nephews. The estate and the Finchley Hoard were important to my family. They wouldn't care about a girlhood plaything." She lifted her chin. "I never played with dolls anyway. I preferred science projects. And shooting."

"Nevertheless." I straightened. "I can't let you sell it—not until you've exhausted every other possibility."

Vivian had brought me another object, a lovely silver coffee pot.

"What's this?"

"That was a gift for the marriage of my fifth-great-grandfather, Melrose Finchley, to Lady Heloise Barkley in 1788," Lady Barbara said.

I turned it over to check the marks—George I, made in London. "See the initials?" I pointed out the letters *PL* over the maker's mark. "This piece was made by Paul de Lamerie, a Huguenot refugee from the Netherlands—the most renowned London silversmith of the eighteenth century. If you're sure you want to sell, you should get a very good price. I hope you don't mind—I asked Tom to check out that new auction house on the Sudbury Road."

"Done and dusted." Vivian crossed her arms over her ample bosom. "The owner is Nigel Oakley. He owned an estate agency in the Cotswolds for thirty years—solid reputation, well thought of locally. Sold up two years ago—made a small fortune, apparently—and invested in an antiques auction business run by his son and a business partner. They bought the old tithe barn near Mills Lane. Spent a year renovating the place. We've already seen it."

Pretty much what I'd learned as well, and it did sound encouraging. Still, I'd have Tom check them out. Where Lady Barbara was concerned, I was taking no chances.

"Shall we make a start with the chairs, the Chinese plate, and the coffee pot?" Lady Barbara asked.

"I'd rather hold off on the lacquer plate if it's all right. Let's start with the chairs and the silver. That way we can get a feel for how the auction house operates without risking your most valuable asset."

"You don't trust them?" Lady Barbara asked.

"I don't know them. Until we've had a chance to meet, talk about terms, examine their contract, I'm not willing to take a chance."

"That can be settled easily enough," Vivian said. "Barb's invited them for cocktails on Wednesday. You're to come as well. Bring that handsome detective inspector."

"In the meantime, have Ivor look at the plate." Lady Barbara laid her small, wrinkled hand on mine. "If you're satisfied, Kate, dear, I'd like to sell everything at once."

A knock on the door announced the entrance of Francie Jewell, carrying a huge bouquet of white tulips in a glass vase. "More flowers, m'lady."

Vivian winked at me. "Our Barb's got herself *another* secret admirer."

"Oh, hush. It's hardly a secret." Lady Barbara's pale cheeks turned faintly pink. "They're from Nigel Oakley. We met at St. Æthelric's when he first arrived. He invited us to the grand opening of the auction house."

"Quite a do. He's been sending her flowers ever since," Vivian said. "Peonies last week. Lilies the week before that. Always white."

I pictured the white, cup-shaped petal on the floor of Ivor's stockroom.

Was Nigel Oakley a shrewd businessman buttering up a potential client, or a thief and a murderer?

# Chapter Eleven

Wednesday, May 8

Wednesday turned out to be the first damp, gray day we'd had since I had arrived in Suffolk. It wasn't raining exactly, more like misting—a *"wee Scottish mist,"* as my husband used to say. I woke to sounds of scuttling in the thatch above my head and pictured tiny creatures taking shelter in the reeds.

I'd spent all day Tuesday at The Cabinet of Curiosities, making sure nothing else had been stolen in the break-in. The storeroom was still off-limits, but I'd made a thorough check of the shelves and cabinets in the display area. Ivor was far too whimsical to maintain an organized shop plan, but as far as I could tell, everything was in its place. I'd phoned Ivor to tell him the good news. Then I'd phoned Tom at police headquarters to find out if our trip to Hapthorn Lodge was still on. It was. The forensics team had completed their search of the house and grounds.

Tom had arranged to pick me up after breakfast. Since the temperature was in the fifties, bone-chilling and damp, I decided on jeans with a white microfleece pullover under a black wool blazer.

Tom arrived at ten AM in his silver Volvo. Vivian was elbow deep in rhubarb. I called goodbye, grabbed my tote bag and raincoat, and dashed to the car.

"Morning." I leaned over and gave him a quick kiss. "I'm still getting used to the idea that I'm part of the investigation."

"We need an expert. Might as well be you. Oh—by the way, the solicitor said no valuation was done after Wallace Villiers's death. They suggested it, but Mrs. Villiers declined."

"So it's up to me. I hope I live up to DCI Eacles's expectations."

"Don't worry." He shot me a smile. "No one ever does."

We drove down Finchley Hall's tree-lined drive. Tom pulled through the huge wrought-iron gates and turned right toward the center of the village.

"Did anyone on Weavers Street remember seeing Evelyn Villiers the day she died?"

"Not a soul. Weavers Street is residential. Not many were home that day except a few old-age pensioners—and they weren't stationed at their windows. If Mrs. Villiers drove herself, she would have parked at the end of the street near the stone wall on Dash End Lane."

"What have you learned?"

"Forensics identified three sets of shoe prints in Ivor's stockroom," he said. "Two have been identified as belonging to Evelyn Villiers and Henry Liu. The third belonged to a man wearing leather-soled shoes with some kind of logo that is being analyzed. Size ten and a half."

If my mental conversion was accurate, that was a man's size eleven in the United States. "Any news on Lucy Villiers?"

"Nothing yet—and we haven't found anyone named Grenfel in the database."

I let that sit for the moment. There had to be some trace of the missing daughter—a driver's license, a job application, a utility bill. "The Villiers's old housekeeper, Ertha Green, will be back in town Friday. I'll ask if she and Lucy kept in touch. Did the crime scene team find anything useful at Hapthorn Lodge?"

"Fingerprints—most belonging to Evelyn Villiers and the part-time housekeeper, a Mrs. Wright. She came in from the village to do light housekeeping and, in her words, 'a little plain cooking.'"

"How about the door-to-door interviews?"

"Several neighbors reported seeing a dark van coming and going from Hapthorn, mostly at night. Some say a plain panel van; others insist it had some kind of logo."

"It makes sense. If Mrs. Villiers never went out, she'd have had things delivered."

Tom turned left at the village green, and we headed in the direction of Little Gosling.

"Did Mrs. Wright identify the body?" I shuddered at the thought. "I'm sure she never guessed her duties would include viewing her employer's remains."

"Cliffe drove her to the mortuary yesterday. She recognized Mrs. Villiers, all right, even though she said her orders were usually communicated in writing—notes left on the kitchen counter. She thought it was an odd way of working, but the pay was enough to allow for a few eccentricities."

"You said you'd identified most of the fingerprints. Were there others?"

"Two sets we've yet to identify and a partial third. According to Mrs. Wright, one set probably belonged to a village man who did occasional work in the garden—and another, a younger man she'd seen once or twice as she was leaving. An odd jobs man—or possibly a relative."

"The owner of the dark van, maybe. Did she say anything about Lucy?"

"She claims she didn't know Mrs. Villiers had a daughter. There were no photographs in the house, something she considered odd."

"But didn't Lucy grow up in Little Gosling?"

"Yes, but Mrs. Wright didn't. She moved from London several years ago to look after her two grandchildren. That ended when her son got a job in Manchester. By that time, the children were in school and she'd gotten used to village life, so when the job at Hapthorn Lodge came up, she decided to take it."

"Does anyone in Little Gosling remember Lucy Villiers?"

"Of course, but no one's heard from her since she moved to Essex."

"What was the name of the town again?"

"Dunmow Parva, about thirty miles south of Long Barston. Cliffe did doorstep interviews there yesterday."

"Did he learn anything useful?"

"No one remembers the girl. Of course, not many lived there eighteen years ago. It's a transient neighborhood—starter homes. Winnifred Villiers—Wallace's younger sister—died about a year after Lucy left. No children, never married. According to the file, she woke one morning to find Lucy and all her belongings gone. No note, no explanation. She notified the police, but as there was no sign of foul play and Lucy was eighteen, the search was called off. Adults have the right to disappear."

"Could she have eloped with Colin Wardle after all?"

"We haven't located him either."

"Another dead end, then."

"That's often the way with a cold case, Kate. Those originally involved have either died or moved on. Memories fade. The evidence has degraded or been lost—or never existed in the first place."

"What are the chances of finding Lucy now?"

"That's turned out to be a bit of a puzzle. There's no record of her death in the UK, but she hasn't held a job or paid taxes in the last eighteen years."

"Maybe she changed her name. Or doesn't want to be found."

"Not even for six hundred thousand pounds?"

"That's what she'll inherit?"

"Plus the art collection and whatever's left from her mother's estate. Quite a motive for murder."

Tom had a point, although the thought of a child killing a parent made me ill. "What if you never find Lucy? Who inherits then?"

"Wallace Villiers had another sister, the eldest, in Melbourne. She went out to Australia with her husband, a civil servant, and stayed. The solicitor is checking to see if she's still living or has children."

*Children who traveled back to England in order to claim the inheritance?*

The sky had darkened. A soft drizzle blurred the windshield. Tom turned on the wipers.

"Almost there."

I leaned back in my seat and thought about Wallace Villiers's art collection. I'd spent part of the previous evening combing the internet. What I'd found was a spread in the September 2002 edition of the magazine *Suffolk Country Life*, glossy photographs and all. One photo had especially caught my attention.

Wallace Villiers stood in front of a black marble fireplace, one gold-ringed hand resting on the high mantel near a Meissen figural group. *Wallace Villiers's latest acquisition,* said the caption, *a rare Meissen figural group,* The Mockery of Age, *modeled by Johann Joachim Kändler, ca. 1740 to 1745.* A second photo of the porcelain grouping alone showed an elderly man, holding a crutch and leaning to kiss a young lady at his side. Behind him, Harlequin poised to crown him with feathers while another Commedia dell'arte figure offered him a plate of celery. The oval base was applied with flowers and foliage.

I'd printed out the images on Vivian's old inkjet printer and shoved them into my tote bag.

Villiers had been impressive, tall and well built, with a square jaw and head of thick dark hair. His wife, Evelyn, had been mentioned in the article, but not pictured. Another indication, I supposed, that she hadn't shared her husband's interest in art and antiques. Or perhaps she was reclusive even then.

At the signpost for Little Gosling, we turned into a narrow lane, bounded on both sides by hedgerows. The road widened every now and again to allow for oncoming traffic, but we met no other cars.

I flinched as Tom swerved to avoid a pothole. "I asked Vivian and Lady Barbara who told them the victim was Evelyn Villiers. They both said it was Briony Peacock from The Finchley Arms. They also said Briony saw Henry Liu pedaling toward the High Street at eight fifteen—not nine as he told you."

"We heard that as well, although it may prove irrelevant. Witnesses are frequently wrong about time. In fact, when they all agree, we begin to worry."

"I almost forgot. You were going to tell me how the intruders got into the shop without setting off the alarm."

"Ever heard of key bumping?"

"Can't say I have."

"It's a lock-picking technique favored by criminals because it leaves no signs of forced entry and does no damage to the lock. All you need is a specially cut key known as a bump key, where all the ridges are cut to maximum depth. You insert the key, then gently bump it with a mallet or screwdriver, forcing the lock pins to the shear line as the key turns and the door opens."

"How do you know they used a bump key?"

"We don't. That's the problem. To prove it, we'd have to catch them in the act or capture them with bumping tools in their possession."

"But what about the security system? Even if they gained entrance, the alarm would have gone off."

"Not necessarily. All wireless alarm systems rely on radio frequency signals sent from the door and window sensors to the control pad, which triggers the alarm—in Ivor's case, a silent alert to the monitoring company. With specialized equipment, the signal can be jammed—almost like preventing someone from hearing by yelling in his ear. The alarm industry has countered with 128-bit encrypted sensors that use frequency hopping—changing the broadcast frequency often and randomly. This makes jamming less of an issue."

I could see where he was going. "And Ivor didn't have the new technology."

"He will now—or should."

"So we're dealing with professionals."

Tom smiled. "I like the sound of that word."

"Professionals?"

"No—*we*."

He slowed down. "And *we* have arrived."

On our right, a gray stone wall, pocked with lichens and greenish algae, stretched ahead of us. Some of the stones lay scattered on the ground, loosened by the leafy vines that grew everywhere. Long tufts of grass had filled in the gaps between the foundation stones. A hundred yards or so farther on, we came to a pair of gray stone columns. A sign said "Hapthorn Lodge. Private. No entrance." Rusty black iron gates stood open."

"This is creepy," I said.

“Wait ’til you see the house.”

Beech trees lined the drive, their high branches interlacing to form a canopy. More vines were tangled, like Absalom’s hair, in the branches. The drive was long and narrow, ending in a round gravel courtyard with a three-tiered fountain in the center, clogged with damp leaves.

Hapthorn Lodge looked like something out of a Gothic costume drama. Early Edwardian, two stories with attic dormers. Light gray stone, nearly smothered in ivy. The house, with its painted bay windows, reminded me of The Willows, except here the ivy had been allowed to run riot. Mist rose eerily from the ground.

Tom pulled into a space near the entrance and turned off the engine. “Ready?”

“Let’s go,” I said, trying to sound plucky.

This house held secrets. And I had a feeling they weren’t nice ones.

# Chapter Twelve

As we got out of the car, the sound of rushing water met us. "What's that?"

"The Stour," Tom said. "I knew we were close."

We couldn't see through the mist and the dense, leafy undergrowth, but the river had to be within a few hundred feet of the house. Having grown up around lakes, I'd often fallen asleep to the gentle rhythm of lapping water, but this swift, unseen current felt menacing.

We picked our way toward the house, following flat slates set into the mossy soil. Leaded-glass panels in the Art Nouveau style, darkened with grime, surrounded the entrance door. Tom punched a code into the keyless lock box, pushed open the door, and we stepped inside.

Hapthorn Lodge was a perfect example of an early-Edwardian country house, built in the first decade of the twentieth century for a prosperous middle-class family with servants. The pale colors and simplicity of design were meant to be a welcome change from the dark, heavy Victorian architecture, but the effect here was spoiled by a lack of light, an air of general disuse, and the unmistakable smell of mildew.

The large, nearly square entrance hall had pale gray wainscoting. A dusty oriental carpet covered the center of the parquet floor. A Dutch still-life I'd seen in the magazine hung on the wall beside a pair of spaniel paintings in gilded frames. No one had loved this house for a long time—or cleaned it. The newel post and bannisters on either side of the wide staircase were thick with dust.

"When Mrs. Wright said 'light housekeeping,' she wasn't kidding." I ran my finger over the surface of a narrow cabinet, leaving a trail in the dust. "She didn't do windows. Or much of anything else from the looks of it."

"To be fair, she told Cliffe she wasn't allowed to do more than tidy up the kitchen, stock the pantry and refrigerator, and do an occasional spot of dusting and hoovering in the rooms being used. Most of the house had been closed up for years. Mrs. Wright came and went through the side entrance. She may never have entered the formal rooms."

Wide pocket doors to the right and left of the entrance hall were shut. Tom rapped his knuckles on the doors to the right. "Dining room through there. Drawing room across the hall. Library at the rear."

"I may as well get started," I said.

"First I'd like you to see upstairs. Let's go the back way."

Instead of climbing the wide staircase in the entrance hall, Tom led me down a hallway, past a butler's pantry, to a large kitchen with a scullery and a back staircase, a typical feature of period houses, enabling servants to lay fires, change linens, and keep things generally clean and tidy without disturbing the family.

The kitchen looked like it had been updated sometime in the 1990s with light oak cabinetry and newer appliances. A wide, windowed bay facing the rear garden had been turned into a breakfast alcove with banquettes upholstered in a dated yellow floral pattern.

"Where does that lead?" I indicated a heavy door to the left of the narrow wooden staircase leading to the upper floors.

Tom opened it, releasing the dank smell of mildew. "There's a partial cellar under the rear portion of the house. Bad drainage. With the floods last December, they probably had standing water for weeks."

"What's down there?"

"The old coal-fired boiler, I'm told. Empty wine rack. A few boxes, which you'll probably have to check—sorry."

We climbed the stairs, making the tight half turn partway up. At the top, Tom flipped the old-fashioned toggle switch, providing much-needed light. The second-floor landing led to a hallway running the length of the house, bisected by the main staircase. The back staircase continued to a third floor.

"What's up there?" I asked.

"The attic and servants' quarters under the eaves. Unused." Tom opened a tall paneled door. "This is the master bedroom."

I felt strange poking around the house. Mrs. Villiers had been a private woman, reluctant to divulge even the most mundane facts about her life. Now her secrets were laid bare. I could only hope they would reveal the identity of her killer.

I peered into the room. The floor was carpeted in densely woven beige wool. The bedroom suite included a king-size four-poster with a mirrored dresser and highboy. Armchairs, upholstered in peach-colored raw silk, faced each other in front of a charming tiled fireplace. The same peach raw silk covered the bed and matching shams. Like the formal rooms on the ground floor, everything was covered in dust. "No one's used this room for a long time, have they?"

"That's part of what I wanted you to see." Tom pulled open a set of painted wood closet doors trimmed in gold. "Everything's still here—clothes, shoes, hats, handbags—his and hers."

Several formal dresses were hung in plastic. I fingered a dry cleaning receipt stapled at the top. "Look at the date—December 2002. We've stepped into a time capsule. After her husband's death, Evelyn Villiers must have simply walked out and closed the door on her former life."

Tom opened the top middle drawer of the dresser. "What does this tell you?"

The large drawer had been fitted with small, double-tiered felt compartments, now empty. "It tells me Mrs. Villiers had lots of lovely jewelry. She said her husband loved buying it for her. Where is it?"

"That's what I'd like to know. Want to see Lucy's bedroom?"

"Of course."

He led the way to a second bedroom, left of the main staircase and toward the rear of the house. I stared at what might have been my own girlhood bedroom, but a decade later. The bed was covered in a patchwork quilt made from faded jeans. A wall shelf held a collection of souvenir dolls in ethnic costumes. The opposite wall was papered with pop star posters. There was Amy Winehouse with her winged eyeliner and beehive hairdo—and Pink in a black leather costume with strategically placed cutouts.

Tom opened a large mirrored wardrobe. "There's nothing here. Same with the drawers—not so much as a hair clip or elastic band. Either Lucy took everything with her to Essex or someone cleaned it out."

"She didn't take this." I picked up a floppy brown teddy bear that lay on one of two cushioned window seats. The well-worn fur made me feel sad. Lucy hadn't been the first young girl to lose her heart to an unsuitable boyfriend. My own daughter, Christine, made a habit of it.

"I'd like to see where Mrs. Villiers slept."

"Saved for last. This way."

We retraced our steps. A small room near the back staircase had once been a nursery, or perhaps a maid's room. A single window faced the front of the house. The furnishings were basic—a single iron bed, a bedside table and lamp, a plain oak dresser, and a straight-backed chair. Over the bed hung a framed photograph of a cottage by a river. On the bedside table lay a small New Testament bound in faux black leather.

One of two interior doors led to a small bath, the other to a closet, which held a meager assortment of skirts, blouses, and cardigans. Everything was clean and neatly pressed. Nothing was new. On the closet floor I saw a pair of leather walking shoes, a pair of low-heeled pumps, and a pair of bedroom slippers.

"This is so strange," I said. "Evelyn Villiers owned this large, beautiful house but lived in one or two rooms. She had plenty of money, yet she let the place go to ruin. She had beautiful clothes but wore only a few plain things purchased decades ago. It's almost as if she stopped living when her husband died."

"Probably depressed. Shame she never got help."

"Too bad she cut herself off from her only child."

I began to notice other things. A hairbrush and comb on the oak dresser. A jar of Nivea face cream on the sink. A towel hanging on a rack in the bathroom. An ironing board, folded and tucked between the dresser and the wall. "She lived like a nun. What do you make of the picture above the bed—the old cottage?"

"Looks like an enlarged photograph."

"Yes, it does." I leaned closer. "Do you recognize anything—the location, I mean?"

"An English cottage beside an English river."

"Well, that's helpful." I shot him a withering look and opened the drawer of the bedside table. Inside was a slim volume entitled *Myths & Legends of Suffolk*. I picked it up and opened to the Table of Contents. One story had been marked with a tiny penciled *X*—"The Green Maiden of Suffolk."

"Tom, look at this." I showed him the mark. "She kept a book about local legends near her bedside. She's marked the story of the green maiden. And the green maiden in the play was the one she spoke to the night she died. Coincidence?"

"The legend of the green maiden is famous in Suffolk."

"I know, but still." I found the chapter and noticed several sentences underlined. "Is it all right if I take this home for a better look?"

"I'd have to get permission. I'll let you know."

I slipped the book back into the drawer.

*The Green Maiden*. Green—the color of life, the color of growth. Also the color of decomposition and decay. Everything about Hapthorn Lodge was green, from the thick ivy climbing along the walls, to the overgrown foliage blocking out the light, to the moss creeping over the stones and the ground.

"I told my mother about Evelyn Villiers's death," I said. "She brought up an interesting question. Eighteen years went by after her husband's death, and suddenly last Monday she decided to sell everything. What changed? Have you checked her bank accounts?"

"She had plenty of money but used little. No large sums incoming or outgoing."

"What was vital enough to make a recluse leave her house? Why was it so important that she sell her husband's art collection? I can't help wondering if she'd heard from her daughter."

"We've considered that."

"A horrible thought—a mother, murdered by her own daughter."

"Most murders happen within family systems, Kate."

"But you said the break-in looked like a professional job."

"Also true." He closed the door to the small bedroom. "Every investigation presents conflicting evidence at first. In time a picture emerges."

"At least my part will be easy." I started down the stairs, leaving him on the landing.

His voice followed me. "You *will* tempt fate, won't you?"

* * *

The sky had partially cleared, and the misty rain had let up—at least for the moment.

"Fancy a look at the river?" Tom peered out the kitchen bay window. "I see more stepping stones."

He was right. A line of flat natural stones led from the side door, around the house, and over the lawn toward the Stour. "Someone's been mowing the grass," I said. "Although it's in need of a trim."

The lawn was bordered by perennial beds, long since gone to seed. Weeds grew up alongside the daffodils, bearded irises, and fringed bleeding hearts. Near the riverbank, a rock garden had been laid out with a central sundial. Whoever designed it hadn't possessed a particularly artistic eye, but perhaps when the summer flowers bloomed, it would be more attractive. Had Evelyn Villiers been a gardener? She must have had some way of passing the time.

Along the bank sat a rustic wooden bench, silvered with age. A pleasant place to read, I thought, when the weather dried out. Willows, alders, and a silver-leafed tree I couldn't identify cast deep green shade on the swiftly moving olivine water. Blackthorn and burdock mingled with other water plants to create a safe habitat for the creatures that depended on the river for life.

"Look," Tom whispered. "A water vole."

A small animal with dark brown fur, a blunt nose, and eyes like jet beads regarded us suspiciously from the long grass before darting away.

"Water's high," I said.

"There's a lock about a mile south of here. The Stour was a means of transport in the past. Look, you can just see the old towpath on the opposite bank."

"Reminds me of the play—the green maiden, drowned in the flood after trying to poison her husband. Justice meted out by God."

"Or by men."

"Wait a minute," I said. "Are you saying there's a historical basis for the story?"

"Some say the story was concocted in Victorian times to compete with the legend of the green children of Woolpit. But every Suffolk schoolchild knows that an eleventh-century chronicle mentions a farmer in Suffolk who found a green-skinned girl hiding in a hedgerow. A cautionary tale." He grinned at me. "Beware of foreign women."

"Well, don't say you weren't warned. But, really—was there such a woman?"

"What do you think?" Tom reached down and righted a tiny turtle, flailing on its back.

"I think legends are based on something, some seed of truth. Expanded and transformed, of course. Like the telephone game—do children play that in the UK?—the one where the original statement changes slightly each time it's repeated so the end result bears little resemblance to the original." A white swan with three fluffy gray cygnets floated past. "You never found any Grenfels in Evelyn Villiers's background?"

"Not a one. Shiptons, Turners, Clarks. That's all I remember. No Grenfels.

I shivered. "Let's go in. I'm cold. And I'm dying for a look at the art collection."

# Chapter Thirteen

We left our muddy shoes in the brick-floored laundry area. "Is there time for me to make a start on the inventory?" I asked, rinsing my hands in the deep porcelain sink and drying them on the front of my jeans.

"I can't stay much longer today, Kate. All hands on deck tonight."

I frowned. "Oh no. Does that mean you can't attend the cocktail party at the Hall? Lady Barbara has invited the owners of the auction house. I wanted you to meet them."

"I'm sorry. I will check the database, though —see if there's anything about the Oakleys you should know. Look, there's time for a quick look-around now. You can come back later with one of the constables. We found Wallace Villiers's inventory records in his library desk, complete with photos. Cliffe made copies for you and left them on the desk."

When Tom opened the wide pocket doors to the dining room, I got the impression the ground floor rooms weren't so much a time capsule as an abandoned warehouse. Dust sheets shrouded the furniture. Paintings had been removed from the walls, leaving darkened rectangles on the sage-green wallpaper. A large number of objects were crowded together on the dining table—more Meissen figural groups but also pieces that looked like Sèvres, K.P.M., Royal Crown Derby. Wallace Villiers had collected the best of the best.

"Did the police do this?" I asked, indicating several empty built-in cabinets.

"No—everything's been left the way they found it."

I picked up a French painted enamel salt cellar, probably early Limoges, and felt a flush of heat. My mouth went dry. *Here I go.*

I knew the sensation would pass, but my immediate reaction to fine objects was intense—and often embarrassing.

"Kate?" Tom looked concerned. "Need some air?"

"No, no." I attempted a laugh. "I'm fine. *Absolutely* fine." My standard response to everything from a hangnail to childbirth. I'm sure those words will be carved one day on my gravestone.

The drawing room was in a similar state. Dust sheets covered the upholstered sofas and armchairs. Paintings, thirty or more in all sizes, had been stacked against the walls. More objects, including more fine examples of Meissen china, had been gathered together on several mahogany cabinets. Except for traces of aluminum powder and large boot prints left by the crime scene team, the layer of dust appeared mostly undisturbed.

I stood in the center of the room and looked around at the chaos. What had been going on here? It looked like someone had been in the middle of a move, then decided against it and left everything where it was. Or had thieves been in the process of cleaning the place out? Is that what Mrs. Villiers had tried to communicate before she died?

"I have an idea," I said. "Maybe Evelyn Villiers didn't know the name of her attacker and was trying to identify him as 'the person who stole the Meissen,' but all that came out was 'Meissen.'"

"Possible. That's why we need you to tell us if any of the artwork is missing." Tom opened yet another set of wide pocket doors. "The photocopies are in here."

I followed him into a handsome wood-paneled room. Curved mahogany bookcases with glazed shelves lined the room. A large desk and chair occupied the space in another of the wide bay windows. Lucy's bedroom had to be directly above. Had she, on warm summer nights when the windows were open, listened in on her father's conversations?

Tom handed me a sheaf of papers. "This may not be as easy as you thought."

I thumbed through the papers, noticing photocopies of what appeared to be old Polaroids, some so badly faded the images were barely visible. "I think you're right."

Last December, when I'd made an inventory of the Finchley Hoard, my problem had been deciphering the often mystifying descriptions. Here, at least I had photographs to help me identify the objects—if I could make them out.

"I'll be back in a few minutes," Tom said. "I want a look in the garage,"

"Okay," I said absently, sitting in Wallace Villiers's big leather chair. I took my time working through the pages. Besides the porcelain and the paintings, he'd purchased all manner of fine things, including a pair of Louis XVI candelabra, a Chinese bronze from the early Five Dynasties period, and a George I gilt gesso side table. He'd spent a fortune amassing the collection. The investment business obviously paid well—or did he have something even more lucrative going on the side? The police would be looking through his financial records.

"Ready to go?" Tom appeared in the library.

"I'd like to check something on the way out." I slipped the inventory sheets into my tote bag. "I found an article on the Villiers Collection in a local magazine. One of the photographs showed a Meissen figural group from the eighteenth-century commedia dell'arte collection. Right there—on that high mantelpiece over the fireplace."

"Commedia dell'arte—am I meant to know what that is?"

"*I'm* sorry." I frowned at him in mock apology. "I thought you said you were an Oxford graduate."

"Ha-ha. Just tell me."

"The commedia dell'arte was an early form of theater with stock characters. It began in Italy, spread all over Europe. I'm sure you know most of the names—Pierrot, Harlequin, Pantalone, Columbine, Scaramouche, Pulcinella. In England, that last chap turned into Punch of the Punch and Judy shows. Anyway, in the eighteenth century, Meissen commissioned a number of figural groups based on the stock characters. Mr. Villiers collected them. They're worth a lot of money, and one of them used to stand right here." I tapped the mantel.

"Maybe Mrs. Villiers sold off part of the collection."

"Maybe." Standing on tiptoes, I peered at the mantel. And felt a sudden chill.

Clearly visible in the dust was an oval shape that looked very much like the oval base of the Meissen piece in the photograph.

* * *

"It's probably somewhere in the house." Tom drove the car around the circular drive in front of Hapthorn Lodge and headed for the road.

"The lack of dust tells me the Meissen figurine was on the mantel until quite recently. Maybe she did sell it—hedging her bets by using several dealers at the same time. I wouldn't blame her."

"We're checking with the local dealers. If you can write up a description, I'll send it out."

"I can do better than that. I can produce a photograph."

The air was still, but the sky had the angry look of an approaching storm. I flinched as the hedgerows whizzed past, too close for comfort on my side. I knew from experience that my sense of impending doom would fade as my brain adjusted to sitting on the left side of the car, but I still felt like I should have a steering wheel in front of me.

The road dipped, then rose. Tom took the blind summit slowly, moving so far to the left I heard branches tapping my side of the car.

"Any theories?" he asked.

I had to laugh. "You told me once police don't begin with theories."

"We don't unless the evidence points strongly in one direction—or when there's no evidence to go on. That's the problem here. A lack of evidence."

"Except for the white petal."

"Yes, but what does that actually tell us?"

I considered mentioning the bouquet of white tulips Lady Barbara had received from Nigel Oakley but decided against it. It would be unfair to implicate the ex-estate agent just because he liked white flowers and knew how to butter up potential customers. "Okay, let's think about what *might* have happened." I fished in my handbag for the small notebook and pen I always carried.

"Kate Hamilton, on the case." He took his eyes from the road and gave me a broad grin.

I laughed. "Just for that, you go first."

"Okay—we have a wealthy widow of sixty-eight, a recluse since the death of her husband eighteen years ago."

"And a missing daughter, Lucy, who'd be"—I calculated the years—"thirty-five or thirty-six. Mrs. Villiers blamed Lucy for her father's death and sent her to live with an aunt in Essex, a single woman. What was her name again?"

"Winnifred—now deceased. Normally in cases like this, we focus our investigation on family members—especially when there's a sizable inheritance at stake. The problem here is a lack of family members."

"Or at least ones you can locate. I'm still thinking about Evelyn Villiers's interest in the green maiden legend. Did she think there was some family connection? In her last lucid moments, she passed by dozens of people and made a beeline for the young actress who played the green maiden. Why?"

"And why did she say *Meissen*?"

"Let's back up a bit," I said, jotting down the questions. "Why was Lucy sent away? I know her mother blamed her for her father's death, but Wallace Villiers must have had a preexisting condition. Lucy was a child—just seventeen. Why was her mother unwilling or unable to forgive her?"

"Vindictive personality? Queen Victoria blamed her son Bertie for his father's death. Some mothers never do develop the motherly instinct."

"I'm hoping Ertha Green can tell us something about the relationship between mother and daughter." I wrote *Why was EV unable to forgive Lucy?*, adding *Ask Ertha Green.*

"Any other questions?" Tom asked.

"Yes—why did Evelyn Villiers live like an unwanted guest in her own home? I guess I can understand moving out of the bedroom she shared with her husband, but she didn't have to live like a hermit. It's almost as if . . ." It took me a moment to put it into words. "Almost as if she felt guilty, as if she didn't deserve to enjoy her wealth."

"Why not move, then?"

I pictured the dust sheets, the jumble of antiques. "Maybe she was in the process of moving, and something—or someone—stopped her."

We turned right onto the B road into Little Gosling. A few fat raindrops, harbingers of the coming storm, plopped against the windshield. Tom flipped on the wipers.

Little Gosling was not much more than a widening in the road. On the north side of the village was the housing estate where Danny, the child who'd helped us solve a murder last December, lived with his mother, Glenda. We passed a village green with a duck pond and a few well-preserved medieval houses, then a petrol station and a pub, The Packhorse.

"Read what you've written so far," Tom said.

I read the questions aloud.

1. *What was Evelyn Villiers's connection with the green maiden?*
2. *Why did she say Meissen?*
3. *Why was Lucy sent away after her father's death?*
4. *Why was EV unable to forgive Lucy? Ask Ertha Green.*
5. *Why did Evelyn live like a hermit doing penance?"*

"Here's a sixth," Tom said. "What made Evelyn so sure Colin Wardle stole that painting? And, if he was guilty, why did Lucy lie for him that night?"

"Oh, that's easy—to protect him. Girls do all kinds of silly things when they're in love."

"Do they indeed?" He flashed me a wicked smile.

"We're focusing on Colin Wardle, remember? That's something else Ertha Green might be able to shed light on. Do you want to sit in on the interview?"

"I don't think so," Tom said. "She'll speak more freely with you alone—but I do expect a full report. I'll compare it to the original statement Ertha gave after Wallace Villiers's death. They say time clouds memories, but that's not always true. Sometimes the passage of time clarifies memories. And sometimes witnesses are willing to be more candid after the initial crisis has passed."

"Any other questions to add to the list?" I held up my pen.

"Quite a few, as a matter of fact. What was that white flower petal doing in Ivor's shop? Where is Lucy Villiers now? What happened to the Chinese jar? Why did Mrs. Villiers fire Ertha Green?"

I scribbled as fast as I could. "I keep circling back to my mother's question."

Tom glanced at me. "What changed in Evelyn Villiers's life?"

"Exactly. I think everything depends on that." I added the question at the top of the list and settled against the car seat, listening to the rhythm of the wipers. Were the questions we'd asked the right ones?

We passed a field of sheep—not the black-faced Suffolks, but the smaller white Merinos raised for their fine, soft wool. The sky opened up, spilling drops of rain against the windscreen and bringing the mineral smell of wet earth.

I wished Ivor were there. I wanted to talk to him about the missing Meissen figural group and the possibility of thieves targeting high-end collectors.

My questions would have to wait. Tonight was Lady Barbara's cocktail party—and my chance to meet the Oakleys. At least one question might be answered.

Were the owners of the new auction house to be trusted with Lady Barbara's future?

# Chapter Fourteen

I slipped my new black dress over my head, zipped it up, and hoped it would do. When Lady Barbara invited friends for cocktails, Vivian had informed me, they put on their finest and came anticipating a delicious selection of hors d'oeuvres, whipped up by the redoubtable Mrs. Francie Jewell, cook extraordinaire and maid of all work. She was a treasure.

My finest was a short black cocktail dress with an asymmetrical neckline, paired with my new black slingbacks and a tiny beaded purse. For the record, all my pretty clothes were chosen by my best friend, Charlotte, an ex-window dresser for an upscale dress shop in Chicago. I am not trusted to shop alone.

Outside, the on-again, off-again rain had passed through, and the gray clouds had given way to a clear evening sky. Since the grass was wet, Vivian and I walked over to Finchley Hall in our rubber wellies, carrying our dress shoes in plastic baggies. Fergus the pug wore his own little rubber boots too, which made him prance along the gravel path like a show pony, but I didn't dare laugh. His feelings are easily hurt.

We gathered, not in the Hall's high-ceilinged formal drawing room, but in the charming coral-pink private drawing room. This room, I'd been glad to learn, would be part of the small suite of rooms Lady Barbara would occupy when The National Trust took possession of Finchley Hall.

If they ever did.

I was surprised to see the Chinese lacquerware plate prominently displayed on an oak sideboard. Lady Barbara must have been planning to show it to the Oakleys.

Francie Jewell, spiffed out in a black dress and frilly white apron, held out a tray of drinks. “Raspberry martini or whiskey sour?”

“Martini, please.” I took a sip and closed my eyes, savoring the intense raspberry ice floating in lemon vodka.

Drifting through the crowd, I ended up near the Portland stone fireplace, where a massive oak log burned on the grate. Year-round open fires are one of the things I loved best about the UK. I knew several people in the room—Vivian, of course, and Fergus, who gazed at the assembled company with benign condescension. Fergus considered mixing with humans a privilege. For them.

In the corner stood Edmund Foxe, the rector of St. Æthelric’s—I’d finally stopped calling him “the dishy vicar”—with his pretty new fiancée, Angela, the local veterinarian. They chatted with Hattie Nuthall, the rectory housekeeper and defender of the faith.

I was more interested in the three men standing near Lady Barbara—a distinguished-looking older man in a tweed sport jacket that whispered “country gentleman,” and two younger men, one fair, in his thirties; the other dark and perhaps a decade older.

“Kate, I’d like to introduce Nigel Oakley,” Lady Barbara said—a bit too enthusiastically for my liking. She’d obviously made up her mind about him already.

The ex-estate agent was, I had to admit, a fine-looking man. If the face is the mirror of the mind, as St. Jerome claimed, Nigel Oakley was open, good-humored, and unassuming. He looked to be in his late fifties, lightly tanned and fit, with brown hair going gray at the temples.

“Delighted to meet you, Mrs. Hamilton.”

The warmth of his smile disarmed me. “Call me Kate.”

“And Nigel, please.” He smiled again. “How is Mr. Tweedy? Recovering well, I hope.”

“He’s doing very well. I hope he’ll be home soon.”

Another guest arrived, and Lady Barbara excused herself.

"I've heard all about you from Lady Barbara," Nigel said. "And of course I read the newspaper accounts of your exploits last year. Chasing a murderer across a roof." He looked up as if he could see through the plaster ceiling. "Very brave."

"It wasn't bravery," I said truthfully. "Desperation. My daughter was in danger. That's what being a parent will do."

"I understand the feeling." A brief shadow passed over his pleasant features. "When my wife died, Peter was all I had left." He indicated his two companions who were examining the lacquerware plate. Based on coloring, I decided the younger man must be his son.

"The auction house was Peter's idea," Nigel said, "along with Martin Ingram's. I was glad to do what I could to help them get started. The opportunity came at the right time, and I must say, I've been impressed with what they've accomplished. Martin's been involved in the antiques trade for years—a virtual goldmine of knowledge and experience. I'm the new kid on the block, learning how things work."

I liked his self-deprecating manner.

"Let me introduce you." Nigel laid a hand on his son's shoulder. "Kate Hamilton, this is my son, Peter Oakley, and his business partner, Martin Ingram. Kate is a dealer in the States and a friend of Lady Barbara," he told them, "She's the one who completed the Hoard exhibition last winter."

"Charmed," said Peter Oakley without looking charmed in the least. His face was pale and narrower than his father's. He wore a tiny-patterned shirt, the collar half in and half out of a rumpled linen jacket. His blond hair had been expensively layered. He brushed it back, and I saw that his fingernails were bitten to nubs.

"Mrs. Hamilton, a great pleasure." Martin Ingram's gaze was so intense I took an involuntary step back. I judged him to be somewhere in his forties, about my age. He had the black hair and crystal-blue eyes of a true Celt—plus the flat abdomen and well-muscled shoulders of someone who spends a lot of time at the gym. There was something mesmerizing, almost predatory, about those translucent blue eyes. He smiled, revealing straight white teeth. I caught a whiff of cologne, something masculine and musky.

"Lady Barbara mentioned some items for possible auction," Nigel was saying. "We've recently completed the renovation of a stunning Grade Two–listed tithe barn. I know you've been advising her. We'd be honored to show you around. I think you'll be impressed."

"I'd like that very much. And perhaps I could see your contract as well." *Might as well just say it.*

"Certainly. I know Lady Barbara values your opinion."

"Do you have an auction scheduled? I'm interested to see how you do things in the UK."

"Next Monday, actually. It's not one of our larger auctions, but it will give you an idea of how we operate. Viewing begins at noon, the sale at three."

Vivian appeared at my side. "What do you think, Kate? Do they pass muster?"

"Well, I—" I turned pink with embarrassment.

Nigel saved me. "She's doing her due diligence, Miss Bunn. I'd expect nothing less from a woman with her obvious experience." He turned to me. "We'll do our best to answer all your questions, Kate. I always think transparency is the best approach, don't you?"

"Did you know Kate is aiding the police with the murder of Evelyn Villiers?" Vivian said. "She even has a title—Antiques Consultant."

*Oh man.* I thought about stepping on Vivian's toe but decided Fergus might consider that a biting offense.

"I'm even more impressed," Nigel said. "My son tells me the Villiers Collection is famous. Plenty of dealers would love an opportunity to see what's there—and bid on it."

Was he hinting that Oakley's would like to be considered? Did he think I'd have some influence? I studied his face, seeing no sign of maneuvering or gamesmanship. Only natural curiosity. "I'm just compiling an inventory. What happens to the collection will be decided by someone else."

"Of course. Mrs. Villiers's solicitor, presumably. Poor woman. Tragic." He stooped to pat Fergus on the head, earning a snort of approval.

On the way home, Vivian apologized. "I'm sorry, Kate. As soon as the words came out of my mouth, I knew they were wrong. It's just that Barb's in such a *pickle*, and time is running out. The *stress* is getting her down. You wouldn't notice—she puts up a good front—but I've known her since she was a bride."

"I agree—time is important, but it's even more important to make sure we're dealing with reputable people who know the right buyers. Otherwise, the auction won't generate enough to solve Lady Barbara's cash-flow problem."

We passed the Chinese bridge and the koi pond. Giant ferns arched gracefully into the water. Above us, a magpie chattered at the pink and lavender sunset. Oh, how I hoped the National Trust would step in and save Finchley Hall. The residents of Long Barston needed this lovely green space with its deep, dark lake and tall old trees, a place of refuge from the world and its problems.

"Nigel Oakley has a sterling reputation," Vivian said. "He's dealt with the aristocracy before. No one has a bad word to say about him in the Cotswolds."

"I liked him. I really did. But what do you know about his son and the other man—Martin Ingram?"

"According to their brochure, Peter studied architecture and design at university. He and Martin Ingram have been business partners for nine years. I figure Martin provides the knowledge of antiques, Peter the vision for the tithe barn, and Nigel the business sense—and the cash, of course."

"What I'd like to see is a track record," I said. "Starting an auction house isn't a matter of hanging out a shingle and expecting clients and customers to show up—even if it is a listed tithe barn. They have to know people—dealers, collectors—to make a success of it. They have to build a reputation, and that takes time. I don't want Lady Barbara to be their guinea pig." I didn't tell Vivian that Ivor's Roman artifacts had brought in only half the expected value. If I expected them to be fair, I should be fair as well.

Presumably they had a website. If an auction was scheduled for Monday, I'd do my homework in advance—check their estimates, gauge the sort of items they dealt with.

"I spoke to Yasmin Green today," Vivian said. "Ralston's driving down to Torquay Friday morning to collect his mother. Yasmin says Ertha always returns home energized. The sea air, you know. Would Sunday work for you? They've invited you for lunch."

"Oh, that's not necessary, Vivian. I don't want to put them out."

"Ertha's an old-fashioned sort, Kate. In her mind, you're a celebrity. She wouldn't think of having you to the house without offering something to eat. Best china and all. Ralston and the boys will be at football practice, so you'll have Yasmin and Ertha all to yourself."

"Tell Yasmin I'll try not to stay too long."

I hoped I could honor that promise. My list of questions for the former housekeeper at Hapthorn was growing by the minute.

When we got back to Rose Cottage, Vivian removed Fergus's little boots, rinsed them off in the deep porcelain sink, and placed them by the back door—ready for their next outing.

My cell phone pinged a text. It was PC Anne Weldon, arranging to drive me to Hapthorn Lodge the following morning. I responded with a thumbs-up and slipped the phone back into my pocket.

I thought of the inventory sheets in my tote bag—line after line, page after page, of meticulously recorded purchases, going back at least twenty years. Would my job be a simple matter of matching objects with their listings?

Somehow I didn't think so. Something sinister had been going on at Hapthorn Lodge—and whatever it was, it had led to Evelyn Villiers's death.

# Chapter Fifteen

Thursday, May 9

I woke at eight thirty the next morning. My eyes felt dry and irritated—not from drinking raspberry martinis (I admit to having two), but from reading Wallace Villiers's inventory records until nearly one in the morning. I was rushing to get ready for my meeting with PC Weldon when my phone rang.

"We got it! The Domesday translation." Ivor was practically crowing.

"That's a good thing?" I couldn't help pouring cold water on his enthusiasm. We hadn't even received a check for the Perseus statue yet.

"It's a *marvelous* thing, Kate. They're sending it by courier from London. Can I give them your mobile number? They'll text you with a date and time of arrival. You'll need to be at the shop to sign for it."

"And how do we pay for it?"

"Let me worry about that. I'm putting in a call to that professor in Essex I told you about. I hope he picks up. Some days he can't manage the telephone. Anyway, I'll arrange for delivery when he agrees to purchase."

"You mean *if* he agrees."

"*When.* It's a sure thing, more's the pity. I wouldn't mind hanging on to the document for a while."

Actually, I wouldn't have either, but a ready buyer in the hand is worth two . . . well, worth two something.

"The police think they know how the thief got into the shop." I told him what Tom had said about bump keys and signal jamming.

"Oh dear. I remember getting letters about that," Ivor mumbled. "They suggested I modernize my system."

"Why didn't you do it?"

"Figured it was another way for the security company to take my money."

"Oh, Ivor."

"I'll call them today. Have them get in touch with you about upgrading."

I didn't have the heart to ask how much that would cost. "How are you getting along?"

"They may release me early."

"That *is* good news. I can't wait to have you back." I meant it. I missed him. Ivor had captured my heart, although I wasn't about to tell him so. I'd been married to a Scot, after all, and if there was one thing I'd learned about the inhabitants of the British Isles, it was their emotional reserve. It's the stiff-upper lip rule: Sincerity is fine; enthusiasm is acceptable in small doses; emotional outbursts are practically treasonous.

"Ivor," I said. "I have a question about the legend of the green maiden. Is there some historic evidence for her existence?"

"Who knows? In the early nineteen hundreds, a history buff from Essex wrote a book about her. According to him, the whole thing happened there, not in Suffolk. He said the green maiden bore a son and is buried in an unmarked grave in a village churchyard. He also claimed her descendants still lived in the area, though no one would tell him who they were. I believe I own a copy. Should be somewhere in the book room if you want to read more."

"Thanks. I have to run. I'm working on the inventory at Hapthorn Lodge today."

"Lucky girl. I'm off to physio for my daily torture session."

PC Anne Weldon picked me up in a Vauxhall Astra police vehicle. I slid in beside her and clicked my seat belt. Anne's honey-colored hair was pulled back into a neat bun, perfect for the round bowler hat worn by policewomen in the UK. She looked young enough to be my daughter.

"Good morning, Mrs. Hamilton," she said cheerily, making me feel even more elderly.

"Please—call me Kate."

"And I'm Anne." She shifted the car into drive and stepped on the gas.

"Thanks for coming with me," I said. "I'm sure there are lots more important things you could be doing."

"Not really. I've only just joined the Force, so it's usually traffic duty or desk work for me. DI Mallory asked me to make sure the house is secure before you start working. Then, if you don't mind, may I leave you on your own for a bit? I won't if you'd feel uncomfortable. It's only my gran lives in Little Gosling. She took a tumble last week, and I'd like to look in on her."

"Of course—go. It's not as if I'm in any danger."

We arrived at Hapthorn Lodge about a quarter after ten. PC Weldon unlocked the side door, which led to the kitchen through the old laundry with its original copper tub and elaborate wooden drying rack. The clean scent of laundry detergent came from a modern washer/dryer unit.

I plunked my handbag and briefcase with my laptop on the plastic laminate counter. "Before I get started, I'd like to run upstairs and get a book from Mrs. Villiers's room. Did Detective Inspector Mallory mention it?"

"Yes—I forgot to say. You're to let him know when you've finished with it."

We climbed the back stairs.

The small bedroom overlooking the front drive felt airless and sad. I leaned across the iron bedframe to examine the photograph again. The cottage was thatched but not especially pretty. The trees were leafless—winter, then. In the background, a gray ribbon of water flowed diagonally. Beyond the opposite bank stretched wide hedgeless fields. I could see nothing to indicate a location, but the warm sepia tones told me the photo had been taken a long time ago.

This cottage had meant something to Evelyn Villiers. Had it been a family home, a much-loved grandmother's cottage, a lovers' retreat?

I opened the drawer of the bedside table, pulled out the slim *Myths & Legends* book, and tucked it under my arm.

"Sure you don't mind if I leave you for a while?" Anne Weldon asked again on our way downstairs. "Knowing my gran, she'll expect me to have a cup of tea and a piece of cake."

"Take your time."

Back in the kitchen, I slipped Evelyn Villiers's book into my briefcase.

"I'll leave off the lockbox," Anne said, "but lock the door after me. Best to take precautions."

Let me know when you get back," I called after her. "I'm setting up in the library, so I may not hear the door."

"Half one at the latest." She gave me a cheery wave.

Once Anne had gone, I set to work. The job wouldn't be difficult—just time consuming, matching the documentation in Wallace Villiers's files with the actual objects scattered in no discernable order around the ground-floor rooms. I'd have to check every nook and cranny in the house, even the cellar, but I had no intention of tackling the house's damp underpinnings alone. I'm not brave when it comes to spiders.

I plugged in my laptop and opened it on Wallace Villiers's desk. Except for the faded Polaroids, his documentation was clear and precise—detailed descriptions, known provenance, date and place of acquisition, and original receipts with purchase price. I'd already set up an Excel spreadsheet with those same columns. I added a final column labeled "Sale price" to my spreadsheet in case I found any sales receipts.

Wallace Villiers had collected a wide variety of antiques, but he had favored eighteenth-century paintings, early Chinese pottery, and European porcelain—especially Meissen.

Forty minutes later I'd successfully matched up seventeen objects, recording them on the spreadsheet, tagging them or marking them with the corresponding numbers, and taking photos with my cell phone. The work was familiar to me. I kept similar records myself. Later, when I had internet access, I would embed links to the images in the file. Finally, I'd load everything on a thumb drive for the police.

Evelyn Villiers's final word haunted me—*Meissen*. If you don't know you're going to die, your last words might be "Don't forget to defrost the chops" or "Watch out for that bus." But if you've been stabbed, your final words are significant.

So what had Evelyn Villiers tried to communicate when she said *Meissen* with her last breath? Wallace Villiers had been particularly fond of Meissen. He'd purchased a large number of wonderful old pieces, mostly figural groups from the eighteenth century. Had she tried to communicate the identity of her killer—or had she hidden an important clue in one of the Meissen pieces?

I was in the dining room, hunting for a large Sèvres sugarbox and cover, when I heard the chink of china in the kitchen.

"Anne—you're back early." I rolled my neck and stiff shoulders.

Silence.

"Anne?" I walked through into the entrance hall.

More silence.

Alert, I backed against the wall, mentally flipping through the possibilities. Had someone wandered inside? A vagrant looking for food? A burglar? I hadn't heard a car drive up, and I'd locked the door from the inside. I'd have heard someone breaking in.

*Should I hide? Run?* I'd left my cell phone in the library. *Crap.*

Slipping off my shoes, I crept barefoot through the butler's pantry and peered around the corner into the kitchen. A thin woman wearing dingy pink workout clothes stood frozen, one hand holding the lid of a ceramic cookie jar. Her hair had been bleached the color and texture of straw. Her face was a mass of wrinkles, her lips a carmine gash.

"May I help you?" I stepped into the room, pretty sure I could overpower her if necessary.

"Lordy," she gasped, clapping her free hand on her flat chest. "Nearly gave me a 'eart attack, you did." She replaced the lid on the cookie jar.

"Stealing cookies?" I thought it was funny, but she gave me an injured look.

"I'm not stealing anything. I saw the police drive off. Thought I'd sort out my wages, long as I were in the neighborhood."

"How did you get in?"

"Got a key, 'aven't I?"

Light dawned. "You're the housekeeper, Mrs. Wright. You'd better give me that key."

Her eyes narrowed. "Who are you, then—police?"

"No, but I'm working with them."

Grudgingly, she handed me the key. "Owes me a week's wages, she does, Mrs. Villiers. I'm sorry she's dead 'n' all, but what's mine is mine."

"Did you tell the police about your wages?"

"Course I did. They gave me a number to call in Bury—solicitor. Took down my details and said they'd be in touch *in due time*, all sniffy-like. Won't 'elp me pay my bills now, will it?"

"What were you looking for in the cookie jar?"

"It's where the missus left cash, in case she wanted something from the stores. 'Just take what you need,' she'd say. Figured I were owed, after all I've been through these past few days. Only there's nothing 'ere." She looked close to tears.

I noticed with relief my handbag was still on the counter. "Stealing will only make them suspect you of something more serious."

"I told you—I weren't stealing." She stared at me defiantly. "Them's my *wages*. I have my rights."

"The police may not see it that way."

"I suppose you'll tell them." Her eyes filled.

She looked so pitiful, I couldn't help feeling sorry for her.

"Look, why don't I say you came for your wages and left, all right?" Opening my handbag, I pulled out my wallet and handed her a twenty-pound note. "It's all I have at the moment, but it should help tide you over until the solicitor contacts you."

"Don't sit well, taking charity," she grumbled. "Always worked for my keep, I 'ave."

"Think of it as an advance on wages due. You can pay me back later."

She sniffed.

"Why don't we have a nice cup of tea," I said, suspecting she was on the brink of tears. "I could use a break, and I'm sure you know your way around this kitchen."

That brightened her up. She got busy filling an electric kettle.

We sat, drinking our tea at the table overlooking the back garden. "Tell me about Mrs. Villiers."

"Oh, she were an odd one. Spent most of 'er time in 'er room upstairs—or in the garden. Fond of the river, she was. In fine weather, she'd sit out there all afternoon."

I thought of the bench along the bank and the photo of the cottage by a river.

"Did you ever hear Mrs. Villiers say anything about a wagon bell?"

I expected her to laugh. Instead she pursed her lips. "Not 'wagon bell,' exactly, but something like it. She were always quoting."

"Quoting?"

"In the old tongue. Couldn't make 'eads nor tails of it."

"Do you know anything about the framed photograph over her bed?"

"Wouldn't know about that. She did for 'erself up there."

"Did you ever ask her why she never left the grounds?"

"That were 'er business. Long as I got paid, she could please 'erself."

"Were you here last Saturday?"

"Police asked that. Only for an 'our or so in the morning to delivery groceries."

"Did she mention driving into Long Barston?"

"No, but then she wouldn't. We weren't friends, like."

"How would she have gotten there?"

"Police asked that too. There's a car in the garage, but I never saw 'er drive."

"Had she seemed different lately? Worried, upset, short-tempered?"

Mrs. Wright wrinkled her forehead in thought. "I 'ardly knew her, did I? Never 'ad a chat—not a proper one like we're 'avin' now. Mostly she'd leave notes on the table, tellin' me what she wanted. Never gave me no trouble."

*The ideal employer.* "How did she pay you?"

"Cash. In an envelope in the cookie jar."

"Did she ever talk about her family? The tragedy of her husband's death?"

"Never. I 'eard about it, o' course, but I never dared ask."

"And you didn't know about Lucy—her daughter?"

Mrs. Wright shifted in her seat. "I may 'ave heard a whisper in the village, but never from 'er. Not a word from 'er."

That wasn't exactly what she'd told the police, but I let it go. "Did Mrs. Villiers receive any mail?"

"Mostly adverts. Every month or so she'd get a letter, official like, from a firm in Bury."

"How did she get cash if she never went out?"

Mrs. Wright blinked. "Must 'ave been that young man who came round in the evenings—the one in the black van. I got the impression 'e did errands for 'er."

"Do you know his name?"

"Never asked—'e weren't local."

"Did the van have a logo on the side?"

"Never paid attention."

"Did Mrs. Villiers ever mention her husband's art and antiques collection?"

"To me?" She hooted. "Not likely. Those rooms were always closed off—although now you mention it, last winter she did ask me to give them a 'ooverin' and a once-over with a feather duster. Right careful I was too. Anything broken, I'd 'ave to pay for it."

"She said that?"

"Stands to reason, don't it? Housekeeper's always to blame." Mrs. Wright drained her cup and set it down on the saucer with a clatter.

I was running out of questions. "Was there ever anything that made you stop and think—especially in the last few weeks? Take your time."

Mrs. Wright sucked in the side of her lower lip. "There was something, now I think on it. It were Friday, the day before she . . . well, you know. I was gathering my things to leave, and there she was, in the kitchen. 'What will you do this weekend?' she asked me. Nearly bowled me over, I was that surprised. 'Fair's on over t' Long Barston,' I said. 'Might catch that play—*The Green Maiden*.'"

"And?"

"She gave me a look—funny-like, you know—and said, 'One day they'll get it right.'"

"What did she mean?"

"I 'aven't a clue."

"Did Mrs. Villiers ever receive visitors?"

"Not while I was 'ere. What she got up to in the evenings, I wouldn't know." Mrs. Wright stood and carried our teacups to the sink. "I should be going."

"You go on," I said. "I'll clean up."

"Ta." She zipped her jacket and turned to face me. "I *will* pay you back."

I followed her through the laundry and locked the door behind her, watching her scurry down the drive without a backward glance.

So the young man who did errands for Evelyn Villiers had a black van. According to Tom, the neighbors reported seeing a dark van in the area at night. Was he a friend of Mrs. Villiers, someone who worked for her?

Or had he taken advantage of her and then murdered her?

Tom needed to hear what I'd learned from Mrs. Wright. The problem was, how could I tell him without getting PC Weldon in trouble?

# Chapter Sixteen

The Three Magpies was busy for a Thursday night. All the tables in the dining room were occupied, so Tom and I grabbed one of the small banquettes in the bar. A new barmaid had been hired recently, a pretty young woman with pink cheeks and a bouncy blonde ponytail. Tom put in our order. Fish and chips, a humble dish, but at The Three Magpies, something to celebrate—filets of locally caught haddock, lightly breaded and panfried to golden perfection. The chips were equally irresistible, served in small wire baskets.

Tom returned to the table with a half-pint of ale and a Sauvignon blanc for me. The lines around his eyes had deepened. I wondered if he'd slept.

"How did things go last night?" I asked, concerned.

"Let's just say not as planned." He laughed ruefully. "We'd been informed about a shipment of drugs headed for a lorry depot near Ipswich. They never showed. Either the informers were playing us, or the bad guys had been tipped off." He leaned back, stretching out his long legs. "I checked on the Oakleys. Nigel, the father, has a spotless reputation. Nothing on Martin Ingram. The son, Peter, had a few drug arrests back in his twenties, but nothing recent."

"No reason to worry, then?" I remembered the cloud that had passed over Nigel's face at Finchley Hall when he'd spoken of his son.

"I didn't say that—just that we have nothing on record to cause undue alarm. I heard you spent a few hours at Hapthorn today. Did you get the book on Suffolk legends?"

"Actually, I brought it with me." I pulled the book out of my handbag.

"And what did you learn?"

"Quite a lot, actually."

"Hmm." Tom lifted his glass and took a long drink. "Read it to me. I need a distraction." He closed his eyes.

I removed the Kleenex I'd used as a bookmark and read.

*"During the rule of Harold Godwinson, Earl of East Anglia, an elderly yeoman farmer in a village on the border between Suffolk and Essex went out one morning to survey his sheep folds near the River Stour. He was surprised to find a young maiden, asleep in a hedgerow. She appeared to be age twelve or thirteen and wore the roughly woven shift of a peasant. She was a pretty child, with hair as black as coal and cornflower-blue eyes, but her skin was as green as the moss on a stone wall, the devil's own hue.*

*"At first the farmer was afraid, but he was a kindly soul, and when the girl began to weep, he took pity on her. As he and his wife had no children, they took the strange child into their cottage and treated her as their daughter. When questioned, the girl said only that she had come from a land of semi-darkness with a great river running through it, giving life and health to the inhabitants. And so they gave her the name Mersia, from the Anglo-Saxon word for river."*

I stopped reading. "The river thing keeps coming up, Tom—the flooding river in the play; the photograph above Evelyn Villiers's bed; her love for the River Stour. Now this."

"Who told you she loved the river?"

*Oh man.* I'd been planning to ease into the housekeeper story. I sidestepped the question. "Why else would she have a photo of a river above her bed?"

He opened one eye. "What does a river have to do with theft and murder?"

"I don't know yet. Just listen."

*"Mersia lived with the couple until she was seventeen, in the full bloom of womanhood. Over time, her skin had faded to the*

*pale green of a moth's wing, and she was said to be the loveliest maiden in all of East Anglia. As the farmer and his wife were now aged, they agreed to give her in marriage to a young yeoman farmer who lived near the village of Borley in Essex.*

*"Sadly, the story of Mersia's history followed her. Some of the women in Borley claimed Mersia was a changeling. Others said she was a witch, casting spells that caused women to miscarry. Even her husband turned against her, testifying that she had attempted to poison him with strange herbs mixed into his drink. Only the intervention of the priest saved Mersia from the gallows. Instead, she was cast out of the village and sentenced to dwell alone in a cottage along the riverbank. There she died in the great flood of 1065."*

"Interesting but irrelevant as far as I can see."

"I'd agree if it wasn't for this." I handed him the book.

He sat up, angling the page toward the candle on our table. Two phrases had been underlined faintly in pencil. After the first, *"agreed to give her in marriage to a young yeoman farmer,"* someone had written in the margin the words *"Not true."* After the second, *"died in the great flood of 1065,"* the same person had written a single word: *Murdered.*

"What do you make of it?" he asked,

"I'll tell you, but first there's—"

A young man in a kilt—his name badge said Angus—interrupted our conversation. After setting down our plates, he pulled a bottle of dark malt vinegar out of his sporran. "Enjoy."

"But first there's what?" Tom uncapped the vinegar and doused his fish and chips.

"While I was at Hapthorn, the housekeeper, Mrs. Wright, showed up. It seems Mrs. Villiers owed her wages, so I—"

He interrupted me. "Where was PC Weldon?"

That was the part I'd hoped I wouldn't have to mention. "She'd gone to visit her grandmother who lives in the village—just for a short while. I locked the door behind her, but then Mrs. Wright showed up with her key, thinking the house was empty. Here it is, by the way." I handed him the key and told him about the cookie jar and the missing wages. "She's living hand-to-mouth, Tom. I gave her twenty pounds."

He put down his fork and turned to face me. "She asked you for money?"

"No. In fact, she was reluctant to take it. But who knows when the estate will be settled, and who knows when she'll get another job. I would have given her more, but that's all I had. She said she'd pay me back."

"You're a soft touch, Kate." He shook his head and gave me a conspiratorial smile. "I would have done the same thing—although let's not mention it to Eacles." He took a chip and dipped it in the vinegar. "I'll have the locks changed tomorrow—in case someone else has a key."

"Mrs. Wright said a man in a dark van would come around from time to time. She thought he did errands or something."

"We know about him. No name yet." He reached out and traced my cheek with his finger. "Now, tell me the rest. I'm betting you didn't let the housekeeper go without a few questions."

He was getting to know me so well.

I went over our conversation in the kitchen, piece by piece, including what Mrs. Villiers said about the green maiden play—*"One day they'll get it right."*

"Something else got my attention. Mrs. Wright said Evelyn Villiers would sit along the riverbank for hours in fine weather. Remember the bench we saw? The river was important to her. I think we should find out where that photograph above her bed was taken."

"Kate—" Tom started to object.

I put up my hand. "I know, I know—the photo may be irrelevant. But what about the notations in the book? And what she said when Mrs. Wright brought up the play—*"One day they'll get it right"*? That has to mean something."

"Have you considered that Evelyn Villiers might have been halfway round the bend? Living in isolation for eighteen years would affect anyone's mental stability."

"She seemed perfectly sane to me, although she was reluctant to answer my questions."

"Lots of people don't like to be questioned—makes my job harder, I can tell you. They hold back bits of information they decide aren't important, sometimes to protect themselves, but often simply because they resent the intrusion." He took a bite of his fish. "How's the inventory going?"

"There's a lot more to do. I haven't found that Meissen piece yet—the one on the mantel in the photograph—but so far nothing else is missing except the jewelry, which makes me wonder about the man in the dark van. Maybe he was taking advantage of her, stealing from her. Everyone knew about the art collection, and her penchant for fine jewelry wasn't a secret. Maybe he took the jewelry, hoping she'd never know it was gone."

An older couple took the table next to us and ordered cocktails.

Tom lowered his voice. "DS Cliffe is going to interview Mrs. Wright again this week. I'll give him the heads-up. She might know more than she said. Anything else?"

"I've been thinking about what Mrs. Villiers said in the shop—'wagon bell.'"

"You've figured out what it means?'

"No, but Mrs. Wright said Mrs. Villiers would often quote things in what she called *the old language*—Old English, I suppose. Maybe Ertha Green can shed some light. She was there when it all happened eighteen years ago."

"If she remembers." Tom took the last bite of his fish.

"Yes—if she remembers."

"Good luck." He looked up as Angus the waiter slid a leather receipt folder on the table.

"No rush," Angus said. "Whenever you're ready."

Tom pulled out his wallet. "I almost forgot—my mother phoned. She'll be home from Devon on Tuesday. She'd like you to come for dinner Wednesday. Will seven o'clock work?"

"Wednesday—seven o'clock?" I tried to smile. "Of course."

* * *

We stood on the doorstep of Rose Cottage. The tiny porch light lit the angles on Tom's face as he bent to kiss me. I felt the ground beneath me sway as the months rolled away, and we were back on the dance floor at Glenroth House in Scotland.

"You have no idea the effect you have on me, do you?" he said.

It was so perfectly my own thought that I almost laughed. Instead, I took a huge breath. "Come inside?"

"Wish I could, Kate. I have an early morning staff meeting. Then an all-day trip to Harwich on the coast. Another tip about drug routes from the Continent."

One more kiss, and I let him go.

Inside on the table, I found a note from Vivian. She and Fergus had dined at Finchley Hall and would be back by nine thirty.

I phoned The Willows. Ivor was still awake, so they put me through. I told him I'd drive out in the morning with Lady Barbara's carved lacquer plate. He was so thrilled, you'd have thought I was proposing to break him out.

After making myself a cup of tea, I sat at the table and thought about what I'd learned. Missing jewelry. A dark van, possibly with a white logo. Wagon bell. Meissen. The green maiden. A river. They were bits and pieces, shards, like broken porcelain. If there were connections, I couldn't see them.

I pictured Evelyn Villiers the day she entered Ivor's shop. There'd been an elegance about her, not only in her bone structure but in the way she moved, in her hands as she held the húnpíng.

I took in a sharp breath as the memory came flooding back.

A wedding, a betrayal, a *death.* I said the last word aloud.

*Get a grip.* Inanimate objects do not communicate with people. And they certainly don't help solve murders. And yet several times in my life, when handling a precious object, a word or a phrase had seemed to distill the essence of a puzzle, a mystery. The source had to be my own brain. Evelyn Villiers had told me just enough about her daughter to plant the idea of betrayal. Somehow the húnpíng had acted as a portal—capturing, then magnifying my unconscious thoughts. That had to be the answer—the one I wanted anyway.

The door opened. "Wait 'til I get the leash off." Vivian's indulgent voice floated in. I heard the tapping of nails as Fergus trotted into the room and gave me a look. *Where have you been all evening?*

* * *

After washing up and putting on my pajamas, I logged into my computer and added the images I'd taken at Hapthorn Lodge to my spreadsheet. Then I telephoned Wisconsin. Sometimes a girl needs her mother.

"Hi, Mom."

"Hello, my darling. I'm trying to pack."

I could see her with the suitcase on the bed, stacks of clothes laid out for her trip to the lake cottage with Dr. Lund. I felt the old stab of jealousy and ignored it.

"It's very casual in the Northwoods," she said, "but the weather can be chilly in May. James says I need to layer." She sounded excited. "What's happening where you are, darling? Any news on the húnpíng?"

I filled her in on my day at Hapthorn. Then I got down to my real reason for calling. "Tom's mother has invited me for dinner next week. I don't want to go. I'm not sure I can face her."

"Of course you can, darling."

I groaned. "But I told her I never wanted to see her again."

"Tom has three women in his life, Kate—his mother, his daughter, and you. However you feel about Liz Mallory, you're going to have to put the past aside and make up your mind to get along with her."

"You mean pretend? I can't do that. She was awful to me."

"Who said anything about pretending?"

"*You* did. 'Make up your mind to get along with her.'"

"My darling girl—in life there are feelings and there are decisions. If we waited to do things until we felt like it, nothing would ever get done. You can't feel your way into right actions, but you can act your way into right feelings. Do the right thing, and your emotions will follow."

"I can't see *that* happening anytime soon."

"Maybe not soon, but eventually. I think she's afraid, you know. Afraid of you, afraid you'll take her son away. He's all she's got."

For a moment, I couldn't speak. She might have been describing me—the fear and resentment I'd felt about her upcoming lake visit with James Lund's family. Or was she describing *herself*, a decision she'd made not to interfere in my happiness, even if it meant losing me to England?

I took a few slow breaths. "So you're saying I should apologize?"

"Certainly not—that *would* be pretending. I'm suggesting you treat her with all the kindness and courtesy you can muster—because she's Tom's mother. If she brings up the day at the Suffolk Rose, listen. Don't rehash it and don't apologize. Tell her you'd like to start again as friends."

"I'll think about it."

"One more thing, darling. Remember, the only one you're responsible for is yourself. Liz may not be willing—or able—to be friends. If that's the case, let it be her decision, not yours."

After we hung up, I pulled back the rose satin comforter and slipped into bed with Ivor's book on Chinese art. In the chapter on the Han dynasty, I skipped over a long section on jade burial suits, thought to preserve the body for eternity, and found the part about soul jars, which the author had spelled "hun-p'ing." My eyes felt heavy.

To keep myself awake, I mumbled the words aloud: *"Among the rarest and most prized examples of Yue ware—first produced in the coastal province of Zhejiang."* I yawned and turned the page. *"Their sudden disappearance at the beginning of the fourth century* CE *is attributed to changes in funeral rites imposed from the north."*

A number of colored plates showed examples. I sat up and adjusted my pillow. The designs ranged from the elegant and restrained to the outlandish and comical. One húnpíng featured a figure gleefully urinating. Each jar was unique, highly individualistic—slices of life captured in clay, a world that had vanished two thousand years ago.

By the time I reached the final paragraph, I was fully awake.

*The ancient Chinese obsession with the afterlife is surpassed only by the obsession of modern Chinese collectors to reclaim what they consider their stolen national heritage. Shrouded in secrecy, the White Lotus Society is said to be dedicated to the repatriation of China's ancient treasures. For more information, see the chapter on the looting of the Summer Palace in Beijing.*

I looked at the clock on the bedside table. Nearly eleven. I thumbed forward, my fingers leaping centuries. I scanned the lines as quickly as I could without missing important details.

*The Old Summer Palace, known in Chinese as* Yuan Ming Yuan, *or "Gardens of Brightness," was built in Beijing in the eighteenth and early nineteenth centuries as the imperial residence of the emperor of the Qing dynasty. In 1860, during the Second Opium War, two British envoys attempting to negotiate a Qing surrender, along with a journalist and a small cadre of Indian troopers, were captured and tortured to death. In retaliation, Lord Elgin, the British High Commissioner in China, ordered the destruction of the palace. It took four thousand soldiers three days to burn it. According to UNESCO, as many as one and a half million treasures—sculptures; carvings; porcelain; jade; silk robes and textiles; and objects of gold, silver, and bronze—were looted and now reside in private collections as well as at least forty-seven museums around the world.*

I remembered the controversy in the art world some years earlier when the Chinese National Administration of Cultural Heritage called for a boycott of the auction of an archaic bronze water vessel known as the *Tiger Ying*, looted from the Summer Palace by a British soldier. The Tiger Ying was purchased for almost six hundred thousand dollars by an anonymous bidder, who promptly donated the vessel to the Chinese government.

The information on the White Lotus Society came near the end of the chapter.

*In 1982, China made the repatriation of its cultural heritage a constitutional mandate. Since then, delegations of so-called treasure-hunting teams have been sent out worldwide to identify and reclaim the looted artifacts.*

The next sentences really got my attention.

*Although never acknowledged by the Chinese government, members of the secret White Lotus Society, named after earlier nationalistic and quasi-religious societies, are reputed to have taken vows to liberate Chinese cultural treasures by any means necessary. Their signature is said to be a white lotus blossom.*

By any means necessary. *Theft? Murder?*

Grabbing my cell phone, I texted Tom: *Has the white petal been identified? Let me guess: lotus.*

# Chapter Seventeen

Friday, May 10

Tom phoned the next morning before I was even out of bed. "All right, what's this about a lotus?"

I told him what I'd read the night before about the White Lotus Society. "I think they have someone operating in the area."

"In Suffolk? Why wouldn't they target a major metropolitan area or one of the wealthier counties like Surrey or Kent?"

"Because right here, in this little corner of rural Suffolk, we happen to have two very fine and extremely rare pieces of Chinese history. That's what they're after." When he didn't respond, I said, "So, was it a lotus petal?"

"Close. The petal came from a water lily—genetically akin, I'm told, to the lotus plant. And plentiful. Water lilies can be found in every lake, pond, and back-garden water feature in Suffolk. Even Blackwater Lake."

"So, not having an actual lotus blossom, they used the next best thing."

"You're jumping to conclusions."

"Point taken—but what if it's true? What if the White Lotus Society targeted the húnpíng and sent someone to retrieve it?"

"Are you talking about Henry Liu?"

"Not necessarily. It could be anyone who cares about Chinese history and culture—or money. Maybe they hire local thieves. But

Henry was on the scene. And he did lie about the time he left the fair, remember? He claims he left at nine, but according to Briony Peacock, he left at eight fifteen."

"Giving him time to kill Evelyn Villiers and hide the jar before calling the police? How do you account for the fact that there were three sets of footprints?"

I pictured the bloody footprints. "Maybe his son was involved."

"We thought of that. Cliffe's team examined James Liu's shoes—every pair. None matched the prints. Besides, someone drove Evelyn Villiers from Little Gosling to Long Barston. Henry and James were at their tent on the green all afternoon and evening. Well, until they ran out of shrimp rolls, anyway."

"I'm not accusing anyone. I'm just telling you what I read last night. The white petal is an odd coincidence, don't you think?"

"I don't like coincidences." His breathing had picked up.

"Sounds like you're running."

"To my car—late for work. I am glad you told me about the Society, Kate. We'll follow up."

"I'm taking the lacquer plate to The Willows later today so Ivor can appraise it."

"Who knows about it besides you and Lady Barbara?"

"Vivian" (I almost added Fergus but stopped myself in time) "and Ivor. Oh, and the guys from the auction house—the Oakleys and Martin Ingram. They were impressed."

"Well, don't mention it to anyone else." He paused. "What are you doing tomorrow?"

"Returning to Hapthorn Lodge if Anne Weldon is available. I'd like to finish the inventory as soon as possible."

"I'm off duty tomorrow. I'll take you."

"You'd be bored."

"No, I wouldn't. I could watch you work—help if I can. And I'll bring something for lunch. We can have a picnic in the garden. Walk along the river if there's time. Talk."

"About the case?"

"No, idiot. About us."

I could see his face, the crinkles around his hazel eyes, flecked with green, the way his hair curled slightly around his ears and at the nape of his neck. The tiny scar on his cheek. That half smile with its remarkable ability to turn me to jelly.

My stomach swooped.

I heard his engine start. "Gotta go. When did you say you're seeing Ertha Green?"

"Sunday."

"Let me know what she says. And say hello to Ivor."

* * *

Ivor held a magnifying glass to his right eye, examining the Chinese lacquer plate with a keenness that landed somewhere between museum curator and small boy with a new toy.

"Look here, Kate," he said, handing me the glass. "Can you see the layers where the angle of the carving is slanted? Narrow stripes of red and black. There may be as many as fifty layers here, black lacquer alternating with red." His cheeks had turned pink. "This plate is the finest example I've ever seen of Chinese lacquer carving—absolute peak of the art. What did your parents call the form, hmm?"

*Pop quiz.* "Cinnabar, because of the red color."

"Correct. Cinnabar is the color, not the material itself. The material, lacquer, comes from the so-called dragon blood tree, common in southern China. The sap is mixed with minerals—charcoal or iron oxide to produce black; arsenic sulfide to produce yellow; and cinnabar, or mercury sulfide, to produce the favored red color. It's an amazing material, painted in thin layers on a base material—turned wood, for example, or metal. When dry, it's resistant to heat and water. Did you know that perfectly preserved lacquer objects have been found in waterlogged Iron Age tombs?"

"I didn't. Amazing."

He held up the plate. "Look at the naturalistic rendering of the flowers, the complexity of the design, the harmony of the elements.

*Magnificent.*" He took off his glasses and wiped his eyes. "I haven't felt this emotional since we saved the tomb of the Empress Nao from the waters of the Yangtze."

"You did?" Ivor's early travel adventures were the stuff of legend.

"A tale for another time, Kate," he said as he always did.

One day I'd pin him down.

The aide, Jay'den, poked her head in the room. "Need anything? Cup o' tea, p'raps?"

"My freedom, since you ask," he said with mock dignity.

"Soon as doctor gives the all clear." She grinned. "Until then we're stuck wi' each other."

"Go on, then." Ivor waved her away. "Find your next victim." This had evidently become a favorite line of banter between them. He resumed his lecture. "I believe this plate—some might call it a tray—was made during the early Ming dynasty, when the art of carving lacquer reached its peak. Say sometime between 1368 and 1430."

"Earlier than I thought. How can you tell?"

"First, the size. Carved lacquer objects of this size became popular in the court of the Yuan dynasty—late fourteenth century. After 1430, smaller items were preferred. Then there's the thickness of the lacquer; the depth and skill of carving; the well-polished finish; the exuberance and complexity of the interwoven floral design; the smooth, rounded outlines—all typical of the early Ming period." He turned the plate over, exposing the line of Chinese characters I'd noticed. "And then there's this."

"A reign mark?"

"Not exactly. The characters say *Zhang Chao zao*—'made by Zhang Chao,' a master carver known to have worked in the late fourteenth century, the Ming dynasty. Think of it, Kate. This plate was created during a time of stability and abundance in China, when art and culture flourished. It lived on to witness upheaval, rebellion, wars, and betrayal."

*Betrayal?* My cheeks went hot. Blood drummed in my head.

"Kate, are you listening?" Ivor touched my arm. "I said this plate had to have been made by the master himself."

I shook myself mentally. "But didn't the Chinese often inscribe objects with the names of earlier artists and earlier dynastic periods?"

"Certainly—not to fool people but to honor their glorious past. Nevertheless, given the size and exceptional quality, the style, and the provenance—the letter, stating this came from the Old Summer Palace in 1860—there's no reason to doubt the attribution."

"So what do we say in the auction description? Nigel Oakley will ask."

"You say, 'Attributed to the master carver Zhang Chao, circa 1368 to 1400 CE.' I'll write something up for you."

"And the value?"

"I've been doing a little research. A similar plate, slightly larger, sold at Sotheby's in 2017 for a million and a half. I'd say between six and eight hundred thousand pounds on a good day."

I tried to take that in. Selling the cinnabar plate would be the answer to all Lady Barbara's problems. "With something so valuable, she'd be better off with one of the auction houses in London rather than a local start-up."

"In that case, prepare her for unpleasant publicity."

"What do you mean?"

"In the past, the Chinese government has tried to block the sale of objects known to have come from the imperial palaces. Lots of adverse press coverage."

"Yes, the Tiger Ying."

"She might rather keep things local—under the radar, so to speak."

It was almost exactly what Evelyn Villiers had said when I'd mentioned Sotheby's and Christie's: *"No public auctions. No catalogs."* Had she known about The White Lotus Society? I wrapped the cinnabar plate in the brown felt bag and slipped it into the braided cotton tote bag Lady Barbara had given me.

"What do you know about the Oakleys? Tom says they're on the up-and-up."

"I know they spent a packet of money restoring the tithe barn. They did well with a collection of Scottish items I gave them. Not so well with the Roman trio."

"But what about the Oakleys themselves—and Martin Ingram?" I swallowed hard as a flash of memory caught me unprepared—those pale crystal-blue eyes.

"The father has a sterling reputation. The son and the Ingram chap are new to these parts, but they're reputed to have a great deal of experience. One of my sources told me they receive shipments from all over the Continent—France, Italy, Germany. Only the finest things."

"Competition for you?" I stood, looping my handbag over my shoulder.

"Yes and no. Many of the objects I carry do best in an auction—in theory anyway. That's why I'm hoping the Oakleys succeed." He breathed out, something between a laugh and a sigh. "I may have to auction off quite a few items to cover the value of the húnpíng. That aside, a reputable auction house will bring trade to this part of Suffolk. Collectors don't simply swan in for an auction and leave. They scour an area clean. More traffic, more sales."

"Then I hope they succeed. Lady Barbara and I will attend the auction on Monday."

"Let me know how it goes."

"I will. I'll call you soon. Oh, and Tom says hello." I was almost out the door when I remembered. "Ivor, what do you know about the White Lotus Society?"

He peered at me narrowly. "Where did you hear about them?"

"In that book of yours, the one on Chinese art. It's supposed to be a secret thing—the members pledged to repatriate China's lost treasures by hook or by crook."

"I ran across them once. Not a pleasant lot."

"Do they ever farm out the work to common thieves?

"I couldn't say. Why do you ask?"

I told him about the white petal found in the stockroom, pledging him to silence.

"Let's hope it's *not* the White Lotus chaps. The looting of the Summer Palace is rather a sore spot for the Chinese. Do you know what they call the era after the First Opium War? They call it *bainian guochi*, the 'century of humiliation.' Even today, with the rise of China as a major world power, the feelings of past humiliation remain. There's a saying in China: *"The flames of Yuan Ming Yuan remain unextinguished."* If I were you, I'd put the lacquer plate in Lady Barbara's safe."

# Chapter Eighteen

Saturday, May 11

I was sleeping soundly when my phone rang. I fumbled to answer, squinting at the clock on the bedside table. Three AM.

"Don't leave the cottage, either of you," Lady Barbara said calmly. "We've had an intruder. The police are on their way."

I pushed myself up on one elbow. "Someone broke into the Hall?"

"Fortunately not. Someone was skulking around in the yard. The new security cameras alerted my mobile."

"What did they look like?"

"You're asking me—with my vision? There's a video clip."

"What did you do?" I pulled the comforter up around my shoulders.

"I opened my bedroom window and shouted, 'Whoever you are, go away. I have a shotgun, and I'm not afraid to use it.'"

"You have a shotgun?"

"Of course not."

"What happened?"

"They went away. Oh, I'll have to ring off—the police have arrived. Don't leave the cottage. I'll explain everything in the morning."

She hung up, leaving me disoriented. Was I dreaming?

I wasn't. I got out of bed and threw on my robe. From my bedroom window, I could see the flashing lights from the police cars, pulsing amber blobs on the wet window glass. It was raining again.

I tiptoed into the hallway. Sounds of snoring came from Vivian's bedroom—whether Vivian or Fergus or both, I couldn't tell. No reason to wake them. The police would make sure the danger had passed.

I lay awake after that, thinking about the White Lotus Society and loyalty to one's country. I was as American as they come, and yet I was beginning to feel very much at home in England. The differences, all those subtleties of language and culture that escape the average tourist, were becoming second nature to me. *Could I live here permanently?*

At six I got up, dressed, and went down to the kitchen to make coffee and boil an egg. Vivian emerged a half hour later, wrapped in her gray wool robe.

"You're up early." She yawned and took Fergus's leash from the hook.

"There was an intruder at the Hall last night. Lady Barbara called the police. She said she'd fill us in this morning."

"Crikey! Is she all right?"

"Perfectly. She frightened them off with a fake shotgun."

The sound of nails clacking on the stairs told me Fergus was awake as well. He maneuvered his sausage-like body down the final steps and headed for the door.

Vivian shoved the leash at me. "Will you take him outside, Kate? I must dress immediately."

By eight we'd donned our rain gear and were tramping through the damp grass toward the Hall. When we arrived, we found Tom having tea and scones in Lady Barbara's private sitting room.

"Join us," Lady Barbara said. "Plenty for everyone."

A log fire burned in the grate, taking the edge off the morning chill. Lady Barbara wore a periwinkle blue wool dress with a patterned shawl, held together at the shoulder with a charming silver Victorian pin.

I took a buttery scone. Vivian poured two cups of tea and topped up Lady Barbara's cup.

"What happened last night?" I asked Tom. "Was someone trying to break in?"

"The video doesn't show much—just a dark shape moving near the Archives building. Impossible to tell if it was a potential burglar or simply a vagrant seeking shelter from the rain."

"I locked the cinnabar plate in the safe in the Archives building last night, but Ivor was the only one who knew that."

"He anticipated a theft?" Lady Barbara asked.

"Not exactly, but when I showed him Lieutenant Finchley's note, saying the plate had been rescued—"

*"Pilfered."* She gave me a stern look.

"That the plate had been stolen from the Old Summer Palace in Beijing, he connected it with the White Lotus Society."

"A horticultural group?" Vivian flicked a crumb from her sweater. "How nice."

"Hardly," I said. "The White Lotus Society is a secret brotherhood, the members pledged to restore China's stolen cultural heritage by any means necessary. I'm wondering if they have an operative in the area."

"An *operative*?" Vivian said. "Who are you talking about?"

"I hope you don't suspect Henry Liu," Lady Barbara said. "He's been a member of the Long Barston community for years. He and his wife keep themselves to themselves."

*High praise.*

"But how about the son—James?" Vivian buttered a slice of banana bread. "Henry claims he's looking for a university teaching job, but I've seen no evidence of it."

"It can't be easy for an immigrant to get a university teaching position," I said. "James helps his parents with the restaurant."

Vivian flicked her eyebrows. "Then why was Penny alone in the tent the night of the May Fair, hmm?"

"Henry's daughter-in-law?" Tom asked. "How do you know James wasn't there?"

"Because I stood in line for ten minutes," Vivian said. "When it was my turn to place our order, Penny told me the shrimp rolls were out, so I ordered duck ribs. People were getting testy—some waiting for their food and others waiting to place orders. Penny was almost in tears. She said, 'I'm sorry for the wait. I'm here by myself.'"

"When was this?"

"Just after the play. Around nine thirty, I suppose."

I could almost see the gears turning in Tom's head. At nine thirty, Penny Liu was alone in the tent, and Evelyn Villiers was lying dead in the stockroom. Around the same time, Tom got the call about a break-in and a body at Ivor's shop, discovered by Henry Liu. A few minutes later, James showed up in the alley, implying he'd just come from the tent.

*Another lie.*

* * *

I walked Tom to his car, hopping over puddles that had formed in the gravel drive. The sky was clearing, but the air smelled of rain and wet soil. The yew hedges around Finchley Hall glistened.

"I don't mind the rain," I said.

"That's good. We're not allowed to have fine weather in England for more than three days running. It's against the rules."

We reached his car. "Come here," he said.

I turned to face him, and he wrapped his waxed jacket around me. "Henry Liu lied about the time he left to replenish the shrimp rolls, and James lied about his whereabouts at the time of the murder."

"They're not necessarily lies, Kate. People get things wrong. Or maybe Vivian misinterpreted what Penny Liu said. We'll interview them all again. Give them an opportunity to explain the discrepancies."

"Hmm." I wasn't convinced.

"I promise you, we're following every line of inquiry" Tom clicked open his car and tossed his umbrella in the rear seat.

"What lines of inquiry?"

"Lucy Villiers, for one. She stands to inherit a fortune, so where is she? And there's the young man who, according to the housekeeper, did errands at Hapthorn Lodge." He ticked them off on his fingers. "The dark van seen in the neighborhood, the general disorder in the house, the Australian connection, the White Lotus Society, even the housekeeper herself."

"You didn't mention the gardener."

"Not a suspect. He was visiting his grandchildren in London when Mrs. Villiers was killed."

"Don't forget the green maiden." I half expected him to say, *How could I when you keep bringing her up?*

Instead, he said, "This is why a police inquiry takes time, Kate. No stone left unturned. When the stones begin pointing in the same direction, we know we're on the right track."

"Maybe the young man Mrs. Wright saw *is* the Australian connection. What if Wallace's sister had a son who came to England, hoping to cash in on the Villiers' fortune, and discovered that his uncle's widow was an easy mark?"

"Then we'll hear from him—or the solicitor will. In the meantime, we're following up with the Australian authorities. As I said, everything takes time."

I made a mental note to ask Ertha Green about the Australian relatives.

A roll of thunder sounded, far away. Tom looked at the sky. "More rain. In some areas, the river has already reached flood stage."

"We're not going to get that walk today, are we?"

"Just as well. With this new development, I'll be spending extra time at the office. If you want to go to Hapthorn later today, I'll ask PC Weldon to drive you."

"No chance of my going alone, I suppose."

"None whatsoever—and not because I don't trust you. Even police work in pairs."

"So you *are* worried about further thefts."

"I'm a policeman, Kate. I'm always worried."

"Tell Anne to phone me when she's free. I want to finish the inventory so I can focus on Ivor and the shop. I suppose you'd tell me if there was news about Lucy Villiers."

"I would, and there isn't. Technically, the missing person case is still open, but there's no record of her living in the UK—or leaving it. She hasn't registered with the National Health, which is how we usually trace missing persons. She hasn't applied for a passport or a driver's license. She's either changed her identity, or—" he stopped, opening his car door.

"Or what?"

"Or she's no longer alive."

# Chapter Nineteen

Sunday, May 12

The Green family lived in a single-story pebbledash cottage, painted white and nearly overwhelmed by giant rhododendron bushes.

"Come in, come in." Yasmin Green beckoned me inside. "Mommy, she's here," Yasmin called over her shoulder.

Yasmin was a lovely young woman with smooth skin, asymmetrical goddess braids, and a figure that could not only stop traffic, but hearts.

The smell of something savory reminded me I was hungry. Rose Cottage had lost electricity for a time during the night, which meant the alarms hadn't gone off. Vivian and I had dashed off to the early morning service at St. Æthelric's with only tea to tide us over.

A huge tabby cat streaked past my legs and out the open door.

"That's Cookie," Yasmin said. "Champion mouser."

I was beginning to feel like a mouse myself—on one of those exercise wheels, going nowhere but getting there fast. My trip to Hapthorn the previous afternoon had been canceled because Anne Weldon's baby, Maddie, fifteen months old, had come down with a cold and had to be kept home from her childminder. Instead, I'd gone to Ivor's shop, finding three e-mails from consignment clients who'd decided to take their items back, plus an ominous-looking envelope from Waltham & Crewe, Solicitors, informing Ivor they'd filed a claim for the húnpíng jar in the Magistrates' Court in Ipswich.

Whoever said "all publicity is good publicity" should have their private cell numbers shared with the friendly telemarketers at "the technical department."

"I promise not to take too much of Ertha's time," I told Yasmin.

"Don't be silly, Kate." She laughed. "This will be the highlight of her day. She insisted on wearing her very best summer dress."

An umbrella stand in the tiny entrance hall was stuffed with cricket bats and shin guards. Two athletic bags had been stowed under a narrow table. The sitting room was crowded with books and potted plants. A half-completed jigsaw puzzle had been laid out on the low coffee table. This was a busy, happy family home.

Ertha Green sat, with her hands folded, in a high-back chair. At ninety-something, she was small and birdlike with close-cropped white hair, velvet-brown eyes, and a face made for smiling. Her best summer dress was crisp cotton in a lavender and white print. White button earrings matched the shawl draped over her shoulders.

"So you're t'e one who wants to know," she said, the rhythm of her speech falling like waves on sand.

"Hello, Mrs. Green. It's so nice to meet you. I'm hoping you can help me find Lucy Villiers. She's missing."

"I heard so. Long time ago now."

I was about to ask her a question when Yasmin bustled into the room, her braids bouncing on her shoulders. "Come, you two. Everything's ready."

According to Vivian, Yasmin's parents had emigrated from Tobago when she was a toddler. She'd grown up in Suffolk and attended the local comprehensive school. Her career with the Royal Mail began with holiday shifts until a job opened up for a permanent mail carrier.

The square kitchen table was covered with a marine-blue cloth. The chairs had cushions in alternating stripes of coral, citrus, and fern green. A wooden cross hung on the wall over a painting of a tropical cove.

"Mommy thought you might enjoy a Caribbean meal." Yasmin filled our glasses. "Mango and passion fruit—hope you like it."

I took a sip. "This is wonderful."

Yasmin uncovered a casserole dish. "*Pelau*, one of Mommy's favorites. Caramelized chicken, rice, coconut milk, spices, and pigeon peas—those little green things. Unfortunately, we settle for tinned in England." The rich stew smelled of clove and coriander.

She handed me a basket. "We call this 'coco bread.'" She laughed. "No one remembers why."

I unfolded the bright orange cloth and took one of the soft, yeasty buns.

"You used to make bread every day, didn't you?" Yasmin smiled at the old lady. "Now only for special."

While we ate, Ertha told me about growing up on her small island in the British West Indies. Her older sister had emigrated first, joining relatives in Birmingham. After Ertha's husband was killed in an agricultural accident, she followed with her son, Ralston, then only two. For almost twenty years, she'd worked in a local Caribbean restaurant. Then, when Ralston was recruited by Ipswich Town, a League One football club, she moved to Suffolk, taking up the post as cook and housekeeper for the Villiers.

After the meal, we carried our dessert, a flaky pastry rolled with currants, onto the back patio, where Yasmin had set out a painted wooden table and three chairs lined with fleeces and soft blankets. A patch of wet green grass was bordered by a riot of rain-soaked flowers—red parrot tulips and orange poppies, pure white stock, and lilacs of the deepest purple, all set against the cool blue-green of lady's mantle and lacy emerald Solomon's seal. A small fountain sent water cascading over rocks.

"Mommy loves to be outdoors," Yasmin said, tucking the blanket around the old lady's shoulders, "even when the air is cool and damp."

I finished the last bite of pastry and pulled my own blanket closer. "What can you tell me about the Villiers family, Ertha? It's not mere curiosity. Mr. Tweedy needs to contact Lucy—if she can be located."

"I was there when Lucy was born, poor child."

"Why poor?"

"Mrs. Villiers was never a mother at heart, you know—God rest her soul. It was hard for her with her husband away so often, and Lucy was never an easy child. High-strung. Secretive. Her parents sent her away to school when she was eight, but it didn't work out." Ertha shook her head sadly. "Couldn't fit in with the other girls, could she now? They brought her home in the end."

"Do you remember Mrs. Villiers talking about a wagon bell?"

Ertha chuckled. "Don't t'ink she ever saw a wagon in her life, that one. Now my father had a cart and an old donkey who refused to take orders, so we—" She stopped herself. "But you haven't come to hear about that. What else do you want to know, child?"

I smiled at her. The truth was, I could have spent the rest of the day listening to her memories. "Why was Mr. Villiers gone so much?"

"Making investments for his firm all over the world."

"And collecting art and antiques?"

"My, yes. Somet'ing new every trip. And he always brought somet'ing for his wife."

"I got the impression she wasn't interested in antiques."

"I t'ink she liked them well enough, especially the jewelry. Somet'ing pretty to wear—a ring, a necklace, a hair clip."

"Was Mr. Villiers a good father?"

The twisting of her mouth was so slight I might have missed it. "I suppose so—when he was home. He always brought Lucy somet'ing too, when he'd been away. Mostly dolls, dressed up in costumes from the countries he'd visited."

I remembered them, lined up on the shelf in her room. "Was he a good husband?"

"Don't want to speak ill of the dead, now." She looked at me, her dark eyes unblinking.

"Even if it helps us find Lucy?"

She seemed to consider this and shrugged. "I don't know this for true, you understand, but I don't t'ink it was a happy marriage. You can't help hearing t'ings, can you, when you live in the same house? The arguments, the tears. Never said a word to me, Mrs. Villiers, but I knew."

"Did you ever hear about relatives in Australia?"

"He had a sister in Australia. Letters would come from time to time."

"Did the sister have a family?"

"That I wouldn't know."

"Were they on good terms?"

"No reason to doubt it."

"Tell me about the young man who worked for Mr. Villiers—Colin Wardle."

"Called himself a *chauffeur*, but he did other t'ings as well. Oh, he was a sly one." Ertha folded her hands on her lap.

"Sly in what way?"

"Couldn't be trusted. He'd lie about little t'ings—driving that big car without permission, taking cash from the cookie jar, coming to work late, leaving early. Taking advantage when Mr. Villiers was away on one of his trips. I told Mrs. Villiers what I saw. She tried to tell her husband, but he didn't want to hear it, did he?"

"And then a painting was stolen."

"Right off the wall, bold as brass. Mrs. Villiers was sure it was Colin, but Mr. Villiers refused to believe it, said she was out to get the boy fired. It all came out later—that he and Lucy were involved, and her just a child. Too good-looking he was, and knew it. Mr. Villiers was furious. Told the boy to clear off. It wasn't two weeks later when I woke to shouting. I looked out my window and saw them on the drive. Lucy had a suitcase. Colin and Mr. Villiers began to fight. I didn't know what to do, child—whether to call the police or wake Mrs. Villiers. Didn't need to in the end. She ran out in her dressing gown and took Lucy inside. T'ings seemed to settle down between the two men. That's when Mr. Villiers fell. Like a tree. Didn't even try to break his fall. Must have been dead already. Then I did call the police."

"And Mrs. Villiers blamed Lucy."

"Lord Almighty, she was in a state. Said Lucy broke her father's heart, and maybe she had." Ertha gazed into the middle distance. "It was cold the day of the inquest. Early spring. Afterward, Mrs. Villiers took to her room, refused to come out."

"Why, Ertha, when the marriage hadn't been happy?"

"I t'ink she was one of those women who depend upon a man too much. I left a tray outside her room that evening. She never took it in.

The next day a woman came—Mr. Villiers's sister from Essex. Packed up all Lucy's t'ings and drove off with her."

"What did you think?"

Ertha closed her eyes. "At the time, I thought it was for the best."

"When did Mrs. Villiers tell you to leave?"

"Later the following day I found a letter on the kitchen counter. I kept it, Lord knows why. Yasmin, will you look in my dresser? Bottom shelf, under my t'ings."

Yasmin brought an envelope, still crisp. Ertha opened it, unfolded the paper inside, and handed me a typed letter.

*14 March 2002*

*Dear Mrs. Green,*

*I regret to inform you that your services are no longer required at Hapthorn. I would be obliged if you would gather your belongings and leave at your earliest convenience, no later than March 17th. In this envelope you will find the sum of £500 as severance, which I hope will enable you to secure a temporary place to live until a suitable position becomes available. Attached is a brief written reference. I shall not respond to any further enquiries about your employment, nor do I wish any prospective employers to call or write to me. Please make this clear when you apply for a new position.*

"She didn't even bother to sign it," Ertha said.

"Why did she fire you?"

"I've wondered about that. Money trouble, I thought at the time. She was a proud woman."

"What did you do then?" I handed the letter back.

"Oh, child." She chuckled. "You know when the Lord closes a door, He opens a window. I kept house for my Ralston. And now for Yasmin and my two grandsons."

"We're a family, aren't we?" Yasmin bent down and kissed her mother-in-law's cheek. "She's been a blessing."

Who was taking care of whom at this point didn't seem to matter.

"Did you ever hear from Lucy?" I asked.

"Never. And then Ralston told me she'd gone missing, poor child."

I could see Ertha was tiring.

"Do you have any idea where she might have gone, Ertha? Friends, other relatives?"

"The Lord, He knows," she said quietly as her eyes closed.

# Chapter Twenty

Monday, May 13

Lady Barbara and I arrived at Oakley's auction house around one thirty in the afternoon. The drive along Mill Lane had been pleasant—farmland sectioned by hedgerows and a few spreading trees. We'd spotted the tithe barn from a distance, a dark, wood-clad structure with a steeply pitched thatched roof and half-hipped gable ends. We parked in the guest lot, and I helped Lady Barbara navigate the stone walk.

"You should have seen the grand opening," she said. "Champagne, cocktails, delicious food, a classical quartet. Very impressive."

"It must have been. Not every auction house is set in a Grade Two–listed building."

In the Middle Ages, almost every village in northern Europe had a tithe barn. It was the place where farmers brought a portion of their produce as payment for land rents and tithes to the local church. The National Trust maintains at least four tithe barns in England. I'd been lucky enough to see two of them. This tithe barn, I'd read on the Oakley's website, had been on private property for four hundred years and was slated for demolition when they purchased it.

We stepped inside. The auction preview was underway—well attended and lively, an excellent sign. What I'd planned to do was stroll around, examining the items to be auctioned off—checking for chips, cracks, reproductions, and what's called in the trade "married pieces"—chests, for example, that have been joined with bases and legs from another chest, combining the two best parts of each to make one charming but not original piece of furniture. It happens all the time.

As it turned out, I was having a hard time tearing my eyes away from the tithe barn itself.

Tiny lights followed the lines of the roof beams, creating a fairytale ambiance. The side bays were lined with goods to be auctioned off—furniture, oriental rugs, porcelain, precious metals. Chairs had been set up in the center for the auction. The selling platform and auctioneer's stand were in place and ready to go. The auction would begin at three. Most bidders were examining the merchandise. A few had already claimed their seats.

"Quite an incredible structure, isn't it?" Nigel Oakley found us staring up at the soaring maze of tie beams. "Built in the late sixteenth century. Fortunately, the original frame and bracing beams were sound—English Oak. We had only to repair and reinforce some of the pegged joints with iron straps and bolts. Sadly, we weren't able to save the elm planking on the exterior, but we left a small section of the original on the west side."

"The thatching looks new."

"The roof was rethatched in 1975, then repaired in 1986 after a fire. We recapped it with natural reed—sedge for the trim cap. Should last another fifty or sixty years."

I spotted Peter Oakley across the room, schmoozing with the clients. He was impeccably groomed and in high spirits—quite different from our first meeting, when he'd appeared bored and restless. Seeing me, he saluted.

Lady Barbara took my arm. "Exciting, isn't it?"

A young man in a waiter's uniform offered us a tray of champagne flutes.

"Glass of champagne?" Nigel asked. "Shameless, I know, but it gets everyone in the bidding mood."

"No, thank you," Lady Barbara said. "I wouldn't mind a cup of tea."

Nigel escorted us through the crowd to the rear wall, where urns of tea and coffee had been lined up on a wooden counter near the kiosk where bidders registered and received their numbered paddles.

"Let's find somewhere more private," Nigel said.

Carrying our china cups, we followed him into an office area behind the kiosk. Here the décor was strictly twenty-first century—glass, wood, and iron with textured upholstery in pale neutrals. Nigel ushered us toward a seating area near a wall-mounted fireplace, where orange flames danced above amber beads. He must have invested a fortune in the renovation.

"Make yourselves comfortable." He handed us each a navy pocket folder, printed on the cover in white with "Oakley's Barn" under a line drawing of the tithe barn. "In the front you'll find information about the barn, our history, and our company philosophy and goals. We've included one of our standard contracts, Kate. Read through it at your leisure. I think you'll find the terms more than acceptable." He addressed Lady Barbara. "Our goal is to provide the highest level of service for our clients. As you can see, we've already gained quite a following in East Anglia and as far as London. We expect your chairs and silver coffee pot to do very well indeed."

His expression was sincere, artless. Either he was a consummate actor or he truly believed what he was saying. Ivor's Roman items hadn't done "very well indeed," but then again, you can't blame a man for optimism. And as Ivor said, you never know with an auction.

Nigel was still speaking, "—and if you're satisfied, we hope you will entrust us with the carved cinnabar plate and anything else you decide to sell."

"Do you solicit bidders from Asia?" I asked. "That could make a difference."

"Martin Ingram has contacts all over the world. Rest assured, Lady Barbara's wonderful things will be offered at the highest levels."

"Do you have an auction date?" Lady Barbara asked.

"Not yet. That's my son's department. We'll pick up the items tomorrow. I'll call you before we put you on the calendar."

"The sooner, the better," said Lady Barbara.

Her mind was obviously made up. I still had questions. "Where do you store objects for future auctions? How are they protected? Can you tell me about your insurance?"

"Excellent questions. We built a steel facility at the back of the property, with the latest in security. Our insurance policy covers every conceivable eventuality—fire, flood, theft. I insisted on it. If you like, my secretary can write something up for you."

"Thank you. That would be helpful."

The flick of his eyes told me he'd expected me to say it wasn't necessary, but he recovered quickly. "Why don't I show you our warehouse? We've just received a shipment from France for next week's auction. Martin's there, unloading."

The sun had broken through the cloud layer. I shielded my eyes as we walked outside. "Do you deal mostly in Continental antiques or English?"

"Mostly Continental at the moment. Martin travels there at least twice a month. Buys whole lots from demolished country estates. The lesser items he sells there. Brings the best back to England. As I said, we're developing a clientele. It takes time, you know, but the tortoise wins in the end."

His cheerful candor and the echo of my own thoughts—that building a reputation in the auction business takes time—added to the general impression of competency. As far as I could tell, the Oakleys were doing things right.

The warehouse facility was a reinforced steel structure with overhead doors at the loading bay. A dark green lorry with the words "Jacques Cailette Transport" printed on the side was positioned for unloading. Men in navy overalls were guiding what looked like the base of a breakfront cabinet down a wooden ramp, into the building.

We heard a chirp as a small bird flew toward a hedgerow.

"A ringed plover!" Lady Barbara exclaimed. "Orange beak, white belly. We don't usually get them this far inland." She was thrilled—more by the fact that she'd actually *seen* the bird, I thought, than by the bird itself.

She and Nigel peered toward the hedges for another sighting.

I continued on toward the lorry.

"This *isn't* part of the preview," growled a male voice. Martin Ingram threw a packing blanket over a small table and shouted to one of the men in overalls. *"Prenez ceci, s'il vous plaît"*—take this away.

Recognizing me, his expression changed. "Mrs. Hamilton—forgive me. I didn't realize it was you."

"It's fine, really." Once again I was aware of those silver-blue eyes. He'd been clean-shaven at Lady Barbara's cocktail party. Today his dark stubble gave him an intensely masculine—and slightly dangerous—look. I forced myself to meet his gaze, determined not to appear flustered. He was a most incredibly handsome man.

Nigel and Lady Barbara joined us.

"I was explaining our security system," Nigel said as one of the navy-clad men waved a sheaf of papers at him. "Would you fill in the details, Martin, while I check the bill of lading?"

"Security—well." Martin appeared to be collecting his thoughts. "We have the latest and best, of course, both here and in the barn. Video surveillance, connected to the local police. Instantly accessible thanks to digital recording and state-of-the art DVRs. Fire alarm and suppression, tested weekly. Perimeter fencing, disguised by hedges—we *are* a listed property—and motion-activated lighting. I get a text every time someone enters the area, day and night. And we're insured for loss or damage up to three million pounds."

*Impressive.* Behind him, several men were loading cartons onto the truck. "Do you ship from here as well?"

"Seldom. Our shipments are almost always individual items, either picked up at the barn or sent overseas by air freight." He'd moved closer, and I caught a whiff of his cologne. Musky, sensual.

"This is where we'll store your items, Lady Barbara." Nigel had returned. He took her arm and led her toward some shelving on the nearest wall.

"Would you like to see today's shipment?" Martin asked me.

Near the loading dock, twenty or twenty-five pieces of fine cabinetry were being inspected and dusted. One was the base I'd seen being unloaded.

"These are very fine things," I said.

"That's our aim." He brushed his dark hair off his forehead. "I'd like to hear how things are done in the States. Are you free for dinner sometime—Wednesday perhaps?"

*Those blue eyes.*

I admit to being tempted—Wednesday was the dinner at Tom's house, and this could be a plausible way of avoiding his mother. "No, I'm sorry. I already have plans."

"Ah—your friend, the detective inspector." He gave me a wry smile. "Another time, perhaps."

I watched him walk away. Why was this man so unsettling? I had no interest in him whatsoever, and yet, in spite of myself, I felt a kind of magnetic pull in his presence.

And the worst part? He knew it.

Lady Barbara and I walked back to the barn.

"What's your assessment, Kate? Are we right to let them handle the sale?"

"Everything looks fine so far. Let me know when your items will be auctioned. I'll attend if I can. Once we see how they do, we'll decide about the lacquer plate, all right?"

We stayed for the first hour of the auction. The items were of high quality, the valuations fair, and the prices realized impressive on the whole.

I would have enjoyed every moment if it hadn't been for a growing awareness of Martin Ingram watching me. There was something predatory about him. Even so, I felt sure he wasn't really interested in me—or in how things were done in the American antiques trade either. His real interest had to be the Villiers Collection. He wanted access and hoped I could grant it.

He was bound to be disappointed there. The fate of the Villiers Collection was up to Lucy Villiers.

If she was still alive.

# Chapter Twenty-One

Wednesday, May 15

The morning after the auction, PC Anne Weldon and I returned to Hapthorn Lodge. We arrived at seven because she had to be back at the station by eleven.

She strolled through the house, admiring the architecture, while I set to work on the inventory.

I still hadn't located Evelyn Villiers's missing jewelry collection, nor any safe deposit keys or other clues to its whereabouts. Even stranger was the fact that Mr. Villiers's meticulous records included no mention of purchasing jewelry, even though both Ertha Green and Evelyn herself said he bought jewelry on a regular basis. He must have kept those purchases in a separate file, and if the jewelry had been stolen, the thief might have removed the records too.

The Meissen *Mockery of Age* figural group was still nowhere to be found either. And now, about halfway through the process, several more Meissen figural groups appeared to be missing as well—both rare and both from the same mid-eighteenth-century commedia dell'arte collection. Normally I'd have assumed Mr. Villiers sold the objects or traded them for other treasures. Collectors buy, sell, and trade all the time. But I'd found no records of sales—strange because in every other way Wallace Villiers had been a nearly obsessive accountant.

One non-sinister explanation occurred to me—that Evelyn Villiers had sold the jewelry and the missing Meissen pieces herself. There were three problems with that theory. First, why? She had plenty of money. Second, where had the profits gone? According to Tom, her bank accounts showed no significant deposits or withdrawals. And third, if she'd sold the Meissen pieces herself, why mention it when she'd been fatally stabbed?

At ten, as Anne and I were preparing to call it a day, we heard a knock on the side door. She hurried to answer it and returned with a middle-aged man in a pin-striped suit. He was carrying a leather briefcase.

"Mrs. Hamilton." He gave a stiff little bow. "Allow me to introduce myself. I'm Simon Crewe of Waltham & Crewe, Solicitors. We represent the estate of Evelyn Villiers. The police said I might find you here." His eyes were pale, hooded, and lashless, giving him a slightly reptilian look.

I wasn't predisposed to like him anyway. "You're the one who sent that threatening letter about the stolen húnpíng jar." I met his gaze. "I can assure you Mr. Tweedy is prepared to reimburse the estate for the full value. Is it really necessary to involve the courts?"

"This is a legal matter, Mrs. Hamilton. No threat intended, I assure you." He placed his briefcase on the floor and folded his hands at his waist as if he wasn't quite sure what to do with them. "With an estate of this size, the courts are automatically involved. We are following standard procedures."

"Maybe so, but I don't think you appreciate what a court case would do to Mr. Tweedy's professional reputation. With the sensational nature of the crime, a legal proceeding is bound to get publicity. The antiquities trade depends upon trust. We've already felt the effects, and it's unfair. Ivor had absolutely nothing to do with any of this. I'm the one who accepted the jar on consignment. You should be after me, not him."

"Noble but irrelevant. Mr. Tweedy is the owner of The Curiosity Cabinet, is he not?"

"It's The Cabinet of Curiosities, and yes, he is."

"That makes him the respondent, not yourself."

This was getting me nowhere. "Have you located Lucy Villiers?"

"Sadly, no. We haven't given up, of course, but after a reasonable amount of time, we will be obliged to proceed with the estate."

"If she isn't found, who inherits—the relatives in Australia?"

He tsked, shaking his head. "I'm afraid that's information I'm not at liberty to divulge."

I tried again. "Well, how about this? I assume you knew Evelyn Villiers. Had she spoken to you recently about changing her will or attempting to break her husband's trust?"

"Certainly not. For the record, I never met the woman. My father knew her personally, of course—he was the original Crewe in Waltham & Crewe—but he's been gone for almost a decade. Now, if we could just—"

"How did she get money to live?"

He glanced at his watch. "Wallace Villiers set up a trust for his daughter and another for his wife—the residue to go to Lucy after her death. We sent Mrs. Villiers a maintenance check every month, which she cashed."

"Did she ever ask for additional funds?"

"Not that I'm aware of." He drummed a finger on the counter. "If she had, we would certainly have obliged."

"Did she ever mention a wish to sell her husband's art collection or her jewelry?" I was pushing my luck, but I might never have another chance to quiz him.

"She did not. Of course, it was her right to do so." He squeezed his eyes shut and pinched the bridge of his nose. "I don't wish to appear impolite, Mrs. Hamilton, but if you're quite finished, I have come here for a purpose."

"And that is?"

He gave a little cough to cover a smile. "A favor. We know the police have asked you to prepare an inventory of the Villiers Collection. Their interest is naturally related to any potential criminal activity. We have a different interest in the collection. The art and antiques form a not-insignificant portion of the Villiers's estate. Unfortunately, we were never provided an evaluation—or indeed even a listing.

Mr. Villiers did not expect to die—nor did Mrs. Villiers, I'm sure. We'd be obliged if you would provide that inventory to us—in our format, of course. There would be a small stipend."

*Another stipend?* This was getting ridiculous. "What information do you need?"

"A listing. Descriptions, date of purchase, purchase price, current valuation."

"Providing valuations will take time and research. In some cases, I'd have to consult with others."

"Understood. Whatever you need." He opened his briefcase and removed a packet of papers. "I'll leave these with you, Mrs. Hamilton. Please contact us at your earliest convenience. I'll . . . erm . . . see what I can do about Mr. Tweedy." He clicked his briefcase shut. "Any further questions?"

"Just one. Mrs. Villiers hired a housekeeper and a gardener. Were you aware of other employees?"

"We were not." He gave an embarrassed little cough. "It was her habit to pay her employees in cash, which, as you might imagine, created a certain, ah, tax problem." His eyes flicked to PC Weldon. "Since she kept no records, we were obliged to . . . erm . . . recreate them." His pale cheeks had colored slightly.

Another dead end. If Evelyn Villiers had been paying the man in the dark van, her solicitors hadn't known about it.

By the time Simon Crewe left, it was nearly ten thirty. I packed up everything, and Anne and I headed back to Long Barston.

* * *

Later, after sharing a quick lunch with Vivian, I walked over to The Cabinet of Curiosities. As I was entering the security code, my cell phone rang.

It was Ivor.

"The Little Domesday translation will be delivered to the shop by courier between two and four this afternoon." he said. "Can you be there?"

"I'm in the shop now."

"The buyer, Professor Markham, is writing a scholarly volume on the history of East Anglia before the Norman Invasion. He's very eager. Could you possibly deliver the package to him tomorrow? His village isn't far over the Essex border. Forty-minute drive, tops."

"Yes, of course. Is he retired?"

"In a manner of speaking. He taught for years at the University of Essex. Forced out during his course on the Boer War when his lecture on the relief of Mafeking turned into a polemic on the King Arthur deniers."

"Can't wait to meet him."

"Yes, hmm. It's a shame we can't hold onto the translation for a few days. I'd quite like to see it."

Precisely my own thought.

* * *

That night, back in my room at Rose Cottage, I forced myself *not* to tear open the brown-paper-wrapped Domesday translation at once. Instead, I texted my mother, attaching the grainy magazine photograph of Wallace Villiers with the missing *Mockery of Age* Meissen figural group.

*Was this sold somewhere recently? If you don't have time to check, no problem.*

Then I opened the package delivered late that afternoon by the courier. The bound document had been preserved in an archival bag and nested in an acid-free, drop-side box. I pulled on a pair of white cotton gloves I'd brought home from the shop.

Since 1977, the original Domesday books have been kept in The National Archives at Kew. This English translation of the Little Domesday book by an anonymous scholar in the late eighteenth century was unknown until it turned up in the archives of a Norfolk country house whose original interior paneling and library shelves were being sold to an architectural salvage dealer.

I lifted the book out of its protective box and peeled back the archival bag with care. My affliction kicked in, of course, but this time the effect was pleasurable rather than alarming.

The book was a *quarto*, approximately eight inches by ten, meaning each page was one fourth of a standard printer's sheet. The linen-laid paper had been bound with faded blue cloth-backed boards. For a book more than two centuries old, the condition was surprisingly good.

I opened to the index, which was arranged according to county—Essex, Norfolk, Suffolk—then (unhelpfully) by the "Holders of Lands," beginning with King William himself. I remembered from my graduate school days that the landholders recorded in the Great Domesday Book were almost exclusively Norman. Few Anglo-Saxons who owned land at the time of the Norman Invasion were allowed to keep it.

The Little Domesday Book was a different story—perhaps because Essex, Norfolk, and Suffolk were the heart of Anglo-Saxon culture. Thumbing through, I noticed that landholders in Essex included both Norman names—Hugh de Monfort, Geofrey de Mandeville, Roger d'Auberville—and Anglo-Saxon names—Ranulf, Wulfgifu, Thorkil, and someone delightfully named Roger God-save-the-ladies, who owned property in Witham and Hinckford, with a manor house, twenty pigs, ten acres of meadows, and two ploughs. Both towns still existed.

Only in England.

At the end of the Little Domesday Book, I found an index of place names.

Long Barston hadn't existed in 1086, but there had been a Little Gosling in Suffolk and a Dunmow Parva in Essex. *Yes!* My primary interest was in surnames, Grenfel in particular. The closest I found was Grenewic, a lost village in Suffolk with twelve households and no mention of green people.

I closed the book, rewrapped it in the archival bag, and placed it carefully in the box. I'd been wasting my time. All this was ancient history—literally. Fascinating, but having no relevance to my current problem, the murder of Evelyn Villiers.

Unless . . . I almost heard an audible click as two pieces of the puzzle locked together.

Ivor had said the professor in Essex was writing a book about Suffolk before the Norman Invasion—the exact time frame when the old yeoman farmer was said to have discovered the girl from another world.

The green maiden had been important to Evelyn Villiers. I needed to know why.

Perhaps Professor Markham could provide the answer.

# Chapter Twenty-Two

Wednesday, May 15

The next morning, energized by the prospect of learning something useful about the green maiden legend at last, I set out for the Essex village of Hatfield Broad Oak. Professor Markham, retired university lecturer and scholar, lived west of Chelmsford and a few miles southwest of Dunmow Parva, the village where Lucy Villiers had been sent to live with her aunt.

Once off the main road, I passed signposts for Helion's Bumpsted, Sible Hedingham, Duck End, and Molehill Commons. If they ever held a contest to see which English county had the quaintest village names, Essex might take the prize.

After two wrong turns, I found the address I was looking for—20 Bedwell Court. An elderly man, stooped and skeletal, answered my knock. Tentacles of greasy gray hair lay plastered across his scalp. His cadaverous complexion matched the tattered gray cardigan that hung on his bony shoulders.

"Yes? What is it?" He squinted at me with bloodshot eyes.

"I'm Kate Hamilton. Ivor Tweedy sent me. The Domesday translation." I held out the wrapped box.

He pounced on it and shoved an envelope at me—the check, I hoped.

"Professor Markham." I put out my hand to prevent him from shutting the door. "Might I ask you a few questions about—"

"I don't have time for that," he snapped, shutting the door in my face.

I stood on the stoop, wondering whether I should ring the bell again. He probably wouldn't answer. He'd be ripping open the package to feast his eyes on his latest acquisition.

Collecting can become as addictive as a drug. *What* one collects doesn't matter. I've seen people spend money they didn't have for a rare comic book from the fifties or a particularly gruesome Victorian postmortem photograph. I've seen collectors sign over pension checks needed to pay rent and buy food. Come to think of it, Professor Markham looked like he hadn't eaten for days.

Well, there was nothing I could do about that. I'd completed my task. Perhaps the elderly academic would respond to a letter or an e-mail.

Since I was only twenty minutes from Dunmow Parva, I decided to drive home through the village where Lucy Villiers had been exiled after her father's death.

Ancient as it was, Dunmow Parva was a disappointment. Whatever medieval charm it might have once possessed had been replaced by postwar prefabs, faux half-timbered shops, and blocks of nondescript terraced housing. The village did have a cricket field, a pub called The Green Maiden—that was interesting—and a market cross, signifying the village had once been granted the right to hold a regular market. And it had an early medieval church.

If the village had fallen victim to an errant German bomb, at least the Church of the Blessed Virgin had escaped destruction. It was early medieval, flint and stone, with a porch of red brick and a red tiled roof. The circular bell tower, with lancet windows and a steep, conical roof, gave it the look of a castle.

The address I remembered hearing in Tom's office was Lark Crescent—thirty-something.

I found the street several blocks from the church.

Rows of nearly identical roughcast terraced houses faced one another. A few satellite dishes jutted from the upper floors. The postage-stamp front gardens were enclosed by fencing or low brick walls. In one, a child's bicycle lay in the mud. In several others, multicolored plastic rubbish bins waited to be collected. Several cars were parked on the street, but no one was out.

I found a parking spot and walked along the street, checking house numbers. I pictured Lucy's bedroom at Hapthorn Lodge—the popstar posters, the denim quilt, the window seat overlooking the back garden. How had she coped with the abrupt change in her circumstances? And why, come to think of it, had Winnifred Villiers lived in this working-class neighborhood while her brother spent a fortune on works of art?

One house stood out from the others because the garden was well tended. Stone planters on the brick wall held pansies in purples, yellows, and whites. Fake stepping-stones led to the front door, which bore a pretty iron plaque with the words "River's Edge Cottage" painted in gold. There wasn't a river in sight.

A pale hand moved along the edge of a lace curtain. Foolishly I waved, embarrassing us both—the resident of the house for spying, me for intruding. The hand disappeared.

I was about to return to my car, when the door opened.

"Are you looking for someone?" The woman wasn't young—in her late forties or early fifties, I thought—but attractive, with a friendly face and chin-length hair dyed a rich auburn red. A pair of tortoiseshell glasses hung from a chain around her neck. She wore black capris. Slim freckled legs ended in a pair of orange canvas slip-ons.

"I'm sorry to bother you," I said. "I don't suppose you know which of these houses once belonged to Winnifred Villiers."

"I do, as a matter of fact. Winnie lived next door, number thirty-four. She was there when my late husband and I moved in more than twenty years ago. Like a granny to our kids—she was that kind."

"My name's Kate Hamilton. I'm staying in Long Barston for the summer, helping out in a friend's antiquities business."

"You've come about the murder." She said it pleasantly, as if we were talking about a day at the seaside. "I read all about it in the papers."

"That's right. The police are trying to locate the daughter, Lucy. I understand she lived briefly in the neighborhood."

"That's what caught my interest." She stepped back from the door. "I'm Sheila Parker," she said, peering past me in both directions. "You'd best come in, luv. I live alone since the hubs passed away, and the neighborhood isn't as safe as it once was. Drugs, you know." Behind the glasses, her light brown eyes were magnified, giving her the look of a friendly Irish Setter.

"I'm a widow too." *Why was I telling her this?*

"We have something in common, then," she said comfortably. "Gets a bit lonely, doesn't it?"

We passed the parlor and went straight into the kitchen, a warm, cheerful room with a white wood table, pale yellow walls, and curtains in a purple pansy design.

"I was making tea when I heard your car door." She filled a mug and placed it in front of me at the table. "Help yourself to milk and sugar." After filling her own mug, she joined me.

I added a splash of milk and a teaspoon of sugar to my tea and stirred. "I heard the police were in the area last week," I said, deciding a direct approach would be best. "No one admitted to having known Lucy Villiers."

Sheila Parker bit her lip. "Never get involved with the rozzers. That's what my Lenny used to say."

I wondered if her Lenny had spoken from firsthand experience. I was glad I hadn't mentioned my connection with the Suffolk police. "It must have been difficult for a single woman like Miss Villiers to take on a girl of seventeen."

"You don't know the half." Sheila Parker's mouth twisted. "That girl was wild, right from the start. Screaming, crying—Len and I could hardly sleep for the ruckus. I don't know how Winnie stood it. I really don't." She blew on her tea.

"Maybe she was homesick. Grieving for her father."

"Grieving for that young man of hers, more like. And him a scoundrel. Too good-looking by half. Lucy insisted he was coming to rescue her, but he never did. Dropped her like a stone. Winnie had her hands full with that girl, she did."

"Didn't Winnie contact Lucy's mother, suggest she return home?"

"Of course. A number of times. Only ever heard back once—and that to say she'd washed her hands of the girl. Nothing poor Winnie could do. She couldn't put Lucy out on the streets now, could she? Still"—Sheila thumped her chest—"she felt it when Lucy took off like that. Worried herself sick, day and night, thinking something terrible must have happened to the girl. Police were no help. Winnie blamed herself, even though I told her it was nonsense. The girl wouldn't so much as lift a tea towel to help out. Then she up and left in the middle of the night, without a note of explanation. That's what killed Winnie in the end—the worry of it, disguised as heart failure." Sheila opened a tin of biscuits and handed it to me.

I took one, to prolong the conversation. "You knew Colin Wardle?"

Sheila Parker set down her mug. "You didn't know? He was a Dunmow Parva lad. Raised on this very street. His father was killed in the Falklands—at least that what his mother said, although some claimed there never *was* a Mr. Wardle. But that's neither here nor there."

"Does she still live in the neighborhood?"

"Moved away years ago."

"How did Colin happen to work for the Villiers family in Little Gosling?"

"Now that's an interesting thing." Sheila took a bite of her biscuit and chewed thoughtfully. "Mr. Villiers visited his sister regular back in the day. He must have met the lad then."

"Did he bring his family with him when he came?"

"Always came alone, far as I knew." She held up a finger. "No—I tell a lie. Lucy and her mother came for one of the village fêtes—back in the nineties. I never saw Lucy again until the day she moved in with Winnie. A pitiful thing—even if she was a wild one."

I pictured Lucy as she'd looked in the newspaper report. Thin face, small round eyes, sloping chin. She'd never been a beauty. What had attracted the handsome Colin Wardle?

For that matter, what had attracted Mr. Villiers to the young man from Dunmow Parva? Had he considered Colin Wardle capable of more than a tradesman's life and decided to give the lad an opportunity to make something of himself?

"I see your local pub is called The Green Maiden. Does the legend have any special significance around here?"

"My, yes. Some say this is the very village where she lived—where her descendants live still."

"Her descendants?"

Sheila made a face. "All part of the myth, isn't it, luv? Brings the tourists, though. Stop in if you're interested. There's a gift shop."

* * *

Back in the car, I started the engine. Before pulling onto the street, I put in a call to Tom.

"I'm in Dunmow Parva. I found a neighbor who knew Winnie Villiers when Lucy lived with her. She knew the Wardles as well. They lived on the same street. Colin's mother moved out a long time ago."

"Did you get her first name? If we can trace Colin's mother, we might be able to locate him."

"I'm sorry, Tom. I never thought to ask."

"Never mind—we'll find out. How are you getting along at Hapthorn?" I heard voices in the background, the clacking of a printer. He was at work.

"Getting there. I still haven't found the jewelry, and now several more objects are missing—both early Meissen figural groups. I *am* beginning to think Mrs. Villiers was selling things little by little and pocketing the cash. Since the solicitors have no listing, she could sell whatever she wanted. As long as she also destroyed the documentation, no one would know, including Her Majesty's Revenue and Customs. No records, no taxes."

"But you found records of the missing Meissen pieces."

"Maybe she just hadn't gotten around to removing those pages yet."

Tom must have closed his office door because it was suddenly quiet. "I've been thinking about you all day, Kate." I could hear his smile. "Remember, dinner tonight. Pick you up at six thirty?"

"You'll have a long enough day. I'll drive myself, meet you at the house just before seven."

"Sure you don't mind?"

"Of course not. Just tell me you can get some time off soon."

"I'll try. I promise."

* * *

Like the village itself, The Green Maiden pub wasn't particularly attractive. Dark wood paneling, fake horse brasses, dingy carpet. Two things caught my eye. First was a series of framed lithographs, each picturing a different aspect of the green maiden legend. Second was the beamed ceiling, decorated with what appeared to be sayings in the Anglo-Saxon language. The gold lettering was one of those complicated medieval fonts that are nearly impossible to read at the best of times, made even more difficult by the fact that the metallic paint had chipped and faded.

"What'll it be, luv?" asked a bored-looking bartender. The middle-of-the-day crowd included a couple in the corner and two men sitting at the bar.

"Club soda with lime."

He brought my drink and parked himself on the other side of the bar. "What brings you to The Green Maiden?"

"The legend."

"Oh." He nodded his head, the glazed look returning. "Gift shop's over there. I can open up if you like."

"I'm not interested in souvenirs. The lithographs are interesting."

"Pub owner had them framed sometime in the seventies."

"What do the words on the beams say?"

"You're asking me, luv?" He hooted. "I can barely read modern English. Local chap painted them around the same time. Needs a touch-up."

"Do you know anyone in the area named Grenfel?"

He shook his head. "Might check the churchyard."

I took my drink to a table and peered up at the words painted on the beams. I'd taken a course in the Anglo-Saxon language once.

A few of the words rang a bell. *Wræcca*—wanderer? foreigner? *Godes þancus*—that one I knew; it meant "God be thanked." *Eallgrêne*—could that mean green? I stared at the ceiling, my eyes squinting as I tried to make out the lettering. My neck was getting sore.

I was about to give up, when two words leapt out at me.

*Wægn belæwung.*

Wagon bell? I did remember the *æ* sound, called the *ash*, was pronounced like the *a* in *apple*. Unfortunately, I had no idea what the words meant in modern English.

"Is there anyone around here who can translate?" I asked the bartender.

"Not any more, luv. Sorry."

Standing, I pulled out my mini Maglite and focused on the beam. A sentence took shape:

*Wægn bel-æwung cópenere brand-hœrm min sefa.*

I copied the words in my notebook. The only word I recognized was *min*. That meant *my*—something, something *my* something. Crap—I should have paid more attention.

Maybe Ivor could translate Old English. Why not? He could read Mandarin Chinese and Egyptian hieroglyphs. I wouldn't be surprised if he knew how to communicate with whales and turn straw into gold.

Things were looking up. A pattern was emerging, and it was all about the green maiden: One, the *Myths & Legends* book in Evelyn Villiers's bedside table, with the underlining and marginal comments suggesting the green maiden was murdered.

Two, her comment to Mrs. Wright, the housekeeper—*"One day they'll get it right."*

Now three, the words she'd spoken (and denied)—*wagon bell*—actually stenciled on a beam in The Green Maiden pub in Dunmow Parva.

Three legs of a stool. My mother always said that about research—two is a coincidence; three is a pattern. But how did this last bit of information fit with the other evidence?

I couldn't wait to talk to Ivor.

First, though, I had dinner with Liz Mallory to deal with, and if the past was any indication, that would take all the patience and courage I could muster.

I downed my club soda, thanked the bartender, and dashed out to the car. No time now to check the churchyard for dead Grenfels. I had to get home and change clothes. I felt like wearing black.

Could I put the past aside for Tom's sake?

I heard my mother's voice: *"Of course you can, Kate."*

# Chapter Twenty-Three

The Mallorys' house stood on the edge of Saxby St. Clare, set back from the road about a hundred yards. The wooden gate was latched. Reluctant to go further without Tom, I parked my car on the street and checked my phone for a message. There wasn't one. He was probably driving.

Lowering the car window, I leaned back against the head rest and breathed in the mild evening air. Liz Mallory was *not* going to push my buttons again. She had no power over me that I didn't give her, and I wasn't about to make the same mistake twice. I'd keep my cool no matter what she said or did. What was the term? *Noncomplementary behavior*. I'd break the cycle by not reacting as she expected.

Five minutes later Tom pulled his silver Volvo into the drive. Stopping the car, he got out to open the wooden gate. I hurried to meet him.

"Kate," he said, gathering me in his arms. He took a deep breath, and I felt him relax against me. "What did you get up to today?"

"I may have cracked the mystery of *wagon bell*—or at least made a start."

"What?"

"I'll explain everything later. Let's get inside before your mother wonders what we're doing out here."

"You ready?" he asked.

"Absolutely." I tried to sound brave and cheerful.

He bent down to look me in the face. "Remember, whatever happens, I love you and I'm on your side."

"I know. Shall I follow you in?"

"No—leave your car where it is."

He pulled back the gate, and we drove in his car toward the entrance to the Grade Three–listed flint-and-chalk farmhouse that Tom and his wife, Sarah, had renovated.

"Does your house have a name?" I asked. Just about every house in England had a name, it seemed to me—from stately homes like Finchley Hall to the humble River's Edge Cottage in Dunmow Parva.

"Some people still refer to it as Scoggins' Farm after the family that lived here before the Second World War. The land was sold off long before we bought the house."

I smiled at him. "You were happy here, weren't you—you and Sarah?"

"We were." He pulled into a parking area near the side of the house. A blue BMW was parked near the walk. "Looks like we have company."

Liz Mallory opened the door. "Tom. Kate, darling. Welcome." She was wearing slim white jeans with a chic black leather jacket—flattering with her trim frame and thick silver hair.

I was feeling less than chic in a plain beige sleeveless dress I'd worn in an attempt to convince myself I wasn't trying to impress her. *I know, I know.*

"It's absolutely wonderful to see you again." Liz gave me a little side-squeeze. "Come in. Make yourself at home."

The large, beamed sitting room was as lovely as ever. Glossy white woodwork, soft butter-yellow walls, comfortable furniture covered in loose, rose-striped slipcovers. The last time I'd been here, there'd been a Christmas tree in the corner and a fire blazing in the brick hearth. Now the hearth was filled with an arrangement of dry flowers.

"Who's joining us?" Tom asked. "I don't recognize the car."

"All in good time," Liz said mysteriously. "First drinks. Kate, what would you like? A glass of white wine? A sherry? Tom will get it for you, won't you, darling?"

Call me suspicious, but she was being way too nice.

Since I was driving home, I opted for a glass of club soda with a splash of white wine.

Liz clasped her hands together. "I have a surprise for you—a wonderful one." She ran to the foot of the stairs. "You can come down now."

A woman descended the stairs, a lovely blonde woman who looked strangely familiar. "Hello, Tom. It's been a long time."

She burst into tears and flew into his arms.

I sank onto the sofa, unable to take in what I was seeing.

*Sarah?* Tom's wife, back from the grave.

* * *

Dinner was awkward.

Liz grinning like the Cheshire cat. Me pretending everything was just fine, thank you. Tom shooting me looks I interpreted as something between confusion and apology.

And the lovely Sophie—this *wasn't* Sarah, of course, but her younger sister and body double—alternating between tears and laughter. She'd just split up with Chris, her husband of barely four years. She'd come to stay with Liz for a while. She needed healing. So why hadn't Tom known about it?

I smelled a rat.

Like her sister, Sophie was a delicate blonde with a pink-and-white porcelain complexion, huge blue eyes, and perfect features. I believe she apologized for intruding on their busy lives at least five times. I was still trying to figure out what Liz had up her sleeve.

"Nonsense," Liz was saying. "We love having you, don't we, Tom?"

"Of course."

"And he's overdue for some time off." Liz gave a little wiggle of pleasure. "I'm sure there's nothing he'd rather do than spend time with you, Sophie dear. We are family, after all."

Sophie dried her big blue eyes.

"I did have some time off," Tom said, taking a sip of his wine. "Unfortunately I'm in the middle of a murder investigation."

"Still, you'll do your best, won't you, dear?" Liz turned to me. "Never having known Sarah, you can't imagine how special it is to have Sophie with us." She reached for Sophie's hand. "It's almost like having Sarah back with us."

"The resemblance is remarkable." Getting those words out was a triumph of the will over inclination. I took a bite of the boeuf bourguignon Liz had prepared—from scratch, no doubt. And a drink of water to force it down. I put on my best meeting-a-new-client smile. "Sophie, where do you live?"

"I'm homeless at the moment. Chris insisted we sell the house."

"Such a shame," Liz added. "They had a smashing house on the Thames near Greenwich."

"Chris is buying a condo in Camberwell with his new girlfriend. He bought me out."

"Where will you go?" Tom asked.

Sophie's smile dawned like the sun. "I thought I might settle near Saxby St. Clare—if you don't mind, Tom."

"Mind?" Tom blinked but recovered quickly. "Of course we don't mind. There are some lovely villages in the area—safe, not too expensive."

Liz was smiling so hard it must have hurt.

*She couldn't have arranged the divorce, could she?*

I made it through dinner and dessert—or the pudding, as Liz called it, a raspberry cheesecake almost too pretty to eat. I love cheesecake. After exactly three bites, I had to put down my fork.

Tom made a valiant effort to draw me into the conversation, talking about my work at Hapthorn Lodge and how helpful I'd been to the investigation.

We moved into the sitting room for coffee. I was exhausted from the effort of acting normal. What I needed was a good reason to leave without appearing upset.

That's when my cell phone rang.

"It's The Willows," I said. "I'll have to take it." *Bless Ivor.*

I jumped up and moved into the entrance hall, expecting to hear Ivor's voice. Instead, the voice I heard belonged to the nursing officer, an efficient woman I'd met only once. "I'm afraid Mr. Tweedy has taken a nasty fall, Mrs. Hamilton. We've taken him to A&E in Ipswich. He's stable but unconscious. That's all we know at the moment. I'm sorry."

My heart jumped to my throat. "I'm on my way."

"No, please. You won't be able to see him tonight. You can visit in the morning after nine. I gave the staff your number. They *will* call you if his condition changes."

I clicked off, feeling numb.

Tom appeared in the doorway. "What's happened?"

"Ivor's fallen. He's unconscious."

"Where is he?"

"Ipswich."

"I'll drive you."

"No. They won't let me see him tonight. Besides, I'll need my car. Stay with your guest. I'll be fine."

"What's wrong?" Liz asked. She and Sophie were sitting side by side on the sofa.

"It's my boss. He's had an accident. They've taken him to the hospital. I'm afraid I'll have to leave."

"Oh no." Sophie looked genuinely shocked.

I put on a smile. "Thank you for a lovely dinner, Liz. So nice to meet you, Sophie. Enjoy looking for a new home."

Liz noticed Tom's jacket, and her face went pale. "You're not leaving?"

"Walking Kate to her car." He put his hand in the small of my back and guided me toward the door. Outside, he pulled me into his arms. "Let me take you home, Kate. I can have Cliffe drive your car over in the morning."

"No, really. I just want to get home and get a good night's sleep. *Liar.*

A bolt of lightning flashed. The rain had started again.

# Chapter Twenty-Four

"What's wrong?" Vivian asked as I burst into Rose Cottage. "Don't tell me you ran over a hedgehog."

"It's Ivor." I shook out my umbrella and hung my wet jacket on a peg. I explained about the phone call from The Willows. "I'm going to see him first thing in the morning."

"Very sensible." Vivian led me to the table. He'll be awake by then and wondering what all the fuss is about."

"I'm sure you're right," I lied. The nurse had sounded grave. Ivor might have sustained a serious injury, screwed up both hip replacements. He could be facing more surgery. This was a major setback.

"Why did he fall? Weren't they watching him carefully enough?"

"I don't know, Vivian." It came out more sharply than I'd intended. "I'm sorry." I reached out to touch her arm. "He was doing so well. They were thinking of releasing him next week."

"I'm sure everything will be fine."

"Will it?" I'd reached the end of my emotional tether. "Ivor may have brain damage. A client was murdered. The húnpíng's been stolen, and Ivor's being sued for the loss. His insurance company is threatening to refuse payment because he didn't update his security system. Clients are reclaiming their consignments. I can't make the inventory at Hapthorn add up, and Tom's mother has—" My throat closed. It was as far as I could go.

I put my head in my hands. "Sorry about the rant."

"Tom's mother has what, dear?" Vivian had the noncomplementary thing down pat.

I looked up. "Tom's mother has produced a gorgeous, young damsel in distress, the spitting image of Tom's dead wife."

After that, I had to explain.

Later, after Vivian and Fergus had ascended the stairs, I made myself a mug of Ovaltine and took it to bed. Tom phoned, as I knew he would.

"Wanted to make sure you'd gotten home all right."

"I'm fine. In bed."

"I'll meet you at the hospital tomorrow if I can get away. In any case, let me know how Ivor is."

"I will."

"He's a tough guy—he'll pull through this."

"Give your mother my apologies again."

"No need. At the moment, she's helping Sophie get settled. We'll talk in the morning. Get some sleep." He clicked off before I could respond.

I held the phone to my chest. He'd completely missed the malicious gleam in his mother's eyes. A detective with a blind spot.

*And your blind spot?* whispered my inner critic.

"Being blind, I wouldn't know," I muttered between my teeth.

I tapped out a text to my mother, telling her about Ivor, but not the lovely Sophie. Then I pulled up the rose satin comforter and leaned back against the soft pillow.

Rain streamed down the windowpanes. A roll of distant thunder rattled the windows. As I sipped the malty liquid, I was transported back in time to my Norwegian grandmother's house. Ovaltine had been her universal cure. It had always worked too—that and the crisp sheets on the bed, the smell of her violet perfume, and the calm orderliness of her house. For a child grieving the loss of a beloved brother, my grandmother's house had been a place of refuge, the cleft in the rock.

I set the mug on the bedside table, turned off the light, and closed my eyes.

I was almost asleep when I heard a noise from downstairs. I sat up in bed. Fergus heard it too. He woofed once, but settled down, satisfied that his attention was not required.

Sliding out of bed, I threw on my old Case Western sweatshirt and tiptoed down the stairs. Someone was rapping on the door.

I flipped on the porch light. "Who is it?"

"Please, let me in." Something in the voice told me this was no burglar.

Turning the deadbolt, I opened the door a few inches.

A woman stood on the stoop, shaking with the cold. Long, dark hair fell in wet strands around her thin face. Her clothing was soaked.

"I'm Lucy Villiers," she said, her teeth chattering. "I need your help."

* * *

Lucy and I sat at the kitchen table. She was in her early thirties but looked younger, especially with no makeup and her hair wrapped in a towel. I'd loaned her my quilted robe and a pair of thick socks while her clothes tumbled in Vivian's combination washer dryer.

I would have made a fire to warm her up, but I didn't want to wake Vivian, who'd have peppered the girl with questions. Instead, I made tea and toasted the blueberry scones Vivian had made that morning. I had questions of my own.

"How did you hear about your mother's death?"

"The newspapers. I've been living in Belfast, but I subscribe to several Suffolk publications. Nostalgia." Her smile was ironic. "That's where I read about you. They mentioned you in the article, how you'd met my mother that very day, and about last Christmas, when you found that killer. I didn't know what to do, so I threw some things in my car and caught the ferry to Liverpool."

"Why didn't you go to the police? Why come to me?"

She bit her lip. "I . . . I guess I felt more comfortable talking to a woman. Someone who knew my mother. It's complicated."

I studied her face, seeing layers of emotion—grief and shock, but the predominant emotion was fear. Fear of what? Had *she* killed her mother and was using me as some kind of advocate with the authorities? I decided to press the question.

"Do you know the police have been trying to locate you?"

Lucy regarded me from beneath her lashes. "They wouldn't have found me. I'm using another name—Lacey Wardle." She must have registered my surprise because she said, "I'm not married to him. I haven't actually seen him for eighteen years."

"Switching identities in the age of computers isn't easy."

"The night my father died, Colin and I planned to run away together. I was underage, so Colin got me a fake driver's license and birth certificate. We were going to Scotland, and from there to Ireland, where he had connections."

"I still don't understand why you didn't contact the police when you learned about your mother's death."

"I told you, Kate. I've been living under a false identity. Using false documents. That's probably against the law."

"You were seventeen—eighteen when you left. No one is going to blame you now for trying to make a new life for yourself. You haven't cheated anyone, have you? Harmed anyone?"

"No, but they won't understand that, will they? "

"I think they might."

"Besides, I read how you found the person who killed that young girl last Christmas. And the thing in Scotland before that. You figured it out before the police did. I hoped you could help me find my mother's killer."

"I'll do what I can, of course, but you will have to talk to the police eventually."

She gathered the robe closer around her neck. "I was so desperate, so unhappy when father died. I tried to find Colin. I didn't see why we shouldn't get married as we'd planned. I guess he didn't want to be found."

"So you went to stay with your aunt."

"I wasn't given a choice. Poor Aunt Winnie—it can't have been easy for her. I regret my behavior. I've learned a lot since then—about love, about telling the truth." Her face crumpled. "The thing is, I really thought Colin loved me." Her thin face colored. "I'd never felt important to anyone in my whole life until I met him. And then he was gone. My mother said he used me to get my money, but I refused to believe it. I still can't believe it."

Was she trying to convince me or herself? If Colin Wardle was "too handsome for his own good," as Sheila Parker put it, would he have fallen for a girl like Lucy Villiers without a wealthy father?

*Unkind.* My conscience stung me. Who knew what kind of upbringing Colin had endured? Who knew what he'd seen in the trusting girl who'd loved him with all her heart?

"I only met your mother once. Tell me about her."

"I know it sounds strange, but I never really knew her. We talked about schedules and school uniforms—never about important things. I learned to keep my thoughts to myself."

"I've been told she loved her jewelry."

"Passionately." Lucy looked at me with her deep brown eyes. "I think it was her way of pretending my father loved her."

"They didn't get along?"

"Oh, they got along very well—when he was away, which was most of the time."

"Did she ever mention the legend of the green maiden? Did it have some special significance for her?"

Lucy looked puzzled. "You mean that pageant thing they do at the May Fair? I don't think so—why?"

"Just a thought. Here." I handed her a cloth napkin to dry her face. "I know it's a sensitive topic, and if you don't want to talk about it, I understand, but why did your mother send you away?" I pictured the lovely, pale face I'd seen at the shop, the way Evelyn Villiers's mouth had hardened when she'd pledged never to let her daughter get her hands on the art collection. That wasn't something Lucy needed to know. At least not yet.

"I was a complication in her life, an unwanted third wheel. Until I came along, she and my father traveled all over the world. They must have been in love then. And of course, she blamed me for my father's stroke. The stress of finding Colin and me sneaking off that night must have sent his blood pressure out of control. I'd never seen him so angry. He wouldn't listen to reason." She sniffed. "Eloping was our only chance at happiness. My parents ended that."

"Do you have any idea where Colin is now?" It occurred to me Lucy might have returned to Suffolk, in part, to find him.

She shook her head. "Probably married, kids. He said he wanted a dozen." She smiled at the memory. "His mother might know." Lucy swallowed.

"Where does his mother live?"

"I wish I knew. She used to live right down the street from Aunt Winnie in Dunmow Parva."

"And she didn't know where her son was either? Back then, I mean."

"I never had a chance to ask her. She'd already moved away."

"How did Colin happen to work for your father?"

"I suppose Father met Colin in Dunmow Parva. He used to visit Aunt Winnie a lot. At the time I assumed he saw himself in Colin—the son he never had. My father grew up in that village. Someone gave him an opportunity, and that made all the difference. He loved me—I know that—but we were never close."

"Lucy, are you aware you stand to inherit a lot of money?"

"The trust fund." She nodded. "I won't pretend it won't help. I'm working in an office, doing fine. Bills are paid. But I'd like to travel, meet someone, have a house of my own one day."

"You never did—meet someone, I mean?"

She shook her head. "I know it sounds pathetic—it probably is—but I'm still in love with Colin."

It was time to mention Ivor. "If you read the newspaper accounts, you'll know about the stolen Chinese pottery. The thing is, Lucy, by taking possession of it on consignment, Mr. Tweedy became legally responsible for its loss. Since no one knew how to contact you, your mother's solicitor is suing him on your behalf. I want you to know Mr. Tweedy is prepared to reimburse you in full, but he'd prefer to do it without involving the courts. Would you consider working out a payment plan?"

"Sure. I don't want to cause trouble, Kate. I just want to find out who killed my mother. After all the grief I caused my parents, it's the least I can do."

All the grief *she'd* caused? From what I'd heard, Lucy was the victim, not the villain. She probably needed counseling, something I was in no position to offer. What I could offer was a safe place to stay the night if she needed one. In the morning, I'd call Tom.

"Where's your car?"

"Parked near the church." She pulled off the towel and shook out her hair. "Stupid to take off without so much as an umbrella."

The dryer beeped.

I stood to retrieve her clothes. "Do you have somewhere to stay tonight?"

"I have a room at the Premier Inn on the Sudbury road." She looked at the watch. "It's late. I should be going."

"The rain's getting worse. Why don't you leave your car at the church and stay here tonight? I'll make up a bed on the sofa. In the morning, we'll call someone I know—a detective inspector. You'll be safe with him. I promise."

She looked at me doubtfully. "I just want to find out who killed my mother."

"Of course you do. That's exactly what my friend—what *Tom* is trying to do."

She massaged her forehead, then let her hand drop. "I suppose you're right. I will have to face the police sometime."

My heart went out to her. She'd been carrying this burden alone for eighteen years. "There's no need to lie anymore."

I hoped it was true.

# Chapter Twenty-Five

Tuesday, May 16

Early the next morning, Lucy and I met Tom at The Dog & Partridge in Bury St. Edmunds. Lucy had refused to go police headquarters, agreeing to meet Tom at the pub only if I would remain with her.

I spotted Tom sitting in a corner with his sergeant, DS Ryan Cliffe, who was probably there to take notes. Tom rose as we approached. "I'm Detective Inspector Mallory." He showed Lucy his warrant card. "Thank you for coming. Can I get either of you a tea or a coffee?"

We opted for tea. The place was empty except for a sleepy-looking woman in a green apron. It occurred to me the pub wasn't actually open yet.

Lucy removed her anorak and hung it over the back of her chair. "I need the ladies'."

The woman in the green apron showed her the way.

"How's Ivor?" Tom asked when she was out of earshot.

"Still unconscious. I called first thing." I hadn't mentioned Ivor's fall to Lucy—not that it made any difference to her, but I didn't want to complicate her meeting with Tom. "I'll stay as long as I can, but it will take me forty minutes to get to Ipswich, and I want to be at the hospital as close to nine thirty as possible. You'll drive Lucy back, right?" I hoped she wouldn't interpret that as abandonment.

The tea came with a rack of buttered toast and three pots of jam.

Lucy returned, looking pale. She wore the same plain brown cotton slacks and oatmeal turtleneck she'd had on the night before—we hadn't had time to stop at the inn for a change of clothes—but she'd washed her hair. It was still damp, hanging in strands.

"I'm sorry about your mother," Tom said. "We're doing all we can to find her killer."

"Kate said you had questions." Lucy crossed her arms as though bracing herself.

Tom went through a few preliminary questions—how she'd heard of her mother's death, when she arrived in England, why she'd sought me out. He was good at his job, managing to pin Lucy down on specific times and places without making her feel like a suspect. The first thing he'd do would be to eliminate her as a suspect. If she'd arrived in England when she claimed, she couldn't have been involved in her mother's death.

DS Cliffe scribbled in his notebook. I don't think Lucy even noticed. Her eyes kept swinging to me, as if looking for support—or approval.

"Would you like toast?" I pushed the toast rack toward her. Vivian had made scrambled eggs with slabs of thick bacon for her surprise overnight guest, but Lucy had refused to eat.

"I couldn't." She'd barely tasted her tea either. "Where's my mother's body?" she asked Tom. "Do I need to see her or something—identify her?"

Tom answered. "I'm sorry, Lucy. That's no longer possible."

"Cremation," Lucy said with a little wrinkle of disgust. "I might have guessed. She insisted on it with father, even though Aunt Winnie protested. And no religious service either, I'm sure. She never believed in an afterlife."

*So why did she have a New Testament beside her bed?*

"Your mother was identified by"—I thought Tom was going to say my name. Instead he said—"the woman who kept house for her, a Mrs. Wright."

Lucy blinked at him. Her lip quivered. "What happened to Ertha—Mrs. Green?"

"Retired," I said, smiling. "Living in Long Barston with her son and his family."

"Let's talk about your father's art collection," Tom said. "You knew about his passion for fine antiques and works of art."

"I could hardly have escaped. It was all over the house. I wasn't interested."

"Did you ever see an ancient Chinese jar called a húnpíng?"

"What's that?"

Tom looked at me.

"The pottery that was stolen. A round jar," I said, "about this size." I used my hands to indicate the dimensions. "Dull gray-green glaze. Lots of figures and details on top."

"Oh, that. I remember he was quite excited when he brought it home. I thought it was weird—and a little creepy."

Precisely my kids' reactions to some of the things I brought home. My son, Eric, had once taken a rare pre-Columbian terracotta figure to school in his backpack along with his books and soccer cleats—passing it off as a voodoo doll to impress his friends. Good thing it didn't break. The money I got for it paid for his freshman year of college.

"We understand your mother didn't share his interest in art," Tom said.

"Oh, she did. Not as much as father, certainly, but she loved the things he brought home—especially the jewelry."

Tom shot me a look. We were both thinking of the plain gold-filled locket—and the empty jewelry drawer at Hapthorn Lodge.

"Do you remember your mother wearing a heart-shaped locket?"

Lucy looked confused. "No. Was she wearing one when—"

"When she died, yes," Tom said. "Do you know anyone named Grenfel? Her maiden name, perhaps?"

"Mother's maiden name was Shipton."

"Did you ever hear your mother mention a wagon bell?" I asked.

"Wagon bell?" Lucy shook her head. "Why would she?"

"It's something she mentioned to Kate," Tom said. "We may have gotten it wrong. Can you describe what happened the night your father died?"

Lucy swallowed. "Colin had promised to come for me at one AM. I had my suitcase all packed, and—"

What she described matched the account in the newspaper. Her parents heard her leave the house. There'd been a confrontation in the drive, an argument that got physical, and her father collapsed.

"What happened after that?" Tom asked.

"Colin called for an ambulance. Mother was screaming. She dragged me inside the house and locked me in my room. Later she came to tell me father was dead, and I was to blame." Lucy's eyes flicked between us, searching for our reaction.

"Your mother shouldn't have said that, Lucy. It wasn't your fault." After eighteen years, my words were a drop of mercy in an ocean of guilt.

"What about the night after the inquest?" Tom asked.

"I don't remember much. Cars in the drive. People coming and going."

"Have you spoken with Colin Wardle since the inquest?"

"No."

As Tom put his questions to her, patiently giving her time to respond, I observed her body language. I thought she was telling the truth.

"Any contact with your mother since you left home?" he asked.

Lucy squirmed in her seat.

Tom tried again. "Did your mother know where you were, Lucy? Did she ever try to contact you in Belfast?"

Lucy shook her head.

"Did you ever try to contact her?"

"I sent her birthday cards every year. She knew where I was."

"You never heard back?"

"No." It was barely a whisper.

My heart stirred. Lucy was an adult, living on her own for eighteen years. Today she was a child again, reliving the pain of blame and rejection.

"I'm sorry." Tom gave Lucy a moment to gather herself.

"I need a tissue," she said.

As Lucy searched in her backpack, I tapped my watch. *I have to go.*

He mimed a cell phone. *I'll call you.*

"Lucy," he said, "Would you come with me to police headquarters? It's only a few minutes' walk. We'll take your formal statement—it *is* necessary. Then I'll drive you to the inn."

"And I'll pick you up on my way home from Ipswich," I said. "It won't be later than two o'clock. You can spend the afternoon with us, have supper. You can sleep at the inn tonight if you prefer, and tomorrow we'll drive over to Hapthorn Lodge." That was the plan Tom and I had agreed upon when I'd called him that morning.

"I guess." She put a shaky hand to her forehead.

Returning to the scene of her father's death and her mother's rejection wouldn't be easy for her. But even after eighteen years, Lucy Villiers was our best hope of finding out what had been going on at Hapthorn Lodge.

* * *

By the time I arrived at the hospital in Ipswich, Ivor had been moved from Accident & Emergency, a separate building, to the nine-patient critical care unit in the main building. I found him near the nurses' station, hooked up to machines. He lay so still under the flannel blanket that the only way I knew he was alive was from the rhythmic beeping of the monitors.

"Don't worry," said a nursing sister. "We're keeping him sedated, letting his brain heal while we wait for the test results." When I teared up, she said, "He's in good hands, dear. We're one of the best neurological units in the country."

I stayed for several hours, alternately sitting by Ivor's bedside and pacing the wide corridors. In the hospital's coffee shop, I turned on my phone and found a welcome text from my mother.

*I'm so sorry, darling. Ivor is tough. Try not to worry.*

My mother's advice, as always, was sound and practical—even if my ability to follow it was crap. When it came to life's challenges, we were polar opposites. She was sure things would turn out all right in the end. I was usually pretty sure they wouldn't.

At eleven thirty a young doctor arrived.

"Mrs. Hamilton, I'm Dr. Chaudhry. I was told you had arrived." He smiled, revealing perfect white teeth. "The Willows gave us your name as Mr. Tweedy's emergency contact." A stethoscope dangled over his crisp white lab coat. After checking Ivor's vital statistics on the bedside monitors, he took a listen to Ivor's heart. He looked up. "Everything sounds normal."

"What can you tell me?" I asked.

"We're completing our tests, but I see nothing so far to alarm me. I assume you're familiar with a concussion. Sometimes, when the brain is traumatized, an overwhelming number of neurotransmitters fire simultaneously, overloading the nervous system and throwing it into a state of temporary paralysis. I believe that's what's happened. Mr. Tweedy will undergo more imaging today and tomorrow. The greatest risk is a brain bleed."

"Has he damaged his hip replacements?"

"Our initial tests showed nothing more than severe bruising. That's hopeful. The next few days will tell us if any revision is called for. At a minimum, his rehabilitation will be delayed."

All that mattered was Ivor's recovery, but could he afford a longer stay at The Willows?

After Dr. Chaudhry left, I remained with Ivor for another twenty minutes, listening to the periodic beeping of the monitors and watching the almost imperceptible rise and fall of his chest. Once I saw his lips move, and I thought he might be waking up.

"It's me, Ivor. It's Kate."

There was no response.

Unable to think of anything else to do, I talked to him.

I told him everything that had happened since our last conversation on Tuesday. I told him about Lucy Villiers showing up at Rose Cottage in the middle of the night and the elderly Professor Markham snatching the Domesday translation out of my hands like it was the gold ring from Tolkien's Middle Earth. I told him about my conversation with Sheila Parker in Dunmow Parva and finding the Anglo-Saxon words on the beams of the pub. I even told him about

Tom and Sophie. Then, because he couldn't tell me not to, I told him I loved him.

My throat tightened. In the five months I'd known Ivor, he'd captured my heart. Not like Tom, obviously. More like . . . *a father*.

I mentally flinched. That was my mother's fear when I'd married Bill, eleven years my senior. Was I still looking for a replacement for the father I'd lost?

"You have to get better, Ivor. I need you."

# Chapter Twenty-Six

I met Lucy in the lobby of the Premier Inn. She'd changed into a pair of gray slacks that had seen one too many washings, and an unflattering puff-sleeved blouse. I know—I'm the last person to accuse someone of ignoring fashion, but it seemed Lucy went out of her way to melt into the background. With her dark hair and sallow skin, she needed a bit of color.

"Come on," I said, taking her arm. "We'll share my umbrella."

The rain had kept up a steady drumming since mid-morning, weighing down the landscape along with everyone's spirits. We dashed to my car, parked just beyond the covered portico. Lucy slid into the passenger's seat. I started the engine and flipped on the windshield wipers.

On the drive to Long Barston, I steered our conversation toward neutral waters. I asked her about Belfast. She asked me about Ohio. What I really wanted to know was what she and Tom had talked about after I left them at the pub, but I decided she'd had enough drama for one day.

I was wrong. She wanted to talk about it.

"Tom is a kind man. He went out of his way to make me feel comfortable." She settled back in the seat and grinned. "Dishy too."

I grinned back. "No arguments here." I waited a moment, then added, "It must have been hard for you, talking about your father's death and what happened afterward."

"The whole thing's like a nightmare. I'm sure I was in shock. Father was dead. Colin left without a word. Mother was treating me like a pariah."

"She blamed you."

"I blamed myself."

"You weren't responsible for any of it. Sometimes, when we've thought a certain way for a long time, it's hard to change. But you weren't to blame, Lucy."

She made a noncommittal sound.

"How about some music?" I turned on the radio, letting her think about what I'd said.

When we arrived at Rose Cottage, Vivian was rolling out dough for a meat and veg pie. We peeled off our coats and shook them out in the small flagstone side entrance.

"I'd forgotten how rainy it is in Suffolk," Lucy said, finger-combing her damp hair.

"Typical English summer." Vivian rubbed her nose with the back of her hand, leaving a smudge of flour. "Disheartening showers interrupted by gales of disappointment." She wiped her hands on a tea towel. "Almost finished. You two make yourselves comfortable in the parlor."

Fergus padded after us, circling his basket an unnecessary number of times before settling down with a grunt. I peered out the window toward the park. On Blackwater Lake, a flock of emerald-headed ducks had hunkered down in the water lilies.

Lucy crouched beside Fergus's basket and stroked his head. "Inspector Mallory was especially interested in the inquest."

I was too. The morning after the inquest, Evelyn Villiers had sent Lucy to her aunt's in Essex. "Did something happen at the inquest?"

"After that my mother shut herself in her room. I thought it was because of Colin. He tried to talk to her, tried to give her some kind of note. I think he was apologizing, asking for forgiveness."

"And she refused to listen?"

"Not just refused. I think she would have attacked him if her solicitor hadn't rushed her away." Lucy stood.

"Come on, sit down." I patted the empty place beside me on the small sofa.

Had Evelyn Villiers experienced a mental breakdown? Losing a husband is traumatic—I know better than most—but Evelyn Villiers's reaction had been extreme. She'd refused to sleep in their bed, to occupy the rooms they'd lived in together, to wear the clothes she'd worn with him or the jewelry he'd given her. She couldn't even bear to see the child they'd borne.

I'd heard of extreme reactions to grief—women who thought they were going mad, felt they'd become different people living in the same body, fantasized about throwing themselves into the grave along with their husband's coffin. Evelyn Villiers's reaction sounded more like anger, as if she blamed her husband for leaving her. She might have received medical treatment if someone had intervened, but Lucy was too young, and Ertha had been dismissed. According to Sheila Parker, she'd refused to answer Winnifred's phone calls.

"How did your Aunt Winnie know to come for you?"

"Mother must have telephoned." Lucy sat with her elbows on her knees and her face in her hands. "Aunt Winnie arrived the next morning and said I was to go with her. I refused, threatened to run away. I told her Colin wouldn't know where to find me. In the end, I went. No choice, really."

"But wasn't Colin living near your aunt in Dunmow Parva?"

"He had been, but he'd taken a room in a house near Little Gosling to be closer to Hapthorn. Actually, Father talked about him moving in, redoing the apartment over the garage. That ended when the painting was stolen. I think Mother forbid it. Anyway, Colin disappeared after the inquest. He wouldn't answer his mobile. None of his friends knew where he was—at least not the friends I knew about."

"You said several people came to the house the night of the inquest. Do you remember who they were?"

"I wasn't paying attention. I was frantic trying to locate Colin. I phoned everyone I could think of, but no one had seen him or heard from him."

"How was your mother in the morning?"

"I don't know. I didn't see her. She left me a note."

"Did you keep it?"

Lucy gave me a pained look. "Why? She made her intentions crystal clear. 'You're no daughter of mine. Your aunt will see to your future.'" Her face crumpled.

Fergus lumbered to his feet and padded over to her chair. He put his paw on Lucy's knee, and she reached down to pet him. He licked her hand. "After all these years," she said, "I still find it hard to accept. Mother and I were never close like some mothers and daughters, but I always thought she loved me a little." Lucy raised her chin. "Could you send a letter like that? Nothing about being sad, nothing about seeing each other again in the future. She didn't even bother to sign her name."

"Did you try to talk to Colin's mother?"

"She wasn't there. I thought Colin must have taken her off to get away from the publicity, but she never came back. A few weeks later someone put up a 'For Sale' sign. That's when I realized Colin wouldn't be coming back either. Not that I didn't hold out hope. I got the idea he'd gone to Belfast as we'd planned—that he'd be waiting for me there. Stupid, right?"

"Not stupid." I sat on the floor next to her chair and petted Fergus. "Human. Our hearts break. We tie them up and go on."

"Do hearts ever heal?"

"They do, Lucy. If we let them." *Did I just say that? I'm turning into my mother.*

"Kate—Lucy, dear." Vivian called out from the kitchen. "Join me for a glass of wine and some cheese straws before dinner. Fresh out of the oven."

Lucy made a move, but I stopped her. "Did your mother ever contact you while you were at your Aunt Winnie's?"

"Why? She'd said it all in that note—'You're no daughter of mine.'"

Something about that note bothered me. Could Evelyn Villiers have meant it literally?

* * *

I drove Lucy back to the inn after supper and made arrangements to pick her up at nine thirty for our trip to Hapthorn. At least Vivian had cheered her up a little with stories from her childhood, growing up in Suffolk after the Second World War.

Tom called while I was getting ready for bed. He'd tried me three times while I was with Ivor, finally leaving a message saying he'd phone later.

I heard laughter and the clinking of glasses in the background. Was he at a party? "Speak up. I can't hear you."

"Sorry. We're at The Trout."

"We?"

"I'm with Sophie. Mother had a headache."

*A migraine?* "How is Sophie?"

"The divorce has been difficult. She's shattered, trying to piece her life together again."

*With all those lovely pounds and pence as glue.* "She must have been young when you and Sarah met."

"She was fifteen, still at school."

I did the math. That meant Sophie was in her mid-thirties. How did she arrange to have the face and body of a teenager?

"Thanks for your help with Lucy today," he said.

"No problem. Can you meet us at Hapthorn Lodge tomorrow?"

"I can't, Kate. I'm sorry. PC Weldon will stand in for me."

I heard a female voice but couldn't make out the words.

"I have to go." It sounded like Tom had cupped his hand over the phone. "Sophie's had too much to drink. Not that I blame her. I'm going to get her home and into bed."

*Right.* When I didn't respond, he said, "Look, I'll call you in forty-five minutes. Will you still be up?"

Oh, I would be now.

* * *

I deserved a medal that night. I really did.

Okay, I stomped around the room for a while. Men can be so naïve. And women can be so devious—some women anyway. Liz's plot to make Tom forget about me and fall in love with Sophie was transparent, but Tom couldn't see it.

*Or is he enjoying it?*

Liz's words circled through my brain: *It's almost like having Sarah back with us.*

To keep myself from obsessing over Tom and Sophie's intimate dinner—courtesy of Liz's *convenient* headache—I threw myself into computer work. Ivor had several auctions going, and I'd have to pack and ship any items that sold. Each had a reserve—an amount below which he wasn't prepared to sell—but they were reasonable sums, and I was sure something would be snapped up. At least I hoped so. Ivor needed the money more than ever.

The warm, damp air in my room felt claustrophobic. I cracked my window, smelling the mineral scent of rain mixed with wet thatch.

It wasn't Tom's fault the lovely Sophie was the spitting image of his dead wife. It wasn't his fault she'd married a jerk who'd left her for an even younger model. It wasn't his fault she'd turned up on his doorstep. Whose fault it was, I felt pretty sure I knew.

Tom called a little after ten.

"I'm sorry, Kate. This thing with Sophie is a real mess."

"I'm sorry, too." A medal *and* a ribbon for valor.

"It's come at a bad time for me. Drugs are pouring into Suffolk. The Yard has agents at all the ports. We've followed every lead, but nothing pans out."

"Ships? Trucks? Automobiles?"

"All of the above, probably. We don't have a tenth of the manpower it would take to put up road blocks—not to speak of the disruption it would cause motorists. We need an inside track." I heard him sigh. "To tell the truth, I'm worn out."

"And now you've got a murder on your hands as well. Which reminds me—have you had any luck tracing Wallace Villiers's Australian relatives?"

"His sister died fourteen years ago. She left a son and a daughter, both living in Australia. We asked the police there to interview them, find out if they've made any recent trips to the UK."

"How about the Liu family? You were going to interview them again."

"We did that. Henry and his wife emigrated from Hong Kong shortly after the Chinese government takeover in 1997. He'd owned a restaurant in Kowloon, so it was natural to open one here. His son and daughter-in-law arrived recently to join them—not surprising, given the recent unrest in Hong Kong. James taught history at Hong Kong University. Penny worked in the administrative offices. Everything checks out except for the time line the night of the murder."

"Briony Peacock seemed pretty sure of her facts."

"Henry admitted he might have been confused about the time. He was under pressure—customers demanding food—and then he found the body."

"Could his wife add anything?"

"She speaks almost no English. All we understood was 'Whatever he say.'"

"What about the son? Why wasn't he helping his wife in the tent?"

"He says he *was* helping—until they had a row over the way he was frying the shrimp rolls or something. He got angry, stalked off, and the next thing he knew the emergency vehicles were screaming into town."

"Henry seems like a nice man—he really does. But there's something about that night that doesn't add up. I just can't think what it is."

"Well, if you figure it out, let me know."

"Everything points to the White Lotus Society. An ancient Han dynasty funereal jar was stolen, and the woman who owned it was found stabbed to death. A white lotus-like petal was left for you to find. That indicates premeditation."

"And a certain arrogance. As if they're daring us to stop them."

"I'm worried about Lady Barbara's cinnabar plate. She has a letter admitting it was looted from the Summer Palace in Beijing—exactly what The White Lotus Society is after. Someone was lurking around the Hall last Saturday night—you saw the video footage. What if they were scoping out the place, figuring out how to get in?"

"We put in a formal request to the Chinese embassy in London for information about the Society, but they're not going to admit anything dodgy, are they? We can hardly call in Interpol on the strength of a flower petal. What we need is someone with connections to the Chinese art market."

"We have someone. He's lying unconscious in the hospital. You could try a few of the major art dealers in London, although they'll probably refuse to reveal information about their clients."

"Actually, that's why I called you earlier. We've identified several recent thefts in England of Chinese antiques and antiquities." I heard the shuffling of papers. "I'm going to read this so I get it right—'a bronze water vessel, a celadon amphora vase, and a pair of clay court figures.' You probably know what all that means. Here's the interesting part—in at least one of the locations, a white petal was left behind."

"What do you mean by 'at least one'?"

"Flower petals are an easy thing to overlook, aren't they?"

"You're taking the White Lotus Society thing seriously."

"I always did, Kate. Now we have something to go on."

"Why can't you go with us to Hapthorn tomorrow? Lucy hasn't been home in eighteen years. This could be important."

Tom groaned. "I know, and I'd arranged to have a few hours off. But Sophie has to file papers with her lawyer in Cambridge. She received a large settlement from the divorce, and there's red tape involved."

"She needs help filing papers?"

"She needs moral support."

"Can't your mother go?"

"She has a dental appointment."

"Root canal?" I muttered.

"Sorry, what?"

"Never mind. When will I see you?"

"How about tomorrow—dinner at The Three Magpies? Just us."

"Perfect. Meet you there at seven."

Feeling better, I checked my computer and found that several of Ivor's items had sold—one for considerably more than the estimate. *Another day at The Willows.*

Putting my phone on vibrate in case the hospital called, I kicked off my shoes. Ivor would know all about the White Lotus Society. He'd know who to contact in England, perhaps even in China.

Where else could I get information?

I peeled off my jeans and my sweater.

*Of course.* Martin Ingram. Nigel Oakley said Martin had contacts in Asia.

*No.* An image of those ice-blue eyes filled my head.

For all I knew, Martin Ingram could be involved.

# Chapter Twenty-Seven

Friday, May 17

"I used to fantasize about coming home." Lucy stood in the entrance to the drawing room of Hapthorn Lodge. She twisted a lock of hair around her finger. "Not to something like this."

On the way to Hapthorn in PC Anne Weldon's police car, I'd told Lucy what we'd found—her mother practically camping out in the small single room, the rest of the house looking like an abandoned warehouse. She'd heard me, but I don't think it sunk in until she saw the state of her former home for herself.

Hapthorn Lodge had been built with the wide, airy rooms; light colors; and the simple, elegant features favored by the Edwardians, but it still felt dark and sad, even after we'd pulled open the drapes and flipped the wall-mounted toggle switches, illuminating a series of wall sconces. The gray skies, the pelting rain, and the drooping ivy around the windows underscored a feeling of desperation that pervaded the house.

I knew Lucy sensed it.

She moved tentatively into the room, her fingers brushing the drop cloths that covered the furniture. "What was happening here?"

"That's what we're hoping you can tell us." Anne was examining one of the paintings propped against the wall. She stood up. "You're the only link to the past we have, Lucy. We need you to look around carefully. You might see something we would never notice."

"Everything's out of place." Lucy put her hands to her cheeks.

I could almost see her brain turning, trying to reconcile what she was seeing with her memories.

"Is anything missing?" Anne asked. "Something that should be here but isn't?"

Lucy thought for a moment. "The photographs. Mother used to have framed photographs—loads of them, on top of those cabinets. Mostly of her and Father, but some of me, some of her parents."

I remembered Mrs. Wright, the housekeeper, mentioning there were no photographs in the house.

"Did you find the albums?" Lucy picked up a paperweight and turned it toward the light.

"What albums?" asked Anne.

"Photograph albums. Mother had dozens—their wedding, their early years together. One for each holiday she and Father took when they were first married. Even a few of me—school photos, sports teams, stuff like that."

"We didn't find any albums," Anne said, "but that's the kind of thing that might help. Why don't we walk through the rooms? Tell us what you notice."

Lucy wasn't much help at first. Except for the kitchen, all the rooms on the ground floor were jumbles of furniture and antiques. A strong musty odor permeated everything.

We climbed the main staircase.

Lucy opened the door to her parents' bedroom. "I remember this, not that I was allowed in here often." Her voice sounded almost wistful. "I do remember one day—Mother must have been in a good mood because she let me try on her jewelry, anything I wanted. Each piece had its own little felt compartment."

"Where did your mother keep her jewelry?" I asked.

"Here." Lucy opened the top drawer of the dresser and furrowed her brow. "It's gone. That's odd."

"Could she have moved the jewelry to a safe deposit box or a storage facility?" Anne asked.

"I suppose, but I can't believe she'd get rid of her jewelry. She adored it."

We left, shutting the door behind us—as Evelyn Villiers must have shut the door on her old life eighteen years ago. Perhaps it had been the only way she could survive.

Lucy stood at the entrance to her old bedroom. She glanced at us over her shoulder. "I'm not sure I want to do this."

"We're right behind you," I said.

She pushed open the door and stepped inside. We followed, the thick wool rug, almost room-sized, muffling the sound of our feet.

Lucy reached out and touched the poster of Amy Winehouse.

"Unhappiness creeps up on you," she said. "I didn't know how unhappy I was until that night—the night father died. I'd never known real love, you see. Then I did, and just when all my dreams were about to come true, everything was torn away." She walked to the window seat and picked up the floppy teddy bear, pressing it to her face before putting it back.

She shook her head as if to dispel the memories.

"There's one more room we'd like you to see," Anne said. "The room where your mother was sleeping."

We entered the small room where Evelyn Villiers had spent her last night on earth.

"But this is Ertha's room. I remember the furniture."

"Is the photograph over the bed Ertha's as well?" I asked. "Do you recognize the cottage or the river?"

Lucy shook her head. "Ertha had a painting over the bed—a tropical scene with a beach and palm trees. I used to fantasize about going there one day."

I pictured the painting I'd seen at the Green's cottage—a cove with a pink sand beach, bending palms, an impossibly blue sea.

Lucy touched the hollow of her throat. "Why would Mother move into Ertha's room?"

Neither of us answered.

I showed Lucy the New Testament and the book of Suffolk legends I'd returned to the bedside table. She just shook her head. "She changed so much."

The question was why.

"Look around. Take your time," Anne said. "When you're ready, we'll be in the kitchen."

"I'll make tea," I said, remembering the porcelain jar where the housekeeper, Mrs. Wright, had found the teabags. With any luck, the milk in the refrigerator would still be fresh.

Anne and I sat at the table, drinking tea and looking out toward the river. The water level had risen alarmingly, swamping the willows along the bank.

When Lucy returned, she seemed frantic, roaming the kitchen, opening doors and cupboards.

"Are you looking for something?" I asked her.

"My life. Something I remember, something that hasn't changed." She opened the cupboard beside the cooker and peered inside. "Everything seems strange, far away. This must be how people with dementia feel. I recognize what I'm seeing, but nothing feels real or right."

"Did you ever help Ertha in the kitchen?" I hoped to focus her mind on something familiar, unfraught with emotion.

Lucy laughed. "The kitchen was Ertha's domain, but she'd let me sit and watch her working. She'd tell me stories about her childhood on the island—swimming in the ocean, catching fish from her father's boat. I envied her, growing up in that sunny world—in a big family with aunties and uncles and grandparents."

"Why do you think your mother told Ertha to leave?"

"Did she?" Lucy raised an eyebrow. "That must have been after I left."

I made a mental note to ask Yasmin if Lucy could visit Ertha. Seeing the old lady again might provide the anchor she needed to the past.

The wind had picked up. Outside the trees swayed in the driving rain. The branches of a forsythia bush tapped against the bay window.

"The new housekeeper told me your mother loved the river," I said.

"I don't remember that," Lucy said sharply. She pulled out a drawer and began sorting through the contents. "I do remember her complaining about the damp. The government engineers did something to the locks downstream. It caused the water level to rise. She made father get rid of everything in the cellar because of the musty smell."

"This rain isn't going to help," Anne said. "One of the sergeants said the foundation might need reinforcement. I'd have a contractor take a look if I were you."

"I'll probably sell the house. I could never live here—not after what happened."

Was she talking about her mother's murder or what happened eighteen years ago?

Lucy pulled a wide-bladed knife from the drawer. "Now *this* I remember. Ertha's favorite knife. She used it to chop vegetables. I picked it up once, and she gave me a bollocking."

I could see why—the knife was huge. "Lucy, you told Inspector Mallory you remembered cars coming and going the night before your aunt came to collect you. Have you remembered anything else about the cars or the people?"

"I suppose they came to offer condolences. I remember Mother arguing with someone in the back garden. She was angry."

"A man or a woman?" Anne asked.

"I couldn't tell. It was mother's voice I heard."

"Did your mother have relatives in the area?" *Like a nephew who drove a dark van.*

"I never heard of any."

"How about your father?" Anne asked. "We know about your Aunt Winnie, but he also had a sister in Melbourne."

"I never knew her."

Lucy stopped dead. She reached out a tentative hand, not quite touching the countertop near the cookie jar. "This is where Mother left the letter for me."

I wanted to comfort her, but there was nothing I could do to make the memory go away.

She pulled her sweater around her body. "Let's get out of here."

I drove Lucy back to the inn. On the way, she was silent, leaning her head against the glass and tracing the raindrops.

"Why don't you come home with me tonight?" I asked. "At least for supper. You shouldn't be alone."

"I *need* to be alone," Lucy said. "I have decisions to make."

"Has your mother's solicitor contacted you? The firm asked me to prepare an inventory of your father's collection. I suppose everything belongs to you now."

"I have an appointment with them tomorrow."

"On Saturday?"

"Mr. Crewe wants me to sign papers. He's going to give me a whole packet of information to read through. I have to decide what to do with Hapthorn and all those antiques. I don't want any of it."

"There must be personal things, Lucy—family mementoes you'll want to keep."

"Mementoes?" She huffed. "As far as I'm concerned, they can tear the place down."

"You should at least have a look. How about the dolls your father sent you?"

"You're right," she conceded. "I will go back."

"If you want help—or just company—let me know."

"That would be nice." She smiled. "I don't think I could face it on my own."

"If you're busy with the solicitors tomorrow, how about Sunday? I have some free time in the morning. You could make a start then."

Later, I dropped Lucy off at the Premier Inn. She looked back over her shoulder once, then disappeared through the entrance door.

Two weeks ago her mother had been brutally murdered.

Lucy was alone and vulnerable. A thought struck me.

Was she also in danger?

# Chapter Twenty-Eight

The Three Magpies in Long Barston was humming. I'd worn my red dress, the one Tom especially liked—the one I'd refused to purchase until Charlotte, my best friend and fashion Nazi, threatened to buy it for me.

Tom hadn't arrived yet. I found Jayne Collier at the bar. She and her husband, Gavin, were Londoners who'd bought the pub several years ago. The first couple of years had been touch-and-go, but they'd finally managed to overcome the local prejudice against newcomers—and a spot of mild harassment from the other village pub, The Finchley Arms, owned by Briony and Stephen Peacock, survivors of the "If it feels good, do it" generation.

"How are you getting along with The Arms?" I asked. "No more dueling sidewalk signs?" Last December, the Magpie's sidewalk billboards—daily specials and upcoming events—had been mocked by rival signs from The Arms, rude but usually hilarious (not that I'd admit it to Jayne).

"At the moment, we're enjoying an uneasy truce. They'll never forgive us for existing, but they've given up trying to compete with us on food." She smiled at me from behind the taps. "I've seen so little of you, Kate. But of course you're busy with this terrible business. How is Ivor?"

"The doctors are keeping him sedated until they determine the extent of his injuries."

"If there's anything I can do—" She handed me a glass of pinot gris. "I've given you and Tom the table in the corner. Have a seat. I'll bring you some bread and olives."

The Magpie's famous homemade sourdough was accompanied by pots of olives in lemon-and-coriander-infused oil. I sipped my wine and speared one of the small, purplish-brown olives.

When Tom arrived, Jayne Collier handed him a glass of Mauldon's Suffolk Pride, his current favorite ale.

"Sorry, Kate. Traffic was brutal." He reached down to give me a kiss before sliding into the banquette tucked under a window. "I didn't even stop home except to change shirts." One corner of his mouth turned up. "It's wonderful to see you."

"How did it go with Sophie in Cambridge?"

"The divorce settlement was far more generous than she'd expected. She can pretty much do what she wants in life."

"Lucky woman. Will she settle in Saxby St. Clare?" *Please tell me she's booked a round-the-world cruise.*

"She says so now, but I have a feeling village life will be too sedate for her. I see her in London—or the south of France."

*Over your mother's dead body* was the response that came to mind. Instead, I said, "Well, wherever Sophie settles, I hope she's happy."

*Did I just say that?* I was either the world's biggest hypocrite or well on my way to sainthood.

Tom tore off a piece of sourdough and dipped it in the oil. "Two bits of good news. Lucy's story checks out. She was on the car ferry from Belfast on the fifteenth, as she said. No previous bookings or flights."

"That's good. And the second?"

"We heard from Australia. The police there have located Wallace Villiers's niece. She's a hairstylist in Melbourne—two kids. Claims to have lost touch with her brother, but a former neighbor said he took a job on an almond farm in the Outback. The police are following up." He took a bite of the bread. "How was Lucy's trip to Hapthorn?"

"Emotional. She's seeing the solicitor tomorrow. I met him, by the way—Simon Crewe. He asked me to provide them with a copy of the inventory."

"Estate purposes, I assume."

"I think Lucy may sell everything. I feel sorry for her—thrust into making decisions about her mother's affairs when they hadn't been in contact all those years. I promised to help her sort through a few personal things Sunday morning."

"PC Weldon says she offered no theories about the state of the house."

"She noticed all the family photographs were gone. It's weird, Tom. Evelyn made a complete break with her past—and yet she remained in the house with all those memories."

"Lucy didn't provide any insight at all?"

"None. She'd never seen the photograph over her mother's bed." I took another sip of wine.

"I can see your mind turning, Kate," he said. "What is it?"

"I think the key to this is Evelyn Villiers."

He laughed. "That's obvious. She was the murder victim."

"I don't mean that. I mean her personality, her character. There were two turning points in Evelyn's life—eighteen years ago, when her husband died, and then sometime prior to last Saturday, when she brought the húnpíng into Ivor's shop."

"How does that help us find her killer?"

"I think each of those events sent her on a new trajectory. Lucy said her mother didn't believe in an afterlife, but she had a New Testament on her bedside table. Mrs. Wright said she loved sitting by the river, and there's that photograph above her bed, but Lucy says her mother complained about the river's dampness. And the jewelry. Both Ertha and Lucy say she adored her jewelry, but it's gone, and the only piece she wore was that inexpensive heart locket."

"What are you saying?"

"I'm saying she changed dramatically—but why? I can understand the shock of losing her husband, but why change your whole way of living?"

"Any conclusions?"

"Just that the solving of her murder has to be tied to those two turning points in her life. I think something happened to her eighteen years ago, something even more profound than the loss of her husband. And I think something happened recently too—something that prompted her to begin selling off the art collection."

"Maybe she needed the money."

"But for what? Was someone blackmailing her? Was she planning on escaping from Little Gosling and starting a new life like Lucy did? Was she afraid? Did she owe someone a lot of money and felt she couldn't go to her solicitors? We need to find out why she did what she did."

"You told me once to begin with what you know. Well, here's what we know: Evelyn Villiers blamed her daughter for causing her husband's death. She told you she was selling the art collection because she didn't want Lucy to inherit. Maybe she knew her daughter would be showing up."

"How could she? Lucy says she came home because she read the account of her mother's death in the Suffolk newspapers, and you confirmed the date she arrived from Northern Ireland."

Angus, the young man in the kilt, flipped the bar flap and strode over to our table. "We have a few off-menu items tonight. Would you like to hear about them?"

We did, and after perusing the menu as well, decided on the daily special, sea bass with scallop risotto and golden beet salad. We settled back against the cushions with our drinks.

"Eacles is pushing hard for a quick arrest," Tom said. "He has his eye on the housekeeper."

"*What?*" I stared at him. "*She* didn't do it, Tom. What motive would she have had? She knows nothing about antiques or how to sell them. She's not a thief. All she wanted was her weekly pay."

"Try convincing Eacles. What we need is someone with both motive and means. Right now I'd say our best bet is the Australian nephew."

"If he's in England."

"Yes—if he's in England."

"What about the Lius? They were both at the crime scene. Maybe The White Lotus Society knew about the húnpíng and sent Henry to England."

"And he's been waiting since 1997 to do something about it? Henry had a perfectly good reason for being on the scene. They ran out of shrimp rolls."

"How about the son, James, then? He lied about being at the tent."

"There still wasn't enough time. He couldn't have driven Evelyn Villiers to Long Barston. People saw him helping out there before the play.

"Hmm." It was a good point.

Our meals came, and we spent the next few minutes enjoying our first bites. Jayne was watching us from behind the bar. I gave her a thumbs-up. I could have happily eaten at The Three Magpies every night for the rest of my life.

Especially with Tom.

They say familiarity breeds contempt—or boredom. Not in this case. Being with Tom Mallory was becoming an alarming necessity. To be blunt, I couldn't get enough of him. *Oh dear.* He'd told me at Christmastime he was a lost man. Well, I was getting lost with him, and enjoying every minute of the journey. The question was, where were we headed? I had no idea.

"Tell me more about your theory," Tom said, setting down his fork. "The turning points in Evelyn Villiers's life."

"It's not a theory—just some interesting connections." I took a bite of risotto and chewed thoughtfully. "The one thing that doesn't fit is the green maiden."

"You were going to tell me something about *wagon bell* the other night."

"That's right—I'd forgotten. I found something in Dunmow Parva—where Lucy was sent after the inquest."

"What does Dunmow Parva have to do with—?"

"Just listen. I told you, the day Evelyn Villiers came into Ivor's shop she said something that sounded like *wagon bell.* We know she was interested in the legend because she had that book by her bedside with the green maiden chapter marked, and she told the housekeeper she hoped one day they'd get the story right.

"I still don't get the connection with Dunmow Parva."

"I'm not finished. I also told you I found Winnifred Villiers's old house in Dunmow Parva. And I met the neighbor, Sheila Parker. After Sheila and I talked that day, I stopped at The Green Maiden pub in the village. Tom, the place is a shrine to the legend—gift shop, lithographs on the walls, quotations from the legend painted on the beams in Old English. I was trying to figure out what the words meant—it's been a long time since I studied Anglo-Saxon—when I noticed two words that could be pronounced *wagon bell*."

I wrote the words out on the bar napkin: *Wægn belæwung*.

"Did you mention it to Lucy?"

"She'd never heard of it."

"What do the words mean?"

"No clue, but I may know someone who can translate."

He looked at me suspiciously. "Kate, what are you planning?"

What I was planning was a return trip to Essex. If anyone could translate the Anglo-Saxon language, I was pretty sure it would be Professor Markham. He may have slammed the door in my face, but I wasn't giving up that easily.

I reached up and kissed Tom on the cheek. "No worries. Only a chat with an aging academic."

"An elderly ex-housekeeper, an aging academic. Who's next? The ghost of Agatha Christie?"

"Why not, if she can help? This case has roots in the past."

Tom held up my empty wineglass. "Another?"

I nodded. "As long as you're driving."

As Tom stepped up to the bar, I thought about those roots into the past. Something was bothering me, flitting around the edges of my brain like a subliminal image in a movie theater. Was it the Australian nephew, hearing that Lucy had disappeared and figuring he was next in line for his English uncle's fortune? The dark van that may or not belong to an unidentified handyman? I frowned. Or was it the charming Nigel Oakley and his partners, practically salivating over the Villiers' art collection? Was it the cinnabar plate they wanted?

"One glass of pinot gris and one club soda." Tom set down our drinks and slid in next to me.

I lifted my glass and smiled at him. "Cheers."

In the morning I'd find out if the Oakleys had set a date for the auction.

# Chapter Twenty-Nine

Saturday, May 18

The morning dawned clearer and dryer than it had in days. I made a quick phone call to the hospital in Ipswich. No change, the nurse told me, but the doctors had decided to wean Ivor off the intravenous sedative. As he regained consciousness, they would further assess any potential trauma to his brain. I arranged to drive over that afternoon.

I thought about calling Lucy, but she'd be at the solicitor's office most of the day. I hoped she'd take some time to rest and process all that had happened to her.

Vivian was out with Fergus. She'd left the previous day's newspaper on the table, folded to the headline: *"Tragedy Strikes Long Barston Again."* They were harkening back to the series of murders the previous December, tragedies that had impacted Lady Barbara directly and led to her decision to transfer ownership of Finchley Hall to the National Trust.

After grabbing a bowl of Vivian's oatmeal—the hardy, thick-textured stuff that sticks with you all morning—I set off for Finchley Hall.

The sky was an innocent blue, but several days of steady rain had left the ground sodden and muddy. The Stour near Long Barston was at its highest levels since the winter floods, and some business owners and residents in low-lying areas were already taking measures to prevent potential inundation. I squelched through the park in my newly purchased wellies, eager to hear if Lady Barbara had heard from Nigel Oakley.

She was in her private sitting room, finishing breakfast. The sun streamed through the windows, picking out the tiny lines around her mouth and eyes. I noticed a strip of wallpaper curling away from the crown molding.

"Good morning, dear. I was hoping you'd stop by. Saves me a phone call." She set down her fragile bone china cup. "Would you like coffee? Morning is the only time I indulge."

"Thank you, no. I'm here to find out about the auction."

"Exactly the subject I wanted to discuss. It's set for Tuesday. Preview at ten, auction at two. They've already sent out an updated electronic catalog to all their customers. Martin Ingram stopped by yesterday evening to show me the lovely photographs. So professional."

"Are you planning to be there for the auction?"

"Vivian and I can't wait. You'll drive us, I hope."

"Of course." Someone had to curb their enthusiasm. And console them if the auction didn't achieve the results they were counting on.

Declining coffee again, I headed for The Cabinet of Curiosities. Between the inventory to complete at Hapthorn and trips to the hospital in Ipswich, I'd neglected my duties at the shop. I didn't expect any actual customers, but there was plenty to do, more than just following the sales. Everything needed a good dusting, and the silver items needed a polish—I'd been in the middle of that task a week ago when Mrs. Villiers had shown up with the húnpíng.

The first thing I did was open the pile of letters pushed through the mail slot.

My heart fell. Still no checks, and now *seven* additional clients wanted their consignment items returned. I had no choice but to be gracious and offer a time when they could pick them up. If this trend continued, the antiquities business Ivor had built up over decades would be permanently damaged. His only chance of survival was the arrest of the killer—and the return of the húnpíng, although that seemed like a pipe dream now.

The morning newspaper had arrived. Usually filled with local events, gossip, and Tesco coupons, the weekly edition featured another front-page article about the murder on the green and the theft at Ivor's shop.

*"Police Admit They Have No Leads in Antiquities Shop Horror"*

First it was a tragedy. Now a horror. What next?

Besides, the problem wasn't *no* leads. If anything, the police had too many leads, each pointing in a different direction. Was the murder of Evelyn Villiers a byproduct of the theft, or was the theft a cover for murder? Was money the motive, or was it revenge for the looting of Chinese national treasures? Had someone been preying on a defenseless widow, or had she been involved in something sinister herself?

Some questions were even more elusive. What had happened in Evelyn Villiers's life to change her so profoundly? And where did the green maiden fit it?

*Betrayal.* I couldn't get that word out of my mind, and that bothered me more than I was willing to admit. Was betrayal the key to everything, or was it a distraction created by my notoriously overactive imagination?

This wasn't getting me anywhere. I balled up the newspaper and threw it in the trash.

Then I got out the silver polish.

At noon, after stowing the supplies and scrubbing the tarnish from my fingernails. I decided to take the bull by the horns and call Professor Markham.

I let it ring twelve times and was about to hang up, when he answered. "Yes? What is it?" Impatient. Snippy.

"This is Kate Hamilton," I said in what my late husband used to call my butter-wouldn't-melt voice. "I'm the one who dropped off the Little Domesday translation last week. I have a few questions about local history. I wonder if I might stop by and—"

"Certainly not. I'm far too busy."

He clicked off, leaving me staring at my phone. Either Professor Markham possessed the natural charm of a boiled egg *or*—my brain made one of those surprising leaps—*or* I wasn't approaching him in the right way.

That had to be it.

*Asking* him for a favor wasn't going to work. What I should do instead was *offer* him something—something he wanted badly enough to answer my questions.

What did Professor Markham want so badly he'd agree to see me? And where was I going to find it?

* * *

"He isn't waking up as quickly as we hoped." Dr. Chaudhry's white lab coat dazzled in the sunlight streaming through the window. "Not necessarily anything to worry about. People respond differently to sedation."

Ivor moved restlessly in the bed. He'd been moved to one of the wards.

"How long of a recovery do you expect?" I asked.

"Impossible to say. We'll know more when he wakes up, but you must expect him to be a bit muddled in the beginning. His concussion was significant. He'll need rest and calm."

I'd originally planned to fly home mid-June. With Ivor's setback, I would almost certainly be needed longer. Normally, with my mother's health and my antiques business to run, I'd worry about being gone so long, but my shop was in the capable hands of my best friend, Charlotte. From the frequent texts she sent, business was positively booming. And my mother wasn't as frail or as lonely as I'd imagined. Besides, she had her own personal physician in the dashing Dr. James Lund.

Ivor made a sound, something between a sigh and a cough. I looked at Dr. Chaudhry. "Is there anything I can do to help him wake up?"

"He may be aware of your presence. My advice is to talk to him. The familiar sound of your voice will give him something to focus on."

Later, after one of the nurses had plumped Ivor's pillows and checked his IV drip, I sat beside his bed. "Well, Ivor, it seems you've dodged a bullet—do you use that expression in the UK? Anyway, all you need to do is wake up and get back to The Willows. I'm sure Jay'den is missing you."

Was the slight movement of his eyes beneath his lids a sign that he'd heard me? I took his hand. "I need you to wake up as soon as you can. A lot has happened since your fall."

I told him again about the White Lotus Society and Lucy showing up at Rose Cottage, adding new information about the Australian nephew, the missing Colin Wardle and his mother, the odd goings-on at Hapthorn Lodge, and what I'd come to think of as the two turning points in Evelyn Villiers's life. "The police are following a number of leads," I told him, "but I'm pretty sure everything connects back to the death of her husband and something that occurred just before she brought in the húnpíng jar. Eighteen years ago, she turned her back on her old life—all her memories, all her contacts. The only thing she didn't do was move out of Hapthorn Lodge, and that may have been due to her agoraphobia. Irrational fears are often triggered by trauma. Two weeks ago today she implied she was ready to sell her husband's entire art collection. Actually, from the state of Hapthorn Lodge, it looks like she'd already taken steps to—"

Had I imagined the slight pressure from Ivor's hand?

"Take your time, Ivor," I whispered. "No hurry. When you're ready, just open your eyes."

A nursing sister bustled in the room. "You'll have to leave for a short while, dear. Time for a little maintenance. Come back in forty minutes or so."

"I think he might be trying to wake up."

"Very possibly." She smiled. "A good sign."

I gathered my belongings and headed for the visitors' waiting room. Most of the seats were already taken, so I stood, leaning against the wall.

Lucy Villiers would be sitting down with her solicitor right now. After living paycheck to paycheck for years, how was she reacting to her new role as heir to the Villiers' fortune? I hoped Simon Crewe would warn her about those who might try to take advantage.

I'd just found a place to sit, when my cell phone rang.

"Hello, darling." My mother's voice was a balm to my soul. "I've been expecting you to call me. Is everything all right?"

"I didn't want to bother you at the lake. Having fun?"

"Oh yes. We've been fishing, walking in the woods. James has developed an interest in personal watercraft. Little boats you ride on—Sea-Doos, I think they're called. His son-in-law owns two. You wear something called a wet suit. James is trying to talk me into going out with him."

I refrained from mentioning she was in her seventies. If she'd forgotten, who was I to remind her?

She went on. "We're having so much fun that James and I have decided to stay until Wednesday or Thursday. That's one of the nicer parts of being retired—the ability to change your plans at a moment's notice." She sounded so lighthearted. So young.

"I may have to change my plans as well." I told her about Ivor's fall. "We won't know for sure until he wakes up, but his recovery will be delayed."

"Do you need me at the shop?"

"Not this time. Charlotte is having the time of her life. As much as she's loved staying home with her boys, I think she's missed having a business to run. She's picking things up faster than I'd expected."

There was a moment's silence. Then my mother said, "You don't need to worry about me, you know. The doctors say I've fully recovered."

"I know, Mom, and I'm very grateful." As usual, she'd read between the lines. The last time my mother had driven down from Wisconsin to run my antiques shop she'd had a TIA, a mini-stroke. Now she was on a blood thinner, but we both knew her chances of having another episode had increased.

"Tell me how things are going with the investigation," she said.

I smiled at her ability to accept things at face value and move on. "At the moment, I'm trying to figure out how to entice a curmudgeonly history professor to talk to me about the green maiden legend." I told her about delivering the Little Domesday book translation. "He's already slammed the door in my face and hung up on me."

"You've always loved a challenge."

"I know Evelyn Villiers's interest in the legend of the green maiden is important. I just can't figure out how."

"Tell me about it."

I went through the whole thing—the marked book in her bedside table, the framed photograph over her bed, her love for the river (denied by Lucy), and the comment she'd made to the housekeeper, Mrs. Wright, about the legend being wrong. Then I told her about what she'd said that day in the shop—*wagon bell*—and then finding the Anglo-Saxon words on a wooden beam in the pub at Dunmow Parva.

"If a theory is sound, Kate, it will account for all the facts, including the ones that appear to have no apparent connection with the others—the outliers. Remember the elephant's amber eye."

Last December, when I was trying to piece together clues to a series of deaths at Finchley Hall, my mother told me a story about seeing a photograph of what you assume is a dry, cracked river bed—until you notice, way up in the corner, the elephant's amber eye. That tiny detail changes everything. "So you think I'm right to pursue it?"

"Your powers of logic and reasoning are impeccable."

"Got them from you, Mom."

"I believe you did. Now, what is it you think the professor can tell you?"

"I think he can translate the Anglo-Saxon phrase, which might tell me why Evelyn Villiers said it, which might tell me what changed in her life."

"And led to her death."

"Exactly. Now I need a reason for the professor to talk to me."

"What did you do last year when you and Ivor wanted that reclusive collector in Bury to agree to see you?"

"We offered him something he couldn't resist."

"And that's what you'll do now."

"Any suggestions?"

"You'll think of something."

"Thanks for the vote of confidence." I heard voices in the background. "Do you have to go?"

"Not before I tell you what I found online. Two weeks ago, an auction house in Paris sold a rare early Meissen figural group called *The Mockery of Age*, like the one you said was missing from the Villiers Collection."

"Actually, several more from that same collection are missing as well—the only name I can remember at the moment is *The Indiscrete Harlequin*. I'll e-mail you the others."

"I'll check the listing and text you the *Mockery* photograph as soon as we hang up."

* * *

The photograph had appeared in the posted results of an auction in Paris exactly a week before Evelyn Villiers brought the húnpíng into Ivor's shop. The selling price, disclosed to online subscription holders only, had exceeded estimates. The Meissen figural group wasn't necessarily the one Wallace Villiers had purchased—exactly how many were produced, I didn't know—but the timing was suggestive. I knew almost certainly that the piece had been on the mantel until quite recently. What I needed was the actual auction catalog, which would give as much of the provenance, the history of ownership, as was known. Requesting the catalog would take time, though. And the auction house was unlikely to disclose the name of the seller—to me anyway. I didn't know what they would do if the police got involved, but I didn't have enough factual evidence to mention it to Tom yet. Maybe Evelyn Villiers sold the pieces herself. She had a perfect right. What bothered me was the possibility—and it was only a possibility—that she'd been the victim of some dishonest person who'd been stealing from her. Had she discovered the theft? Was that the trigger that sent her to Ivor's shop?

I returned to Ivor's bedside. The linens had been changed, and the clean scent of soap suggested he'd been bathed. He seemed more settled now. Perhaps he felt more comfortable. Once I thought I saw his eyelids flutter, but he didn't open his eyes.

I pulled up the visitor's chair close to the bed. "I know you can't help me right now, Ivor, but I need to find something to offer your professor friend in Essex—some piece of information that will gain his trust. Maybe then he'll tell me more about the green maiden legend and translate the phrase I saw in the pub. So what can I offer him—and how do I contact him?"

Ivor slept as soundly as an infant.

I leaned back and slipped off my shoes.

The machines blinked reassuringly. Several get-well cards, formerly displayed on Ivor's tray table, had fallen to the floor. I picked them up and slipped them in the drawer beside Ivor's watch and cell phone.

*Ivor's cell phone.* The professor's e-mails would be in the history.

Had he heard about Ivor's fall? Not likely. He probably hadn't heard about the moon landing.

I picked it up.

*Don't you dare,* my conscience warned me. *Invasion of privacy.*

Too late. I was already scrolling through Ivor's texts. There weren't many.

There it was, the back and forth about the package delivery.

Quickly, before my conscience could come up with a scathing rebuke, I tapped out a message:

*Ivor Tweedy here. My friend Kate Hamilton has discovered some interesting new information about the green maiden.*

I deleted *interesting* and substituted *startling*. Then I added *Are you interested?* and pressed "Send."

"I'm sorry, Ivor," I said to the sleeping form, but somehow I knew his only regret would be missing out on the action.

The reply came in less than five minutes.

*Monday. Nine AM.*

*Yes!* Now all I had to do was come up with that startling new information.

I checked my watch. Five o'clock.

I had less than forty-eight hours to find it.

# Chapter Thirty

Sunday, May 19

Lucy and I met at Hapthorn at nine AM. This time she drove her own car. Thankfully, the rain had subsided, but the skies were hazy and the river hadn't receded. A mist hovered over the soaked earth, nearly obscuring the half-submerged wooden bench along the bank.

I punched the code in the lockbox, and we entered through the old laundry.

"The musty smell is getting worse," Lucy said. "I think it's coming from the cellar."

"Should we go down and check?"

"No." She shook her head. "Mother's solicitors are sending someone over to examine the house before we list it. I'll let them deal with it."

"How did it go with Simon Crewe?" I asked, plopping my handbag on the kitchen table.

"He was trying hard to impress me." Lucy rolled her eyes. "He kept saying what a terrific job Waltham & Crewe had done for my mother and how ready he was to help me 'navigate the rough waters'"—she put air quotes around the words—"of probate and taxes."

"Did you make any decisions?" I leaned against the sink.

"Not yet." Lucy opened the refrigerator and frowned at the sour smell. "Mr. Crewe is lining up a few estate agents. In the meantime, he needs your inventory to complete the papers for the courts."

"I'm about two-thirds of the way through your father's records, although setting valuations will take a bit more time. Do you mind if I come back myself to finish up?"

"Of course not." She hopped up on the counter and sat swinging her legs. "I should say I'd be glad to help, but it wouldn't be true. I was never interested in my father's art collection. That disappointed him. The more time and money he spent on his art collection, the less important Mother and I became to him.

"That can't be true, Lucy. You were important to him. He may not have been right, separating you and Colin, but I'm sure he thought he was protecting you."

She made a face. "He said he was saving me from the worst mistake of my life. He was absolutely beside himself when he caught us that night. Snobbery. That's what killed him."

"I thought he liked Colin."

"I know—he did. Dad *always* stood up for Colin—no matter what mother said about him. He refused to listen at first when she accused him of theft."

"So why didn't you and Colin talk to your father before eloping?"

"Dad had plans for me. I was meant to be studying for my A levels so I could get a place at uni. Not Oxbridge—we all knew I wasn't up to that—but maybe Birmingham or Leeds. He wanted me to have a career in finance." She gave me a rueful smile. "Maths was never my thing."

We began in Lucy's bedroom.

"There's nothing left," she said, opening the closet and staring at the empty space.

"Your teddy bear's still here—and the dolls."

Lucy reached for a doll with dark curls. She was dressed in a colorful striped skirt and lace petticoat with a black shawl and a straw hat. "This one's from Spain." Lucy smiled, running a finger along the felt shawl. "Dad bought me a straw hat just like this one—and he bought Mother a pair of diamond and ruby earrings. I remember her putting them on, admiring herself in the mirror."

"How old were you?"

"Nine or ten." Lucy put the Spanish doll back on the shelf. "That one's from Bavaria." She pointed out a doll wearing the traditional dirndl skirt and puffed sleeve blouse with a sueded leather bodice. "And this one's from Japan. I thought the red silk obi was so beautiful."

"I think your father loved you very much, Lucy. Maybe he just didn't know how to show it."

Her dark eyes shone. "Maybe I didn't either."

"Vivian sent a few empty boxes from Rose Cottage," I said. "They're in the car. Should I get them? You can wrap the dolls in tea towels."

"Yes, please. I'll put them on the bed for now."

I carried the boxes in from the car and pushed the door shut with my foot. Choosing one I thought would hold all the dolls, I filled it with tea towels from the kitchen.

"Lucy?"

I found her in her parents' bedroom, sitting in one of the peach silk chairs, staring at the cold fireplace.

"What is it?" I asked, taking the other chair.

"I thought I'd search for the albums. Mother kept some of the older ones in her wardrobe. Do you know I have no photos of my parents or myself as a child?" She opened her hand. "I found this." Lying in her palm was a tiny gold triangle, one of the self-adhesive photo corners people used years ago.

"Where do you think the albums are?" I asked.

"Thrown out? Burned? I have no idea."

"Why would your mother burn old photos?"

"Getting rid of memories, I guess." Lucy laughed, a small angry sound. "Ironic, isn't it? All those valuable paintings and antiques, and all I care about are the photographs."

"What will you do once the estate is settled?"

"Return to Belfast. I have friends there—good friends."

"Have you thought about how your life will change?"

"I won't have to worry about money for one thing—that'll be a new experience." She grinned. "Now when I have my annual two-week holiday, I can actually go somewhere warm."

"Will you keep working?"

"Not sure. I'll do something. Maybe invest in a business. That's what my mother should have done. Mr. Crewe said she could have taken money out of the trust any time—it was hers to use during her lifetime. She never did anything except pay the bills."

"Tell me about your mother, Lucy."

She shook her head regretfully. "I wish I could. I can describe her to you, but that's just the outside."

"Start there then."

Lucy took a deep breath. "She was about my height—a little taller. Kept herself slim so she could wear the pretty clothes she liked." Lucy laughed and lifted her jeans-clad legs. "I didn't take after her in that department, did I?"

"How *did* you take after her?"

"Her coloring, I suppose. Maybe her sense of insecurity. No one else would have thought so, but she was always trying to prove herself, wearing expensive clothes, jewelry. Like those dolls. They're all the same—identical faces and bodies. The only thing that makes them distinctive is the clothing."

"What was her family like? Your grandparents?"

"I never knew Grandma and Grandpa Shipton. They died when I was a baby. Mother was their only child, so there weren't any aunts or uncles or cousins. That's why I loved Ertha's stories. I always dreamed of having a brother or sister—a big family with lots of laughter and teasing." She blushed. "I'm sorry. You don't want to hear all this."

"I do as a matter of fact. I've been trying to understand why your mother turned her back on her former life. She could have remarried. She could have done anything she liked. Instead, she lived like a hermit."

"If I knew why, I'd tell you. All I know is she blamed me for my father's death—and that made her hate Colin even more."

"Did your mother grow up near a river?"

Lucy stared at me. "Near a river? Not that I know of—why?"

"The housekeeper said she loved the river. She would sit along the bank for hours, watching the water go by."

"She never did that when I was home."

"I think she developed an interest in the legend of the green maiden."

"You mentioned that."

"She had a book of local legends and myths in her bedside table. She'd marked several passages in the chapter about the green maiden of Suffolk."

"She had to be interested in something, I guess."

"Did your mother ever go with your father to visit your Aunt Winnie in Dunmow Parva?"

"She might have done. I don't remember."

"Did she study the Anglo-Saxon language?"

Lucy raised one eyebrow. "Now, that *is* a strange question, Kate."

"The day she was murdered, the day she brought the húnpíng jar into the shop for consignment, she said something I didn't understand at the time—it sounded like *wagon bell.* Now I believe it was an Anglo-Saxon phrase."

"Mother always said she was rubbish at languages—barely passed her O levels in French. What did the phrase mean?"

"When I find out, I'll let you know."

# Chapter Thirty-One

Lucy and I left Hapthorn Lodge before one o'clock. She headed back to the inn, in her own car, with the dolls and a few other items she'd packed. I headed for the shop.

Tomorrow, Monday, Lucy had another appointment at the solicitor's office to go over the list of estate agents vying to sell Hapthorn Lodge. Tomorrow I had an appointment in Essex with Professor Markham. I winced inwardly, remembering my minor deception.

*Minor?* queried my inner conscience. I thought I caught the term *slippery slope*, but I brushed it away.

The professor had agreed to see me—that was the important thing. My job now was to find something to impress him.

Ivor said he owned a copy of the book written in the early twentieth century about the green maiden. I'd find it in the book room—but where? Ivor's filing methods bore no resemblance to any known cataloguing system in the universe. He filed by theme—or whim. That meant the book about the green maiden might be shelved under "Local History" or "Myths" or "Ancient Britain" or some other designation known only to Ivor. Green women, maybe.

With no time to waste, I plunged in, setting up the library ladder. Starting with the top shelf in each section, I scanned the book titles one by one.

*Lemons to Lemonade: Paint Spills on Chinese Export Porcelain*
*Cloning the Pharaohs: Another Jurassic Park?*
*The Poisons of the Ancient Sumerians*

*Elizabethan Mousetraps: Deciphering Clues in Shakespeare's Plays*

I was on the third stack of shelves when I found it: *The Legend of the Green Maiden: Fact or Fiction?* by Arthur A. R. Cockrill, Esq., B.Litt., MA, FSA.

Ivor had filed it under "Folklore." I might have guessed.

A quick look-up on my phone told me FSA meant Fellow of the Society of Antiquaries of London. Was the Society still in existence?

Was Ivor a member?

Cockrill's book was less than two hundred pages long. I turned to the title page.

Arthur A. R. Cockrill had been born in 1859. He'd published his slim volume by subscription in 1901, the year Queen Victoria died. Ivor's copy was twenty-third in a run of one hundred.

I was about to check out the Table of Contents when the sky suddenly darkened. Needles of rain pricked the windows. *Oh man.* Just what we didn't need.

Shoving the book in my carryall, I armed the security system and dodged the raindrops all the way home to Rose Cottage.

* * *

I found Vivian and Fergus in the sitting room, watching a documentary on the restoration of York Cathedral after the Second World War.

"Hello, dear. I was hoping you'd be back in time for supper." Vivian lifted the remote. "I'll just switch this off."

"No—finish your program," I said.

She clicked the TV off anyway. "We'd rather hear about Ivor. Come sit."

I gave her the latest—that Ivor was taking longer than expected to wake up from the sedation. "The doctor says we shouldn't worry."

"*Humph.* That's what they told Lady Barbara before her husband died."

"Vivian." I put up my hand to stop her. "Ivor *isn't* going to die."

I was afraid I'd offended her, but she appeared not to have heard me.

"I have news." She lifted her eyebrows and gave me a knowing smile. "Remember when I told you Briony Peacock saw Henry Liu on his delivery bicycle the night of the May Fair?"

"Yes—at eight fifteen."

"That's right, but here's the thing: after discussing it further with her husband, she's changed her mind."

"You mean it happened later after all?"

"No, it happened at eight fifteen all right—they were both clear on that point. But it wasn't Henry they saw."

"What?"

"Stephen got a better look at the man on the bike than she did. He insists it was the son, James, they saw. Not Henry at all." Vivian gave a nod and settled back in her chair.

"Are they sure? The two men do look alike, especially from a distance."

"Positive. They called the police to amend their statements."

I stared at her, trying to decide what this meant. While the new information might clear up the discrepancy in Henry Liu's time line, it didn't explain how James could be on the delivery bicycle at eight fifteen and Henry on the same bike forty-five minutes later. There wouldn't have been enough time for two trips, plus the time Henry said he spent with his wife in the kitchen. Something still didn't add up.

Vivian clearly wanted to talk further about this new development, but pleading work, I headed to my room under the eaves. Bright and early the next morning I had to deliver startling new information to Professor Markham. So far I had zip.

Settling back against the big pillows on my bed, I opened Cockrill's book and started with the Preface.

> *The legend of the Green Maiden of Suffolk is thought to have emerged in the mid-eleventh century, which, if true, means it predates the better-known legend of the Green Children of Woolpit, recorded in the* Cronicon Anglicanum *by Ralph of Coggeshall, English Chronicler and sixth abbot of Coggeshall Abbey.*

Oh, joy—a pedant on his hobby horse. This could take all night.

*Folklorists claim both tales originated with the ancient myth of the Green Man, a personification of Nature and a pre-Christian god, worshipped by the Celts in Britain. In an age of superstition, green was the colour of elves and fairies, creatures of the forests, malevolent sprites who preyed upon children. Some scholars theorise that tales of strange creatures developed in the tumultuous times during and after the Norman Invasion, when the old Anglo-Saxon way of life was being threatened and parents sought to warn their offspring about the dangers of associating with foreigners.*

*Did the Green Maiden of Suffolk exist? I hope my efforts will provide a definitive answer.*

*Arthur A. R. Cockrill, Esq., B.Litt., MA, FSA*
*Moreton Appley Hall, Chelmsford*

I hoped so too. Cockrill had taken on quite a challenge.

The first chapter had to do with the surprising number of variations on the legend, each with its own tradition of origin. I skimmed through, marking interesting paragraphs with Post-it Notes.

Several versions of the legend claimed that rather than marrying a farmer, Mersia had married an important landowner in Essex named Randúlfr Leofwine and bore him a son named Wulfmær. The strength of this argument lay in the details. According to these accounts, Randúlfr died soon after the boy's birth, leaving his dowager a fine manor house and many acres of farmland, which she spurned, preferring to dwell in a simple cottage by the river. I thought of the photograph hanging over Evelyn Villiers's bed. That cottage was old, but not nine centuries old.

Several versions agreed with the May Fair pageant's—that Mersia's husband accused her of being a witch after she tried to poison him. One version insisted it was the son who had betrayed her in order to claim his inheritance.

All versions agreed that Mersia died in a flood, but exactly how that happened was a matter of controversy—an unfortunate accident or deliberate murder?

With the concept of betrayal submerged in my brain like an iceberg, my only real takeaway was the reference to rivers—rivers were becoming a theme. But I could hardly tell Professor Markham my startling revelation had to do with two women living nine hundred years apart who both liked flowing water.

I read on.

Cockrill had dedicated several chapters to tediously detailed scientific explanations of his day for green skin. In the end, he'd landed on two theories. The first associated a green cast to the skin with arsenic and copper poisoning. Arsenic, he noted, was favored by medieval alchemists, and copper was used as a mordant in the plant-based green wool dyes of the eleventh and twelfth centuries. That sounded plausible, especially since the alternative theory claimed green skin was produced by *green sickness*, an ailment apparently common to Victorian virgins, which, like hysteria and "wandering uterus," was cured by sexual relations and childbirth. *Right.*

When I Googled "green sickness," though, I found something interesting. The actual name for it, chlorosis, is a real medical condition, known today as hypochromic anemia, a rare blood disorder that occurs when red blood cells lack normal levels of hemoglobin.

Interesting but hardly startling. Professor Markham would already know the medical explanations. I needed something more.

At six thirty Vivian called me down for Welsh rarebit, made with local cheddar and brown ale. She was spoiling me, and I knew it. To be fair, I had offered to share the cooking. She'd refused, saying that foreign food didn't agree with her stomach.

Fortified, I returned to my bedroom and pushed ahead toward the final chapters.

By eight I was getting sleepy. And discouraged. Could I bluff my way through the meeting with Professor Markham? Could I spin a few curious facts into something solid enough to win his trust, or would he throw me out before even looking at the Old English phrase?

So far I'd learned nothing except that the version presented at the May Fair wasn't the only one. Is that what Evelyn Villiers meant when she implied they'd gotten the story wrong? Did it even matter after nine hundred years?

One thing I've never been is a quitter. As Vivian and Fergus had retired, I slipped down to the kitchen and made myself a mug of Ovaltine before finishing Cockrill's book.

Like so many things in life, the final chapter was a game changer.

*Where Lies the Truth?*

*Like many legends, the tale of the Green Maiden of Suffolk rests upon stories handed down from generation to generation. We have already proved that, scientifically speaking, such a woman might have existed [cf. Chapters 2 and 3]. Now, based upon hitherto unknown records uncovered by the author in the archives of the Church of the Blessed Virgin in the Essex village of Dunmow Parva, we shall endeavour to prove that she actually did exist.*

Dunmow Parva? Suddenly I was no longer sleepy.

*The earliest known parish records in England date from 1538, when Henry VIII issued a mandate that every parson, vicar and curate in the realm was to record all weddings, christenings and burials. Over time, the information entered into the parish registers became more fulsome and personal.*

*In the years after the restoration of the monarchy under Charles II, the current incumbent of the Church of the Blessed Virgin in Dunmow Parva, Robert Bisbie, LL.D. (1633—1688), recorded not only details of the church sacraments but also, on occasion, his thoughts and opinions concerning such village events as the defacing of tombstones by village ruffians and the number of souls lost in the plague year, 1666.*

*Salient to our current investigation is the following notation, entered by Bisbie in February of 1671:*

> Sir John Grenfel, by declaration, bearing date 12 February 1671, in gratitude to God for restoring his son, Henry, gives to the church the sum of £420, for the maintenance of four poor people of the parish, to be nominated by the mayor, aldermen, and common council of Dunmow Parva, or the major part of them. And he directs that said £420 should be put forth at interest at six per cent, the profits thereof to be bestowed upon the said four worthy people annually in perpetuum.

*Grenfel?* I sat back, stunned. The locket Evelyn Villiers was wearing the night she died had a curl of black hair and the inscription: *M. Grenfel, born Mar 5, 1805, died Feb 4, 1853.*

Finally I was getting somewhere. I read on.

> Sir John, wool merchant of the parish, dwells with his good wife and three daughters in a manor house along the River Stour. Their fourth child, Henry, was born with the affliction common amongst his forbears. The child was restored to health by the grace of God and the prayers of his pious parents. Sir John claims to be a descendant of the green maiden of Suffolk. The truth of this cannot be proved, but the family's strange physical affliction is well known in the parish.

> *Strange, indeed! You may wonder as I did, dear reader, if descendants of the family reside today in Dunmow Parva. When the author enquired, he was assured that although the surname Grenfel dropped out of usage in the late nineteenth century, the family has survived and, like their ancestors, still dwell along the River Stour. No one in the village was willing to disclose the names. A future researcher may have more success.*

Bells were going off like mad in my head. This was it—the first actual evidence I'd found of the connection between Evelyn Villiers and the green maiden legend. Was she related to the descendants mentioned by Cockrill—or did she believe she was? Was this the significance of the cottage by the river?

I needed to examine that photograph.

The first thing I did was call Lucy Villiers and ask her permission to borrow it.

"Of course," she said. "I honestly have never heard of anyone named Grenfel. It's strange mother never mentioned anything about the legend. If you learn something, please let me know."

Then I dialed Tom.

# Chapter Thirty-Two

"DI Mallory." He sounded tense.

"I'm sorry. Did I wake you?"

"Kate." I pictured him running his hand through his hair. "I was afraid it was Cliffe with bad news. One of our detective constables was pretty badly injured tonight. He's in hospital. Cliffe's with him."

"Injured on duty?"

"Yes. He may have broken a leg."

"I hope he's okay. I've called about information I found linking Evelyn Villiers with the Grenfel family."

I thought I heard a groan. "Can this wait until tomorrow?"

"Tom, are you sure there were no Grenfels from Dunmow Parva in Evelyn Villiers's family line?"

"Not a one. Her family came from Sussex."

"Okay, but there's something I need to check out right away—tonight, actually—at Hapthorn Lodge."

"Tonight? That's impossible. No one's available."

"I can go alone—it will only take a few minutes. In and out."

"No, Kate. Not at night."

"What if I get Vivian to go with me? I swear the whole thing won't take more than five minutes."

"You won't be able to get in."

"Yes, I will. I've watched PC Weldon punch in the key code often enough."

"What's so important it can't wait until morning?" As if to underscore his point, a rumble of thunder was followed by a flash and the crack of lightning.

"I may have a clue to Evelyn Villiers's murder."

"What clue?"

"Her possible connection with the green maiden." I scrunched up my face, knowing how that must have sounded.

"Kate." There was a warning in his voice. "I'm struggling here."

"Hapthorn Lodge isn't a crime scene anymore, right?"

"No, but—"

"And I got Lucy's permission, so I wouldn't be breaking in."

Silence.

"Trust me on this, Tom—please. It's that photograph. All I need to do is get into the house, dash upstairs, and grab it. I'll call you when I'm back in the car and explain the whole thing."

Silence.

"Tom?"

"Call me when you arrive. And leave the line open." This time the groan was unmistakable. "I hope I don't regret this."

* * *

Thirty minutes later, *I* was beginning to regret my decision.

Navigating the back roads of Suffolk in the middle of the night isn't easy. Believe me—there's nowhere darker at night than the English countryside. On top of that, rain made the roads slick.

Vivian and Fergus were crammed into the passenger's seat of my Mini Cooper. She'd insisted on bringing the dog along. "Protection," she said. "Fergus has the heart of a pit bull."

*And the body of a slug.*

Vivian was keeping up a steady stream of advice—"Not so close on the left, dear . . . watch that puddle . . . a little slower around the corner." Fergus was panting, steaming up the passenger-side window.

Actually, the whole car was fogging up. I flipped on the defrost and cracked my window, feeling spits of rain on my right cheek.

"We're having an adventure," Vivian told Fergus in the voice of a parent calming a child during a tornado watch. I think he believed her. He stopped panting but kept up a low rumble in the back of his throat, half growl, half whimper.

My own sentiments exactly.

At the junction of the unpaved single-track road, the surface—awash with runoff—seemed to disappear.

I was seriously considering turning around, when Vivian said cheerfully. "I believe we've arrived. Sure you don't want us to go in with you?"

"Absolutely not. Stay in the car. I'm going to leave it running."

We followed the ruined stone wall for about a half mile. As I pulled the car through the open gate, Hapthorn Lodge rose up, shrouded in darkness.

"Looks like Dracula's castle," Vivian said, probably intending to sound witty. "No wonder Lucy wants to sell the place."

The car bumped into a pothole, sending up a spray of muddy water.

*Whatever made me think this was a good idea?*

I parked at the front entrance and pulled up the hood of my jacket.

"Here's the torch." Vivian produced the small flashlight she used when taking Fergus for his nightly walkies. "When you get upstairs, flash twice. I'll get the message."

"What message—'split up and meet up in Istanbul'? We're not spies, Vivian."

"So I'll know you're still alive."

"Thanks for the encouragement." I got out and closed the car door.

Rain pearled the thick ivy climbing the stone walls. I skirted the dense, overgrown shrubbery and found the side entrance. Using the flashlight and dialing my cell phone at the same time was awkward, but I managed to punch in Tom's number.

He picked up instantly. "Everything all right?"

"I'm here. Hold on—I'm using a torch the size of a fountain pen." I keyed in the code on the lock box. "I'm in now. Looking for the light switch."

"Use the torch, Kate. We don't want the neighbors reporting a burglar."

"There aren't any neighbors, but I take your point. Here goes." I kept up a steady monologue which, in spite of my earlier protestations, felt comforting. "I'm on the staircase, going up. Okay—I'm in the upstairs hallway now. Entering the bedroom."

I followed the narrow beam of light into the small room overlooking the front drive. To give Vivian a thrill, I flashed twice at the car below—the least I could do when she'd gotten out of bed to go with me. Grabbing the photograph off the wall, I headed for the stairway.

I was near the top of the landing when I sensed something.

A disturbance in the air. A faint trace of warmth.

Someone was there—or had been.

I clicked off the flashlight and held my breath.

"Kate? Is everything all right?" Tom's voice cut through the silence.

"Shh." I covered my cell phone with my hand.

I squinted into the darkness. "Hello? Is someone there?"

The swift movement of air took me by surprise. Someone slammed past me, sending me, my phone, and the flashlight flying.

A dark shape hurtled down the stairs as I lurched backward into a chest of drawers. A lamp crashed in an explosion of shattered glass.

"Kate? *Kate?*" I heard Tom's voice from a distance.

I followed his voice, wincing in pain. I'd landed on my hip.

The phone lay near the wall—intact. "I'm okay. Someone was in the house. He's gone."

Wild barking in the distance reminded me that Vivian and Fergus were sitting ducks. Moving as fast as I could with my bruised hip, I raced down the stairs and out to the car.

"Thank goodness you're safe." Vivian's round face was pale. Fergus was pawing at the window.

"What did you see?" I held the phone between us so Tom could listen in.

"A man. Dark clothing—a hoodie, I think. Ran off in that direction." She pointed north toward the village.

"At least I got the framed photograph," I said into the phone. "I'll go back and lock the house."

"Leave it. Just get out of there. Can you drive?"

"Of course." I didn't tell him my hands were shaking.

"Drive carefully," he said. "Don't stop. I'll meet you at Rose Cottage in twenty minutes."

* * *

Tom paced back and forth between Vivian's kitchen and the parlor, his long strides turning her snug cottage into a child's playhouse. He slid his phone into his jacket pocket. "Cliffe and Weldon are at Hapthorn now."

I was still in my damp jeans and sweater.

Vivian had changed into her gray wool robe and slippers. She poured me a cup of tea. "When we saw that man running from the house, we thought he'd killed you."

Fergus made a low rumble of agreement.

"I don't think he had any intention of hurting me," I said. "He just wanted to escape."

"They found a smashed window on the lower level at the rear of the house." Tom sat next to me at the table. "Looks like someone took up residence in one of the spare bedrooms. Did you see any evidence when you were there with Lucy?"

"No, but we didn't check all the rooms. I'll call Lucy in the morning. Until they find him, she shouldn't go there alone." I took a sip of tea. "If she had reservations about selling the place before, she won't now."

The framed photograph lay on the table in front of us.

Vivian peered at it through the magnifying glass she'd found in a kitchen drawer. "It's just an ordinary old cottage by a river. The photo was taken a good while ago—that's obvious."

"It's a sepia print," I said, "which means the original was probably taken sometime before the First World War."

Tom turned the frame over, bent back the metal prongs, and pulled out the stiff cardboard. He removed the photo and handed it to me. "Spot on with the date."

Written on the back of the thick card stock were the words *River's Edge Cottage, 1912*.

"That's it?" Vivian said. "No family name or location?"

"Kate, what is it?" Tom bent to look at me.

*"River's Edge Cottage."* I'd been holding my breath, and my voice came out high-pitched. "Sheila Parker, Winnifred Villiers's neighbor in Dunmow Parva, has that same name on her house."

"Lots of houses are probably called River's Edge."

"When there's no river within fifteen miles?" Something dark leaped up in my brain. "I know it's a legend, Tom, but one version of the green maiden story says she was banished to a cottage along the River Stour in Essex. In 1901, villagers in Dunmow Parva claimed her descendants still lived in the area."

"There's probably a logical explanation," Tom said. "Ask Sheila Parker."

"Not tonight," Vivian said. "It's nearly midnight."

I was beginning to wonder if the merry widow of Dunmow Parva had been lying to me. "Sheila Parker has the name River's Edge Cottage on her house, and Evelyn Villiers had a photograph of a cottage with the same name over her bed. Yet Sheila claimed they'd never met." I folded my arms, daring Tom to explain it away.

"It's curious, I admit," he said, "but what does it have to do with Evelyn Villiers's death and the theft of the húnpíng?"

"All right, I don't know. We're obviously missing something."

"Maybe Lucy knows more than she thinks she does," Vivian said.

"Or more than she's willing to tell us." Tom began reassembling the photograph in the frame. "I'll take this to the lab in the morning." He pulled an evidence bag out of his inside jacket pocket. "Maybe they can learn something in spite of our fingerprints."

Images hung like mist in my head, but I couldn't persuade any of them to settle. "Lucy said her father really liked Colin Wardle. Why not as a son-in-law?"

"Class distinction?" Tom asked.

"It can't be that," I said. "Wallace Villiers was from a working-class family too."

"You know what they say—no snob like a new snob."

"What did Lucy say her mother's maiden name was?" Vivian asked.

"Shipton." Tom gathered up his jacket and umbrella.

"Will you mention this to Eacles?" I asked him.

"Not if I can help it." Tom hunched into his jacket and slid the evidence bag into an inside pocket. "If I bring him an old photograph and the name of a cottage that probably doesn't exist anymore, he'll send me on a mental health course. Now, the intruder he'd like—something he can get his brain around. Kate, talk to Sheila Parker tomorrow. Cliffe will be interviewing people in Little Gosling. Someone has to know something."

He thanked Vivian for the tea and kissed me goodbye.

The lights of his car swung an arc as he backed up and pulled toward the road.

I watched him drive off into the darkness. Tomorrow I'd tackle Sheila Parker and Professor Markham—two birds with one stone.

That night the rains began in earnest.

# Chapter Thirty-Three

Monday, May 20

I stood outside 20 Bedwell Court in the pouring rain for so long I was afraid Professor Markham's neighbors would call the police.

When the professor finally answered, he was less than thrilled to see me. "Yes—what is it?" he scowled at me through a pair of spectacles with one lens cracked. A blob of what looked like congealed strawberry jam clung to the front of the same baggy gray cardigan he'd worn the day I'd met him.

"I'm Kate Hamilton," I said, trying to keep my teeth from chattering. "I believe you were expecting me at nine."

Professor Markham consulted his wristwatch. "Oh, very well," he said grudgingly. "I suppose you'd better come in."

I furled my umbrella and left it on the doorstep. Inside, I hung my raincoat on a Victorian coatrack and dried my feet on what looked like a large, hand-knitted tea cozy.

The interior of the professor's house was an expanded version of the man himself—shabby, cheerless, untidy, and smelling of unwashed hair. He'd never been married—I'd found that out by Googling him the night before. His furniture, mismatched and grimy, had been repurposed as repositories for piles of scholarly journals and magazines. A sixties-style pole lamp with exposed wiring was trained on a row of pine shelves, sagging under the weight of books. More books were stacked in tottering mounds on the stained mauve carpet. The only relatively tidy area of the room was a wooden desk, on which stacks of books and papers appeared to have been recently reorganized.

"I suppose you want tea." He glared at me.

"No, no—please don't bother."

He seemed not to hear me and filled a cracked mug with a suspiciously dark liquid. "Milk's off. Take a seat," he said, shooing a gray cat from a ladder-back chair near the desk. The cat hissed, springing testily off the fur-covered cushion.

The professor handed me the mug, and I searched for a spot to set it down.

"What is it? I don't have all day." He threw himself into his desk chair.

I opened my handbag and pulled out the Essex book. "Are you familiar with Arthur Cockrill's work?"

"Cockrill? Of course. There's a copy around here somewhere." He waved a hand vaguely in the direction of the bookshelves.

"Then you know about Cockrill's assertion that the green maiden married a wealthy Anglo-Saxon landowner and bore him a son."

"Yes, yes." He rolled his hand impatiently. "Common knowledge."

I swallowed hard and kept talking. "According to Cockrill, certain villagers in Dunmow Parva insisted the son's descendants still lived in the area, and some of them, including a boy born in February of 1671, inherited the green skin of his famous forbear."

"What are you talking about?" He narrowed his eyes.

"I'm talking about the archives of the Church of the Blessed Virgin in Dunmow Parva. Cockrill discovered a record of the boy's birth, along with his parents' offering of thanks when the color of his skin faded." This wasn't strictly true—there'd been no mention of green skin—but sometimes you have to read between the lines.

"Those records don't exist. They were destroyed in the flood of 1937."

"Check it out for yourself." I handed him Ivor's copy of Cockrill's book. "The final chapter."

He snatched the book out of my hand and began riffling through the pages.

"This isn't the same book." He glared at me accusingly. "Cockrill must have issued a second printing with new information." He turned to the title page and stabbed a yellow fingernail at it. "See—I was right 'Second edition, enlarged.'"

He grabbed a stenographer's notebook and began scribbling furiously.

"Were there Grenfels living in Essex in the eleventh or twelfth centuries?"

"Grenfels?" He plucked a circular card file off the windowsill and began thumbing through the cards. "Ellis, Forsdyke, Frostich, Gildersleeve, Goslan, Grimwood—"

*Golly—an eleventh-century Rolodex.*

His head jerked up. "Where was this cottage?"

"Cockrill doesn't say, but I may have a clue." *In for a penny, in for a pound.* "They named it River's Edge—a small cottage along the River Stour. It's probably gone now, but it still existed in 1912."

"That's not very helpful, is it?" He raised a finger and leaped out of his chair. "Aha! Kelly's."

"What's Kelly's?"

"Victorian postal directory," he said, weaving his way through the stacks of books. "Nineteen twelve, you say?" He climbed a step ladder, balancing precariously.

"Professor Markham, do you think that's wise?"

His head swiveled toward me. "*Wise*? It's essential. If I can prove— " He probably completed his thought, but he'd ceased verbal transmission. He pawed through a row of books bound in faded red cloth.

I'm sure the cat still held me responsible for an unwarranted usurpation. He prowled around, fixing me with one malevolent green eye.

The professor pulled a book free, causing the entire row of red-bound volumes to collapse. Several landed on the floor with a thud, sending the cat flying into the air in a yowling cloud of fur.

"It's not here." He climbed down, muttering, "Strange."

"Professor Markham," I said, reminding him I was present.

He scowled at me. "Can't you see I'm busy, woman?"

"I'm busy too," I said, raising my voice. "I've come all the way from Suffolk to give you information. The least you can do is allow me a few moments of your time."

"What for?"

"Translation. Anglo-Saxon."

He huffed. "Oh, very well. Make it snappy."

"Please look at these words and tell me what they mean." I pulled a paper from my handbag and handed it to him. I'd copied the entire sentence from The Green Maiden pub.

*Wægn bel-æwung cópenere brand-hœrm min sefa.*

"What does this say in modern English?" I asked.

He gave it a brief glance. "It's nonsense."

"It's painted on one of the beams at The Green Maiden in Dunmow Parva."

"Well, that explains it, then," he said as if any fool would have known. "This was written in the sixties by the history teacher at the comprehensive school. The idiot cobbled the words together from an Old English dictionary. "

"They have to mean something." I folded my arms and held my ground. "Just give me a rough idea."

He tsked and bent his head over the paper. "*Wægn bel-æwung*—'treachery' or 'betrayal.'"

I swallowed hard.

"*Cópenere* is 'lover,' or sometimes 'the one I love.'"

He handed me the paper.

I pushed it back. "And the rest, please?"

"If you insist," he growled. "*Brand-hærm* means 'torch' or possibly 'burning sword.' *Min sefa*, 'my heart.' The fool's left out the verbs. You might say, 'The betrayal of a lover is a flaming sword in my heart."

*Betrayal—again.* I did the mental version of a head slap. *This is the last time I will ever listen to an ancient—*

Realizing the absurdity of my thought, I shut it down.

Professor Markham clambered over me. "Perhaps I missed it." He was on his knees, surrounded by books—a modern-day Robinson Crusoe, shipwrecked on an island of research materials.

I stopped at the door. "If you locate River's Edge Cottage, will you let me know?"

He mumbled something under his breath, but I don't think he was talking to me.

Back in the car, I dialed Lucy's cell phone. No answer.

* * *

"You're telling me Lucy has come back from the dead? Well, I never."

Sheila Parker dropped two sugar cubes into a purple mug and stirred. "And to think poor Winnie died without ever knowing the girl was alive and well." She passed the glass sugar bowl to me. "If she comes round here, I'll give her what for. Winnie faded away with worry."

"Lucy was a child, Sheila. She'd lost her father. Then she was rejected by her mother and abandoned by her fiancé."

Sheila shot me a guilty look. "And here's me, blaming the girl, when I did the same. Ran away at sixteen. Lucky I found my Lenny before the hoolies got their paws on me." She gave a dreamy smile. "Never had eyes for no one but me, Lenny. Good provider too—when he was around."

"Sheila," I said, turning the conversation back to the subject at hand. "I'd like to ask you a few questions—just to clear things up. It won't take long."

"I'm not talking to the police." She crossed her arms.

"You don't have to." I should have added *at least not yet*, but I didn't want to raise any alarms. "You have a lovely old name plaque outside. It looks Victorian—maybe older."

"Silly, I know, giving myself airs. But ever since I was a child, I dreamed about living in a house with a name." She held her mug with both hands and took a sip.

"Where did you come up with the name River's Edge Cottage?"

"I didn't steal the plaque, if that's what you're implying."

"What do you mean?"

"Did the police send you?" She narrowed her eyes. "If they think they can do me for theft, it's too long ago. I know the law."

"This has nothing to do with theft."

"Besides, everyone was helping themselves, weren't they?"

"Helping themselves to what? When?"

"When Mrs. Wardle moved out. I told you—she took her clothes and some personal things. Left most of her furniture behind—not that it was worth anything. She'd been on the dole long as I knew her. The neighbors cleaned the place out. Only thing I took was the plaque, I swear. I thought it was pretty."

"It is pretty. Did she ever talk about the name, River's Edge Cottage?"

"No, but I got the impression it had sentimental value—that's why I was surprised she left it behind. I told myself I was saving it for her—in case she ever came back."

"Weren't you worried about her?"

"I would have been, except that son of hers came and packed up a few boxes, so we knew she'd moved away for good."

"Colin came back? When was that?"

"Must have been around the time of the Villiers' scandal—or shortly after. Caught sight of him one night, moving the boxes out."

"Did Lucy know?"

"I shouldn't think so." Her face clouded. "Should I have said something to Winnie?"

"I'm sure it wouldn't have made any difference. Was there a connection between the Villiers and the Wardles? Were they distant relatives or something?"

Sheila shook her head. "Winnie never mentioned a connection with the Wardles—and she would have done, since they lived just down the street."

"Did Winnie tell you much about her family?"

"She and Wallace grew up in Dunmow Parva. They had an older sister, but she moved away. Their mother worked in a bakery, I think. Not sure about their father."

I thought again about Winnie, living in a two-up two-down on Lark Crescent while her brother spent a fortune on fine art and antiques and indulged a wife with a taste for fine jewelry. Had Winnie been resentful? What about the sister in Australia and her children? The only person Wallace Villiers had shown an interest in helping was a young working-class lad.

"Tell me about Colin Wardle."

"Lovely looking boy, he was. His mother was that proud of him, always dressing him up and showing him off like he was the Prince of Wales. Colin got himself into trouble when he was a teenager—shoplifting, joyriding, coming home all hours. He could be sweet as anything one day and a right baiter the next. Bullied his mother. I think she was afraid of him, although she never said. He must have been nineteen or twenty when he got a job as a driver for an appliance outlet. Next thing we knew, they had a satellite dish."

"When did he meet Wallace Villiers?"

"Must have been shortly after that." She chewed thoughtfully on one of her orange-painted nails. "He started wearing smarter clothes, got his own transport. He wasn't popular around here, I can tell you."

"Why was that?"

"Put on airs, didn't he? Like he was something special, when we all knew better. Liked to give the impression he knew something we didn't."

Ertha Green had said he was sly.

I thanked Sheila Parker and stepped out into the deluge. Rain had beaten down the lovely flowers and sluiced topsoil over the concrete walk.

In the car, I tried Lucy Villiers's cell phone again. This time it went straight to voicemail.

I was about to leave a message, when a call from Tom beeped in.

"Where are you?" he asked.

"Dunmow Parva. Sheila Parker just told me—"

He cut across my words. "Tell me later, Kate. Can you get to Bury? Eacles heard about your visit to Hapthorn Lodge. He's on the warpath."

# Chapter Thirty-Four

I found DCI Dennis Eacles waiting for me in Tom's office. He looked about as glad to see me as a bride discovering a blemish on her wedding day.

"I hear you used another of your nine lives last night, Mrs. Hamilton." He stared at me with his piggy eyes. "If you'd care to give me your version." His annoyance showed on his face—literally. He'd nicked himself twice while shaving and had missed a bristly patch on his neck altogether.

I told him what I'd read in Cockrill's book about the cottage along the River Stour. "Evelyn Villiers had a thing about rivers and the legend of the green maiden. I wanted to know if the photograph over her bed would reveal anything—and it did. The name on the back of the photograph, River's Edge Cottage, is the same name as a house plaque once owned by Colin Wardle's mother in Dunmow Parva."

Tom raised an eyebrow. I gave him a look that said *I'll explain later.*

"And what does all that have to do with Evelyn Villiers's death?"

"I don't know," I admitted, pretty sure he wouldn't be interested in my mother's theories about puzzles and elephants with amber eyes.

"What if you'd been seriously injured?" Eacles waived a newspaper in my face, and I realized my close encounter at Hapthorn Lodge had made the front page. "The press are on our backs as it is. Imagine what they'd do if we'd put a civilian in harm's way." He threw the paper on Tom's desk and glared at him. "We have drugs pouring into

Suffolk, a constable in critical care. It's been fifteen days since Mrs. Villiers was murdered—*fifteen days*—and there's been no arrest. Not even a viable suspect."

"We're following every lead—you know that." Tom appeared unruffled, but his left eye was twitching.

"Yes—including airy-fairy notions like maidens with green skin." Eacles looked like a warthog with acid reflux. "We're the Suffolk Constabulary, not the Society of Folklorists. Next thing you know we'll be consulting mystics and conspiracy theorists."

I wanted to tell him about Professor Markham and the archives of the church in Dunmow Parva, but this definitely wasn't the time. Tom would have to deal with Eacles in his own way.

"We've been conducting interviews in Little Gosling," Tom said. "A number of residents reported seeing a stranger in the area. We think it's the intruder. When we find him, we'll bring him in. In the meantime, I've posted a guard at Hapthorn Lodge."

"When the cow's out of the bloody barn?" Eacles ran a finger around his collar as if it were choking him.

Tom stood. "If you have a better idea, sir, please share it."

"A better idea, you say? I do, as a matter of fact. Bring this case to a conclusion before both of us are transferred to Traffic Division." He turned to me. "We hired you to take an inventory, Mrs. Hamilton, not conduct clandestine operations. Is the report complete?"

"It'll be on your desk by Thursday."

Eacles was halfway out the door. "Here's another idea for you, Mallory. Do it all again—witness statements, doorstep interviews, dustbin searches—the lot. And don't come back without evidence we can actually use."

* * *

If the day had been sunny, we'd have walked in the Abbey gardens. As it was, rain bucketing down, the gutters overflowing, Tom and I took shelter in the pub. The Dog & Partridge was crowded with patrons, folding their dripping umbrellas and stashing their rain gear on the coatracks near the entrance.

While Tom put in our orders, I texted Lucy: *Call me.*

"I'm sorry, Tom. Eacles is taking potshots at you, and I'm handing him bullets."

We found a seat near the fire. I sat, warming my hands and feet. We'd barely gotten settled when the food came. While the Dog & Partridge didn't exactly offer gourmet cuisine, the food was tasty, the prices reasonable, and the service fast. I'd ordered a bowl of tomato basil soup. Tom had ordered a ham and cheese panini.

"It wasn't your fault." Tom sliced off a corner of his panini. "Mind you—haring off to Hapthorn in the middle of the night wasn't the wisest move."

"I'll be more careful from now on." I rubbed my hands together to thaw them out.

He ruffled my hair. "I know you will. Now, tell me about Sheila Parker."

"The sign on her house—'River's Edge Cottage'—actually belonged to the Wardles. Somewhere around the time of Wallace Villiers's death, Colin's mother moved away from Lark Crescent, leaving most of her furniture and no forwarding address. The neighbors helped themselves. Sheila took the house sign because she thought it was pretty. She was surprised Mrs. Wardle hadn't taken it with her because it had sentimental value."

"Kate—" Tom rubbed the back of his neck. "Are you trying to say the Wardles are descended from the green maiden?"

"No, I'm not. Most people have a hard enough time tracing their family back three or four generations, much less to the eleventh century. But I've given this a lot of thought. Proving something is true isn't nearly as important—or as powerful—as believing it is. Take the Loch Ness monster. For all the photographs, spurious and otherwise, for all the underwater explorations and DNA testing, no one has produced an iota of actual physical evidence that a large, prehistoric creature lurks in the loch's murky depths. Most people don't care. If they want to believe it, they will. Same thing for the green maiden. Did she exist—even in some less spectacular form than the legends suggest?

Do her descendants still live in Dunmow Parva? The important thing is an emotional attachment to the myth. What I want to know is what emotional attachment both Mrs. Wardle and Evelyn Villiers had to the legend. Sheila swears they weren't related. I don't even think they knew each other." I put my hands around the warm bowl of soup.

"You're saying Evelyn Villiers's belief in the green maiden played a part in her death."

"I can't say that yet, but as she was dying, she specifically sought out the actress playing the green maiden. That has to mean something. If we can find the missing connection between the two women, we'll be on the way to solving her murder. I texted Lucy, but she hasn't answered yet."

"You may be right." Tom shook his head at a server who asked if we needed something else. "I have news. Wallace Villiers's nephew—his name is Patrick Allen—left the Outback almond farm a month ago and bought an airplane ticket for London Heathrow. Immigration says he arrived in April, two and a half weeks before Evelyn Villiers's death."

"He could be the intruder at Hapthorn last night."

"More to the point, he could be the killer—and if he's killed once, he won't hesitate to do it again."

"Why would he murder his aunt?"

"For the inheritance. If he knew about Lucy's disappearance—and he probably did—he might have figured he was next in line for the Villiers' fortune."

"I thought that too," I admitted. "But still, why kill her, and why now?"

"I can't answer the last part. Maybe he suddenly needed money. Maybe he got sick of working in the Outback. The point is, if he contacted his aunt and she sent him packing, he might have lost his temper. It happens all the time, Kate."

"So what were they doing in Ivor's shop?"

"If he knew about the húnpíng and didn't find it at the house, he could have forced her to show him where it was."

"You think Evelyn was trying to sell the art collection before her nephew could steal it? That makes sense. Maybe he took the missing jewelry too."

"If he did, he's holding onto it. None of the local jewelers or pawn shops have been offered a collection of jewelry lately. We checked."

I refrained from pointing out that a savvy thief would never unload his takings locally. On the other hand, how would a chap from Down Under, squatting in an abandoned house, know where to sell expensive jewelry?

"The point is," Tom said, "Lucy may be in danger. Let me know when she contacts you."

"Did you ever talk to the solicitor, Simon Crewe, about what happened the day of the inquest?"

"He confirmed Lucy's story. According to old Mr. Crewe, Simon's father, Colin Wardle tried to give Evelyn Villiers a piece of paper. She pushed him away—in fact there was a bit of a tussle. The elder Crewe separated them, but Wardle managed to stuff the note in her handbag."

"An apology?"

"He never knew. She refused to talk about it."

"I'm getting a headache. Where does all this lead?"

"Nowhere so far, but I'd better come up with something soon or Eacles will have my guts for garters."

I laughed. "Guts for garters? That's something Vivian would say."

Tom stood. "That's right—laugh at me. Come on. I've been sitting too long, and people are waiting for tables."

Reclaiming our coats, we headed out into the rain.

I held his arm under the umbrella, matching his steps. "How's your injured constable?"

"Off duty for eight weeks. Broke his leg in three places."

"How did it happen?"

"The on-site manager of a lockup near Ipswich alerted us to the possibility of stolen goods—trucks coming and going in the middle of the night. Cliffe and the PC caught two lads loading a van. As soon as they realized they'd been spotted, they jumped in the van and took off. Cliffe gave chase. He thought he had them at the roundabout west of town, but one of them bolted, headed on foot for an open field. The PC followed—fell into a burrow."

"Ouch. What happened to the van?"

"Nearly caused a smash-up in the roundabout, but the driver got away too. Fortunately Cliffe got the plate number. The van belongs to a vehicle hire company. They're checking their records, but it won't do any good. Criminals never use their real names. The best we can hope for is CCTV footage."

"Good luck."

"Just what we need."

The streets were nearly empty. The sky was leaden. A gust of wind caught Tom's umbrella, threatening to turn it inside out.

"Have you learned anything about The White Lotus Society?"

"None of the dealers in London will talk about it," Tom said, struggling to keep the umbrella over our heads. "The Chinese authorities haven't responded."

"It does seem unlikely that a local businessman like Henry Liu would suddenly decide to steal a valuable Chinese húnpíng. Besides, there's no evidence he even knew Evelyn Villiers."

We'd reached the small parking lot on the north side of the police station. I clicked open my car door. Tom held the umbrella as I slid into the driver's seat. "It has to be the Australian nephew."

He bent down and kissed me. "That statement lacks conviction."

He was right.

# Chapter Thirty-Five

Back in Long Barston, I found a parking place on the street, just two buildings down from The Cabinet of Curiosities, and took it. Unusual, even for a Monday. The rain must have been keeping people at home. As I hurried down the street, the wind whipped at my umbrella.

I turned the key in the lock, stepped over the pile of mail on the floor, and punched in the security code. The alarm company still hadn't called about upgrading Ivor's system. That made me uneasy. If one thief had made it inside without alerting the police, why not others?

Except for the ticking of a Georgian mantel clock, the shop was silent.

I flipped through the mail. Thank goodness—no more official letters from Waltham & Crewe, demanding reimbursement for the húnpíng. Either things weren't done that way in the UK or Lucy had persuaded them to drop the lawsuit. And no more demands for the return of consignment items either. I refused to even hope we were turning a corner. Fate loves nothing better than a good laugh.

My plan was to check for phone messages, then head to the hospital in Ipswich. I'd called the nurses' station that morning and learned that Ivor was woozy but awake and asking for me.

I couldn't wait to see him.

Lucy hadn't returned my call or my text. I texted again. *Is everything all right? Call me.*

I was gathering my things and heading out when I heard a noise coming from the back alley. It sounded like someone was doing something with the rubbish bin.

Monday wasn't the day for collection.

Leaving my things on the counter, I crept into the stockroom and peered out one of the barred windows. Henry Liu was mounting his delivery bicycle. A large blue and white striped umbrella covered both the rider and the insulated cargo box.

Rain hit my face as I opened the door. "Mr. Liu," I shouted. "Is there something you need?"

I must have startled him because he jumped. "I . . . erm, I didn't think anyone would be in today. How is Mr. Tweedy?"

"Awake, thank goodness. I was just on my way to see him."

"Give him my regards. Tell him if there's any way I can be of help, he has only to ask."

"That's very kind. Was there something you wanted? I heard a sound."

Mr. Liu blinked. "I was checking his rubbish bin. We've had some rodent activity."

He pedaled off, leaving me puzzled. Rats would have to be either desperate or deranged to bother with Ivor's bin—not with a Chinese takeaway a few doors down.

Dashing out, I lifted the lid, finding nothing but the rubbish bag I'd tossed in there last Saturday.

* * *

Ivor was asleep when I arrived. Most of his tubes and lines had been disconnected. He was snoring softly.

Dr. Chaudhry met me in the hallway outside the ward. "Mr. Tweedy is doing well, very well indeed. Still quite sleepy, but that's to be expected." He beamed at me. "It will take another day or so before the sedation is completely out of his system, but I believe we can transfer him to The Willows by Wednesday."

"The nurse on the phone warned me about stress."

"His brain needs time to heal. No computer work, nothing mentally taxing at first. He'll be monitored at The Willows for dizziness or mood changes. Depression is common after a head injury like this. His thought processes will take time to normalize."

I couldn't imagine Ivor, the optimist, struggling with depression. Even so, I wouldn't bring up Evelyn Villiers and the missing húnpíng unless he asked.

I thanked the doctor and returned to Ivor's bedside.

"Hello, Ivor," I said softly. "Before you ask, everything's fine at the shop. I shipped out a few items that sold last week. Henry Liu said to tell you if there's anything you need, just ask." When he didn't respond, I pressed on. "I delivered the Little Domesday translation to Professor Markham last week. He's quite a character, by the way. Oh, and tomorrow is the auction at Oakley's Barn. Lady Barbara is selling a set of Regency chairs and a Georgian silver coffee pot. If things go well, we might try the carved cinnabar plate."

I sounded like Pollyanna. If Ivor was alert, he'd see through me in a minute.

I looked at him, all five foot four of him, tucked up under the flannel sheet. Shouldn't he be awake? Had he fallen back into unconsciousness? I felt a frisson of fear.

All of the nurses were busy attending to other patients.

I was about to alert someone, when I felt him squeeze my hand.

I jumped. "*Ivor*? It's me—Kate."

His eyes were closed, but a slow smile spread across his face. "I know. I love you too."

* * *

I left the hospital in high spirits. Ivor hadn't said another word—he'd drifted back to sleep almost immediately—but it was enough. Not only was he lucid, he'd actually heard all the soppy things I'd said to him while he was unconscious. The human brain is amazing.

I tried Tom's number. When I didn't get him, I left a text message: *Ivor's awake! Transfer to Willows possible Weds. Talk soon.* Then, because I just had to share the good news, I called my mother. It was mid-morning in the Central Time Zone.

She picked up immediately. "Linnea Larson here."

"Hi, Mom. Ivor's awake and talking. He's going to be okay."

"Well, that's a relief. I've been wondering about him but didn't want to disturb you. I know you have a lot on your mind."

"And I haven't wanted to bother you on vacation."

"Hearing from my daughter is never a bother. Tell me about Ivor."

"He's sleepy but pretty much over the sedation. They're going to move him back to The Willows before the end of the week. What have you been doing?"

"Just now? Packing up sandwiches. The weather is surprisingly warm for May in northern Wisconsin. We're taking a picnic on the pontoon boat—their lake is part of a chain, so we'll cruise around, maybe stop and take a dip if the water's warm enough." She laughed. "I never imagined myself wearing a bathing suit in public again. James says I look rather nifty."

Her voice was different—lighthearted, joyful, almost like a young girl in love for the first time. I ignored a prick of . . . it wasn't jealousy this time. Was it fear? Of what?

"Tell me what's going on with the investigation," she said. "Any luck tracking down the húnpíng jar?"

"How much time do you have?"

"As much as you need, darling girl. James knows it's you on the phone."

I filled her in as well as I could while glossing over my encounter with the intruder at Hapthorn Lodge. I would tell her, just not at that moment, when she was so lighthearted. "The húnpíng is either on the Continent or in China by now," I said. "We'll never see it again anyway. As far as the murder is concerned, the police are focusing on the Australian nephew. He's somewhere in England, and he's the only one so far with a clear motive and opportunity. I'm wondering how he knew about the key bumping thing and jamming alarm signals."

"Maybe he has a police record."

"Maybe," I said, remembering the frightened young man I'd encountered in Hapthorn Lodge. "The thing is, I can't get the green maiden and the cottage by the river out of my head. I'm sure Tom thinks I've gone off the deep end, but I know Evelyn Villiers had a fascination with the legend. I keep asking myself why she had a photograph of River's Edge Cottage over her bed if she blamed Colin Wardle for her husband's death?"

"I'm not sure I follow you."

"Colin's mother in Dunmow Parva named her house River's Edge Cottage, remember? And the photograph over Evelyn Villiers's bed had 'River's Edge Cottage, 1912' written on the back. Why would Evelyn want to be reminded of the man who caused her husband's heart attack?"

"It could be a coincidence—two cottages named River's Edge."

"That's not likely, is it?"

"Maybe you should try looking at things the other way around."

"What do you mean?"

"I'm talking about assumptions—not you in particular, Kate. We all do it. We construct a theory from the ground up, building logically on what we think we know. Every step in the argument rests on something that came before. But sometimes the logic collapses under its own weight, not because the conclusions we've drawn are faulty, but because the foundations on which they were built—the underlying assumptions we never questioned—are false. What if you worked backward, starting with the facts you've uncovered and tracing each one back to its underlying assumptions?"

"I think you've lost me."

"Do you remember the diamond brooch I was asked to appraise a few years ago? The provenance was impeccable—and added greatly to the value because the brooch had once belonged to a famous German actress, a gift from her first husband, an Austrian arms dealer who supplied the Nazis with iron. The owner had bought the brooch at auction for a little over thirty thousand dollars and was hoping to sell it for twice that. He had everything—bills of sale, names, dates, photographs of the actress wearing the brooch. The white gold setting was marked eighteen carat and bore the patent of Schreiber & Hiller, the famous German jeweler of the 1930s. He even had the original pale blue silk presentation box. Only one thing was wrong. The stones weren't diamonds. They were white sapphires—lovely to look at, but worth a fraction. In all the focus on provenance, the owners simply assumed the stones were diamonds and never questioned it. Of course, a gemologist would have spotted the sapphires at once."

"So you're saying I need to question the assumptions I've made—that we've all made—unwittingly. How do I do that if they're unwitting?"

"I'm not saying you *have* made false assumptions. I am saying be aware of the possibility that you've gotten something wrong, something you took for granted and never questioned. For every statement you make, ask yourself, 'Is that true? How do I know?'"

"Hmm."

"Oh, sorry, darling—I will have to go. They're ready to take off. Much love to you. Stick with it and question everything."

As always, her advice was sound.

Timely, too, because tomorrow was the auction at Oakley's Barn, and the assumptions everyone had made about the Oakleys might very well determine Lady Barbara's future.

# Chapter Thirty-Six

Tuesday, May 21

I had to hand it to them—Oakley's had pulled out all the stops.

In spite of the rain, the tithe barn positively glittered. Bidders had arrived for the preview in droves, parking their BMWs and Range Rovers on the sodden gravel and dashing into the building under a sea of black umbrellas. Now, at nearly one PM, they waited for the auction to begin, wine spritzers or sparkling waters in hand. Runners stood ready to display the objects. A bank of phones and computers lined one wall, already connected to the overseas and online bidders.

Nigel Oakley was bursting with high spirits. "I have a good feeling about this, Lady Barbara." He took her arm and escorted her to a chair near the rear of the bidding section. Vivian and I followed.

"I told you he's top notch," Vivian said, giving me a poke with her elbow.

"Let's wait for the bidding, shall we?"

While Lady Barbara and Vivian chatted, I checked my phone. I'd texted Lucy first thing that morning to find out how her meeting with the solicitor went. She still hadn't responded. "Excuse me for a moment," I said and slipped away. I dialed the hotel.

A young man answered. "Premier Inn, Sudbury."

"Could you ring Lucy Villiers's room, please?"

After a moment, he said, "I'm sorry. We don't have anyone by that name staying at the hotel."

"How about Lacey Wardle?" I winced, knowing how that would sound.

"Miss Wardle isn't in residence. She left her key at the desk."

I thanked him and returned to my seat. A bell indicated it was time for the auction to begin. I was surprised to see Martin Ingram take the podium.

"Goodness. He's a hunk," Vivian said.

He was, too, with hair the color of black coffee and those startling blue eyes. He wore jeans and a crisp white shirt under a fitted wool sports jacket. *Very GQ.* Was it my imagination or did our eyes meet? I looked away, feeling . . . churlish. *Always wanted to use that word.*

He clapped his gavel. "Welcome, everyone, to this eclectic auction of Continental and British antiques, including several items from Suffolk's own Finchley Hall. Let's get started, shall we? Lot one is this magnificent George the Third mahogany serpentine serving table, attributed to Ince and Mayhew, circa 1775, the property of a gentleman. Perfect for that country cottage." The audience laughed appreciatively as two burley young men held the table aloft. "We'll start the bidding at five thousand pounds. Who will begin?"

A man in the fourth or fifth row raised his paddle.

"We have five thousand. Who will make it six? Yes, in the blue sweater. And seven?"

In the end, the table sold for twelve thousand pounds, well over the eight- to ten-thousand-pound estimate. Everything was selling well. The bidders were in a good mood.

Lady Barbara's Regency chairs were lot fifty-seven. I thought Oakley's had taken a risk, selling them as a set.

After what seemed like a long wait, the lot came up.

"A set of fifteen Regency mahogany dining chairs ," said Martin. "Possibly by Gillows, early nineteenth century, including one armchair. Each chair has a curved bar top rail with ebony stringing and horizontal splat above a padded seat on tapering turned and reeded legs. From Finchley Hall, Long Barston."

One of the runners lifted the armchair, the other a side chair.

"Where is the second armchair, you ask?" Martin Ingram lowered his eyebrows in mock suspicion. "I have it on good authority—the chair met its end, if not its maker, at Christmas dinner, 1956, under the not-inconsiderable bulk of a certain gentlelady, whose identity"—he put a finger to his lips and winked—"shall remain undisclosed." The audience actually clapped.

Martin Ingram was charming them—and adding to the chairs' value by incorporating intriguing details about their provenance. Exactly what my mother had always done. "Give them as much information as you can," she used to say. "That way they're not just buying an object; they're buying a piece of history."

"We'll start the bidding at fifteen thousand pounds."

In the end, the chairs sold for thirty-four thousand pounds and the silver coffee pot for an astonishing thirty-eight thousand pounds.

Lady Barbara was ecstatic.

I felt foolish for having had doubts about the Oakleys.

The auction was drawing to a close. Some of bidders had already claimed their purchases and left. A number of the telephone bidders had disconnected.

"Lot one hundred forty-three," Martin Ingram said, "a molded blue-and-white dragon bottle vase, Qing dynasty, eighteenth century, the property of a gentleman."

I was surprised Oakley's had placed such an important piece near the end.

"We'll start the bidding at three thousand pounds."

"That's low," I whispered to Vivian. "I should have registered for a paddle myself."

One of the runners displayed the vase, including the unmarked bottom, a sign of age.

Four bidders raised their paddles, but they were trumped by an online client who put in the winning bid of four thousand five hundred pounds.

The vase should have brought a lot more. Had Oakley's deliberately sabotaged the sale? Why would they do that?

Nigel Oakley appeared at Lady Barbara's side. "Were you pleased with the results?"

"Kate tells me we got top prices." She was positively glowing. "Congratulations, Nigel. You've certainly earned your commission."

"Does that mean we'll have the privilege of handling the lacquer plate?"

I cut in before she had an opportunity to respond. "We'll let you know very soon. In the meantime, when can Lady Barbara expect to receive the proceeds?"

"As soon as the checks clear—a day or two at the most." He addressed Lady Barbara. "I'll bring the check myself, personally."

"No rush," Lady Barbara said. "I enjoyed this afternoon more than I imagined."

"I'm sure you've attended countless auctions, Kate," Nigel said. "I hope you were pleased with the outcome today."

"Very pleased," I admitted. "Especially with the chairs. Martin did a masterful job of turning a liability into a selling point."

"That's his specialty—making spending money fun. The mark of a true salesman. And he's got an eye for quality. Smart lad. Always popular with the ladies."

"One thing surprised me—that dragon vase, near the end. Why didn't you place it earlier in the lineup, before so many bidders dropped out. It should have gone for twice the winning bid."

A cloud darkened Nigel's pleasant, open expression. "Do you think so? I'll mention it to Peter and Martin. They set the bidding schedule."

I mumbled something about auctions being unpredictable, but the bidding on the dragon vase bothered me. Why would an experienced auctioneer with an eye for quality, like Martin Ingram, handicap a sale before it even began?

* * *

By the time we'd pulled onto the A road, Lady Barbara and Vivian were already speculating on how high the bidding might go on the cinnabar plate.

The windshield wipers kept up a steady rhythm. I backed off an articulated lorry that was sending up sheets of muddy water, making it impossible to see.

"If I didn't need the money, I'd donate the plate to one of the Chinese museums," Lady Barbara said from the rear seat. "It ought to go home."

"The plate will probably return to China anyway," Vivian said over her shoulder. "Kate says wealthy Chinese businessmen are buying up things like that and donating them to the State."

"At least the money will repair the damage in the Chinese bedroom." Lady Barbara chuckled at her own joke.

"What damage?" I asked.

"There's rain pouring into the east wing." Vivian said. "Mind you, that happens every spring."

We turned right onto the B road toward Long Barston and waited as several sheep decided if life would be drier on the other side of the road.

"Such a charming man," said Lady Barbara. "So clever."

"Isn't he just," agreed Vivian, yanking on her seat belt to loosen it. "A dreamboat."

"Dreamboat?" Lady Barbara leaned forward. "I'd hardly call him that."

"Then your eyesight must be worse than I thought. He made me feel quite weak in the knees."

"Honestly, Viv. I can't imagine what you mean."

I was trying not to laugh. "You're talking about Nigel, Lady Barbara, and Vivian is talking about Martin Ingram."

"I should have thought that was obvious," Vivian said huffily.

"At least we're agreed on the auction." Lady Barbara smoothed things over as usual. "If I have to keep Finchley Hall going without the National Trust, I know how to turn assets into cash."

I didn't bother to argue. First I'd talk to Ivor, then get involved if necessary. The fact that the only object to sell *under* the estimated value was a Qing dynasty vase was curious.

"Join us for a light supper, Kate?" Lady Barbara asked.

"Wish I could. I have some appointments at the shop. I'll probably grab something from the Chinese takeaway."

After dropping both ladies at the Hall, I headed for The Curiosity Cabinet.

Three of the ten clients who wanted their consignments back were scheduled to arrive between six and eight that evening. I parked in the alley and entered through the rear door, quickly disabling the alarm. Each object would be marked "reclaimed by owner" on the computerized inventory, then securely packed up.

At the front desk, I stashed my handbag under the counter and powered up the computer. Most of the consignment clients hadn't included their consignment number in their communication, so I'd have to find them by name. Unfortunately, Ivor's listing was by date rather than alphabetical. My biggest problem would be finding the objects in the shop. Ivor knew the location of each item by heart, down to the tiniest ushabti, the turquoise faience funerary figures tucked within the folds of an Egyptian mummy's linen wrappings. I would have to search.

No time for shrimp rolls and stir-fried pork. I gathered packing materials and began.

An hour later, I'd found exactly one of the items, a soft-paste figure of a cockerel from the French porcelain maker Saint-Cloud. Fortunately that owner was the first to arrive. She accepted the parcel I'd made up and left without even a thank-you.

Having failed to locate the other two items, and feeling more tired and hungry than I liked to admit, I phoned the two remaining clients and asked them to allow me another day.

A meal at the Hall was sounding heavenly.

The wind had picked up, and the sky had darkened alarmingly. Another squall was on the way. Unsettling news, as the river was already at flood level. The shop would be fine—at least I hoped so. We were near the high point of the road sloping from St. Æthelric's Church down to the river. The Suffolk Rose Tea Room, overlooking the river, had already erected a flood fence around its foundations.

I was about to phone Lady Barbara and ask if it was too late to join them, when I heard knock at the rear door. *Please—not another dissatisfied client.*

It was Henry Liu. Rain had plastered his dark hair across his forehead. He held a damp cardboard box, covered with a pink bath towel. He was crying.

"Mr. Liu, what's wrong? Do you need help?"

He stepped into the shop, glancing behind him as if he were being followed. Without a word, he placed the box on the floor and removed the towel.

I gasped. Inside was the húnpíng jar.

"It was James," he said miserably. "My son is a thief."

# Chapter Thirty-Seven

Henry Liu looked blankly at me when I told him I was calling the police.

While we waited for Tom and DS Cliffe to arrive, I sat him in one of the campaign chairs and made him a cup of strong tea.

He didn't touch his tea. He didn't try to leave. We didn't talk.

For once, I restrained my curiosity. The police needed to hear his story, fresh from his own lips. Restraining my emotions was more difficult. On the one hand, Henry Liu had risked a lot to return the jar, saving Ivor from the potential loss of his life savings. That was huge. On the other hand, he'd concealed his son's actions, damaging Ivor's professional reputation, not to speak of the fact that he'd helped cover up a brutal murder.

My mother's admonition about jumping to conclusions—or jumping to the wrong ones—came to mind. Okay. I'd listen first. I owed him that much. He'd taken a risk, coming to me. Whatever his story, the húnpíng was back, safe and sound.

Lucy needed to know. I moved out of earshot. Since she didn't seem to be responding to texts, I left her a voicemail. "Amazing news, Lucy. Call me the minute you get this—even if it's late." I was really starting to worry. Where was she, and why wasn't she answering my calls and messages?

Forty minutes later, Tom and DS Cliffe arrived, Tom in his silver Volvo, the sergeant in a panda car. I dragged two Chinese Chippendale side chairs over, and together we filled the cramped space between the glassed-in display units.

"Does your wife know where you are?" Tom asked. "Do you need to phone her?"

"She knows." Henry bowed his head. "Our son has brought shame on our family."

*Family shame*? Was that all he was worried about? I pictured Evelyn Villiers, clutching her belly, the spreading red stain, the blood dripping through her fingers.

I found a box of tissues and handed it to Henry.

"We'll have to go over the events of that night again, step by step." Tom said.

Henry pulled out a tissue and swabbed his eyes.

"Start at the beginning," Tom said. "What time did you set up at the fair?"

Henry took a breath, visibly calming himself. "Mid-afternoon. James and Penny helped. My wife was at the restaurant, preparing the ingredients we would need. It's a big job. I bicycled over for the first batch of rolls and pork ribs, and at five we began serving customers."

"Where were you at eight fifteen?"

"Still at the tent. Customers were beginning to queue up because I was the only one cooking. The ribs aren't a problem. We wrap them in foil and keep them hot in the steamer. But the shrimp rolls must be made fresh. My wife assembles them at the restaurant, and we deep fry them just before serving. There's only a thirty-minute window—otherwise the rolls will be dry. We were doing fine until James left."

"What time was that?"

"Just before eight. He and Penny had a row. He left the tent."

"Where did he go?"

"He didn't say."

"So you and Penny were alone in the tent. What happened then?"

"She was taking orders. The shrimp rolls were running low. That was a problem because my wife doesn't drive. One of us would have to leave the tent. Penny suggested she text James and ask him to pick up the rolls. She did, and he agreed. I phoned my wife and told her to begin assembling another batch, but by eight forty-five, James still hadn't arrived, so I told Penny I'd have to go myself, even if it meant leaving her alone. I'd parked my bicycle behind the tent, but when I went to find it, it wasn't there. I realized James must have taken it, so I set out on foot. I hadn't gotten far when he phoned me. He was distraught."

"What did he say?"

"I couldn't understand him at first. He was in shock, really shaken up. He told me about seeing the back door of Ivor's shop open."

"And the húnpíng jar?"

Henry looked up, clearly in agony. "James didn't tell me he'd taken the jar. Two days ago my wife found it hidden in his bedroom. We confronted him, told him he had to return it to Mr. Tweedy. He refused, demanded it back. We couldn't do that." Henry put the heels of his hands on either side of his forehead. "I've been wracking my brain ever since, trying to decide what to do."

"Is that why you were poking around in the alley yesterday?" I asked.

He nodded. "I considered leaving the jar in the rubbish bin, but the risk was too great. You might not find it before the collectors came. I realized I had to return it myself."

"Where are James and Penny now?" Tom and DS Cliffe exchanged a look.

Henry sighed. "They arrived in Beijing two hours ago. He left me a voicemail as they were boarding the plane, telling me they'd left the van in the Heathrow parking lot." His eyes filled. "You'll never see them again. Neither will we."

"What color is your van?" I asked, wondering if James had been the driver of the dark van at Hapthorn.

"White." He looked puzzled.

"Back to the night of the May Fair," Tom said. "When we arrived, you had blood on your hands and your shoes. You told us you went inside to see if someone needed help."

"That wasn't true. James was the one who went inside. We exchanged clothes and shoes. We wear the same size."

"And you never saw Mrs. Villiers?"

He shook his head. "I knew something terrible had happened. There was so much blood."

*But there were three sets of footprints. Who was the third person?*

"I understand you were protecting your son," Tom said, "but weren't you afraid you'd be arrested?"

"I am a British citizen, a local businessman with no criminal record and a reputation for honesty. We knew you were more likely to believe me than him. That's why I agreed to switch clothes."

"And then you phoned the local police and pretended you'd been passing by and noticed the open shop door. Where was James?"

"He went to the flat. Took a shower and changed clothes. Then he circled around through the High Street to join the crowd that had gathered."

"What was his plan?"

"To return the jar to China, of course. In Han culture, a húnpíng is a sacred object. We have a duty to our ancestors, Inspector. James has dedicated his life to that duty, finding and returning the precious cultural objects stolen from us. Ironically, in fulfilling that duty, he brought shame on his parents."

"Your son is a member of the White Lotus Society," I said.

Henry's eyes swung to me. "How do you know that?"

"They've committed thefts all over the world. The international police are involved."

Henry pulled himself up. "I sympathize with their cause, even if I cannot agree with their tactics."

Tom asked, "How long has James been involved with the Society?"

"His resentment against the English began when we sent him to the international school in Hong Kong. The same one I attended. We wanted him to speak English without an accent. We thought it would help him in his future career, but he was never happy there. They favored the British students. James was slated to attend university in England. Instead he chose Beijing. After earning his graduate degree, he took a position as an assistant professor of history at Hong Kong University. Someone from the White Lotus Society approached him and convinced him that reclaiming our stolen heritage is a restoration of justice."

"And does the restoration of justice include murder?" Tom asked.

"Certainly not."

"Come now, Mr. Liu. How did Mrs. Villiers manage to get away from your son?"

"Wait a minute." Henry Liu shot out of his chair. "My son isn't a murderer. He saw the open door, the blood, the húnpíng. He didn't stab that woman."

"Someone else was there?"

"Obviously, but James never saw him. When he got there, the door was open. No one was inside."

"Are you saying the killer left without the húnpíng?" Tom asked. "Why would he do that?"

"Yes. It is strange." Henry sat down again. "James and I talked about that. The woman must have gotten away somehow and ran for help. If her killer gave chase, he must have realized it was too risky. He'd have been covered in blood. We figured that's when James arrived on his bicycle. He saw the open door and the blood. He went inside, and there was the húnpíng—just sitting on the floor. He took it. It wasn't planned, Inspector."

"On the floor? Kate, I thought you said you hid it."

"Obviously not well enough." I turned to Henry. "If the theft wasn't planned, where did James get the white petal?"

"White petal?" Henry looked confused for a moment, which surprised me. I'd expected him to flinch.

"Someone left a white petal on the stockroom floor," Tom said.

Henry put a hand to his forehead. "The flowers. That night Penny told James she was expecting a child. She wanted to return to China. They'd been having arguments. She wasn't happy here, working under my wife's thumb. James was upset. He stormed out of the tent, said he had to think. By the time Penny called about the shrimp rolls, he'd calmed down. He'd been walking near Blackwater Lake. He wanted to bring her flowers as an apology, so he took off his shoes, waded in, and gathered a bouquet of water lilies. He was still holding them when I got there." We must have looked scandalized because his mouth hardened. "I realize it's against the law."

The legality of picking wild flowers was the last thing on our minds. Tom and I sat there, stunned. We'd all taken it for granted that the theft and the murder were committed by the same person—one of those false assumptions my mother had talked about.

I felt cold. If the theft and the murder were committed by two separate people, that meant the murderer was still out there. And Lucy wasn't answering my messages.

Tom rubbed the bridge of his nose.

"And neither you nor your son thought this information was important enough to mention to the police?" His tone was clipped. "You've been wasting police time, Mr. Liu—and possibly allowing a murderer to go free."

"I'm sorry."

"Did James see *anything* that might be helpful?"

"He saw a van. Black, he thought, with a white logo on the side."

Tom closed his eyes and rapped the table. He was clearly struggling.

"What will happen to me?" Henry Liu asked.

"That's up to the prosecutor. Go home, get some sleep. Tomorrow DS Cliffe will arrange for you to be driven to the police station in Bury. There will have to be a formal interview."

Henry left with DS Cliffe.

Tom began pacing.

"What do you think?" I asked him. "Was it Patrick, the Australian nephew, in a rented van?"

"Reasonable," he said. "Except the elusive Patrick Allen happens to have an alibi for the time of the murder."

"An alibi?"

"He was in police custody that whole weekend."

"*What?*"

"Drunk and disorderly. The local police let him go with a warning."

"When did you find that out?"

"This morning. We're trying to locate the lad now. He couldn't have killed his aunt, but he may know who did."

"Tom." I took a step toward him. "Lucy isn't returning my messages, any of them."

"Well, keep trying." Tom let out a defeated breath. "Eacles is going to love this."

I pictured Eacles' piggy eyes and his meaty slab of a face. "I promised him I'd have the inventory report on his desk by Thursday. I'm going to have to return to Hapthorn tomorrow."

"Fine. I'll have PC Weldon get in contact." He shut his eyes and ran a finger along one eyebrow.

His face was so familiar to me—the tiny scar on his cheek, the long bridge of his nose, the high cheekbones and the line of his mouth. Now there were bruise-like shadows under his eyes, and the lines on his forehead and around his mouth had deepened.

I forced myself to blink. "You'll find him, Tom. You will."

I held out my arms, and he reached for me, pulling me close.

He rested his cheek against my hair. "We're missing something."

I'd said the very same thing, but was it true?

*Were* we missing something—or was there something else we thought we knew that wasn't so?

# Chapter Thirty-Eight

Wednesday, May 22

PC Anne Weldon picked me up in her Vauxhall Astra. "The rain just won't give over," she said. "The weather presenter said there's a bubble of low pressure stuck right over Suffolk."

The rain wasn't my biggest worry. I'd tried Lucy three more times that morning. Still no answer. Had I made her angry in some way? Hurt her feelings?

The roads on the way to Little Gosling were wet but passable—until we reached the final leg of the trip. It seemed Hollow Lane had more rain-filled potholes than road surface, and Anne struggled to maneuver her small car around the rough patches. If a tire went in, we'd never get the car out on our own.

"We've had 15 centimeters of rain in the last twenty-four hours," Anne said, "The river's already two meters above flood stage, and a surge is expected tonight. The authorities are warning those in low-lying areas to turn off gas and electricity, and move their families, pets, and valuables to higher ground."

I thought of the gorgeous day I'd met Evelyn Villiers. Everything had seemed so idyllic then.

"Ready?" she asked when we finally parked outside Hapthorn Lodge.

We opened our umbrellas and ran for the side entrance. I was grateful I'd bought my wellies. At least my feet were dry.

When she unlocked the house, the stench of mildew hit us like a wall of water.

*"Ew."* I waved my hand in front of my nose. "That smell is getting worse. I'm sure breathing it isn't healthy. If Lucy wants to sell Hapthorn, she's going to have to do something about it soon."

"Apparently there's mold growing everywhere in the cellar," Anne said. "And the rear wall—toward the river—has huge damp patches eating away the mortar. Rats have moved in."

I shuddered. *And probably spiders. I hate spiders.* "At least we won't be here long."

Anne had promised to pick up her baby, Maddie, from the childminder before two, and I needed to get to the hospital to see Ivor.

"Look at the river now," she said, beckoning me to the window.

At least half the back garden was underwater, and the river had yet to crest.

I got to work. All the antiques and artwork listed on Wallace Villiers's inventory had been accounted for except the seven items I'd already determined were missing. All but one were Meissen figurines, a fact I'd noted in my report to DCI Eacles, but without drawing conclusions. Even if my mother found more matches in the online auction sites, the police would have to do interviews, check records, and possibly get international search warrants to delve into the computer data.

All I had left to do now was make sure there was nothing in the cellar. Going down there was the last thing I wanted to do, but it had to be done. Then I'd take some final photographs, embed them in my spreadsheet, and save everything on a memory stick. Copies would go to DCI Eacles and the solicitor, Simon Crewe. Then I'd start on the valuations for probate.

"I'm going to toss out the food in the fridge," Anne called from the kitchen, where she'd made a pot of tea—sugar, no milk. "Then I'll have a look downstairs. I'll let you know if I find anything."

"Bless you," I called back, rejoicing in my escape from rats and spiders. Anyway, given the mildew problem, it seemed highly unlikely that Evelyn Villiers had stored anything of value in the cellar.

I'd just set up two of the final objects to be photographed—a pair of Paris porcelain biscuit vases—when Anne appeared in the archway. "Kate." She had a funny look on her face. "I think you'd better come see this."

*Crap.*

Anne went first down the set of narrow, open stairs into the cellar, a low-ceilinged space under the rear portion of the house. I brushed a web away from my face.

"There's a switch and some bare bulbs, but I don't dare turn on the electricity." Anne held a torch, the beam widened out to give maximum coverage. "We'll have to make do with this."

The smell was overpowering. "We're taking years off our lives," I said. "We should be wearing gas masks." The cement floor was slick with wet mold. *Ick.*

We moved slowly, holding onto each other and trying not to bump our heads on the maze of scabbed ironwork pipes suspended from the ceiling. An old, unused brick boiler stood next to a modern steel version.

Anne shone her torch ahead of us. An abandoned coal bin held the remains of a wine rack, the wood swollen and furred with fungus.

The unmistakable sound of dripping water echoed in the enclosed space, making me think of wells—one of my childhood fears. I tightened my grip on her arm.

"Just over here," she said.

The rear wall of the cellar had bowed inward, swollen by the damp. The cellar and the foundation of the house had been constructed of lime-mortared rubble. Here, below ground level, the stones were pocked with damp, sickly patches of black mold.

Something small and dark darted past us into the shadows.

Anne squealed. *"A rat."*

I screamed, imagining a furry horde, waiting to attack.

Laughing to cover our nerves, we held onto each other. Anne aimed her light toward the rear corner of the cellar, where the back wall met the side wall to our left. A jumble of cardboard boxes had collapsed under their own weight, melding together in a pulpy pile.

"It's the photo albums," Anne said. "Look."

I peered in. Sure enough, the boxes—or what was left of them—held photograph albums, stacks of them, their fabric covers thickly mildewed and encased in cracked and clouded plastic.

"Why would Mrs. Villiers store photograph albums down here?" Anne asked.

"No idea. Let's see if any of the photos have survived. This album on top is probably our best bet." I pulled on the box to reach it.

The soggy cardboard came away in my hand, releasing hundreds of tiny pale brown spiders that scattered in every direction, across the floor and over our shoes.

I screamed again, stamping my feet to get them off me. *"Ew, ew, ew."* My skin was crawling. "Let's get out of here."

"Right behind you." I felt her hands on my back.

But Anne had managed to grab the photo album.

* * *

We laid the soggy album on the kitchen table.

Anne opened it cautiously. I took a step back, half expecting another swarm of baby spiders to jump at me.

"The photos are ruined," she said. And they were—sticking to the mounting paper and to each other. The coated paper had turned pulpy, the images dissolved like wet glue.

"The albums underneath will be even worse." I pried another page loose and turned it.

"Did you notice the cover? It said *1994*." Anne was running a dish cloth under the water in the sink. She brought it over so I could clean my hands.

"Give me a minute," I said, turning another page. "I want to see if any of the images are still visible. In 1994, Lucy would have been eight or nine. She should have some record of her childhood." I turned pages, finding more of the same.

Not one of the photos had survived.

I spread my hands. "This is Lucy's family history, her past—erased, dissolved, destroyed. Why would her mother do that? I don't get it."

"What a shame," Anne said. "At least you tried."

I'd reached the final page of the album.

"Wait a minute—look at this." Attached to the back cover of the album was an opaque plastic pocket sleeve.

"That's where you store photos until you have a chance to organize them," Anne said.

I unwound a heavy string from the two metal discs and folded back the flap.

"There's something here." I drew out a five-by-seven family portrait, the image spotted with mold but still visible. A family of three. "That's Wallace Villiers. I recognize the square jaw and head of thick hair. And there's Lucy." The little girl clung to her father's hand and seemed to melt into the arm of his tweed jacket. Her thin face and small dark eyes were unmistakable. I looked closer. "But who's the woman?"

"Evelyn Villiers."

"No it isn't." I looked up. "That isn't the woman I met."

Anne examined the photo. "Are you sure—the photo was taken, what—twenty-five years ago? People change."

"Not their eye color, they don't. Look—this woman has dark eyes like Lucy. The woman I met definitely had pale eyes—blue or gray."

Anne whipped out her phone. "I'm calling the station."

"And I'll call Lucy. She was there."

I dialed Lucy's cell phone. Still no answer. A feeling of dread closed around my heart.

Anne had someone on the line—I didn't know who. She held the phone against her shoulder. "When was the last time you actually spoke to Lucy in person?"

"Sunday night. I've left messages and texts, but I can't be sure she got them."

While Anne relayed this information, I phoned Tom. He didn't answer either, so I punched out a text.

*The dead woman wasn't Evelyn Villiers. Lucy isn't answering her phone. Meet me at the Premier Inn ASAP.*

# Chapter Thirty-Nine

PC Anne Weldon's panda car flew over the wet Suffolk roads. She even knew a few shortcuts, skirting sections where the road was awash. Everywhere, the rainwater was moving—flowing, streaming, rushing to find its level.

"Hang on," she said, swerving to avoid a section where the road surface had fallen away. "Are you sure it's all right if I drop you at the inn? I'm expected at the childminder in less than forty minutes."

"No problem. If Tom's hung up for some reason, I'll call Vivian." I realized instantly that wasn't going to happen. No way would I ask Vivian to drive in this storm.

We entered Long Barston from the northwest, turning south at the green. Tea-colored water sluiced down the High Street toward the swollen river. I hoped the flood fence at The Suffolk Rose was working.

"Is it safe to drive?" I asked, picturing TV shots of cars swept away by rising waters.

"It's not deep enough here to cause a problem," she said. "The water's heading for the river. We're turning off before the bridge."

"Anne—look." A crowd had gathered around The Finchley Arms. Some were watching. Others were relaying buckets, hand to hand, from inside the pub toward the street.

"The cellar must be flooding," Anne said.

A truck pulling some kind of motorized pump had arrived. Gavin Collier from The Three Magpies was helping the driver uncoil a heavy plastic hose.

We turned off toward Sudbury. Rain streamed down the windscreen. Even with the wipers on the fastest speed, Anne had to lean forward to see the road.

"When we get there, take my umbrella," she said. "It's on the floor of the back seat."

"No—you'll need it for Maddie. I have a hood, and Tom will have an umbrella.

The road was clear, but the fields on either side were swamped.

"It's a good job you checked the whole album," Anne said. "I was ready to throw it in the bin with the spoiled food."

"How am I going to break the news to Lucy? How do you tell someone the woman claiming to be her mother was someone else?"

"I understand about the eye color," Anne said. "The real Evelyn Villiers had dark eyes. The woman in the shop had light. But didn't the housekeeper, Mrs. Wright, identify the body as Mrs. Villiers?"

"Yes, but she'd only worked at Hapthorn Lodge for a short time. No one we've talked to actually knew the real Mrs. Villiers from eighteen years ago. Not even her solicitor."

"Except Ertha Green," Anne said.

"True. Ertha could tell us the woman in the photo is Evelyn Villiers—we know that already. Too bad I didn't snap a photo of the imposter when I had the chance."

"And now the body has been cremated."

"Do undertakers take photographs before cremation?"

"I don't know." Anne slowed down to take a curve. "Do you think Lucy will know who pretended to be her mother?"

"I hope so, but I think she's going to be more interested in what happened to her mother."

The photograph, encased in a plastic baggie, was in my handbag.

My cell phone rang. Tom—*thank goodness.*

"I just arrived at the Premier Inn. What's all this about?"

"I'll tell you when I get there." I looked at Anne, who flashed five fingers twice.

"Be there in ten minutes. Try to find Lucy. See you soon."

I'd forgotten about Ivor. Feeling guilty, I called the hospital and was told they'd made arrangements to transfer him back to The Willows on Thursday. "He can have his old room back then," said the nurse, "and it gives us another day to make sure he's stable. He's asking for you, dear."

"Tell him I have news about the húnpíng jar."

"The *hunting* jar?"

"Hún-*píng*. He'll know what that means. And tell him I'll be there as soon as I can."

I'd no sooner hung up than my phone rang again. This time it was my mother.

"Mom, you'll never believe what we—"

"*Kate*, just listen." Something in the tone of her voice made me sit up. She never interrupted. "It's James." I heard her breath catch.

"What is it? What's happened?"

"He's had a heart attack. He was just admitted to the hospital in Minocqua."

"Oh no—Mom, I'm *so sorry*. How is he?"

"We don't know yet. It's bad." Her breath was coming fast. They said at his age—" She didn't finish the sentence. I heard a sob. "What am I going to do? I can't lose him now, Kate. I just can't."

* * *

Tom was waiting for me in the lobby of the Premier Inn.

"Lucy's not in her room, and she isn't answering her mobile. The desk clerk hasn't seen her—which doesn't tell us much because she would normally use the side entrance to come and go. It's nearer the elevator." He reached out to unzip my jacket. "Take this wet thing off. What do you mean the dead woman wasn't Evelyn Villiers?"

"I have something to show you," I said. "Can we find a place to sit?"

We found chairs near a Costa Coffee kiosk.

I handed him the photo. "The Villiers family, taken in 1994. Lucy was eight or nine. That's her father," I pointed out the tall, well-built man in the tweed sports jacket. "And her mother. Notice anything strange?"

Tom peered at the photograph. "It's not a clear image."

"We're lucky to have an image at all." I told him about the pile of photo albums in the cellar. "I tapped my fingernail on the face of Evelyn Villiers. "Take another look and tell me what you see."

"A thin woman, mid-thirties, with dark hair."

"What color eyes?"

"I don't know—dark, anyway. Quite dark."

"Exactly. And the woman who came into Ivor's shop with the húnpíng jar—the one who said her name was Evelyn Villiers—had light eyes. Very light." I sat back and watched him take this in.

"So who was she?"

"I don't know."

"Where is the real Evelyn Villiers?"

"I don't know that either. That's why we have to talk to Lucy. I'm afraid for her, Tom. I think we should check her room."

The desk clerk was a young man with limp sandy hair and gold-rimmed eyeglasses. When we informed him we wanted a key for one of the guest rooms, he frowned theatrically. "I can't allow that. Miss Wardle is a registered guest. She has a right to privacy."

"Her real name is Lucy Villiers." Tom flashed his warrant card. "We can get a court order, but we may not have time for that."

"What's she done?" the desk clerk demanded.

"Nothing as far as we know," Tom said. "It's important we talk to her—or find out where she is."

The desk clerk insisted on escorting us to Lucy's third-floor single. He opened the door with a passkey and stood aside as we entered the small room.

The curtains were drawn. The bed was made and the room tidied. Lucy's clothes—she hadn't brought much in her backpack and carryall—were hung neatly in the closet. In the bathroom, a red fabric toiletries kit had been stashed in the corner.

"When was the room cleaned?" Tom asked.

"We do changeovers first, so sometime between noon and"—he checked his watch—"now."

"Did she sleep here last night?" I asked.

"Let me check." He unclipped a wireless intercom from his belt and punched in a few numbers. "Was the small single on the third floor, east wing, used last night?" He waited a minute or so. "Say that again, please." He switched the intercom to speaker.

The voice sounded a long way off. "That's Aisha's floor," said a female voice. "She says the room hadn't been slept in, so she gave it a quick once-over. Is everything all right, luv?"

"Fine. Thank you." The desk clerk clipped the intercom back on his belt.

"She's got her mobile with her," Tom said.

"How do you know?" I asked.

He pointed at the charger cord, plugged into the lamp.

"Is her car still in the parking lot?" Tom asked the desk clerk.

"I'll have someone check."

Back in the lobby, the desk clerk consulted his records, found Lucy's vehicle registration number, and used the intercom to alert security. The answer came quickly. Lucy's car, an older model Ford Fiesta, was parked near the side entrance.

Tom and I looked at each other.

"What do you think?" he said.

"If Lucy decided to spend the night somewhere, I think she would have called me," I said, feeling increasingly uneasy. "More to the point, she wouldn't have taken off without her toiletry bag."

"When was the last time you actually spoke to her?"

"Sunday night—just before I called you. She had an appointment Monday with Simon Crewe. I texted her to ask how it went. I never heard back, so I called her room. No answer. That night I left a message. I've been leaving them ever since." My stomach tightened. "Tom, I should have said something last night."

"You weren't to know," he said. "Look, I'll contact the solicitor. He may know something." He turned to the desk clerk. "We'll need your CCTV footage. Both entrances and the parking lot from Monday morning until now. Your cameras are working, I assume."

"Oh yes. We're very careful about security. It'll take time to go through all the footage."

"Don't bother." He handed the man his card. "I'll send someone."

Tom called DS Cliffe on the way to his car.

"Cliffe says they've gotten a lead on the Australian nephew." Tom fastened his seat belt. "He rented a van. They believe he's been sleeping in it."

"A van with white lettering?"

"No. I think there were two vans, both dark. One with white lettering."

We pulled out of the parking area and headed for Long Barston.

"That photograph," Tom said as he turned left onto the main road. "Can you tell where it was taken?"

I pulled it out of my handbag and examined it through the plastic baggie. "They're standing in front of a church. Wait a minute—there's a sign. No, I can't read it." I fished for my lighted magnifier. "Pull over. I'm getting carsick."

Tom pulled into a turnout and parked.

I laid the photo on the middle console and held the lighted magnifier directly over it. "No, it's no good. I can't make it out. You try." I handed the lighted magnifier to him.

"There's mildew right where the name of the church should be." He turned the photo so we could both see it. "It looks like some kind of a celebration—a wedding, maybe."

"Not a wedding. Mr. Villiers wouldn't have been wearing tweeds."

"A celebration then. Look—you can see a string of flags and other people in the background. Maybe we can identify the church."

"The church could be anywhere."

"It's not the church in Little Gosling, and it's not the one in Long Barston."

"Thank you for that." I gave him a wry smile. "That's two out of how many in rural England?"

"Laugh if you want." He took another look. "Hold on—look at the edge of the photo. What do you think that is?"

I moved the magnifier. "Part of the church building. A tower."

"Exactly. But look at the shadow—just there. The tower's round. That's unusual. There's a society dedicated to English churches with round towers. Most are thirteenth century, and the majority are in East Anglia."

"Tom—the church in Dunmow Parva has a round tower. I remember thinking it looked like a castle. That's where Wallace and his sisters grew up. It's just blocks from the house where Winnifred Villiers lived. Where better to attend a celebration than your hometown?"

"We need Lucy."

"I think I know someone else who can help."

# Chapter Forty

On the way to Dunmow Parva, I convinced Tom that Sheila Parker was more likely to be candid if I saw her alone. "She doesn't trust policemen, but she's a kind soul and a bit of a gossip."

"An ideal witness, then." Tom flicked me a smile.

Flooding on the roads and a few necessary detours added fifteen minutes to a trip that should have taken no longer than half an hour. It was four o'clock when we pulled up to the Church of the Blessed Virgin.

I held out the photograph. "That's the church, all right. No question."

In the churchyard beyond us, a clutch of black umbrellas bobbed around an open grave.

We found the exact spot where the photograph had been taken—the yew-lined walk leading to the church entrance. The pollarded trees had filled out since the day the Villiers family had posed for the photographer.

I slipped the photograph back into the plastic sleeve. "Lark Court is just around the corner. Park at the end of the street."

"Here, take this." Tom reached in the back for his umbrella and handed it to me.

I dashed across the street, trying to avoid the puddles, but my shoes were soaked by the time I reached Sheila Parker's door. She answered on the first knock.

"Didn't expect to see you again so soon, luv. Come in out of the deluge." Sheila wore a long brocade caftan with a gold chain around her neck and bangles at her wrists. "Good timing 'n' all. Neighbor from down the street just left. Lost his wife last year, poor man. He likes a bit of company. Would you care for some rhubarb crumble? From my own garden."

"Sounds heavenly, but I'm in a bit of a rush today—trying to place a photograph taken some years ago." I removed the photo from the plastic baggie. "I'm hoping you might recognize the people."

Sheila put on her glasses. "I recognize the photo, of course. Oh my—Wallace Villiers was a good-looking man, wasn't he? And little Lucy. I suppose that's her mother, poor thing."

"Lucy's the reason I'm here. We don't know where she is."

"Scarpered again?"

"Not this time. We think she may be in trouble. Was this a village fête?"

"Nine hundredth anniversary celebration—July of 1994. Grand day. I remember it well."

"Do you recognize any of the other people?"

She shook her head. "You can't see them properly, can you? I have some photos of my own. Would that help?"

Sheila trotted off and returned moments later with a photograph album.

She turned to the first page. "That's my Len—there." The young Lenny Parker had been a good-looking young man with a suave, super-gelled haircut and an impressive tattoo on his left forearm. She flipped pages. "Here we go—June of ninety-four." She handed me the album.

The photos were the usual kind—meant to record an event, with no attempt at artistry. Lenny must have been the photographer because most shots were of a young woman with bright red hair and freckles. "How old were you?" I asked her.

"Twenty. Bun in the oven. Len bought me a candy floss, and I was sick all over his shoes." She sighed dreamily.

"Do you have a photo of Winnie?"

"Didn't know her then, did I?" She took the album. "My, I haven't looked at these in donkey's years." She studied the photos. "Wait a tic—that's Winnie, right there. And Wallace beside her."

Winnifred and Evelyn Villiers stood under a blue-and-white-striped awning. Evelyn was bending over a table, studying a row of necklaces. Winnie stood next to her sister-in-law, looking bored. Wallace was a step or two behind them. He was glancing over his left shoulder at a young woman and a boy.

"Who's that woman, the one Wallace is looking at?"

Sheila peered closer. "Oh my. That's Emily Wardle—the one I told you about, remember? Colin's mother."

Even in a snapshot, Emily Wardle's beauty was striking. She was so slim a stiff breeze might have toppled her. Her hair was glossy black, her eyes light—gray or silver-blue. There was something familiar about her—the shape of her face, the way she held her head and shoulders.

"Do you mind?" I held my lighted magnifier over the image.

Around the woman's neck was a heart-shaped locket.

I stopped breathing. The face I saw was Evelyn Villiers—*my* Evelyn Villiers, the woman who came into Ivor's shop to sell the húnpíng.

"—always said her looks would get her in trouble." Sheila was still speaking. "Claimed her husband was killed in the Falklands, but why didn't she take his name, I ask you?"

"Is that Colin she's holding onto?"

"Got his mum's looks, all right. Dark hair—and oh, those eyes. Like fairy pools, they were. You could almost fall in—and many did, more's the pity."

I trained the lens on the child. He looked to be around eleven or twelve, half twisting away from his mother.

Oh, there was no mistaking those blue eyes.

"Could I borrow the photograph?" I asked. "I'll return it as soon as I have a copy made."

"Sure, but"—Sheila frowned—"what do you want with an old photograph?"

"It might help us find Lucy."

* * *

Tucking the photo inside my jacket, I flew out of Sheila's house, neglecting to raise the umbrella. By the time I got to the car, I was soaked—and seriously out of breath. "Tom—" I tossed the umbrella in the back and shoved Sheila's photograph at him. "Look at the woman holding the boy's hand." I made an effort to slow my breathing. "That's Emily Wardle and her son, Colin."

"Okay, but—"

"Except they're not. I mean, they *are*, but—" I stabbed at the photo, catching my breath. "That's the woman who told me her name was Evelyn Villiers. And Colin is now calling himself Martin Ingram, the antiques expert who works with Nigel and Peter Oakley at the Barn."

Tom turned in his seat to face me. His eyes hardened. "You're saying Colin Wardle installed his mother at Hapthorn as Evelyn Villiers. What happened to the real Evelyn Villiers?"

"Exactly."

The look on Tom's face could have stripped paint. "Bloody hell."

"Oh, Tom—I should have picked up on it when Lucy told me she'd inherited her mother's coloring—dark hair, dark eyes."

"No wonder Emily Wardle pretended to be a recluse all those years," he said. "No wonder she fired Ertha and hired housekeepers new to the village."

"I had all the evidence—I just didn't make the connections. The real Evelyn Villiers wasn't religious; the fake one had a New Testament by her bed. The real Evelyn Villiers didn't like living so close to the river; the fake one loved the river." I clicked my seat belt. "I was looking for a connection between Emily Wardle and Evelyn Villiers based on the assumption they were two separate people. All the time, they were the same person."

Tom turned the key and started the engine. "I'm betting she left Hapthorn whenever she wanted to—just not as Evelyn Villiers."

"She couldn't allow anyone who'd known the real Evelyn Villiers to see her or hear her voice—including her solicitor—so she communicated by text. Oh!" A new thought occurred to me. "The letters she left for Lucy and Ertha Green were typed. That seemed so cold, Tom, but they of all people would have recognized her handwriting."

His mobile rang.

"Mallory." He listened, then rang off.

"That was Cliffe. The CCTV footage shows Lucy getting into a dark blue van with white printing on the side—Oakley's Barn."

I opened my mouth, but nothing came out.

Tom slammed the gearshift forward. "Now all we have to figure out is whether Lucy Villiers is a victim or an accomplice."

# Chapter Forty-One

The tithe barn was locked up tight. A sign on the door announced that auctions were held every two weeks on Mondays and Tuesdays. Enquiries should be directed to either Peter Oakley or Martin Ingram. I jotted down the contact information.

We found Nigel and Peter Oakley in the warehouse.

"Mrs. Hamilton, how lovely to see you." Nigel wiped his hands on his jeans and came to meet us. His friendly, open face was pink from exertion. "We received a new consignment. Checking things in, cleaning them up."

Peter was rubbing down a rosewood Pembroke table. He glanced up briefly and went back to his work. He wasn't in one of his ebullient moods.

"Nigel, this is Tom Mallory."

"Pleasure to meet you at last." Nigel held out his hand. "Shall I call you Inspector?"

"Tom is fine. Is Martin Ingram here today?"

"I'm afraid not." Nigel turned toward his son. "Where's Martin today?"

Peter straightened up. "In-house appraisals."

Nigel frowned. "What's this all about? Is there a problem?"

"We need to get in touch," Tom said. "Did he take one of the Oakley vehicles?"

"I believe he did." Nigel looked at his son again. "But I'm not sure—"

Peter threw down his rag. "Why all the questions? Martin meets potential clients in their homes by appointment, all right? He looks over what they have to sell, and if it fits our stock, he puts the item in the back of the van and goes on to the next location." He hooked his thumbs in his belt loops as if daring us to question him further.

*Why is he so belligerent?*

Tom asked, "Do you have a list of the clients he was planning to visit today?"

"We don't keep track." Peter's lip curled. "Martin leaves. He comes back with antiques to sell."

"That's right." Nigel laughed. "We call him the Scarlett Pimpernel. We never know what he's up to until—" He closed his mouth, the seriousness of Tom's expression sinking in.

"When do you expect him back?" Tom asked.

"When we see him." Peter returned to his task.

The tips of Nigel's ears were turning red. "Inspector, it would help if you'd tell us what this is all about."

"A woman is missing. She was seen getting into an Oakley's van Monday evening. She hasn't been seen since."

"That doesn't sound right." The corners of Nigel's mouth turned down. "Where was this?"

"There's no mistake," Tom said, ignoring the question. "It was caught on CCTV footage."

Nigel swallowed hard. "Martin can be a bit of a lad, I'll admit, but he's no kidnapper."

"No one said anything about kidnapping," Tom said smoothly, "but we need to find her."

Nigel got out his phone and punched a few numbers.

We waited.

"He's not answering his mobile." Nigel glanced at his son. "Peter—text him. Tell him to call in immediately."

Peter scowled but did as his father asked.

"Does Martin have a computer?" Tom asked.

"He'll have his laptop with him, but all business communication is synced with our main computer in the office. I insist upon it."

"I'd like to see the computer."

"Is that necessary, Inspector?"

"I'm afraid so."

Nigel set his jaw. "In that case, you'd better come this way. Peter, you too."

Peter looked like he was about to protest but thought better of it.

Nigel led the way into a small office—not the ultrachic space in the tithe barn, but a real working office with metal desks and files. He powered up a desktop computer connected to a flat monitor and a keyboard. "Peter, what's Martin's password?"

"How would I know?" Peter looked like a schoolboy caught writing test answers on his forearm. "Anyway, Martin doesn't keep much on the computer—not the important stuff anyway."

"What?" Nigel threw up his hands. "Everything goes into the main data bank. You both know that."

"What's the 'important stuff'?" Tom asked.

"You know—where he gets the merch." Peter was starting to sweat. He wiped his face with the back of his arm. "List of clients, that kind of thing."

"And where does he keep that information?"

"Personal files." Peter licked his lips and ran a hand through his expensively layered blond hair.

"And where are they?"

"With him, I suppose. On his laptop."

Tom tapped on the keyboard and a password screen appeared.

Peter leapt forward. "Hey—you need a search warrant for that. I know our rights."

"Peter." Nigel's voice held a warning. "If you know something, you'd better say so—now, son."

Peter caught his father's eye and seemed to deflate. "Look—all I know is he was talking about a source. Someone had died, and—" He stopped and swallowed.

"And?"

"And he said he could talk his way in."

"What does that mean?"

"You know—schmooze, flirt."

"Meaning a woman."

"Suppose so."

"Any names?"

"No, man." Peter blinked and rubbed at the corner of his eye. "Martin never said."

*He's lying.*

Peter Oakley was an enigma—sometimes affable and charming like his father; other times tense and sullen. Today he looked ill, shifting his feet and picking at his cuticles.

Several ideas were forming in the back of my brain—and one of them had to do with the police drugs investigation. I put a slight pressure on Tom's arm.

He looked at me. *Go ahead.*

"How often do you ship out of this warehouse?" I asked.

"This is where we *receive* goods," Nigel said. "If there's anything to ship, we have the items packed and shipped by DHL in Ipswich. They provide insurance."

"I wondered because the first day Lady Barbara and I were here, the day you received the shipment from France, I saw several boxes being loaded onto the transport vehicle."

"Those weren't ours—were they, Peter?"

"I . . . ah, I'm not sure. I mean, it's possible Martin, ah—" Peter Oakley's sentence stumbled and fell.

Tom handed Nigel one of his cards. "If you hear from Martin, let me know."

As soon as we were out of earshot, I said, "I think Peter was talking about Lucy. We'd better get to Hapthorn Lodge."

"What was all that about packages and shipping?"

We slid into the car and shut the doors. "You said drugs are shipped in from the Continent—possibly by truck—and distributed to small-time dealers all over East Anglia. What better cover than a shipment of high-end antiques?"

"And the packages shipped back?"

"Cash payment? Antiques they can turn into cash? I don't know. It's a hunch." I clicked my seat belt.

"Based on what?"

"On the fact that starting an art and antiques auction house from scratch takes more than a lovely venue. Nigel Oakley invested a lot of money in that tithe barn—fine. He probably fronted some cash as well. But consignments are only a percentage of their business. Peter told me Martin buys whole lots from estates in France and Italy. That takes serious money, and I think I have an idea where it came from."

Tom looked at me. "The missing jewelry." He got on the phone. "Cliffe, get down to Oakley's Barn. Get a search warrant for the computer. Bring in the father and son for questioning." His mouth tightened. "Keep it friendly." He listened. "Any charge you want. Just make sure you hold them for twenty-four hours. Kate and I are headed for Hapthorn.

* * *

"So, is Lucy working with him?" Tom asked.

The flooded fields rushed by in a gray, watery blur.

"I honestly don't know. She's still in love with him, but I don't think she's been lying to me. She really had no idea where he was all those years—or why he'd abandoned her without an explanation."

"Why *would* he abandon her? If he was after her money, they could have gotten married—even without her mother's blessing. Eventually she would have inherited that big trust fund."

"Maybe that was his plan, but I think something happened the night of the inquest."

"We know Colin tried to give Evelyn Villiers a note—hoping to win her over?"

Bits and pieces of what Lucy told me were coming back. "Lucy heard her mother arguing with someone that night in the back garden. She never saw her mother alive after that."

Tom turned to look at me. "You think Evelyn Villiers is dead."

"I think she died eighteen years ago, the night of the inquest."

"Murder?"

"Or suicide. Either way, Colin Wardle saw his chance to cash in by keeping her alive in the person of a substitute—his own mother. The real questions are, why did Emily Wardle agree, and why did she have to die too?" I settled back in my seat and listened to the rhythmic *whap-whap, whap-whap* of the wipers. "A young man from a small village in Essex is given the chance of a lifetime because he reminds a wealthy investor of himself at that age. Instead of being grateful, the young man betrays the trust placed in him and steals a valuable painting. He also romances the man's naïve daughter and plans to elope with her, no doubt assuming her father will come around in the end. When they're caught and the man dies of a stroke, the young man disappears. Next thing we know, the wealthy widow is dead and the young man's mother takes her place. Why would she agree to impersonate Evelyn Villiers?"

"A chance to live in wealth?"

"But she didn't live in wealth, Tom. She lived like a nun—never used the money she had access to. She must have felt guilty about what she was doing. I think she did it to save her son—and partly out of fear. Sheila Parker said Colin Wardle bullied his mother."

Tom braked behind a farm tractor. The farmer, soaked to the skin, moved far to the left to allow us to pass. "And then one day, she decides to sell a valuable Chinese jar. Why?"

"Maybe she was tired of living like that and wanted to escape. Or maybe something happened, and she feared for her life."

"Afraid of her own son."

"That's *it*, Tom—" I grabbed his arm. "That's what Emily Wardle said when she was dying. Not Meissen—*my son*. She was telling us who killed her, except we never put it together because we assumed she was Evelyn Villiers."

The road ahead of us had been closed with barriers. A policeman in a neon-yellow rain slicker was waving a torch.

Tom turned onto a smaller road heading north. "Do you think Lucy knew about her mother?"

"You mean did she know her mother died the night of the inquest? I'm sure she didn't. She was truly heartbroken over her mother's death. She thought it had just happened."

"Why heartbroken when they'd never gotten along?"

"She must have held out hope her mother would forgive her. Wounds do the most damage when they're inflicted by someone who's supposed to love us."

The tires thumped over the uneven road surface. *Betrayal, betrayal, betrayal.*

Fields, now lakes, hemmed us in on both sides. Spills of dirty water blurred the edges of the road, forcing the car toward the center. Was the rain letting up?

We'd reached a railroad crossing. "How long until we get there?"

"Next left." Tom turned the wipers on slow. "You know we have no actual proof for any of this, don't you?"

"We need a confession."

Tom braked to avoid a massive sinkhole in the road. "Or a body."

# Chapter Forty-Two

We pulled up to the broken-down stone wall near Hapthorn.

"Stay in the car." Tom said. "This could get dicey."

"Why? Colin doesn't know we suspect him."

"Even so, I'm doing this alone."

"Tom," I put my hand over his on the steering wheel. "If Lucy's with him, you're going to have to convince her to leave Colin and come away with you. She's much more likely to agree if I'm there."

He looked at me. "All right. But at the least hint of trouble, you head for the car—promise?"

"Of course. The important thing is to get Lucy away from Colin until you can figure out what's going on."

"Agreed. We'll play it by ear—but no confrontation. Invent a plausible reason why Lucy should come with us. I'll deal with Wardle—give him just enough to put the wind up, but not enough to know we've figured it out. With any luck, he'll decide to escape while he can."

We bumped over the gravel drive. Tom parked about fifty feet from the house, and we got out. No Oakley's van—but a light emanated from somewhere toward the back of the house.

The mist was as thick as cotton wool. The sound of rushing water and a low groaning reminded me of a lake icing up in winter.

We followed the slate pavers to the side door. Tom knocked.

No one answered.

He knocked again, louder this time.

I was beginning to think we'd made the trip for nothing, when a light flipped on. Colin Wardle appeared at the door and turned the bolt.

"Stay behind me," Tom said.

"Remember to call him Martin," I whispered.

Colin opened the door. "Can I help you?"

"Martin Ingram?"

"Hello, Martin," I said, peering at him from around Tom's shoulder. "We're sorry to bother you, but I've been really worried about Lucy. Is she here?"

"Ah, yeah. I offered to drive her out here, give her a hand with the art collection."

"May I speak with her?"

Colin hesitated a fraction of a second too long. "Sure. I should tell you, Lucy's decided to sell everything. Oakley's will handle the auction."

"Lucky you," I said, moving past him into the kitchen.

A large number of objects had been gathered on the counter and the kitchen table. I smelled moldy plaster and damp wood.

Lucy was standing near the kitchen sink. "Kate—I'm so sorry. I got your messages, and I should have phoned, but we've been so busy." Her face was alight with joy. "Colin's helping me. I couldn't face it on my own." She held up a hand. "Before you say anything, I *know* he's been calling himself Martin Ingram. That's why I couldn't find him. And he's been looking for me all this time too, not knowing I was still calling myself Lacey Wardle." She laughed. "Comedy of errors, right?"

*Hilarious.* "So you found each other. How did that happen?"

"Colin heard I'd returned to England after my mother's death. He called me at the hotel."

"It was quite a shock." Colin's expression of friendly candor was starting to congeal.

Tom stood near the old-fashioned gas range, his hands in his pockets and his I'm-not-a-cop-just-an-ordinary-guy smile on his face.

I focused on Lucy. "Is everything all right? I was concerned when the hotel said you hadn't been there in two days. And you hadn't taken anything with you." *Crap.* I held my breath, hoping she wouldn't figure out we'd searched her room.

"Oh, that." Lucy looked embarrassed. "We went out for dinner, then back to Colin's flat. I hadn't planned to stop the night." She shot him a look. "It's just that we were talking, and it got late, and it was raining—" She spread her hands.

"Nothing happened," Colin cut in abruptly. "I mean we're just getting to know each other again, right, Luce? It's been eighteen years."

"Perfect gentleman. Today we decided to drive out here." Lucy reached out to touch him.

*Is it my imagination, or is he trying not to flinch?*

"So you've decided to go with Oakley's."

"No hard feelings, Kate?" She made a moue of apology. "I *so* appreciate all you've done for me. I really do. But this is going to be a new start for Colin and me."

"You've been working hard here." I tried to smile. "You must be exhausted."

"I am a bit. And I really should get cleaned up."

*Perfect.* "Of course you should. Why don't Tom and I drive you back to the hotel? That way Colin doesn't have to go out of his way. Or better yet, why don't you spend the night at Rose Cottage? I can lend you everything you need."

Lucy looked at Colin. "I don't know."

"I'll take her back to the inn," Colin snapped. His eyes were chips of ice. "We have things to talk about, don't we, Luce?"

The atmosphere was heating up. I needed to find a distraction.

"Lucy, have you checked the back garden? I was here this morning, and the river was really high."

"Oh, I know. Come look." She cleared a circle in the window condensation with her sleeve.

I peered out the window. All I could see was water.

The house groaned.

That's when I noticed the crack. It extended from the corner of the bay window to the wall. "I'm not sure the house is safe," I said. "Why don't you come home with me now, Lucy. Tomorrow we'll call a builder to have a look."

"*I'm* taking Lucy home, Kate." The steel edge in Colin's voice chilled me to the bone.

Tom cut in. "Did you hear from Peter? He said he was going to text you."

Colin shrugged. "Going to have to blow my cover, aren't I?" He took out a packet of cigarettes and lit one. "You don't mind, babe, do you?"

"No, no. I—" Lucy looked confused.

I threaded my hand through her arm. *If I could just get her to step away from that bay window.*

Colin's eyes followed me.

"Why *did* you change your name?" Tom asked.

If the question surprised him, Colin didn't show it. "Good for business. Martin Ingram's a bit more upmarket than Colin Wardle."

Tom had positioned himself between Colin and the door. "I understand your mother moved away from Little Gosling about the time Lucy's father died. Are you still in touch with her?"

Colin took a long pull on his cigarette and stubbed it out on the porcelain sink. "She and I went our separate ways."

"So she isn't living in the area?"

"No, she isn't." He blew a ribbon of smoke toward the ceiling.

"What's this about your mother, Colin?" Lucy asked.

"Nothing important." He was getting rattled.

So was I. The tension in the room was thick enough to cut with a . . . *knife*.

*Oh man.* Ertha's wide-bladed chopping knife lay on the counter.

I looked at Tom. His eyes gave nothing away, but he'd moved closer to Colin, allowing us a way of escape.

If Lucy would take it.

"You've been here before, right?" Tom asked Colin.

"No—first time."

"That's odd because the neighbors told police they'd seen an Oakley's van at the house."

That wasn't true—no one had mentioned Oakley's—but I wasn't about to contradict him.

"Hoping to handle the Villiers' estate, perhaps?" Tom smiled.

I put pressure on Lucy's arm and whispered. "This really isn't safe. Let's get out of here."

I didn't see it coming.

Colin sprang forward and ripped Lucy out of my grasp.

He held the knife at Lucy's throat.

"Nobody's going anywhere."

# Chapter Forty-Three

"Well, that's not brilliant, Colin." Tom sounded almost chummy.

"Stay back." Colin's left arm was wrapped firmly around Lucy's waist. With his right elbow, he'd pinned her shoulder against his chest.

The knife was huge—eight inches at least, with a blade that still looked sharp. I could see an indentation in Lucy's neck. She was whimpering.

All he had to do was flick his wrist, and Lucy would be gone.

Her eyes were huge. Her breath came in shallow pants.

"It's going to be okay, Lucy," I said with no justification. It's what moms say.

"Stay back," Colin growled.

I held up my hands, picturing Colin's mother staggering onto the stage at the May Fair.

"Let's all calm down, shall we?" Tom actually smiled. "Why don't you tell us what all this is about, Colin."

Colin tightened his grip on Lucy's waist, but he lowered the blade.

Lucy gulped for breath. "Why are you doing this? I don't understand." She tried to twist around to look at him, but he jerked her back.

"Shut up while I think."

"Good idea," Tom said. "Let's think this through before someone gets hurt." He took a small step toward Colin and Lucy.

"Stay where you are," Colin raised the knife again. He'd taken a step backward, pulling Lucy toward the table and the bay window.

They say, in a crisis, the first thing to leave is your hearing. It wasn't working for me. The house was making weird sounds.

"We know about your mother," Tom said. "She lived here for eighteen years, didn't she? What I'd like to know is what you did with Evelyn Villiers."

*"What?"* Lucy was frantic, holding her chin up and trying to pull back from the knife. "Colin—what's he talking about?"

"Shut up."

"Col-*in*," she moaned. "You said—"

He lowered his knife hand and smacked her in the jaw. "I need to think."

Lucy screamed, then started to cry.

The house shuddered. There was a sharp crack as somewhere above us wood splintered.

Lucy screamed again. "What's that?" She was wriggling in his grasp. "Let me go, Colin. *Please. Please.*"

Colin ignored her. His mouth hardened. "Show me your mobiles."

"Mine's there," I said, pointing at my handbag on the counter.

Tom pulled his mobile out of his pocket and held it up.

"Put it on the floor. Kick it away from you."

Tom did.

Colin raised the knife to Lucy's throat again. "All right—this is how it's going to be. My van's parked in the bushes on the other side of the house." He nodded at me. "You're going to drive it around here and leave it running. The keys are there, on the counter. Don't even think about getting away or she's dead."

Tom gave me a nod. *Do what he says.*

I left at once. The ground was so wet my feet sank into the gravel. Keeping my balance was tricky. Plus I was shaking.

The van was parked, as Colin said, in the bushes on the west side of the house. I got in, started the engine, and backed up slowly.

*Crap. Where's the switch for the headlights?*

I had no idea—and no time to consult the owner's manual. Putting Colin's van in drive, I squinted into the darkness as I drove across the front of the house, past Tom's Volvo, and over the soggy grass toward the side door.

*Please, don't let me get stuck.*

Thoughts crowded together in my mind. Was Tom counting on me to do something, like radio the police? If he had a police radio in his car, I hadn't seen it. And who knew what Colin might do if I delayed long enough to find out? The look on Lucy's face was enough to convince me the best course was to do exactly what Colin said. And pray.

I got out and went back inside. "The van's running."

"Now open the back and bring in the boxes and packing materials. Start packing up this lot—as much as will fit."

"Then what, Colin?" Tom's voice had a dangerous edge. "You know I can't let you take Lucy."

"No problem, mate. I don't want her." Colin laughed. "I'll drop her off somewhere—safe and sound."

Lucy was weeping. "Why, Colin? You said we could be together now."

"Silly cow." Colin sounded almost tender. "I would have had to tell you sometime. Even if I did love you, we could never marry. Your father made sure of that."

"What do you mean?"

"What I mean, my dear girl, is that you and I are brother and sister—half, anyway. My mother and your father had a child—me."

"My God—you knew all along?" Lucy was pale, breathing hard. "You knew when we—"

"Of course not. He told me the night he died."

"Did my mother know?"

"I told her at the inquest—or tried to."

"So that's why you never came for me."

"I was never in love with you, Luce. You must have realized that."

"No, Colin, I didn't." She sagged.

"Water over the bridge, old girl."

The moment the words left his lips, the house gave a violent shudder, and the floor beneath the table dropped. Porcelain began to slide toward the bay.

Colin was trying to move away, but Lucy's weight was too much for him.

"The cellar wall's collapsing," Tom said. "We need to get out of here. Lucy, grab my hand. Kate, leave—*now*."

It was too late.

With a mighty groan and the sound of cracking wood and breaking glass, the bay window shattered and the rear wall of the house collapsed. A blast of wet mist hit me in the face, almost taking my breath. The ceiling hung over a gaping wound in the floor. Everything was sliding. We heard a splash, then another and another as parts of the banquettes broke off and fell.

With the floor tilted at an angle, Colin struggled to stay on his feet.

Another crack and the kitchen table disappeared into the hole.

Colin fell to his knees, slipping backward on the wet floorboards toward the hole. He held onto to Lucy, to save himself now, but that wasn't helping because she was sliding too.

I reached out for her hand, but they were already beyond reach.

"Move away, Kate. You'll go with them." Tom was edging toward them along the cabinets.

Lucy screamed, scrabbling in vain against the floorboards as Colin held her waist.

Tom dropped to his knees.

"For god's sake do something," Colin screamed. His legs had slipped over the edge.

Tom lay flat on his stomach and stretched out his arm. "Lucy—take hold."

"Be *careful*." I couldn't watch.

There was another ferocious crack and a further section of the floor disappeared.

Taking all three of them into the pit.

* * *

"Tom! *Tom!*" I was blinded by tears. "Where are you?"

I couldn't get close enough to see what had happened. I could hear gasping, splashing. At least someone was alive.

Lucy screamed.

"Ahh," someone moaned in pain.

"Kate, the cellar's completely flooded." Tom's voice reached me from the pit. "I think we're standing on the table—the water's up to Lucy's neck. Colin's been badly injured." He sounded breathless. "We have to get out of here, Kate—now. Look at the ceiling."

A huge bulging crack had opened above what had been the bay area. Chunks of plaster and lathe were falling into the chasm. The ceiling had seriously bowed. Soon it would collapse, bringing two floors of wood, plaster, and who knew what else down on Tom, Lucy, and Colin.

"What should I do?"

"We need a rope," Tom said. "At least thirty feet."

"There's one in the back of the van—*ahh.*" Colin sounded breathless. He was in pain.

"Yes, I saw it," I said, wondering if he'd had plans for that rope.

"Get the rope," Tom said. "Tie a knot at one end. Tie the other end to the van undercarriage."

"How do I do that?"

I heard Colin mumble something.

"Reach under the front bumper," Tom said. "Find the toe eye—it's a metal ring, off to one side. Thread the rope through and make a double knot. Hurry."

It took me only minutes to complete the task.

"Here's the rope." I threw the knotted end into the hole. In the time I'd been gone, the ceiling crack had opened further. Something had wedged itself into the gap—a piece of furniture, maybe. Plaster dust floated down, mixing with the mist and making visibility worse. Much worse.

"Got it," Tom said, coughing. "Lucy, wrap your legs above the knot and hold the rope. Watch your hands at the rough edge of the floor. I'm going to boost you up. Kate, get in the van and back it up—as slowly and smoothly as you can. Just five feet or so. Then come back in."

I rushed out to the van and put it in reverse. *Slow, smooth.* I couldn't feel my hands. When the van had moved what I thought might be about five feet, I put it in park and ran back into the house.

The upper half of Lucy's body was visible. Suddenly she shot over the edge.

"Don't let go of the rope," Tom called to her. "Kate, see if you can pull her toward you."

I pulled. Slowly, Lucy slid toward me along the sloping floor. She scrambled to her feet, dripping with foul-smelling water.

"We have to do it again," Tom said. "Kate—get back in the van and move it forward. Lucy can throw the rope toward us. Colin, this is going to hurt like hell. Grab the rope with your good arm. I'll boost you up."

The crack in the ceiling opened wider. More debris fell.

"We have only a few minutes, Kate," Tom said. "The whole house is collapsing."

This time things didn't go as smoothly. Colin screamed as Tom pushed him toward the surface. His left shoulder hung at an unnatural angle. His left leg was bleeding profusely through his jeans.

Somehow Tom managed to boost him up. He lay on the sloping floor, moaning.

It took both Lucy and me to haul Colin to safety.

"I'm ready whenever you are," Tom said, trying to sound breezy and unconcerned. We both knew there was no one else down there to give him a boost.

Everything went according to plan—until the end. We were at the end of our rope—literally. Colin was useless. He lay on the floor, writhing in pain. Lucy and I would have to pull Tom's weight up and over the edge of the floor.

"Pull," I screamed. "Harder, Lucy." I couldn't see because my eyes were filled with tears.

As we pulled, the ceiling gave way with a sound I hope never to hear again.

Everything came crashing down in a cloud of dust.

I couldn't see.

"Tom," I croaked. My throat was so tight, I could barely get the word out.

I lay on the floor, still pulling on the rope. Suddenly it went limp.

*No. Please, no.*

A hand grabbed my wrist.

Tom scrambled to his feet. *"Get out, get out, get out!"*

Lucy went first. Tom and I hoisted Colin on his good leg and practically carried him outside.

We ran toward Tom's car as quickly as we could in the mist.

Suddenly the noise stopped and everything seemed to settle.

I turned back to look.

The house sighed once, a deep, convulsive moan of utter defeat, and the entire structure collapsed in an explosion of dust and debris.

We got in the Volvo and closed the doors. Tom started the engine and shot backward down the drive, fifty feet or so.

He pulled a police radio from his glove compartment. "Hapthorn Lodge. We need medical assistance—EMTs and police backup. *Now.*"

# Chapter Forty-Four

Lucy and I huddled in the back of Tom's Volvo. She was shaking—from shock or the cold, or both. Colin lay moaning in the front passenger's seat. I couldn't see the extent of his leg injury, but it was bleeding badly. He needed medical help right away.

All three of them were going to need serious antibiotics and antifungals. The stench from their wet clothes was enough to make me sick, but I didn't care.

Tom was alive.

Colin was still moaning. "My shoulder."

"I'm more worried about your leg," Tom said. I'm going to try compressing the injury until the EMTs arrive. Kate, may I have your jacket?"

Tom folded my jacket into a tight coil and positioned it over Colin's thigh. Then he whipped off his belt, wrapped it around Colin's leg, and pulled it tight.

*"Aah."* Colin grimaced in pain.

Lucy was sobbing. "What did you do to my mother, Colin?"

"It wasn't my fault." Colin grimaced. "She attacked me. *Aah.*"

Tom was breathing hard. "Colin Wardle, I'm arresting you on suspicion of murder in the death of Evelyn Villiers." He stopped and took a breath. "You do not have to say anything, but it may harm your defense if you do not mention, when questioned, something you later rely on in court. Anything you do say may be given in evidence."

"You murdered her!" Lucy flung herself at him from the back seat. I pulled her back.

"Never laid a hand on her, I swear." The words came through gritted teeth. "*Aah*. My leg." Colin breathed in and out several times through his nose. "Went to see her after the inquest. I was Wallace Villiers's son. I deserved something after all those years of poverty, after all my mother had put up with to preserve his precious reputation. I thought she'd see the justice of it—at least give me something to get started in life."

"And then what, Colin?" Lucy hissed. "When she wouldn't agree, you killed her?"

"It wasn't like that, Luce." He was wheedling now, getting weaker. "She wouldn't let me in the house. Said to meet her by the river. She offered me five hundred pounds to go away. *Ha!* Five hundred measly pounds when my father was worth millions." Colin's breath was coming in ragged spurts. "I ripped up the check and threw it at her. Told her I'd take her to court. She came at me with her claws, scratching, gouging at my face. She was wild, Luce. Next thing I knew she was on the ground. Must have hit her head or something."

"You're saying it was an accident?" Tom said.

*Was that the truth? How would we ever know?*

"What did you do with the body?" Tom asked.

"Dragged her into the long grass and hid her while I drove to Little Dunmow to get my mother. I didn't know what to do. She was the one who came up with the idea of pretending to be Evelyn Villiers—it wasn't me. I found tools in the shed. She helped me bury the body. Later, we gathered rocks and made a sort of garden over her."

"All that same night?"

"Finished at daybreak. *Aah.* Mother told me to leave. She'd take care of everything. Said she'd call Winnifred Villiers." He cried out again in agony. "I'm going to die!"

"Not if I can help it," Tom said. "Hang on. Help's on the way."

"Wouldn't Winnie have recognized Evelyn's voice?" I asked.

"They hardly knew each other." Colin stopped to catch his breath. When he spoke again, we could barely hear him. "Mother pretended to be crying, told her she had to . . . get Lucy."

"And she needed to get rid of Ertha," I said. "She typed those letters, didn't she—the ones to Lucy and Ertha."

Colin nodded. "Had to. Police would have blamed me."

"What about your mother, Colin?" Tom asked. "What happened the night of the May Fair? Colin? *Colin?*"

Colin's head had dropped against the window.

"I think we're losing him," Tom said. "He's lost too much blood."

We weren't getting any more answers out of Colin that night—maybe we never would.

Lucy was sobbing quietly.

We heard the sound of the ambulance. Minutes later, the flashing lights lit up the car interior.

* * *

DS Cliffe and PC Weldon arrived together.

Colin was loaded into the rear of the ambulance. The EMTs bundled Tom and Lucy into Cliffe's car. Anne Weldon slid into the driver's seat of Tom's Volvo, and we followed the ambulance to the NHS hospital in Bury St. Edmunds.

Colin was taken immediately into surgery. His shoulder was dislocated, as I thought, and his collarbone was broken. The most serious injury was the gash on his leg. He'd severed the superficial femoral artery. He was lucky to be alive.

Tom and Lucy were put on IV meds and admitted overnight for observation.

I was allowed to see Tom for a brief moment. He lay, pale and exhausted, under a cotton blanket.

"Do you believe Evelyn Villiers's death was an accident?"

"Not for a minute." Tom's eyes closed. They must have given him a sedative.

"I thought I'd lost you," I said and had a sudden memory of him saying almost the same words to me in Scotland. "How did you pull yourself out of that cellar?"

"Hand over hand." He grinned sleepily. "Police academy rope training comes in handy every once in a while. You're stronger than you think, Kate. You and Lucy were holding my weight."

"Amazing what you can do when you have to." I wrinkled my nose. "I'd kiss you but you smell like a sewer."

"I'll claim my kiss later. We have time, you know."

*We have time, you know.* I was still thinking about those words when I met Liz Mallory in the waiting room.

"Is he going to be all right?" She looked terrified.

I took pity on her. "He ingested some of the filthy water, so they've put him on anti-something. But yes, he's going to be fine. He was a hero, Liz. Cool as a cucumber. He saved three lives—including his own."

Her eyes filled with tears. She wiped them away with an impatient hand.

"Why don't you go in? He'd like to see you."

"You really think so? He was so angry with me after the dinner party. He said I treated you unfairly. Have I, Kate? If I have, I'm sorry."

Liz rushed off toward the nurses' station. *Was that an apology?*

DS Cliffe was waiting to drive me back to Rose Cottage.

Now that Tom was going to be fine, all I wanted was to hear my mother's voice.

* * *

I slipped out of my muddy shoes. Third pair I'd ruined in the UK so far.

Vivian was waiting up for me. Someone from the police had called her, which was thoughtful.

"Oh, my dear. Sit down. Have a cup of tea, and tell me *all* about it." She was practically vibrating with curiosity.

"Vivian, do you mind if I don't? I'm ready to drop."

"Of course." Vivian also has a kind heart. "You take a nice hot bath and climb into bed. I'll bring you a tray in the morning."

"No need for that." I yawned. "Ivor's being released from the hospital in the morning. I'll be up bright and early to visit him at The Willows."

I climbed the stairs and peeled off my wet, filthy clothes, laying them out on the bathroom rack to dry. The sour smell of mildew and plaster dust would probably never come out of them. Small price to pay. Tom was going to be all right.

I had no idea if Colin would be all right—or if the police would find enough evidence to convict him of murder. All they had at the moment was circumstantial, but he had admitted to being there when Evelyn Villiers died.

I pictured Lucy lying alone in her hospital bed and wished I could comfort her. The shock of learning that Colin was her half brother would be harder to overcome than any strange organisms floating around in that filthy water.

After a hot bath, I put on my Mickey and Minnie Mouse flannel pajamas, my comfort pajamas—the ones the kids bought me years ago at Disney World—and slipped into bed, feeling almost human again.

I dialed.

"Linnea Larsen here."

"It's me. How's Dr. Lund?"

"Sweet of you to call, darling. He's so much better. The attack was serious, but the doctors were able to limit the damage to his heart because we got him to the emergency room so quickly. I think he's going to be all right." She laughed. "Maybe no more Sea-Doos."

"Oh, Mom, I'm so glad."

"Kate, I've been thinking."

"About what?"

"About catching monkeys."

"Catching *monkeys*?" I had to laugh. "Why?"

"It's how you catch them. If you want to catch a monkey, you cut a hole in a gourd, just big enough for the monkey's little hand to fit inside. Inside the gourd you put something the monkey likes—nuts or fruit. The monkey smells the treats, puts his hand in to grab a fistful. But then he can't get his fist out because it won't fit through the hole. He's stuck because he refuses to let go."

"I know the feeling."

"What I've really been thinking about is life—life and alternatives. Sometimes life gives you two paths, two choices. You can't have them both."

"You're talking about James. He's asked you to marry him."

"Yes. Before his attack."

"What did you say?"

"I haven't answered him yet, but I'm going to say yes. Do you mind?"

"Of course not. I'm so happy for you." It was the truth.

"Kate—you sound tired. Is everything all right?"

"Everything is fine—or it will be. We can talk again tomorrow."

It wasn't the time to tell her I'd almost lost Tom—or that she might have lost me.

She'd chosen a new path in life, and I hoped the view was amazing.

# Chapter Forty-Five

Thursday, May 23

Ivor was back in his old room at The Willows, dressed in his paisley dressing gown and ensconced in the big leather armchair near the French window. The nurse's aide, Jay'den, was serving us tea and getting Ivor settled back in.

"Thought you'd got rid of me, did you?" Ivor teased Jay'den.

"You know what they say about old pennies," she chirped back. She poured two cups of tea and placed them between us on the table. "Have a lovely visit. I'll be back to wheel you down for your dinner at one."

Once Ivor had regained full consciousness, Dr. Chaudhry had been impressed with his recovery. Now all he needed was to regain his strength and stability so he could resume physiotherapy.

Every muscle in my body ached. Even so, I couldn't have been happier. Tom had been discharged from the hospital with a load of pills to protect him against the noxious substances he'd swallowed in the Hapthorn cellar. I was to meet him that afternoon at police headquarters to give my statement. Not only that, he'd gotten an entire week off, starting Monday. If the Stour had receded enough, we'd spend one of those days taking the river walk he'd talked about.

I spent twenty minutes bringing Ivor up to speed on all that had happened while he was (in his words) "napping."

"I'm sorry for pretending to be you with Professor Markham."

"You can pretend to be me any time you please, dear girl. I just wish I'd been able to help."

"The professor is a bit—well, eccentric."

"Completely barking, but harmless enough."

The sun picked out the silver cloud on Ivor's head. His face was a healthy pink again and his eyes that electric blue I remembered. I felt a lump in my throat. I might not have seen those eyes again.

Ivor chose a finger of Vivian's shortbread. "What will happen to Martin Ingram, or Colin What's-it—"

"Wardle."

"Will Colin Wardle be charged with murder?"

"I might find out today—if his surgery doesn't delay things. He admitted fighting with Evelyn Villiers but swore her death was accidental. He says he and his mother buried her body. Then she took Evelyn Villiers's place at Hapthorn Lodge."

"So his mother went along with it."

"He claims it was her idea, but I'm not buying it. That's what happens when a parent shields her child from the consequences of bad behavior. The child never learns his lesson because he's never held accountable for his actions. I think Colin was terribly spoiled as a child—partly, I suppose, because he was so beautiful. He must have grown up believing he was special, more important and deserving than other people. That idea was reinforced when Wallace Villiers took him under his wing. Or maybe he's a sociopath—one of those people who never develop a conscience."

"And the drugs? That shocks me. Nigel Oakley seemed like an honest man. Will they charge all three of them?"

"Right now it's just a theory, Ivor. When I learn more, you'll be the first to know." I stood and dropped a kiss on Ivor's head. "Now get some rest—and get better."

I was fitting the lid on Vivian's tin when he stopped me. "Kate, do you mind if I ask about your plans?"

"Don't worry. I've already made arrangements to stay until you're back on your feet."

"It's not that. It's just . . . just—" He dithered a bit. "What I'm trying to say is, I don't want you to leave at all. At least not for good. Having you to chat to about antiques has been the best thing in my life. I have no children, no close relatives. All my friends were born before the ark. When I fall off the perch, I want you to have the shop, Kate."

"Ivor—you're not dying."

"Not yet. What I mean is I want you to be my business partner—co-owners. And one day—when my clock runs down—I want you to have it."

I burst into tears.

* * *

The headquarters of the Suffolk Constabulary was a hive of activity. Tom's investigators were gathering evidence more quickly than the crime scene manager could process it. Fortunately, they had enough to keep Colin Wardle, still recovering in the hospital, and the Oakleys in custody.

"Step this way, Mrs. Hamilton." A middle-aged police sergeant named Janice ushered me through the waiting room and up the stairs toward the second floor of the building. "Inspector Mallory is with Chief Inspector Eacles. He'll join you shortly."

I found Lucy in one of the conference rooms. She and Tom had been released from the hospital early that morning with instructions to get some rest, take their pills, and call if any unusual symptoms cropped up. DC Weldon had driven her back to the Premier Inn so she could change into clean clothes.

"Oh, Lucy." I teared up. "Come here." I opened my arms, and she flew into them.

"I'm so sorry." She clung to me. "If I hadn't fallen for Colin's lies, the whole thing wouldn't have happened."

"It wasn't your fault. Colin knew what he was doing—and he was clever."

"Clever enough to fool me twice. He convinced me his lack of affection was out of respect—and the eighteen years we'd been apart. He said we should take our time, get to know each other again." I felt her shiver and pictured the way Colin had almost flinched when Lucy touched him. She'd been too deliriously happy to notice the body language.

We sat at the conference table, waiting for Tom to join us.

Lucy lowered her eyes. "I keep wondering how it would have turned out if you and Tom hadn't shown up."

"The house would have collapsed anyway."

"I know that. I mean what would have happened with Colin. Would he have kept stringing me along until he got his hands on the art collection and then disappeared?"

*Or murdered you.* "We'll never know—thankfully. What will you do now?"

"I'm going home to Belfast next week. Simon Crewe will send a salvage team to Hapthorn. Something will have survived."

"I have some very good news—the húnpíng jar is safe." Her eyes widened in surprise. "It is, truly. Remind me to tell you about it later."

"The house is a complete loss."

"I'm sorry."

"Don't be. I've spent too much time in my life mourning over what I couldn't have. I'm ready to start living."

I smiled at her. "You know what I think? I think if your mother had lived, she would have contacted you. I'm just so sorry you never had that chance."

"I'd like to think that. For all those years, I wasn't able to draw a line under my past and move on. Now that the line has been drawn, what I feel isn't regret. It's relief. I've got the trust fund to keep me going the rest of my life as long as I'm not extravagant."

"Will you quit your job?"

"Not right away. I like my work. My boss is great. My coworkers are like family. And there's a bloke, one of our suppliers—I've never given him a chance because of Colin."

"I hope we can keep in touch, Lucy. If there's ever anything I can do, just ask."

"Thank you. If any of the antiques have survived, I'll have to decide what to do about them."

"I have something for you." I found the plastic photo sleeve in my purse and handed her a copy of the family photograph. "The police will return the original after the court case. You might be able to have the image restored."

Lucy traced her father's face with her forefinger. "He wasn't ever going to win father of the year, but he did love me. He must have loved Colin too, and wanted to give him a start in life. His mistake was keeping Colin's parentage a secret. He never imagined we'd fall in—" She broke off and started again. "Never imagined I would fall in love with him."

"Colin didn't know you shared a father until the night you'd planned to elope?"

"That's what he says, and I believe him—on that point, anyway. He thought marrying me would earn him a permanent place in the Villiers family. Not knowing he already had one."

"Colin is going to need a good lawyer."

"I'll make sure he gets one." She must have seen the look of surprise on my face. "He is my brother, Kate."

The door opened.

"Ready?" Tom smiled at us. "Let's get your statements out of the way. Then I'll take you both out for lunch at The Dog & Partridge."

# Chapter Forty-Six

Monday, May 27

Five days after the arrest of Colin Wardle and the Oakleys, Tom and I got our walk—but not along the River Stour. While the flood waters had mostly receded, the towpaths were still impassable, some stretches washed away completely. We walked instead on higher ground, along sheep meadows and through wooded bowers from Long Barston to Little Gosling. Far in the distance, church bells rang out—a practice session, no doubt, for the change ringers.

Sunlight dappled the hawthorn hedges, their glossy oak-like leaves dotted with clusters of fragrant white flowers. Tom walked ahead of me along the narrow foot path, helping me through the kissing gates and over the styles. In the fields, the younger lambs nursed. The older ones butted heads in mock battles while their patient mothers munched grass and enjoyed the sun on their wooly backs.

After two and a half hours, we stopped where the path widened, found a convenient log, and sat. I retied my hiking boots. "You haven't mentioned the case once today. What's happening? If you can tell me, that is."

"You of all people deserve to know." Tom pulled a water bottle out of his backpack and handed it to me. "Forensics deciphered the logo on the bottom of the third set of shoe prints in Ivor's stockroom—Bally, the luxury Swiss shoemaker. We matched the prints to a pair in

Colin's closet. He'd cleaned them, but we found blood traces in the stitching."

"He must have been confident he'd never be suspected."

"We can now place him at both murder scenes."

"Enough to convict?" I took a long drink of water.

"Not quite, but there's more. I said we needed a body, and we got one. The floods at Hapthorn Lodge swept through the rock garden, partially uncovering the skeleton of a woman, about the same age as Evelyn Villiers. We're checking the DNA with Lucy's, but there's little doubt. A forensic examination showed the hyoid bone had been broken. Rare except in cases of manual strangulation when the killer's hand gets up high underneath the victim's chin. Information like that impresses a jury."

"Is that enough?"

Tom stretched out his long legs and smiled. "There's more. We identified the two men in the van chased by Cliffe—CCTV footage at the car hire lot. They confessed and fingered Peter Oakley as their contact. When we presented Peter with the evidence, he crumbled. Most bullies are cowards at heart, Kate. He's agreed to testify against Colin Wardle."

"Peter knew about the murders?'

"He says no, but he saw Colin the night of the May Fair with blood on his shirt and trousers. And he knew about Colin's nefarious activities in France. He has facts, dates."

"How about Nigel Oakley?" I was almost afraid to ask.

"He had nothing to do with any of it. Come on." He pulled me to my feet. "Two more miles to Little Gosling. Lunch and a glass of white wine at The Packhorse?"

* * *

We gathered that evening in the small dining room at Finchley Hall—Lady Barbara and Vivian, Lucy, Tom, and me. Ivor was the only one missing, but I'd have plenty of time in the coming weeks to answer his questions. Or try. Some things, like the true circumstances of Evelyn Villiers's death, might never be known.

Francie Jewell had prepared an amazing dinner of English beef with small roasted potatoes, fresh peas from the garden, and all the trimmings. She'd filled our crystal wineglasses with a vintage cabernet from the Lady Barbara's wine cellar. Finchley Hall's fine old Royal Crown Derby china gleamed in the candlelight.

I reached for Tom's hand under the table, overwhelmed with gratitude for his life and with love for the people I'd come to care about in this small, perfect English village.

With Lucy's permission, Tom had outlined Colin's story about confronting Evelyn Villiers the night of the inquest and about their argument in the garden, ending in her accidental death. Then he'd explained about the skeleton and the broken hyoid bone.

"So he strangled her," Lady Barbara said. She glanced at Lucy. "Oh, my dear. Is this too much too soon?"

Lucy was looking pale, but she squared her shoulders. "Hearing the truth is hard, but not as hard as believing all those years that my father's death was my fault. Now I know my mother didn't send me away. And she didn't write the note I found the morning after the inquest." She looked at Tom. "I want to know everything."

"Colin really thought Evelyn Villiers would *welcome* him as her husband's heir?" Vivian huffed. "He must be delusional."

"I think he was trying to salvage something out of the deal," I said. "He'd just learned he could never marry Lucy. He must have hoped he could charm his way into Evelyn Villiers's good books—it had worked for him in the past. Or at least he might leave with a substantial sum of money to keep quiet. She probably laughed in his face."

"That's exactly what she would have done," Lucy said.

"We may be able to prove he stole her jewelry," Tom said. "He hasn't admitted to that yet, but the Yard is tracing sales in France and Italy."

"I think the jewelry provided the cash he needed for a start in the antiques trade," I said.

"He probably convinced himself it was his due," Lucy said, "in lieu of the inheritance he thought he deserved."

"Did he take the missing pieces of Meissen as well?" Vivian asked.

"We found proof of that on his laptop," Tom said. "Colin learned about an auction of old Meissen in Paris and couldn't resist selling the commedia dell'arte figurines."

"I'm surprised he didn't sell the entire art collection," Lady Barbara said.

"According to Peter, that was his original plan," Tom said. "He'd been gathering objects to pack up, but his mother was a very superstitious woman. She put her foot down, insisted it would bring them bad luck. That's why she refused to sleep in the master bedroom or wear Evelyn Villiers's clothes—she felt they were tempting fate."

"And that's why she got rid of the photograph albums, I suppose," Lucy said. "Seeing them reminded her of what they'd done."

"You're the one who said it, Kate," Tom said. "When we still thought it was Evelyn Villiers who died at the May Fair that night, you said, 'It was almost as if she felt she didn't deserve to enjoy her wealth.' Emily Wardle knew she didn't deserve it, and in the end, her guilt overwhelmed her. Colin admitted his mother was planning to leave for good. When she learned he'd sold the Meissen, she was convinced they'd be found out and decided to save herself. All she had to do was raise enough cash to make her escape."

"That's why she refused to use the phone or the mail," I said. "If Colin found out what she was doing, she knew he'd stop her."

"And that's exactly what he did—he stopped her." Vivian drained her wineglass and slammed it down on the table so hard I thought the stem would snap. "Is he claiming self-defense for his mother's murder? Diminished capacity? Another accident?" Vivian trained one skeptical eye on Tom.

"Colin's statement will be compared with the evidence." Tom said.

"Did he say anything about his mother's fascination with the legend of the green maiden?" Lucy asked.

"That's the one topic he would talk about," Tom said. "Colin said his mother was obsessed with the idea that she was descended from the green maiden through the Grenfels, an old branch of her mother's family. The photograph over her bed was of her grandmother's cottage along the Stour—River's Edge Cottage. Emily Wardle grew up with the legend. She'd memorized the words on the beams of the pub in Dunmow Parva."

"Mrs. Wright said she was always quoting things in the old tongue," I added. "When I heard her say *wagon bell* the day she came in the shop, she was actually quoting the words painted on the beam: *The betrayal of the one I love is like a flaming sword in my heart.* She loved Colin too much for his good, if that's possible. He betrayed that love by forcing her to play the part of her rival, Evelyn Villiers—the one role guaranteed to cause her maximum guilt."

"Colin claimed his mother came up with the idea of pretending to be Evelyn Villiers," Tom said, "but I think he was lying. I think he forced her into it."

"When she brought the húnpíng jar into Ivor's shop," I said, "her son's betrayal must have been uppermost in her mind."

"Why did she cling to that young actress, the one playing the green maiden?" Lady Barbara asked.

"We'll never know," Tom said.

I laid down my fork. "I think in her final moments, she saw the girl in the green makeup and focused on her."

"I understand that." Lady Barbara wrinkled her brow. "Family legends are powerful. At that moment, everything she'd been brought up to believe would have come back to her."

"Fatally stabbed, she ran toward the lights on the green," Tom said. "If she'd gotten medical attention sooner, she might have lived. As it was, she'd lost too much blood."

We were silent for a moment, reliving the shock of Emily Wardle's death.

"So *was* she related to the green maiden?" Vivian asked.

"She believed she was," Tom said. "That's what counts."

"What *does* Colin say about his mother's death?" Vivian asked.

"He says he was provoked. The night of the May Fair, he noticed the húnpíng was missing and confronted his mother. He hasn't admitted it, but we think he roughed her up. The coroner found extensive bruising on her face and body. Colin forced her to show him where she'd taken the jar. Once they were inside the stockroom, Emily must have reached the breaking point. Colin says she grabbed the húnpíng and threatened to smash it on the floor. He tried to get it away from her. They struggled, and Emily was stabbed—accidentally, he claims. The húnpíng flew into the air, and while Colin was trying to save it, she fled."

"He couldn't catch her?" Lucy asked.

"He did go after her, but she'd gotten a head start, and with so many people on the green, he realized he'd be spotted."

"Why didn't he go back for the húnpíng?"

"He did, but James Liu had gotten there first. The fact that Colin's mother died before she could tell anyone her name was a stroke of luck for him—in his eyes, another sign of his charmed life."

"Will Colin be charged with murder?"

"That's the prosecutor's decision," Tom said. "I think we're building a compelling case."

"What about Nigel Oakley?" Lady Barbara asked. "I can't believe that charming man was involved in drugs."

"We have no evidence Nigel Oakley knew anything, Lady Barbara. He's cooperating fully with the investigation."

"Poor man." Lady Barbara, who knew about errant sons, shook her head.

Francie Jewell carried in a round silver platter. "Treacle tart with a shortbread crust," she said. "Lady Barbara's favorite. Clotted cream on the way."

In time, the full story would be revealed—or as full a story as the prosecutors could put together so long after the facts. The bottom line was, Colin Wardle would spend a very, very long time in prison.

Lucy could finally get on with her life.

# Chapter Forty-Seven

Friday, May 28

"It's Henry Liu I feel sorry for." Vivian passed me the toast rack. "Have another slice. The honey's from local bees."

I looked at my half-full plate. Vivian had gotten up early to prepare eggs with sausage and smoked salmon, topping it off with mountains of whole grain toast. "I couldn't possibly."

I was still stuffed from the night before. After dinner and the treacle tart, Vivian and I had waddled back to Rose Cottage while Tom drove Lucy to the Premier Inn and headed for police headquarters. With two murders and a drugs case to conclude, his team had a long night ahead.

Vivian tsked. "Imagine James Liu betraying his parents like that. We heard they feel so ashamed, they're thinking of closing the restaurant. Naturally, we can't allow that, so Lady Barbara has organized a community dinner at the church hall tonight—Chinese takeaway. We want the Lius to know the village supports them. Will you join us?"

"I'm sorry—I'm having dinner with Tom." I pulled my feet up on the soft chair and hugged my knees. Nothing on England's *sceptr'd isle* was going to rob us of our evening together.

"That's a shame. Barb has an announcement."

"You can tell me in the morning."

"I can't wait that long." Vivian mimed unzipping her lips. "An anonymous benefactor has given the National Trust a substantial donation to be used for the renovation and permanent upkeep of Finchley Hall."

"Substantial? You must mean monumental. Do you have any idea who it is?"

"The donor wishes to remain anonymous. It's a secret."

"Nothing is secret for long in this village. Come on, Viv. Who it is?"

"We don't know." She raised one eyebrow. "Or let's just say we *do* know, but we don't."

"Wait a minute—it's that collector from Bury St. Edmunds isn't it? The one who sends Lady Barbara flowers every week. Charles, with the title even I would recognize."

"Just don't say I told you. He sent Barb a huge bouquet of white roses this morning. She's over the moon."

"That'll make the national news."

"The collapse of Hapthorn Lodge made the news. You're lucky to be alive."

Yes, I was. And so were the others. I was deciding how much I should tell Vivian about that awful experience, when we heard a knock at the door.

Fergus woofed.

Vivian jumped up to answer it. "If it's those pesky reporters, should I tell them you've come down with a fever—or you're too shattered to talk?"

I laughed. "Just tell them I have no statement to make."

Vivian returned with a puzzled look on her face. "It's for you, Kate. She says she's Tom's sister-in-law."

I went to the door.

Sophie was wearing a lapis-blue silk wrap dress with silver high-heeled sandals. Her hair fell over her shoulders in a golden curtain. "Do you have a few minutes?"

"Of course. Come in."

Sophie turned to Vivian. "Would you mind leaving us alone for a minute?"

"I shall withdraw." Vivian left the room, closing the door behind her. It occurred to me she might eavesdrop, but I heard her footsteps on the stairs.

"Please sit down, Sophie. Have you decided on a house in the area?"

She sat on the edge of the sofa and crossed her shapely legs. "That's why I'm here. I've come to say goodbye."

"Oh? Where will you go?"

"London for now. Then maybe somewhere warm for a while. Or a cruise. I'm not ready to settle down."

"Liz must be disappointed." I couldn't help myself.

Sophie laughed. "It was her idea I come. You'd probably worked that out. For a while I thought it might be the best thing, but rural Suffolk isn't for me."

"Liz was hoping you and Tom would get together."

"I can't pretend it wasn't tempting. Tom is a gorgeous man. But I can't see myself as the wife of a policeman, can you? Besides, I would never have lived up to my sister."

"In Tom's eyes?"

"In Liz's eyes. She thought Sarah was perfect."

"So I've been told."

"Sarah *wasn't* perfect, Kate. Don't get me wrong. She was a wonderful woman—kind, smart, generous. A terrific wife and mother—smashing cook. But she wasn't perfect."

"No one is."

"No. But sometimes we *are* perfect—for someone. I hope one day I find someone who thinks I'm perfect. In the meantime, I'm going to have some fun."

She uncrossed her legs and stood. "He's in love with you, Kate. I'm sure you know that. Don't let Liz stand in the way of your happiness."

* * *

The Trout, an ancient pub outside Saxby St. Clare, was low-ceilinged, cozy, and quiet. Tom and I had finished a wonderful dinner in the tiny dining room. At present we were curled up on an ancient leather sofa near the fire, drinking cognac from small lead-crystal snifters.

"I ordered a chilly night so we could enjoy the fire," Tom said.

"*Mmm.* Very wise." I kissed the side of his neck, breathing in the woodsy scent of his cologne and thinking of starry nights and bonfires. "Remember the last time we were here?"

"I do remember. You'd just met Ivor Tweedy." He slid his hand down the back of my hair.

"That's right. I'd forgotten." I teared up.

"Kate—Ivor's all right isn't he?"

"He's fine. It's not that." I wiped my eyes with the backs of my hands. "Yesterday he told me he wants to give me the shop. Not right away—when he's gone. And in the meantime, he wants me to join him as a partner."

"Did he, indeed." Tom gave me that half smile that always shorted out my mental synapses. "And what did you say?"

"I'll tell you. But first, tell me what you've learned about Peter Oakley."

"There's a lot more to discover, but we've been able to piece a few things together. Selling drugs was Peter's thing in the beginning. He's an addict."

"Oh—I suppose that accounts for his changeable moods."

"When he met Martin—Colin Wardle—they went big time. On Colin's trips to the Continent, he would hook up with suppliers and conceal packets of powder and pills in the antique furniture. The rest was Peter's operation, distributing the drugs to small-time dealers in East Anglia—like the two charmers in the leased van."

"How did Peter and Colin meet?"

"Colin had become involved with an antiques auction house in London. He'd learned quite a bit from Wallace Villiers and knew how to sound more knowledgeable than he really was. Most of the stock auctioned off was legitimate, but the principals weren't fussy about provenance. Colin began accepting stolen goods and either selling them through the auction house or privately to dealers in the home counties. Soon he began selling abroad as well. That's where he met his shady contacts on the Continent. We think he may have been involved in a few burglaries in France. In the meantime, Peter had applied for a job as a runner at the same London auction house. He needed money to fund his habit."

"And Nigel didn't know?"

"Nigel was never involved with any of it, Kate. As a teenager, Peter got hooked on drugs. His parents had him in rehab several times—not cheap. But he continued to get into trouble. When Peter developed an interest in the antiques trade, his father was relieved, took it as a sign the lad was finally going straight and wanted to do anything he could to encourage him. After Peter's mother died, Nigel sold his estate agency and looked for somewhere to invest his money. Peter introduced him to Martin Ingram—Colin—and Nigel was impressed."

"So impressed that he agreed to finance the new auction house venture." My eyes stung. "What will happen to Nigel? Will he lose all his money?"

"I hope not. The tithe barn is worth a fortune, and Nigel still has lots of connections."

Tom got up to put another log on the fire. He poked the burning embers, sending sparks flying up the chimney.

When he sat back down, I curled up beside him.

"By the way," Tom said, "we located the Australian nephew—Patrick Allen. After you found him hiding in Hapthorn Lodge, he'd taken to dossing in the rented van, trying to figure out how he was going to raise enough money for a return ticket to Melbourne."

"Had he visited the woman he thought was his aunt?"

"Tried to. She refused to see him. Actually, he said she seemed confused about who he was."

"No wonder. She had no idea."

"When he heard about her death, he decided to lay low. I told Lucy. She wants to see him. I won't be surprised if she buys him a ticket."

"Back to the auction house." I laid my head on his shoulder. "I'm still puzzled about a Chinese vase that sold for far less than it should have."

"Scotland Yard is looking into that part of it. They've been tracking a cabal of dealers who work together to keep prices artificially low."

"We have that kind of thing in the States. Dealers agree to suppress bidding. One of them buys the item well below estimate, and later they have a private auction among themselves."

"With the collaboration of the auction house."

"Of course."

He put his arm around my shoulders. "Kate, what will you tell Ivor about the shop?"

"I don't know yet—but I have been thinking."

"About what?"

"Catching monkeys."

He laughed. "Tell me you're not planning to open a pet shop."

"See my hand?" I made a fist and then slowly uncurled my fingers, one by one. "I'm thinking about what happens when you finally let go."

"I'm sure you have a brilliant explanation for that, Kate, and I'd love to hear all about it sometime. But right now I want to tell you what I'm thinking."

He slid down in front of me on one knee. "I want to marry you. As soon as possible."

I stared at him. "But we've never talked about marriage."

"No, we haven't."

"I own an antiques business in Ohio."

"Yes, you do."

"We've never talked about any of it—where we would live, who would move."

"You're right."

"I've never met your daughter. She might not like me."

"She might not. So will you?"

I pictured the monkey's fist. Letting go.

"I will."

# Acknowledgments

Readers familiar with the English county of Suffolk will know there is no village called Long Barston. That wonderful place, including its inhabitants, history, and folklore, is entirely a product of my imagination. So is the shadowy organization I've named The White Lotus Society, although the history of the sacking of the Old Summer Palace in Beijing during the Second Opium War (1860) is a historical fact. It is also true that in 1982 the Chinese government made the repatriation of its cultural heritage a constitutional mandate.

Even so, I would like to think that although the events in this book did not happen, they might have, and for that I must thank a number of people in the United Kingdom: Detective Inspector Tamlyn Burgess of the Suffolk Constabulary; Harry Boswell, Director of Operations and Consultancy for the National Trust; Lauren Booth of the Suffolk Coroners Service; and Henry Heath, Assistant Priest at Holy Trinity Church, Long Melford.

I owe a huge debt of gratitude to those who read and commented on my manuscript at various stages—Grace Topping, Charlene D'Avanzo, and Lynn Denley-Bussard. I value their wisdom and treasure their friendship. Lynn, in particular went well beyond the call of duty in correcting, advising, and encouraging me in the process of writing this book.

Thank you to the crew at Crooked Lane Books, especially my editor, Faith Black Ross. And thank you to my agent, Paula Munier. Without their help, this book wouldn't exist.

## Acknowledgments

Finally, I am immensely grateful for the love, support, and encouragement of my husband, who, in lieu of travel this year, has watched enough British television to develop an accent.

This book is dedicated to my sons, David and John. Love you forever!

*Soli Deo gloria*